I0592158

George A. Townsend

Events at the National Capital

and the Campaign of 1876

George A. Townsend

Events at the National Capital
and the Campaign of 1876

ISBN/EAN: 9783337239411

Printed in Europe, USA, Canada, Australia, Japan

Cover: Foto ©Andreas Hilbeck / pixelio.de

More available books at **www.hansebooks.com**

NATIONAL CAPITAL

AND THE

CAMPAIGN OF 1876.

A COMPLETE HISTORY OF THE FOUNDATION AND GROWTH OF OUR GOVERNING CITY, A
DESCRIPTION OF THE PUBLIC BUILDINGS AND MANNER OF LIVING THERE, A
SEARCHING EXPOSURE OF THE VARIOUS JOBS AND SCANDALS WHICH HAVE
EXCITED PUBLIC INDIGNATION, FULL BIOGRAPHIES OF HAYES,
WHEELER, TILDEN, AND HENDRICKS, BESIDES
VARIOUS POLITICAL STATISTICS.

By GEO. ALFRED TOWNSEND, AND OTHERS.

HARTFORD, CONN.:

JAS. BETTS & CO.

S. M. BETTS & CO., CHICAGO; J. H. CHAMBERS & CO., ST. LOUIS;
A. L. BANCROFT & CO., SAN FRANCISCO, CAL.
HABER BROS., MINNEAPOLIS, MINN.

1876.

ILLUSTRATIONS.

FULL PAGE.

TABLE OF CONTENTS.

CHAPTER I.

INTRODUCTORY.

CHAPTER II.

HOW WASHINGTON CITY CAME TO BE.

CHAPTER III.

THE JOB OF PLANNING THE FEDERAL CITY.

CHAPTER IV.

THE ARCHITECTS OF THE CAPITOL AND THEIR FEUDS.

CHAPTER V.

THE LOBBY AND ITS GENTRY.

CHAPTER VI.

A RUNNING HISTORY OF GOVERNMENT SCANDALS.

CHAPTER VII.

SOCIETY AND THE CITY FROM THE MADISONIAN TO THE EMANCIPATION PERIOD.

CHAPTER VIII.

THE ROMANCE OF THE CAPITOL BUILDING.

CONTENTS.

CHAPTER IX.

SOME OF THE ORGANIC EVILS OF OUR CONGRESSIONAL SYSTEM.

CHAPTER X.

STYLE, EXTRAVAGANCE, AND MATRIMONY AT THE SEAT OF GOVERNMENT.

CHAPTER XI.

DOMESTIC HISTORY OF THE WHITE HOUSE.

CHAPTER XII.

SOME OF THE BUREAUX OF OUR GOVERNMENT VISITED.

CHAPTER XIII.

A PICTURE OF MT. VERNON IN 1789.

CHAPTER XIV.

CHAPTER XV.

CHAPTER XVI.

CHAPTER XVII.

CHAPTER XVIII.

CHAPTER XIX.

SOCIAL SKETCHES OF THE OLD AND NEW IN WASHINGTON.

CHAPTER XX.

JOBBERY COEVAL WITH GOVERNMENT.

CHAPTER XXI.

THE WHISKEY FRAUDS.

CHAPTER XXII.

OUR NATIONAL DISGRACE.

CHAPTER XXIII.

THE REPUBLICAN CONVENTION OF 1876.

CHAPTER XXIV.

RUTHERFORD B. HAYES.

CHAPTER XXV.

WILLIAM A. WHEELER.

CHAPTER XXVI.

THE DEMOCRATIC CONVENTION.

CHAPTER XXVII.

SAMUEL J. TILDEN.

CHAPTER XXVIII.

THOMAS A. HENDRICKS.

CHAPTER XXIX.

VARIOUS POLITICAL STATISTICS.

INTRODUCTORY CHAPTER.

THE public mind is at last exercised on the subject of scheming and jobbery.

The Crédit Mobilier investigation accomplished what many years of unthanked agitation and challenge failed to do. It reached such eminent reputations and made such general wreck of political prospects and accomplishments, that every class of citizens—even those who came to scoff, remained beside their Capitol to pray. This was the first element of encouragement; for it proved that in every extremity of the American nation there is still a public sentiment to be found, and it will rally on the side of good morals and the reputation of the state if it understands the necessity.

The people must not be blamed if, in the great variety of affairs and investigations, they often look on confused and apathetic. Our government is so extensive in area and so diversified in operations, that it requires men of state—statesmen—to keep its machinery in order and prevent waste, neglect, interference, and incendiarism. No amount of mere honesty and good negative inclination can keep the ship of state headed well to the wind. A reasonable experience in civil affairs, education, and executive capacity are requisite, and it is when the accidents of war and the extremities of political parties bring men without these qualities to the surface that the enemy of public order and well regulated government seeks and finds his opportunity.

Such is our present condition. It is to our noble system of schools and our unhampered social civilization that we owe the moderate capacity, even of men of accident, for public affairs.

From the time of President Fillmore, all our Chief Magistrates have been of this popular growth. Mr. Lincoln proved to be the possessor of powers extraordinary in their combination, ranging from the Jesuitry of the frivolous to the depth and gravity of the heroic, and, at last, the tragic. He kept in view great objects of human performance, and showed how profoundly his inherited idea of the equality of rights and his belief in the destiny of America to protect and teach them, animated his conduct. He bore the sword of the country while constantly possessed of the ambition to preserve its nationality and expel slavery; his amiable nature added to these achievements the softness and sweetness of a personal mission, and his lofty fate the solemnity of a personal martyrdom.

The elements of corruption, inseparable from human nature, had long existed in a more or less organized form in the United States, and they waxed in strength and took enormous proportions during Mr. Lincoln's administration. He was a statesman and kept his mind steadily upon the larger objects, preferring to leave the correction of incidental evils to the administrators who should succeed the war. Had he been of a desponding spirit, and nervous and violent upon errors of omission and commission by the way, we might never have kept in view the main purposes of the war, but would have been demoralized by the ten thousand peculations and intrigues which marked the course of that extraordinary conflict.

It is our province and the task of statesmanship in our time, to return along the course of those war-ridden years and take up their civil grievances, exhibit them clearly and correct them unflinchingly. If we do not do so the Union is too great for us and emancipation has been a mockery.

The opportunities for gain at the public and general expense, had been too vast during the war to be suddenly relinquished at the peace. President Johnson was as honest personally as President Lincoln, but the division of arms was now succeeded by a conflict of policy in which the harpies who had studied the Government to take advantage of it plied between both sides, and by the common weakness of the administration and Congress continued their work. They set up the audacious proposition that the schemes which prevailed in the war and the grade of taxation consequent upon it were the declared national policy. A large proportion of the capital and enterprise of the country took the same ground. The currency was maintained in its expanded amount, and war was even declared upon gold, the standard of valuation throughout civilization. High prices and high wages were advocated as evidences of national happiness, and, of course, high salaries were demanded to make public and private conditions consistent with each other. The prevalence of money, work, and rank during the war were not suffered to relax, and Congress undertook to supply artificial means of prosperity by laying out schemes, subsidizing and endowing corporations, increasing offices and commissions, and altering the tariff and the tax list. The victorious side in the wrangle about policy was soon represented in congress by a great number of adventurers, foreigners in the constituency they affected to represent, and shameless and unknown.

At this period the third President of the new era was elected, a brave and victorious soldier, who was in part a pupil and associate of the loose notions of the period. He had a modest person, and this, with his historic exploits, affected the sensibilities of his countrymen, including many of the larger men in literature, criticism, and society, so that this personal sympathy, added to the financial necessities of the time, and the well organized Northern sentiment of the majority of the people carried him again into the White House. Whatever might have been the capacity, or incapacity, of General Grant to direct the law makers and give example to the laws, he sank into a relatively inconspicuous place almost at the moment of his second inauguration by the nearly simultaneous exposure of a series of old and new corruptions in congress which involved the Vice-President of the United States, the Chairman of the three leading committees of Congress, the head of the Protection School in public life, half a dozen senators and as many members of the House, of both parties.

The Vice-President departing and the new Vice-President acceding, both complicated in the celebrated Crédit Mobilier corruption, confronted the public gaze as actors in the same ceremonial with President Grant, who was waiting to deliver his second inaugural address to the public. Five senators, Bogy, Casserly, Clayton, Caldwell, and Pomeroy, were at that moment under accusation of purchasing their seats in the Senate. Three judges of the United States Courts, Delahay, Sherman, and Durrell, were under impeachment or imputation for complicity in the Crédit Mobilier intrigue. The proudest foreheads in the national legislature were abashed. It was a melancholy and disgraceful spectacle, and it saddened the Capital and cast a cloud over all the country.

The purpose of this book is to make Washington at the present day visible to voters, so that they can be guided in criticism upon abuses such as have been related. The course of the chapters is purposely made discursive so that the mind can be carried through a variety of scenes without flagging.

CHAPTER II.

THE American Capital is the only seat of government of a first-class power which was a thought and performance of the Government itself. It used to be called, in the Madisonian era, "the only virgin Capital in the world."

St. Petersburg was the thought of an Emperor, but the Capital of Russia long afterward remained at Moscow, and Peter the Great said that he designed St. Petersburg to be only "a window looking out into Europe."

Washington City was designed to be not merely a window, but a whole inhabitancy in fee simple for the deliberations of Congress, and they were to exercise exclusive legislation over it. So the Constitutional Convention ordained; and, in less than seven weeks after the thirteenth state ratified the Constitution, the place of the Capital was designated by Congress to the Potomac River. In six months more, the precise territory on the Potomac was defined, under the personal eye of Washington.

The motive of building an entirely new city for the Federal seat was not arbitrary, like Peter the Great's will with St. Petersburg, nor fanciful, like that of the founder of Versailles. It was, like many of our institutions, an act of reflection suggested by such harsh experience as once drove the Papal head from Rome to Avignon, and, in our day, has withdrawn the French Government from Paris to Versailles. Four years before the Constitution was made, Congress, while sitting at Philadelphia, —the largest city in the States,—had been grossly insulted by some of the unpaid troops of the Revolutionary War, and the

Pennsylvania authorities showed it no protection. Congress with commendable dignity, withdrew to Princeton, and there, in the collegiate halls, Eldridge Gerry, of Massachusetts, (whose remains now lie in the Congressional Cemetery of Washington,) moved that the buildings for the use of Congress be erected either on the Delaware or the Potomac.

The State of Maryland was an early applicant for the permanent seat of the Government, and, after the result at Philadelphia, hastened to offer Congress its Capitol edifice and other accommodations at Annapolis. Congress accepted the invitation, and therefore, it was at Annapolis that Washington surrendered his commission, in the presence of that body. The career of Congress at Annapolis—which was a very perfect, tidy, and pretty miniature city—left a good impression upon the members for years afterwards, and was probably not without its influence in making Maryland soil the future Federal District. The growing "Baltimore Town," which was the first place in America, after the revolution, to exhibit the Western spirit of "driving things," appeared in the lobby and prints, as an anxious competitor for the award of the Capital; and the stimulation of that day bore fruits in the first and only admirable patriotic monument raised to Washington, while Washington City was yet seeking to survive its ashes. With the jealousy of a neighbor, the snug port and portage settlement of Georgetown opposed Baltimore, and directed attention to itself as deserving the Federal bestowal, and counted, not without reason, upon the influence of the President of the United States in its behalf.

Many other places strove for the exaggerated honor and profit of the Capital, and it is tradition in half-a-dozen villages of the country,—at Havre de Grace, Trenton, Wrightsville, Pa; Germantown, Pa; Williamsport, Md; Kingston, N. Y., and others— that the seat of government was at one time nearly their prize. Two points, however, gained steadily on the rest,—New York and some indefinite spot on the Potomac. The Eastern Congressmen, used to the life of towns, and little in love with what they considered the barbaric plantation life of the South, desired to assemble amongst urbane comforts, in a place already established. Provincialism, prejudice, and avarice all played their part in the contest; and, in that day of paper money, it was thought by many that the currency must follow the Capital. Hence, according to Jefferson, whose accounts on this head do not read very clearly, the financial problems of the time were offset by the selection of the Capital. Hamilton deferred to the South the Federal City, and had his Treasury policy adopted in exchange for it. When Jefferson and Hamilton came to write about each other, we are reminded of the adage that, when the wine is in, the wit is out; but it is agreeable to reflect that they were both accordant with Washington on this point, and Jefferson had great influence over the young Capital's fortunes.

Congress made a reasonable decision on the subject. The comforts of a home were to be accorded at Philadelphia for ten years, to quiet Philadelphia, and meantime a new place was to be planned on the Potomac River, and public edifices erected upon it. The actual selection and plan were to be left to a commission selected by the President; and thus the Federal City is an executive act, deliberated between Washington and private citizens.

Mortifying, indeed, was the early work of making the Capital City for the three Commissioners, whose ranks were renewed as one grew despondent and another enraged.

It was July 16, 1790, that President Washington approved the bill of six sections which directed the acceptance of ten miles square " for the permanent seat of the Government," "between the mouths of the Eastern Branch and Conogocheague." The bill had become a law by a close vote in both Houses, and the Capital might have been placed, under the terms of it, at the Great Falls, or near the future battle-site of Ball's Bluff, or under the presence of the Sugar-Loaf Mountain, in the vale of the River Antietam. It is possible that Washington himself, who held discretionary control over the Commissioners, was not firmly of the opinion that the future city

should stand on tide-water; for he had previously written letters, in praise of the thrifty German country beyond the Monocacy, in Maryland. But the matter of transportation and passage was greatly dependent, in those days, upon navigable
water-courses, and it is probable that, when the law passed, the
spot of the city was already appointed.

About five years before selecting the site for the Federal Capital, Washington made a canoe upon the Monocacy River, and,
descending to the Potomac, made the exploration of the whole
river, from the mountains to tide-water, in order to test the
feasibility of lock and dam navigation. It is apparent, from
his letters to Arthur Young, the Earl of Buchan, and others,
that he was aware that the value of his estates on tide-
water was declining, and he wanted both the city and the canal
contiguous to them. A noble man might well, however, have
such an attachment to the haunts of his youth as to wish to see
it beautified by a city.

The bill was passed while Congress sat in New York; six
months later, on January 24, 1791, Washington, at Philadelphia, made proclamation that, "After duly examining and
weighing the advantages and disadvantages of the several situations within the limits," he had thrown the Federal territory
across the Potomac from Alexandria.

The site of the new district was not entirely the wilderness
it has been represented. The Potomac had been explored up
to this point, and as far as the Little Falls above, by Henry
Fleet, one hundred and sixty years before. Fleet was the first
civilized being who ever looked upon the site of Washington,
and his manuscript story of ascending the river was never published until 1871. When Leonard Calvert arrived in the Potomac, in 1634, he went up to confer with this adventurous fur-
trader, who had been many years in the country.

"The place," said Fleet, evidently alluding to the contracted
Potomac just above Georgetown, "is, without all question, the
most healthful and pleasant place in all this country, and most
convenient for habitation; the air temperate in Summer and

not violent in Winter. It aboundeth with all manner of fish. The Indians in one night commonly will catch thirty sturgeons in a place where the river is not over twelve fathoms broad. And, for deer, buffaloes, bears, turkeys, the woods do swarm with them, and the soil is exceedingly fertile ; but, above this place, the country is rocky and mountainous, like Canada. * * * * We had not rowed above three miles but we might hear the Falls to roar."

The early settlers of Maryland and Virginia kept to the navigable streams, and the earliest pioneers of the terrace country of Maryland were Scotch and Scotch-Irish, some Germans, and a few Catholics.

Georgetown and Bellhaven (or Alexandria) were rather old places when the surveys were made for Washington City, and the former had been laid out fully forty years. The army of General Braddock had landed at Alexandria, and a large portion of his army marched from Rock Creek, as the infant Georgetown was then called, for Fredericktown and the Ohio. As early as 1763, the father of Gen. James Wilkinson purchased a tract of " five hundred acres of land on the Tyber and the Potomac, which probably comprehended the President's house ;" but the purchaser's wife objected to a removal to such an isolated spot, and the property was transferred to one Thomas Johns. In 1775, the young Wilkinson " shouldered a firelock at Georgetown, in a company commanded by a Rhode Island Quaker, Thomas Richardson," in which also the future Gen. Lingan was a subaltern, and this full company drilled for the Revolutionary struggle " on a small spot of table-land hanging over Rock Creek, below the upper bridge." As Wilkinson lived " thirty miles in the up-country, and was always punctual at parade," we may infer that Georgetown was the most considerable place in all this quarter of Maryland. As early as 1779, William Wirt, whose parents resided at Bladensburg, went to " a Classical Academy at Georgetown ;" and he and others long bore remembrance of the passage of the French and American armies from north to south over the ferry at that place, of

encampment at Kalorama Hill, and wagons loaded with specie
crossing Rock Creek. Gen. Washington also designated
Georgetown as one of the three great places of deposit for military stores; and so important was Alexandria that Charles
Lee, in his plan of treason, had proposed to cut the Northern
States from the South by occupying it with a permanent detach-
ment of British troops, who should keep open the ferries between
Alexandria and Annapolis, and, by menacing the rich farms of
the German settlers in the up-country, compel them to starve
out the Patriot armies.

The port-town of Bladensburg was now just upon the decline,
and the period had come when the interior parts of Maryland,
Pennsylvania, and Virginia were showing forth their promises.
Maryland had contained considerably more population than
New York during the Revolutionary War, and we may conceive
Georgetown and Alexandria to have been amongst the best grade
of secondary towns at that period. They stood, as now, in full
sight of each other; and the ridgy basin and lower terraces
between them, where the Federal City was to rise, presented a
few good farms tilled by slaves, and was already marked for a
couple of rival settlements before the Commissioners adopted it.

One of these prospective settlements was located near the
present National Observatory, and took the name of Hamburg,
afterward Funkstown, the other was projected near the present
Navy-Yard, and was named after the proprietor of the estate,
Carrollsburg. At any rate, there were enough people on the site
to give the Commissioners a great deal of trouble with their
bickering and rapacity; and it is likely that the idea got abroad
in advance of the official choice, that here was to be the mighty
Capital, and therefore lands and lots had been matters of considerable speculation.

Few who had passed the ferry at Georgetown, and beheld the
sight from the opposite hills of Virginia, could fail to have
marked the breadth of the picture, and the strong colors in the
ground and the environing wall of wooded heights, which rolled
back against the distant sky, as if to enclose a noble arena of

landscape, fit for the supreme deliberations of a continental nation.

Dropping down from those heights by stately gradations, over several miles, to a terrace of hills in the middle ground, the foreground then divided, parallel with the eye, into a basin and a plateau. The plateau on the right showed one prominent but not precipitous hill, with an agreeable slope, at the back of which the Potomac reached a deep, supporting arm, while around the base meandered a creek that changed course when half-way advanced, and then flowed to the left, parallel with knolls, straight through the plain or basin,—defining to the inspired eye, as plainly as revelation, the avenues, grades, and commanding positions of a city.

As such, Washington must have builded it up in his own formative mind; for many a time he had passed it in review. He did not require to take note of the shiftless slave farms for which the ground had been already broken. Where yonder orchard grew, he saw the Executive Mansion, with its grounds extending down to the river-side cottage of that curmudgeon Scotch planter who was to be among the last to say words of impudence to the father of the city. Where the pleasant hill swelled up to the clear skies in the night, Washington saw the spiritual outlines of the fair white Capitol, soon to be embodied there. Flowing down into the plain, and extending back over the hill of the Capitol, he realized the lower and the upper city, on which a circle of villas in the higher background should some day look down; and all the undulating space between the blue heights of Georgetown, from the river back to the table-land, should, by another century, smoke with population, worship with bells, and march with music to honor the founder of this virgin Capital.

Having named the three civil Commissioners to whom Congress—wiser than Congresses of a later period—committed the business of Capital-making, Washington set out from Philadelphia, to confer with them on the spot.

It is characteristic of Maryland roads in those days, in March,

2

that the President drove down the Eastern shore of Maryland,
instead of crossing the Susquehanna, and was ferried over from
Rockhall to Annapolis.   At the latter place, he rested all Saturday, receiving hospitality ; and, on Sunday, continued his
journey by Queen Ann to Bladensburg, where he dined and slept.
Next morning he took breakfast at Suter's tavern, a one-story
frame in Georgetown,—having occupied one week in fatiguing
and perilous travel from Philadelphia.

From the heights of Georgetown, Washington could look
over the half-uncultivated tract, where the commissioners had
plotted a part of their surveys for the Federal City, and Pennsylvania Avenue was then a path through an older swamp from
Georgetown to Carrollsburg.

On Tuesday, a misty and disagreeable day, Washington rode
out at seven o'clock, with David Stuart, Daniel Carroll, and
Thomas Johnson, the three Commissioners, and with Mr.
Andrew Ellicott and Major L'Enfant, who were surveying the
grounds and projecting the streets of the city.   "I derived no
great satisfaction," says Washington, " from the review," and
this we can readily suppose from our present knowledge of
what might be the condition of the soil of the District in the
spring of the year, on a damp day, with the landholders of
Georgetown and Carrollsburg contending with each other by
the way, with the numerous uninvited idlers pressing after,
and the crude and tangled nature of the region.

That night at six o'clock, Washington endeavored to con-
trive an accommodation between the Georgetowners and
Carrollsburgers, and it was probably at this time that he
had reason to designate Davy Burns, the Scotch farmer and
father to the future heiress of the city, as " The obstinate Mr.
Burns."   He dined that night at Colonel Forrest's, with a large
company.   The next day, the contending landholders agreed to
Washington's suggestions, and entered into articles to surrender half their lots when surveyed ; and, having given some of
his characteristically precise instructions to the engineers and
others, the President crossed the Potomac in the ferry-boat,

his equipage following, and dined at Alexandria, and slept that night at Mount Vernon, his homestead.

There is a statue of Washington in one of the public circles of the Capital City, representing him on a terrified steed doing battle-duty; but a local treatment of the subject would have been more touching and thoughtful; the veteran of war and politics, worn down with the friction of public duty and rising party asperity, riding through the marshes and fields of Washington, on the brink of his sixtieth year, to give the foundling government he had reared an honorable home. Could a finer subject appeal to the artist or to the municipality of Washington; the virgin landscape of the Capital, and this greatest of founders of cities since Romulus, surrounded by the two engineers, the three commissioners, and certain courteous denizens, and seeking to reason the necessities of the state and the pride of the country into the flinty soul of Davy Burns, that successor of Dogberry,—for he is said to have been a magistrate?

The new city was one of the plagues of General Washington for the remainder of his days, because he was very sensitive as to its success; and it had to suffer the concentrated fire of criticism and witticism, domestic and foreign, as well as more serious financial adversity. He never beheld any of the glory of it; and the fact that he had been responsible for it, and had settled it in the neighborhood of his estates, probably weighed somewhat upon his spirits in the midst of that light repartee which a grave nature cannot answer. Greater is he who keepeth his temper than he who buildeth a city. That Washington did both well, the latter century can answer better than the former. The extravagant plan of Major L'Enfant has not been vindicated until now, when the habitations of one hundred thousand people begin to develop upon the plane of his magnificence. The neighbors of General Washington had no capacity in that early day to congregate in cities, and the Federal site had to wait for a gregarious domination and a period of comparative wealth. It is yet to be tested whether the ornamentation of the city is to conduce to an equally Republican rule with that of more squalid times; for, New York excepted, Washington is now the dearest city in America.

The trustees of the Federal City in whom at law nominally reposed the conveyed property, were Thomas Beall and John M. Gautt. The chief owners of the site were David Burns, Samuel Davidson, Notley Young, and Daniel Carroll.

The cost of the ground on which Washington City stands was truly insignificant as compared with the remarkable expenditures of the years 1871, '72, '73.

The few property-holders agreed to convey to the Government out of their farm-lands as much ground as would be required for streets, avenues, public-building-sites, reservations, areas, etc., and to surrender, also, one-half of the remaining land, to be sold by the United States as it might deem fit,—receiving, however, at the rate of twenty-five pounds per acre for the public grounds, but nothing for the streets. In other words, the Government through its three commissioners, was to plot out the Federal City in the first place, delineating all the grounds required for buildings and reservations, and surveying the parts to be inhabited. It was then to divide these inhabitable lots equally between itself and the landholders, and sell its own lots when, and on what prices and terms, it pleased, and, out of the proceeds of such sales, to make its payments for the national grounds and reservations.

· In this way the Government took seventeen great parcels of ground out of the general plan, such as now surround the Capitol, the President's House, etc., and the same amounted to five hundred and forty-one acres. At sixty-six dollars and sixty-six cents per acre, this yielded to the farm-holders thirty-six thousand ninety-nine dollars,—a very small sum indeed if we compute interest upon it, and subtract principal and interest from the present value of the ground.

The building lots assigned to the Government numbered ten thousand one hundred and thirty-six. The amount of sales of these lots, up to the year 1834, was seven hundred forty-one thousand twenty-four dollars and forty-five cents, and an assess-

ment upon the unsold lots, made at that time, brought the
Government's share up to eight hundred fifty thousand dollars.
Besides this handsome speculation, the State of Virginia voted
to the Government the sum of one hundred twenty thousand
dollars, and the State of Maryland seventy-two thousand dollars, as a concession for planting the great city on their borders. With equal courtesy, the Government gave away a great
many lots to such institutions as the Columbian and Georgetown Colleges, and the Washington and St. Vincents Orphan
Asylums; and it also squandered many lots upon less worthy
solicitors, giving a depot site away to a railway company in
1872, which was worth several hundred thousand dollars.

In the entire area included under the above agreement, there
were seven thousand one hundred acres, with a circumference
of fourteen miles. The uneven plain of the city extended four
miles along the river, and averaged three-quarters of a mile in
breadth. The only streams were the Tiber, which divided the
plain nearly equally; James' Creek, emptying into the mouth
of the Eastern Branch; and Slash Run, emptying into Rock
Creek. These streams still preserve the names they received
long before the Capital was pitched. The first dedicatory act
was to fix the corner-stone at Jones' Point, near Alexandria.
James Muir preached the sermon, Daniel Carroll and David
Stuart placed the stone, and the Masons of Alexandria performed their mystic rites.

A glimpse of the United States as it was at that day (1791)
will complete the impression we may derive on thus revisiting
the nearly naked site of the "Federal Seat." Virginia led all
the states with nearly seven hundred fifty thousand people;
Pennsylvania and New York combined did little more than
balance Virginia with four hundred thirty-four thousand and
three hundred forty thousand respectively. North Carolina
outweighed Massachusetts with three hundred ninety-four thousand to the Bay State's three hundred seventy-nine thousand.
All the rest of New England displayed about six hundred thousand population. South Carolina and Georgia with three

hundred thirty thousand people together, were inferior to Maryland and Delaware together by fifty thousand. There were only two Western States, Kentucky and Tennessee, whose one hundred eight thousand people lacked seventy-five thousand of the population of New Jersey and altogether, four millions of Americans were watching with various human expressions the puzzle of the capital town. Such was the showing of the census of 1790, but by the year 1800, when the infant city was occupied by its government, the country was one third greater in inhabitants. It was not until 1820 that any state passed Virginia, but in 1830 both New York and Pennsylvania had bidden her good-bye.

The Capital was staked out the year after Franklin's death, thirty years before the death of George III, in Goethe's fifty-second year and Schiller's thirty-second, sixteen years before the first steamboat, two years before Louis XVI was guillotined, when Louis Phillipe was in his nineteenth year, while Count Rochambeau was commander of the French army, two years after Robespierre became head deputy, five years after the death of Frederick the Great, while George Stephenson was a boy of ten, the year subsequent to the death of Aden Smith, the year John Wesley and Mirabeau died, two years before Brissot was guillotined, in Napoleon's twenty-second year, the year before Lord Nott died, the year Morse was born and Mirabeau was buried, in the third year of the London Times, just after Lafayette had been the most powerful man in France, three years before the death of Edward Gibbon, while Warren Hastings was on trial, in Burke's sixty-first year and Fox's forty-second and Pitt's thirty-second, three years after the death of Chatham, in the Popedom of Pius VI, while Simon Bolivar was a child eight years old, the year Cowper translated Homer, and in Burns' prime.

CHAPTER III.

THE JOB OF PLANNING THE FEDERAL CITY.

ACCORDING to the whole of many authorities and a part of all, the city of Washington itself was a scheme and the public buildings severally were sown in corruption. That they have been raised in incorruption, however, is clear to the cheerful, patriotic mind: for the Capitol is the ornament in some manner of nearly every American dwelling. The White House is the most beautiful building in the world to a politician aspiring toward it. Thousands of people would be glad to get as much as a hand in the Treasury or even a name in the Pension office.

These buildings make a continuous romance in respect to their design, construction, and personal associations. In their day they were esteemed the noblest edifices on the continent, and educed praise even from such censorious strangers as Mrs. Trollope. To this day the Capitol and President's house remain as they were exteriorly, the same in style and proportions, and the additions to the Capitol have been made consistent with the old elevation. The public is better satisfied with the Capitol from year to year, and many men of culture and travel even prefer the old freestone original edifice to the spacious and costly marble wings. The President's House has lost somewhat of its superiority as a residence, owing to the progress made in household comforts during the last half century, but it is still admired by the visitor for the extent, harmony, and impressiveness of its saloons. Both buildings and the city as well invite at this day our inquisitiveness as to how the young republic became possessed of architects and engineers of capacity equal to such ample and effective constructions.

The material for this inquiry is to be found in the journals and letter books of the early commissioners of the Federal City, which are kept on the crypt floor of the Capitol and are partly indexed. The personal story of the early architects must be obtained by family tradition and partly by recollection. The printed documents of congress continue the story of those constructions to our own day, but many of them are rare and some missing, because the Capitol has been three times devastated by fire which twice chose the library as the point of attack.

Let us first note the lives of the planners of the city itself.

They assembled at Georgetown with tents, horses, and laborers, and proceeded to plot the city upon the site, while the commissioners, acting for the executive, raised and supplied the money, dealt with the owners of the ground and negotiated with quarrymen, carters, and boat owners. Every step was a matter of delicacy, and conflicts were frequent between all parties. A high degree of personal independence prevailed in the late colonies and in military, political, and professional life, amounting in many cases to sensitiveness and jealousy.

The commissioners had little consonance of temperament with the professional men, many of whom were foreigners, and both had reason to dislike the natives who began by craving the boon of the city, and ended by showing all the forms of querulousness and discontent which rise from excited avarice.

First in consideration is the man out of whose mind and art were drawn the design of Washington city as we find it still. Peter Charles L'Enfant was born in France, 1755, and made a Lieutenant in the French provincial forces. Touched at an early period in the American revolution with the spirit of the American Colonies and the opportunities afforded in the new world for a young officer and engineer he tendered his services in the latter capacity to the United States in the autumn of 1777. He received his wish and the appointment of Captain of Engineers February 18, 1778. At the siege of Savannah he was wounded and left on the field of battle. After cure he took a position in the army under the immediate eye of Washington and was promoted Major of Engineers May 2, 1873. Hence the rank with which he descends to history.

At the close of the Revolution L'Enfant commended himself to Jefferson who almost monopolized the artistic taste and knowledge of the first administration, and as the project for a Federal city developed L'Enfant was brought into very close relations with President Washington. The artistic and the executive mind rarely run parallel, however, and very soon Washington heard with indignation that L'Enfant, enamored of his plan of the city, had refused to let it be used by the Commissioners as an incitement and directory to purchasers. The excuse of L'Enfant appears to have been that if acquainted with the plan speculators would build up his finest avenues with unsuitable structures. Washington's letter displays both the ability and weakness of his architect and engineer:

"It is much to be regretted," he says, "that men who possess talents which fit them for peculiar purposes should almost invariably be under the influence of an untoward disposition * *. I have thought that for such employment that he is now engaged in for prosecuting public works and carrying them into effect. Major L'Enfant was better qualified than any one who had come within my knowledge in this country or indeed in any other I had no doubt at the same time, that this was the light in which he considered himself."

This letter was written in the autumn of 1791, eight months after Jefferson instructed L'Enfant as follows:

"You are directed to proceed to Georgetown where you will find Mr. Ellicott in making a survey and map of the Federal territory." Jefferson then distributed the responsibility by prescribing as L'Enfant's duty "to draw the site of the Federal town and buildings." He was to begin at the Eastern Branch and proceed upwards, and the word "Tyber" is used thus early in the history of the city as applying to the celebrated creek of that name, long afterwards the eye-sore of the city.

As between the immortal patron of the new city and the poor military artist posterity will expend no sympathies upon L'Enfant.

but there was probably a provincial hardness amongst the Commissioners and a want of consideration for the engineers, for even " Ellicott," also a man of uncommon talents in his way and of a more placid temper, was incensed at the slights put upon him.

Jefferson wrote to L'Enfant Nov. 21, 1791, that he must not delay the engraving of his map by over nicety and thus spoil the sale of town lots, which it appears brought as good prices without the map as with it ; for he had written in October that " the sales at Georgetown were few but good." They averaged two thousand four hundred the acre.

The Map was not produced, however, and his appeals over the heads of the Commissioners on points of difference were decided against the artist. His task lasted but one year and was abruptly terminated March 6th, 1792, as the following letter of Jefferson to the Commissioners shows :

" It having been found impracticable to employ Major L'Enfant about the Federal City in that degree of subordination which was lawful and proper, he has been notified that his services are at an end. It is now proper that he should receive the reward of his past services and the wish that he should have no just cause of discontent suggests that it should be liberal. The President thinks of two thousand five hundred dollars or three thousand dollars, but leaves the determination to you. Ellicott is to go on and finish laying off the plan on the ground and surveying and plotting the district."

L'Enfant's reputation and acquaintance were such that he might have done the new city great injury by taking a position to its detriment, and Washington wrote that " the enemies of the enterprise will take the advantage of the retirement of L'Enfant to trumpet the whole as an abortion." It appears, however, that L'Enfant was loyal to the Government and the city, for he lived on the site and in the neighborhood all his days, and several times afterwards came under the notice of the executive and was a baffled petitioner before Congress.

We hear of him in 1794 in the public employment as Engineer at Fort Mifflin below Philadelphia and after a long lapse as declining the Professorship of Engineers at West Point, July, 1812.

Christian Hines, referred to elsewhere, told me that he had seen Major L'Enfant many a time wearing a green surtout and never appearing in a change of clothes, walking across the commons and fields followed by half a dozen hunting dogs. Mr. Hines reported with some of his company to L'Enfant at Fort Washington in 1814 to do duty, and that officer, who was in temporary command, filled him a glass of wine in his old broadly hospitable way and told him what to do.

The author of the plan of the city led a long and melancholy career about Washington and died on the farm of Mr. Digges in Prince George's County, about eight miles from the Capital he planned. The Digges family were allied to the Carrolls of Duddington, and had pity upon the military gentleman who had been

MAJOR L'ENFANT'S RESTING PLACE—THE DIGGES FARM.

at once so capable, so willful, and so unfortunate. The banker Corcoran has a distinct remembrance of L'Enfant as he lived, a rather seedy, stylish old man with a long blue coat buttoned up on his breast and a bell-crowned hat, a little moody and lonely like one wronged. He wrote much and left many papers which Mr. Wyeth of Washington told me he had inspected. He would not abate a particle of his claim against the Government, being to the last as tenacious of the point of pride as when he refused his maps to the Commissioners to be the accessory of the auctioneer and the lot speculator. The Digges farm was purchased by the banker, George Riggs, Esq., many years after L'Enfant's death, and a superb stone mansion and a chapel for worship were erected upon the pleasant hill where the architect of the ruling city sleeps. In the garden planted by the Digges family there had been one of those private burial grounds not uncommon in Maryland and quite common to Catholic families. Amongst the people who closed his eyes he was laid to rest in June, 1825, at the age of seventy. Mr. Riggs says that subsequently a member of the Digges family committed suicide and the negroes buried this person crosswise to L'Enfant's body. The leading members of the family were disinterred afterward and the old soldier left there nearly alone. Some measures were suggested for giving him a monument at the time I made these inquiries.

L'Enfant's judgment was not equal to his imagination, but he had taste, knowledge, and amplitude, and with a richer patron than the American Nation might have made a more sounding fame. His plan of the Capital City is gradually vindicating itself as the magnificent distances fill up with buildings, and the recent happy expedient of parking the streets has made it possible to pave them all without extraordinary expense. Such as it is, the city is irrevocably a part of his fame. One cannot fail to see that he drew it from the study of LeNotre's work in the city of Versailles and in the forests contiguous to Paris, where aisles, *routes*, etc., meet at broad open *carrefours* and a prospect or bit of architecture closes each avenue. Washington city in its grand plan is French; in its minor plan Quaker. It is the city of Philadelphia griddled across the city of Versailles. Anybody who will look at the design of the house which L'Enfant built for Robert Morris at Philadelphia after he was discharged from the public service,—that house which so far exceeded the estimates, that it was pulled down after the ruin of Morris and the materials made a quarry of—will observe that it is very much in the style of Mansard and the French architects of the seventeenth century. Thus the French alliance with America brought to our shores the draughtsman

of the government city, and few men have had it in their power
to define so absolutely a stage for historical and biographical
movement.   As L'Enfant made the city it remains, with little
or no alteration.   And his misfortunes and poverty contrasted
with his noble opportunity will always classify him with the
brotherhood of art and genius, and make him remembered as
long as the city shall exist.

The first quarrel which L'Enfant had with the commissioners related to the destruction of a mansion belonging to one of
the proprietors of the ground, the aged Daniel Carroll, who had
begun to build a great brick house which he called " Duddington," in the middle of New Jersey Avenue right under the
Capitol.   As this house embarrassed the engineer's much
beloved plan and assumed for itself the importance of a public
edifice, L'Enfant issued an order for its demolition.   The commissioners protested but the artist gave orders to his Lieutenant, Isaac Roberdeau, to pull down the structure in his absence
while he meantime should be at Acquia Creek where he had
leased the quarries of Brent and Gibson.   Roberdeau was
stopped by Carroll who sent a courier to Annapolis to get an
injunction, but seeing the speed the Frenchman was making in
the interval Carroll served a local magistrate's warrant upon
him.   When L'Enfant returned and found his orders unfulfilled
he quietly organized a gang of laborers and in the evening these
set to work and reduced the presumptuous edifice with a hearty
diligence which led to a shower of complaints from both proprietors and commissioners.   Carroll proposed to sue L'Enfant ;
Roberdeau was discharged and the artist in chief kept his place
only two months longer.   The Administration directed Duddington House to be reconstructed as it was before but in
another spot, and there it remains to-day, a grim old relic surrounded with a high brick wall and a park of forest trees.

Andrew Ellicott, the consulting and practical engineer of the
new city, was a native of Bucks county, Pennsylvania, where
his English father emigrated in 1730.   He and two brothers
had moved from Pennsylvania in wagons in 1772 and started

the town of Ellicott's Mills and were promoters of the fortunes of Baltimore and enterprising merchants, manufacturers, agriculturists, and inventors. They were the fathers of good road building, of iron rolling and copper working in Maryland, and inventors of many useful things, such as the wagon-brake. Andrew Ellicott was in the prime of life,—thirty-seven years old,—when he rode out with Washington to inspect the embryo city. Of all the party he was the most intellectual unless we except L'Enfant; for although a Quaker he had commanded a battalion of militia in the revolution, and it gives us a wondering insight into the resources of the American Colonial mind to find that this companion of Franklin, Rittenhouse, and Washington learned the elements of what he knew at the little Maryland milling place he established.

Ellicott had surveyed portions of the boundaries of New York, Pennsylvania, and Virginia, executed a topographical map of the country bordering on Lake Erie, and made the first accurate measurement of Niagara Falls. He had besides been a member of the Maryland Legislature. His more tractable and accommodating disposition secured him the honor of finishing the work of L'Enfant, and it appears that he was paid while on this service five dollars a day and his expenses.

In 1792 he became Surveyor General of the United States, laid out the towns of Erie, Warren, and Franklin in Pennsylvania, and constructed Fort Erie. In 1796 he determined the boundary line separating the republic from the Spanish possessions, and for many years subsequently was Secretary of the Pennsylvania state land office. His acquaintance and correspondence were with the most eminent people of his day in America and Europe, and in 1812 he was made Professor of Mathematics at West Point, where he died August 28, 1820, at the age of sixty-six. One of his family, Mr. Jos. C. G. Kennedy, was Superintendent of the United States census in 1860, and is now a resident of Washington. Amongst the assistants to run the lines of the new city was one man entitled to the future consideration of all his race, Benjamin Banneker, a negro.

He was at this time sixty years of age and a native of Ellicott's Mills and the protégé of the family of Andrew Ellicott. He is represented to have been a large man of noble appearance with venerable white hair, wearing a coat of superfine drab broad cloth and a broad brimmed hat, and to have resembled Benjamin Franklin. He was honored by the commissioners with a request to sit at their table, but his unobtrusive nature made him prefer a separate table. He was not only considerately cared for by these gentlemen, but Mr. Jefferson with his broad encouragement for learning and ability had praised an almanac he constructed, and the black man's proficiency in the exact sciences had given him a general reputation. He was sometimes too fond of a glass, but made it a matter of pride that at Washington he had carefully avoided temptation. Banneker died in 1804, and his grave at Ellicott's Mills is without a mark.

Thus much for the makers of the plan of the city. The trials and quarrels of the architects will be found even more romantic.

With all his discouragements concerning it Washington kept up the gleam of belief in the fortunes of his namesake city and called attention to it in letters to the Earl of Buchan and his old neighbor Mrs. S. Fairfax. To the latter, who was in England, he wrote the year before his decease:

"A century hence, if this country keeps united, it will produce a city though not as large as London yet of a magnitude inferior to few others in Europe."

Three quarters of that century have expired and Washington is a city of one hundred and fifty thousand people. By the year 1900 this should increase to two hundred and fifty thousand. At the time Washington wrote, London had eight hundred thousand inhabitants.

CHAPTER IV.

The first architect of the Capitol in the proper sense of a professional man was Stephen S. Hallet, whose name is also spelled *Hallate*. About this gentleman, whose career on the public buildings was very brief, no recollections and scarcely a tradition prevails. It has been generally said that he was an Englishman and a pupil of the celebrated John Nash of London. It is apparent however, from the books of the Commissioners, that Hallet was a Frenchman. He is addressed by them as Monsieur Hallet and referred to by them as a French artist. They also apologize for writing him a letter by saying that the difficulty of making explanations between themselves and him verbally suggests the former manner of communication. Hallet sent his plan to the Commissioners and they received it July 17, 1792. They were struck with the evidences of his professional capacity, and invited him to visit the spot as soon as he could. These were the old Commissioners, Johnson, Stewart, and Carroll. It appears that Hallet's plans, which were several in number, had about commended him as the author of the building, and he was employed in that capacity when Dr. Thornton, an Englishman, also presented a plan which the Commissioners requested him to lodge with the Secretary of State at Philadelphia. This latter plan, although drawn by an amateur, affected both Jefferson and Washington to such a degree that a letter was at once despatched to the Commissioners requesting them to adopt it and to substitute it for Hallet's, but to do this with as much delicacy as possible and to retain Hallet in the public service. This peremptory order probably gave the Com-

missioners much relief if we may believe the statement of George
Hadfield, another architect who wrote twenty years later to the
following effect :

" A premium had been offered of five hundred dollars and a
building lot for the best design for a capitol, at a time when
scarcely a professional artist was to be found in any part of the
United States ; which is plainly to be seen from the pile of
trash presented as designs."

It does not appear that Monsieur Hallet received in a cordial
way this assurance that an English amateur had made a superior elevation to his own, and he drew again and again designs
while Thornton's were also amended after the foundations of
the Capitol had been raised to the ground level. The situation
was further embarrassed by Thornton's appointment as one of
the Commissioners where he came into conflict with his predecessor in an administrative as well as a professional way. Mr.
Hallet, in deference to Jefferson's suggestion, was employed at
four hundred pounds per year, November 20, 1793. More than
nine months previously, on April 5, 1793, the Commissioners
wrote to Thornton : " The President has given his formal approbation of your plan." The changes in Thornton's design were,
however, made so nearly like that of Hallet's, particularly as
to the interior, that Monsieur demurred to the premium being
accorded to Doctor Thornton. Quarrels ensued and Hallet
withheld his drawings and wrote a letter to the Commissioners
June 28, 1794, saying : " I claim the original invention of the
plan now executing and beg leave to lay hereafter before you
and the President the proofs of my right to it." Thereupon
the Commissioners demanded the plans and Monsieur Hallet
refused to surrender them. He was then verbally acquainted
with the order that their connection with him had ceased and
he was no longer in the public service. From this time forward there is no notable mention in the Commissioner's books
of this unfortunate architect, and I have not been able to find
any traditions respecting him. His successor was George
Hadfield, who continued on the work until May 10, 1798. Mr.

Hallet's account, amounting to upwards of one hundred and seventy-six pounds, was allowed by the Commissioners.

His name, however, had been deposited in the corner-stone as one of the architects, and subsequent developments have in a great measure vindicated his claim as a principal suggestor of the building. About seventy years after his disappearance from the public view a son of B. H. Latrobe, the real builder of the wings, returned to Washington Hallet's drawings. Mr. Clark the architect passed them over to the Librarian of Congress in 1873. I was permitted to make sketch copies of Hallet's plans, and Mr. Clark came into the library while I was drawing from these plans and expressed his opinion that Hallet was the real architect, that what he called his " fanciful plan " had been borrowed by Thornton and changed to such a degree that Hallet was overridden in the premises. He called my attention to this memorandum in Hallet's handwriting:

" A grand plan accompanied this (elevation) which Dr. Thornton sent for, together with my plan in pencil."

On another drawing the following memorandum in Hallet's handwriting appeared:

" Sketch of the groundwork : part of the foundations were laid by sometime in August, 1793, now useless on account of the alterations since introduced.   S. HALLET."

Other drawings by Mr. Hallet were endorsed as follows :

" The ground floor of a plan of the Capitol, laid before the board in October, 1793."

" Plan of the ground and principal floor sent from Philadelphia to the board in July, 1793."

Doctor William Thornton came to America, like Alexander Hamilton, from the West India Islands. He was a man of a good deal of amateur talent, and his introduction to Jefferson brought him to live on the Capitol site where he remained for the remainder of his days. He would appear to have been of an officious, buoyant, persevering disposition, and after he was relieved as Commissioner he gathered together models and curiosities in an abandoned hotel which stood on the site of the present general Post-office, and these curiosities were spared at his intercession from the British incendiary and became the nucleus of the present Patent Office collection, of which, while nominal clerk, Thornton was really the first Commissioner. He was also the founder of the first race track at Washington, and took delight in blooded horses, entering the lists with the great John Tayloe, the chief stock breeder and the richest citizen of the District. Dr. Thornton always insisted with vehemence that he was the original architect of the Capitol, and no doubt his picture of the elevations brought the administration to a conclusion. Jefferson says of it: "The grandeur, simplicity, and beauty of the exterior, the propriety with which the apartments are distributed and economy in the mass of the whole structure recommended this plan." The next day he says that Thornton's plan has captivated the eyes and judgment of all. "It is simple, noble, beautiful, excellently distributed, and moderate in size. * * Among its admirers no one is more decided than he whose decision is most important," meaning Washington.

Mr. Jefferson, at the time above referred to, was held in great consideration by Washington. He had been stationed at the Court of France and was known to have a fine fancy for the arts and to take a patron's delight in the legislative edifices of his country. We can get an idea of his sentiments on art from a letter which he wrote April 10, 1791. He says:

" For the capitol I should prefer the adoption of some of the models of antiquity, which have had the approbation of thousands of years—and for the President's House I should prefer the celebrated fonts of modern buildings."

A controversy sprang up amongst the architects, which outlived the life of Washington, and Thornton was put upon the defensive. In 1804, Mr. Latrobe addressed a report to Congress in which he denounced Thornton's plan and animadverted with some severity upon the principle of competition for designs of great public buildings, saying that " A picture " was not a plan, and intimating that Thornton's work in the premises was merely pictorial. To this Thornton rejoined in a pamphlet, of which a copy exists in the Congressional Library,—a purchase with Mr. Jefferson's collection. Thornton says:

"Mr. Hallet was not in the public service when or since I was appointed commissioner, which was on the twelfth day of September, 1794. *Mr. Hadfield* was appointed to superintend the work at the Capitol, October 15, 1795." Thornton says further:

"Mr. Hallet changed and diminished the senate room, which is now too small. He laid square the foundation at the centre building, excluding the dome; and when General Washington saw the extent of the alterations proposed he expressed his disapprobation in a style of such warmth as his dignity and self-command seldom permitted. * * * Mr. Hallet was desirous not merely of altering what might be improved, but even what was most approved. He made some judicious alterations, but in other instances he did injury * * *. When General Washington honored me with the appointment of commissioner he requested that I should restore the building to a correspondence with the original plan."

It further seems that Washington addressed the commissioners, Gustavus Scott, William Thornton, and Alexander White, February 27, 1797, expressing his " Real satisfaction with their conduct," which involved an endorsement of Thornton's ideas.

Mr. Hallet's first design for the capitol, as well as the modifications and amendments of the same, show that he was an architect of very perfect knowledge. Mr. Clark, as we have said, the architect in 1873, told me that he had heard that Hallet was a pupil of Nash, who was the leading English architect of his period. Nash was born in London in 1752, and after undergoing a course of training in his profession and practising it for some time, withdrew under the delusion of speculation and lost considerable sums of money. When he returned to his profession he met with very great success and opened an office in London in 1792. He designed and constructed numerous splendid mansion houses for the nobility and gentry in England and Ireland, and performed some of the most celebrated street improvements in the British metropolis. He was an inventor as well, and in 1797 obtained a patent for improvement in the construction of arches and piers of bridges, which led him to assume the credit of introducing the use of cast-iron girders. His work in London has been quite celebrated, including the fashioning of Regent Street and its beautiful blocks, the Langham Place Church, the Haymarket Theater, the terraces in Regent's Park, and the pavilion at Brighton. England contains many superb interiors and imposing mansion-houses accredited to him, and he lived until 1835.

It would be interesting only to architects to go at length into a discussion of the relative cleverness of Thornton's original plan, of Hallet's plans and of the amended Capitol as we see it to-day, the work of Latrobe and Bulfinch. The building has received the general approval of the public sentiment, and with the magnificent marble extensions of Mr. Walter,—which are a pattern with the old Capitol,—is one of the most imposing buildings in the world. Thornton's original design of the Capitol had but one dome, a great eagle in the pediment, a statue with a club on the top of the pediment flanked by two female statues on the balustrade, and oak or laurel encompassed the rounded top of the chief window in each wing.

The original plan by Hallet placed the dome outside of the rectangle of the center and put the Senate Chamber in that rotunda. The center of the building was made a square open court with a covered walk around the sides and a carriage turn in the middle. The Supreme Court took the place of the subsequent senate chamber and the Vice-President's room was semi-circular and facing the long main corridor which traversed the edifice lengthwise.

It would appear that Hallet was in Washington until February 22, 1795, for in the bunch of drawings recently consigned to the library and which were doubtless sent to the authorities by Hallet to prove his right to the premium—there is one

"A fanciful plan and elevation which the President having seen accidentally in September, 1793, agreed with the commissioners to have the Capitol planned in imitation thereof."

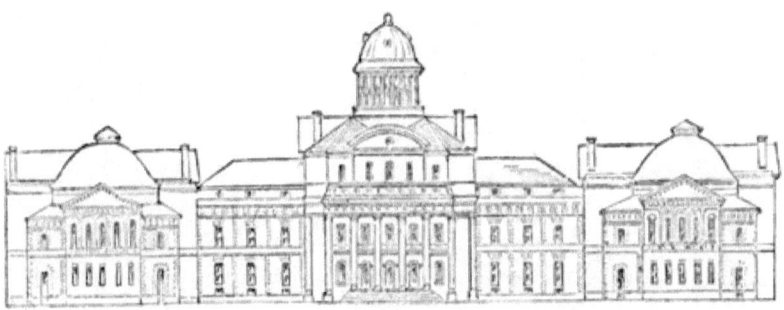

HALLET'S PLAN OF THE CAPITOL.

Hallet's "Fanciful plan" was surmounted by a dome with drum pillars and a light open cupola. Six Doric columns supported the center which upheld a curved pediment with a large eagle in the tympanum, and below were four standing colossal figures of WAR, PEACE, JUSTICE, and TIME. Three columns flanked the portico, which had four doors of equal size and low flights of steps. Shallow curtains with one door and one window connected in the center with the wings, which consisted of a basement and one story. The basement was of stone rusticated, and the portico above had four Ionic columns flanked by windows flush with the portico. In the pediment of each of the wings was a group of statuary of half a dozen figures, representing war and peace. In the recess under the porticoes were three designs in relief over the three doors which opened upon the portico. Hallet's "Fanciful plan" was borrowed by Thornton.

We may congratulate ourselves that the present state of the arts and the unity of official direction in this country prevent such scandals in public construction as attended the building of the old Capitol. It does not appear that any harmony prevailed, and dishonesty was often charged and sometimes proved. The early commissioners accused L'Enfant, Roberdeau, Baoreaf, and others of circulating on the spot infamous falsehoods to

NATIONAL CAPITOL, WASHINGTON.

Design from Harper's Magazine.

the prejudice of our character. Hadfield says that unfavorable reports were taken to General Washington of Thornton's ground plan, and he was ignorantly advised to retain the elevations' and change the interior plans. The corner stone had no sooner been laid than " squabbles began ; differences, factions, and broils were the order of the day." The contractor for the foundation was displaced for another mason, " who used what is called the continental trowel, which was wheelbarrows filled promiscuously with stones and mortar and emptied on the walls. When the foundation was completed or nearly so, the whole was condemned and the second contractor or continental trowelist was dismissed."

It is very certain that the foundations of the first Capitol were condemned and obliged to be rebuilt. After the first crop of commissioners had passed away it was found that at least two of their successors were short in their accounts or had kept no responsible accounts whatever. Mr. Hadfield, to whom we shall come directly, who resided in the city until his death and lived to see the reconstruction of the wings, published at the time a dignified criticism upon the edifice with these admissions :

" The proper way to have built the Capitol was to have offered an adequate sum to the most eminent architect in any of the European cities, to furnish the design and working drawings, also a person of his own choice to superintend the work. In that case the Capitol would have been long ago completed and for half the sum that has been expended on the present wreck."

The second architect in order is Mr. Hadfield, an Englishman who had been requested to come to this country and give some responsibility to the work on the public buildings. He received the endorsement of that undoubted genius, Latrobe, who employed him between 1803 and 1817 after the commissioners had cast him off, and he bore testimony that Hadfield had " talent, taste, and knowledge of art." Mr. Hadfield left behind him abiding proofs to the same effect in the City Hall and in the two remaining department buildings which he constructed

" Of brick in the Ionic order with freestone basements," two
on each side of the President's house, namely, Treasury and
State, War and Navy buildings. He could agree with the commissioners but a short time, one of whom was Thornton aforesaid, and instead of discharging Hadfield courteously it appears
by their minutes that on May 10, 1798, they gave notice to a
citizen, Mr. William Brent, to tell Hadfield that he was no
longer in their employ. Hadfield died in Washington, February, 1826. His successor was James Hoban, who must have
then lived elsewhere, probably in Maryland, where he had
married, for he was ordered May 28, 1798, to superintend the
building of the Capitol, to remove to the city, and to occupy
Hadfield's house, or if he did not get it to charge his rent in
some other dwelling to the Government.

At this time Hoban was architect of the President's house
as well as of the Capitol, and he was allowed for the moment to
draw his full salary on both buildings. He received a hundred
guineas a year for his subsequent attention to the President's
house. Hoban was a native of Kilkenny County, Ireland, and
was educated and taught the profession of an architect at Dublin. His living grand-son, James Hoban, is possessed of a medal
awarded to the architect by the Dublin Society, for the best style
of ornamental brackets. In 1780, Hoban, still unmarried, sailed
from Ireland to Charleston, S. C. where he settled and soon
received employment on the public and private constructions of
the place. South Carolina has had the honor of furnishing
two architects and a sculptor to Washington, Hoban, Robert
Mills and Clark Mills.

At the conception of the Capital City, Mr. Laurens (Henry
Laurens, long a State captive in the tower of London) gave
Hoban a letter of recommendation to Washington. He speedily drew the prize for the President's palace and was employed
to construct it, which he did with equal particularity, stability,
and speed, so that it was habitable in 1799. It is traditional
in the Hoban family that President Washington took exception
to the style and proportions of the White House as inviting

criticism from severe Republicans, but that he gave up the point to the architect. It was revived, however, by Jefferson, of whom Tom Moore, Hoban's poet countryman, wrote in 1803: "The President's House, a very noble structure, is by no means suited to the philosophical humility of its present possessor, who inhabits but a corner of the mansion himself and abandons the rest to a state of uncleanly desolation. This grand edifice is encircled by a very rude paling through which a common rustic hill introduces the visitors to the first man in America."

As an instance of the boorish feeling prevailing between the Commissioners, citizens, and architects, we may mention that David Burns, who owned a large part of the ground taken up by the city, resisted the opening of a cartway over his land to haul stone from the landing to the White House, and also threatened to sue the Commissioners, and complained of Mr. Hoban for cutting his wood, saying: "Such persons are not responsible, because they have no property any body can lay hands on, but are miserable speculators and without thrift." Mr. Hoban built the first post-office at Washington and many other good buildings, but he also failed to please the civil authorities although he reconstructed the White House after 1814 and maintained his influence in the city to the end. Captain Hoban died in the year 1831, possessed of about sixty thousand dollars in property, and having lived a comfortable and active life. He was at first interred in the old graveyard of St. Patrick's Church, but the remains were removed at a later date to N. Olivet cemetery on the Bladensburg turnpike, where they lie at present. He left an efficient posterity, two sons in the U. S. Navy, another a priest, and a fourth, James, who was a fine Speaker and was United States Attorney of the District in the administration of President Polk. Hoban's residence is still standing at this writing on F street in the rear of 15th, on the north side, a landmark in itself. Sharp-gabled and very decrepit, and pointing toward the street. He married after he removed to Washington, and his wife was Miss Sewell of Maryland. He was a devout Catholic, and those who most distinctly recall him at this day are clergymen like Fathers Lynch and McElroy. During the early building of the Capitol the clerk of the works, Lenthall, Blagden, the chief stone mason, and a citizen, Cocking, were killed upon it. The stone quarries used for the early public edifices were at Acquia creek and at Hamburg near the mouth of Rock Creek, the latter within the city limits; these quarries for stone and slate were purchased outright and cost twenty-nine thousand five hundred and fifty-eight dollars. The since celebrated Seneca stone was also used at a very early period for flagging and steps; the former cost about seven dollars a ton and the latter about fifteen dollars, delivered.

The fourth professional Architect of the Capitol was one of the remarkable men of the country. His constructions of both a public and private character are numerous at Washington and in other cities of the country. One of his sons, B. H. Latrobe, Jr., was afterwards made engineer of location and construction of the Baltimore and Ohio railroad, July 1, 1836. He was the genius of that great mountain highway. He had been educated by his father, the architect, for a lawyer, but took to engineering, while his brother John H. B. Latrobe, educated for an engineer, became a lawyer of Baltimore, equally celebrated. The elder, Benjamin H. Latrobe, was born in Yorkshire, England, May 1, 1767, and was the son of Rev. Henry Latrobe, a Moravian clergyman of Huguenot descent, who figured as Superintendent of the Moravian establishments in England and as an author in the Church. The architect was educated at a village near Leeds, at the Moravian school of Weisky in Saxony and at the University of Leipsic. He was a cornet of Prussian Hussars, and made the tour of Europe, examining all the public buildings of note before he returned to England in 1782. He entered the office of Cockrell, an eminent English architect, and married the daughter of the rector of Clerkenwell parish. The death of his wife gave him such desire of change that in 1796 he resolved to come to America and visit an uncle, Colonel Antes. The ship brought him to Norfolk where by good luck he fell in with the officer of customs who introduced

MARBLE HALL, CAPITOL, WASHINGTON.

him to Judge Bushrod Washington, a nephew of President Washington, which led to his visiting Mount Vernon and becoming one of the fast young friends of that father of the Capital.

Richmond, Virginia, was then rapidly growing, and Latrobe designed the penitentiary and several fine private mansions. In 1798 he was established in Philadelphia where he built the old water works on Penn square and the old Banks of Pennsylvania and Philadelphia, and he also designed the Bank of the United States which was built by his pupil, Strickland. It is to be remarked that as Latrobe was the preceptor of Strickland, Strickland was the preceptor of Walter and Walter of Clark. As Latrobe availed himself of the services of Hadfield there has been a close succession of minds of the same order and of mutual inspiration at work on the Capitol for eighty years. Few buildings in the world have commanded the services for so long a time of men who knew each other.

At Philadelphia Latrobe married his second wife, the daughter of Robert Hazelhurst, who had been a partner of Robert Norris, the early speculator in Washington lots and buildings. From this second marriage arose the two eminent sons above referred to. Mr. Latrobe was summoned from Philadelphia to be surveyor of the Public buildings at Washington in 1803. He made a report at the beginning of the following year to this effect: "The hall in which the house of Representatives are now assembled was erected in part of the permanent building. I am, however, under the necessity of representing to you that the whole of the masonry from the very foundation is of such bad workmanship and materials that it would have been dangerous to have assembled within the building had not the walls been strongly supported by shores from without."

After due inspection Mr. Latrobe reported that the south wing of the Capitol required rebuilding from the very foundation. He also resolved upon a reformation of the outer plan and a very thorough change of the inner. This led to the criticism from his associate Hadfield, "That there is no conformity between the outer parts and the interior of the Capitol, the original designs having been totally disregarded." Particularly does Hadfield denounce the raising of the entire floor throughout the building from the ground story to the principal order over the casement, excluding the light, making catacombs of the basement and turning an inferior part of the edifice into the superior uses." We may regard the east front and wings of the old freestone Capitol in mass as we see it as the design of Mr. Latrobe, who had sufficient influence with Mr. Jefferson to make him modify his extravagant praise of Thornton's design. The embargo and non-intercourse acts of that administration made money so scarce that very little was accomplished beyond finishing the interior of the wings, and when the Capitol was burnt in 1814, Latrobe, who was then absent at Pittsburg building the first steamboat to descend the western waters (jointly with Fulton, Livingstone, and Nicholas I. Roosevelt, his son-in-law by his first marriage) hastened back to the Capitol and took charge of its reconstruction in a more methodical and comprehensive way than any of his predecessors. He first made an inspection of the mined building and reported part of the walls and all the foundations sound and the more delicate work of the interior little injured although the incendiaries had labored all night to make the devastation complete, using powder, etc., of their rockets for that purpose. It was Latrobe who designed what Madison called the American order of architecture, using the cotton blossom, the tobacco leaf, and the Indian corn, shaft and ear, in his columns and capitals. He made a personal visit to the Catoctin and London hills to find quarries, and discovered the breccia or blue mottled marble which is used in the old hall of Representatives and in the corridors. The hall of Representatives, the Senate Chamber, the old Supreme Court Room, and the old lobbies, as well as the ground plan of the two wings, were Latrobe's work. He also erected St. John's Church, the Van Ness and Brentwood mansions, the arched gate of the Navy Yard, and was conferred with as to public buildings in many parts of the country. Latrobe had been on good terms with the commissioners fourteen

LADIES' RECEPTION ROOM, CAPITOL, WASHINGTON.

years when President Monroe appointed a one-armed Virginia
Colonel, Samuel S. Lane, with whom he soon came into collision, and he resigned in 1817.   Removing to Baltimore he built
the noted Cathedral there and a part of the Commercial
Exchange.   His son, Henry S. Latrobe, had been sent to
New Orleans to build the water works in 1811 and died there
in 1817.   Following him upon the same errand, the architect of
the Capitol met with the same fate September 3, 1820.

Mr. Latrobe has left behind him letters, compositions, constructions, and a posterity which will give him a permanent
fame in the Republic.   He was well acquainted with the Latin,
Greek, Hebrew, French, Spanish, Portuguese, Italian, and German languages.

The fifth architect on the Capitol was Charles Bulfinch, the
senior of Latrobe, who had been born in Boston, August 8, 1763,
the son of a physician.   He saw the battle of Bunker Hill
from the housetops of the city, and graduated at Harvard in
1781.   Finding life in a country house distasteful he made the
tour of Europe to further his desire to be an architect, and
returning to Boston—he married his cousin, Hannah Apthorp,
and became at the same time a constructor, merchant, and
selectman.   It was he who laid out the streets and filled up
the marshes of Boston, built the Boston State House, and was
one of the partners to dispatch the ships Columbia and Washington to the Pacific Ocean whereby Captain Gray discovered
the Columbia River.   He twice failed in business, once by
putting up Franklin Place, Boston, on too ambitious a scale,
and again by the endeavor to fill up the Charles River marshes.
His work is plentiful in Boston, as in the Court House and the
North and South Churches.   He also built the State House at
Augusta, Me.

Bulfinch made the acquaintance of President-elect Monroe
in 1816.   At this time he was a lame man, having crippled
himself for life by slipping on the steps of Faneuil Hall, and he
was visiting Washington and other cities to obtain suggestions
for a hospital for Boston.   President Monroe renewed the

acquaintance while making a tour in the East subsequently, and was struck with the elegance of Bulfinch's buildings. The architect refused to take Latrobe's place until the latter had resigned absolutely, and then he proceeded to complete the wings on Latrobe's plan and to build the rotunda, old dome, and library, and to give area to the west front of the Capitol, which had been built too near the brow of the hill, by putting up the glacies and architectural terrace. In 1830 when the Capitol was virtually completed, Bulfinch resigned and returned to Boston, where he died April 15, 1844, at the age of eighty-one. He built two other buildings at Washington, the church for the Unitarian Society of which he was a member, and the old penitentiary at Greenleaf's Point, where the conspirators were imprisoned, tried, and hanged in 1865.

The criticism of Hadfield, already twice referred to, was written in 1819 in the period of Bulfinch. That artist throws some light upon the cost and style of the edifice. He begins by calling it " A very singular building," ascended by " uncouth stairs in the south wing." The plan of the Representatives Hall, he says, was taken from the remains of a theater near Athens as described by Stewart, an authority. It had gained " some advantage in appearance of form and costliness of materials " over the former hall, which was, however, more consistent, being all of native freestone. The capitals of the columns in this hall were executed in Italy " and are a copy from the capitals of the well-known remains of the lantern of Demosthenes at Athens. Had the entire columns been in Carrara marble they would have cost less money. Hadfield rebukes the coupling of the form center columns, the screen between the columns of the peristyle, the gallery door, and the principal entrance crowding each other, and the screen of columns on the south side of the hall, which " would be better among the ruins of Palmyra."

Such criticisms as Hadfield's lose their effect upon the public mind by their minuteness. The building stood for a quarter of a century complete as Bulfinch left it, and meantime

HOUSE OF REPRESENTATIVES, CAPITOL, WASHINGTON.

persons of every quality from all parts of the world bestowed their encomiums upon it. For many years a contest raged about the difficulty of hearing in that ambitious domed, column-encircled Hall of Representatives, but no portion of the building is more admired to-day, and perhaps people of wisest censure prefer the involutions, quaint workmanship, economy of space, and classical simplicity of the old freestone building to the marble wings which are modeled upon the former plan.

The old Capitol, including the works of art which belonged there, cost about two million seven hundred thousand dollars. It covered considerably more than an acre and a half of ground. It was three hundred and fifty-two feet, four inches long, seventy feet high to the top of the balustrade, one hundred and forty-five feet high to the top of the old dome, and the wings were one hundred and twenty-one feet, six inches deep. These dimensions show a sufficient edifice for the period to have been truly a national Capitol. The part which the British burnt had cost about seven hundred and ninety thousand dollars; to restore those parts cost about six hundred and ninety thousand dollars; the freestone center cost about six hundred and ninety thousand dollars. The park enclosing this old Capitol contained about twenty-two and a half acres.

Within that old building happened all the contests of the first social civilization of the Republic. Every room and lobby and recess of it is full of reminiscence. Attempts are now being made on the score of architectural harmony to demolish it and erect a new center in keeping with the wings. We may hope that this will not take place until reverence and innovation, the historical and the artistic spirit, have a full debate on the subject in which the country can take sides.

The successor of Mr. Bulfinch was Robert Mills, who was appointed government architect by Andrew Jackson in 1830. He was a man of mediocre talents, whose opportunities allowed him to impress himself favorably upon the country. He was born in Charleston, S. C., and placed under the tuition of James Hoban in 1800, with whom he remained two years. Mr.

Jefferson introduced him to Latrobe. He had very extensive employment in the country, and constructed churches, public buildings, and mansions from Pennsylvania to Georgia; he built the second Treasury, of which the façade remains, and commenced the Patent Office and the general Post-Office, all three of which retain the impression of his style. He designed the Washington Monument, made a design for the Bunker Hill Monument, built the Monument Church at Richmond, the State Capitol at Harrisburgh, the Philadelphia Mint, and was the engineer of South Carolina when the Charleston and Hamburg Railroad was constructed between 1830 and 1834. Mr. Mills completed Bulfinch's work on the Capitol but got into a wrangle about the Patent Office which led to his removal. He long inhabited a tall brick house on New Jersey Avenue, Capitol Hill, and died in Washington, March 3, 1855. Mr. Mills had very little connection with the Capitol building, and for twenty years after its completion there was nothing more of architecture except a wrangle about the acoustics of the Hall of Congress.

New states were, however, admitted to the Union, and the increase of population in all the states multiplied Congressmen so that in 1850 it was determined to extend the old wings by greater wings named "extensions," to be constructed of more durable materials and upon the original plan. Proposals were invited and the fortunate architect was Thomas W. Walter.

He held and keeps the rank of the foremost classical architect in America. The corner-stone of the additions was laid by President Filmore, July 4, 1851, more than fifty-nine years after Washington laid the south-east corner stone of the old Capitol. Mr. Walter was born in Philadelphia, September 4, 1804, and was the son of a builder. In 1819 he entered the office of Mr. Strickland and, working with the trowel, supported himself and became a fair artist in colors. In 1830 he became an architect on his own account and the following year designed Moyamensing Prison. His plans for Girard College were accepted, and from 1833 to 1847 he superintended its construction, visiting Europe in 1838 to make studies for that institution.

SENATE CHAMBER, CAPITOL. WASHINGTON.

In 1843 the Venezuelan Government employed him to construct a mole and port at LaGuayra, and from 1851 to 1865 he was the architect of the Capitol and had an influence in the Treasury, Patent Office, and Post-Office extensions. Mr. Walter was accused of influencing contracts on the public works in Washington, and the disposition of funds on the Capitol building was mainly committed to an able engineer officer, Montgomery C. Meigs.

The first estimate for the Capitol extension was two million six hundred and seventy-five thousand dollars and five years time. In 1856 Captain Meigs called upon Jefferson Davis for two million eight hundred and thirty-five thousand dollars and said that the additional cost was on account of the low estimates of Mr. Walter and in the substitution of marble, iron, encaustic tiles, etc., for wood, plaster, and stone. And he added: " I have labored faithfully and diligently to construct this building in such a manner that it would last for ages as a creditable monument of the state of the arts at this time in this country." At that time the expenditure was about ninety thousand dollars monthly.

Captain M. C. Meigs reported in August, 1856, that above two million five hundred thousand dollars had been expended on the new wings up to that time, that the work had no debts, and that everything had been bought for cash. The Berkshire marble shafts, monolitho, cost one thousand four hundred dollars each, and the shafts for the corridors of the south basement two hundred dollars each. The following were the prices of marbles per cubic foot. Massachusetts, two dollars and fifty cents; Tennesee, six dollars; Vermont Green, seven dollars; Potomac Breccia, four dollars; Levant from Barbary, five dollars; Italian Statuary, seven dollars and ninety-five cents; Common Italian, two dollars and seventy-five cents. Meigs changed Walters' design somewhat, putting in one hundred and ninety-two columns in all instead of two hundred and fifty-two. Bricks, from all cities, cost from five dollars and fifty cents to nine dollars and

twelve cents per thousand.   To lay the bricks cost five dollars
and eight cents per thousand.

The cost of the Capitol extension was about eight million dollars, of the new dome about one million two hundred and fifty
thousand dollars, and of the new library enough additional to
make the entire cost upwards of ten million dollars.   Works
of art and ornaments made three hundred and fifty thousand dollars more.   The extensions are about one hundred and forty-three
by two hundred and thirty-nine feet each exclusive of porticoes.
The whole Capitol has therefore cost about thirteen million
dollars.

LOBBY OF SENATE, CAPITOL, WASHINGTON.

CHAPTER V.

The word "Lobbyist," as any body might guess, is derived
from the part of the Capitol where people go, who have objects
to attain on the floors of Congress but not the right of access.
In the Latin *lobby* signifies a covered portico-pit for walking,
and in the Capitol at Washington the lobbies are long, lofty,
and lighted corridors completely enclosing both halls of legislation. One of the four sides of this Lobby is guarded by door-
keepers who can generally be seduced by good treatment or a
douceur to admit people to its privacy, and in this darkened
corridor the lobbyists call out their members and make their
solicitations.

The lobby at Washington is referred to by the architect
Latrobe as early as 1806. He explains that " The Lobby of the
House is so separated from it that those who retire to it cannot
see and probably will not distinctly hear what is going forward
in it. This arrangement, he says, "has been made with the
approbation of the President of the United States and also
under the advice of the speakers of the two houses at the time
when the designs were made. It is novel, but it is supposed
that the inconveniences to which the Lobby now subjects the
House will be thereby avoided."

This shows the high antiquity of the Washington Lobby.

I have no doubt that many of my readers may be asking
themselves, what kind of a fellow is a lobbyist to look at ?

A lobbyist is an operator upon his acquaintance, his wits,
and his audacity. Your lobbyist may be an old man, whose
experience, *a plomb*, suavity or venerableness may recommend

him. He may be a strong man in middle life, who commands what he is paid for doing by a knowledge of his own force and magnetism. He may be an adroit young man, full of hollow profession, who dexterously leads his victim along from terrace to terrace of sentimentality, until that dell is reached where the two men become confederates, and may whisper the truth to each other.

The average lobbyist must seem an agreeable man, whether he be so or no. He is seldom so foolish as to risk a quarrel for no end, and therefore a newspaper-writer can readily approach him and learn the news,—there being a tacit truce understood between them, by which the writer gets his news on the understanding that he will give trouble, in the way of revelations, to none less than the lobbyist's principals. The native lobbyist rather likes to read quick-witted accounts of such operations as he is about, and, if somebody in his own line other than himself, be described, enjoys the matter hugely.

I recollect, on one occasion, having it suggested to me that a sketch on the game of poker as played at Washington might incidentally trench upon a character of lobby influence not generally understood. The intimation that I received was, that certain prominent men in Congress and the government were very fond of the Western game of draw-poker ; and that certain gentlemen in the Lobby, knowing this fact, humored the inclination, and played a losing game with the aforesaid dignitaries, in order that the acquaintance might be closer, and the legislative business in hand easy to approach. It is well established that, if you can deceive a man into believing that he has plundered you at cards, he feels under a sort of chivalric obligation ; and hence a strong lobbyist will permit himself to lose heavily at the poker-table, under the assumption that the great Congressman who wins the stake will look leniently upon the little appropriation he means to ask for. As the appropriation is sure to be twenty-fold the loss at cards, it is plain that the loser really plays the best game at poker.

On this occasion, I went directly to a couple of fellows whom

I knew to be prime hands at the draw game, and stated to them that I could not play poker, and wanted to get an idea of it *sans* experience, and also some points with which to point my article. Both men entered into the spirit of the proposition, and while one sat down, with a mischievous twinkle in his eye, and gave me some inside information, the other slipped off and bought a book called "The American Hoyle," which he sent to me under the frank of the very member of Congress who was to be the subject of the article.

Amongst the lobbyists at Washington, is one very agreeable, well-behaved, and most learned man, who is on excellent terms with some of the most prominent of the judges, senators, etc., at the Capital. He formerly enjoyed the advantage of a partnership-at-law, and in a distant state was quite an influence in politics and at the bar. I believe that an unfortunate streak of luck came to him in the course of his practice, by which he was able, upon a speculation, involving some legislative proceedings, to make very much more money in a short space of time than he could do in a year or two by methodical practice. Whatever the cause, he slipped his moorings as a fair lawyer, and took to the legislature every winter, but never in support of any small matter. His propositions were all imperial, and to hear him talk you would think his ends were his country's, his God's, and truth's. He had a fine way of talking about "The equities," which he explained to be something superior in morals to mere points of law and evidence ; and, with his fine grave face, suave manner, and enormous determination, he never failed to be respectable, and I always wondered how he ever could fail. Yet he always did fail, that is, he could inspire sufficient confidence in those who backed him with money to be kept at Washington from year to year at their expense, but his proposals were so preposterous in the amount asked, that nobody dared to vote for them.

On one occasion I was bound to New York, when this gentleman was discovered to have the adjacent berth to mine, and to be my companion in those agreeable hours one spends sitting

up until the berth shall be made, the lights put down, and the
last passenger turned in.   I was but imperfectly aware of his
business at Washington, where he had always addressed me
respectfully, and with a lazy man's privilege, I turned to him
more unguardedly than on previous occasions, and soon found
myself under the glamour of a very remarkable mind. ' He had
spent much of his life in a distant part of the country, among
associations interesting in themselves, and the grade of his
acquaintances was high, and often eminent.   He was President-
making on this particular evening, and called my attention to
the force, record, and consistency of some gentlemen whom I
had never thought of in association with the Chief Magistracy.
As he proceeded in his talk, I felt a luminous mind near me as
truly as if I had been sitting under some shining orb.   His literary tastes were just crude enough to be original and honest.
His acquaintance with men was that of one who never took a
suggestion but he gave one back like an equal.   There was
bearing in the man also, and that feeling of warm interest in
my youth which had the effect to make me feel that there was
something to pity in my associate.   Without any clear knowledge that he had ever been wronged, I got to feel that his desert
had been unequal to his aspiration, and imperceptibly the
impression was made upon me that he had lost his grasp upon
fortune by too much courage, rather than by the abandonment
of his friends; for, like every man in the Lobby, as I afterwards
found out, he placed much stress upon personal fidelity.   You
never find a genuine lobbyist but he makes it a point of honor
that friendship is the last manly element to be given up, and I
suppose that this is an approximate notion to that older relation
we express when we say that there is honor among thieves.
At Washington one hears much more of loyalty to one's friends
than of loyalty to one's country.   In fact, one would soon become
unpopular in that promiscuous society by affecting any undue
or juvenile consideration for his country.   They expect John
A. Bingham, or Daniel Voorhees, or some of the professional
orators, to attend to that kind of sentiment exclusively.

Time ran on, and I discovered what my quondam companion of the sleeping-car was working his brain upon during the pending session. He had a fine scheme, based upon the nicest principles of equity, to take sixty million dollars out of the Treasury to refund the cotton tax. I have never been able to persuade myself that he did not believe he was engaged in a highly meritorious duty in seeking to have that cotton-tax taken out of the Treasury and refunded, because, as he expressed it, the Supreme Court had been equally divided on the subject, and would certainly have made a decision as he argued it, except that two unjudicial Justices had been added to the Bench to anticipate certain railway decisions, and were not to be relied upon when a fine point of law and honor came up. The sixty million dollars were not to be grossly shoveled out of the Treasury, for my friend was no such gross disturber of the revenues and the tax-scale. Like every other lobbyist, he preferred the pleasant form of a bonded restitution.

The Treasury was merely to listen to the courts, as the courts were merely to do justice to a war-ridden people. If the courts should be so lost to judicial integrity as to slip the matter over from term to term, he did not entertain the supposition that a Congress of his countrymen would be equally tardy in doing their duty. When this Congress had shown, in a chivalric way, its origin with the constituency, and its respect for law and "equity," by passing the little bill which he proposed, nothing else was necessary than for the Treasury to issue sixty million dollars of bonds, redeemable in forty years, with the proper coupons attached. Having your coupons attached, you, as a friend of the outraged planter, were merely to collect the interest annually; and here my friend was wont to stop and say, with a look which was as impressive as Chevalier Bayard's: "What is interest at seven per cent to a nation like ours, which owes so much to the cotton interest?"

You can see it all in a twinkling. The whole thing involved but four million or so per annum; while, meantime, with his three cents per pound on cotton refunded to him, the planter would take new heart, believe again in the generosity of the country, put this annual amount into gins, seed, and labor, and push the country so far ahead that, when the bonds came due at the end of forty years, so far from anything being lost, there would only be a magnificent investment on all sides. It would bless him that gave and him that took.

If there could be such a thing in our days as a simple-minded man in Congress, it might not be hard to suppose that a scheme like this might carry conviction to his mind. But my friend, probably, had a less sentimental backing than this to his proposition. All that portion of the press, all those Congressmen, all the commercial interests, in the cotton area, were, perhaps, already driven up and prepared to vote for this job as a sectional issue; for he makes a great mistake who thinks we have got out of sectionalism by getting out of slavery. It was the cotton which made the sectionalism before fully as much as the slave; because the slave might grow anywhere, but the cotton would not. In this scheme, however, there was still another powerful interest lying back in the rear, and that was a combination of disinterested gentlemen who paid my friend's expenses in Washington, and had already secured nearly the whole sum to be restored from the Treasury, by obtaining the refusal of nearly all the said claims for the cotton which had been seized.

Although sixty million dollars were to be represented by the bonds which the Treasury were to issue, it might take but a few thousand dollars to get control of the bonds in anticipation of their issue. These few thousand dollars would, perhaps, come from some plethoric banker who was to be promised the negotiation of the bonds when the Treasury should put them out. In order to make everything fair, perhaps a stock company, with no capital to see, but plenty to talk about, had arranged to distribute stock in anticipation of the bonds, to redeem the stock with the bonds when they were at last printed, and perhaps the whole Confederacy was to be " taken in " somewhere between the passage of the bill and the insurance of the bonds.

Another of our sterling knights of the Lobby of Washington is the gentleman who is responsible for the great tunnel project.

This man is a Columbus, a Lesseps, and a De Witt Clinton of his kind. He is, I believe, a native of Prussia, and a fine-looking man, with Oriental features, a dark eye, excellent address, in despite of his German accent, and he is both an author, a pleader, and a diplomatist. Some say he is no engineer ; but, if this be the case, he has performed an enormous amount of work as a mere assumer, which it would have been hard for a real professional mining engineer to do as well.

I made this gentleman's acquaintance the first year I came to Washington, while visiting, as I was in the habit of doing, Mr. Riley, clerk of the Mining Committee.

Mr. Riley had led a life of adventure ; had edited a newspaper in British Columbia, and subsequently made a journey to the diamond fields of South Africa, to write a book for a Hartford publishing house. He died of cancer in the face before his book was completed.

One day while speaking to Mr. Riley, he called my attention to some large and beautiful albums filled with the richest photographs of Kings and Queens, works of art, fine architectures, and people prominent in literature, opera, and adventure, which could be collected in Europe. I had never seen, even in Europe, such a perfect and exquisite library of photographs, and they have been uniformly the admiration of all who have seen them. They were the property of the tunnel-maker. Adjacent to these photographic books was a magnificent collection of gems, minerals, etc., from the various mines of Europe. I was told by Mr. Riley, as a mark of confidence, that he would see to it that I should become possessed of a copy of an extraordinary book on mining which his great friend and collector was at that time publishing.

In due time this book came out, and it was, indeed, an expensive and entertaining work, and of a somewhat technical character.

The title of this work was, " The Comstock Lode, and the Evils of the Present System of Mining."

It began with a description of the Comstock Lode,—a mighty vein of gold and silver in the State of Nevada, which was discovered in the year 1869, and on which nearly forty companies owned claims.   These companies had already produced the incredible sum of one hundred and thirty million dollars in bullion.   The shafts into the lode had been sunk more than one thousand feet, so that, between the cost of labor, the interference of water, and the loss of power, the whole lode was in danger of abandonment.   If abandoned, one hundred thousand people would be deprived of their occupation and means of subsistence ! Such a calamity Providence had done its part to avert by raising the lode a thousand feet or more above the adjacent valley, which was thus manifestly designed to be used for the propulsion of a tunnel beneath the lode, which would at once draw off the water and carry off the ore by an inclined plane, and permit economical and vastly ramified mining for a hundred years to come.   This tunnel, which would be called after its proposer, would have a length of twenty-one thousand feet, with shafts making the amount total forty-three thousand.   The scheme had been already proposed to eminent " experts " in Europe, who forthwith came to the aid of the engineer with letters of indorsement, all duly printed in this beautiful volume.   The mining companies working far above the lode had agreed to pay two dollars a ton for the ore which the great tunnel should carry out for them.   The Tunnel was to have two substantial railroad tracks.   Such tunnels had been built in Germany and elsewhere, as in the Hartz Mountains; and the engineer staked his reputation, and gave the whole tunnel, liberally, as security, that, if Congress would issue bonds and come to the aid of the work to the extent of five million dollars, fifty million dollars per annum of precious metal could be brought out, science would be benefited, the mineral domain would be filled with immigration, the burdens of the people in taxation would be reduced, and the national debt paid off!

Some years have passed since this book was placed in my hands, and every year the indefatigable engineer adds another tome, if possible more agreeable, more eloquent, and more convincing, in favor of the proposition. He has obtained some private credit, and has had sympathy among the miners, hundreds of whom have given parts of their work for nothing; while, in Congress, men like William D. Kelley, Gen. Banks, and Senator Nye, have made such speeches in his favor as Queen Isabel might have delivered before the King of Arragon in aid of Columbus. Every session of Congress finds the engineer in good apartments at Washington, patiently reasoning out the cause, showering his scorn upon those too blind to see and too selfish to help ; and, in the face of the opposition of the most powerful Capital on the Pacific Coast, he has succeeded in getting two or three reports from the Mining and other Committees, indorsing his project. Horace Greeley committed the editorial columns of the New York Tribune to it. If never achieved, it has become one of the notorieties of the period.

There is a certain kind of nature in your fine old lobbyist, which grows tough and sturdy by opposition. In the amount of opposition, it avows that it finds at least the bitter half of the appreciation which belongs to it. This tunnel, however, has not risen above the usual cares of such popular propositions, and the handsome shares of stock of the Tunnel Company, which represent the golden meed of victory, if ever that time comes, are not uncommon on the streets of the Federal City.

But, " Pshaw !" says your fine old lobbyist, " what is there wrong about our stock ? What is our property we have a right to divide, as we are a chartered institution under the laws."

The great banking institution which is fighting the tunnel proposition has, however, its own suggestion for the development of the country and decrease of taxation on a scale scarcely less extraordinary, in the matter of irrigation.

While our engineering friend wants to take all the water out of the Comstock lode, the quartz company and bank which oppose him want to flood all the San Joaquin Valley with

water, and redeem an empire from the drought.   They have
had engineers from India to demonstrate the entire feasibility
of the project, and I believe that their bill passed Congress
near the close of the session, sustained, as it was, by all the
powerful influences which resist the scheme of the tunnel.

What will become of us if the great tunnel and the great
irrigating scheme combine and drench all the Pacific Coast
with the water pumped out of the lode ?   If both the schemes
be successful, our heads will fly off; and, if both fail, where
will be our pockets ?

The next of our exalted lobbyists is the gentleman who
watches the claims for French spoliation.   He advertises with the
regularity of the original Jacobs, whenever the prospect revives
for paying these seventy-year-old losses.   Does the Alabama
Treaty arrange to pay losses inflicted by British slavery-corsairs ?
So much more the reason for beginning in the right way with
the wrongs of our grandfathers!   Is there a Venezuelan claim
commission prepared ?   Then why do we expect other governments to deal restitution to us who began with swindling our
countrymen during the French republican wars?   We think
our gifted friend deceased sometimes ; like Mr. Hood's infant ;

> We thought him dying when he slept,
> And sleeping when he died ;

for, after we have ceased to regret him, hard as his loss has
been, up turns that familiar advertisement in the Washington
journals :

"The French claims agency.   In uninterrupted existence
for forty-five years.   Justice is to be done to us at last, friends !
I have never doubted the integrity of the United States Government, if the matter were pressed steadily upon its attention.
The prospects at the present time are light almost unto the
perfect day.   Send us the name of your grandfather's step-
father.   If the middle name is remembered, please put it in ;
otherwise no matter, for we shall be sure to know all about it.
We keep a list of ships, captains, breadth of beam and keel,

and damages at compound interest. Broken hearts, assuage
your tears! All will be well by addressing Brobiggan, post-
office box 41,144."

What kind of looking man is this French claim agent? I
often wondered! Is he the son or grandson of himself, having
inherited the business in direct line, or is he like "Pecksniff,
architect," possessed of the designs of Chuzzlewit, merely a
clerk of the original Jacobs, who has wormed into the scheme
or purchased it for the heirs? If he be himself, the same in
memory, faith, and perseverance, the same stalwart old-hunker
of the Lobby whom Benton fought, and who stood with fortitude
the thunder of Silas Wright, let him come forward and give
us a specimen hair from his brave old wig. Let him organize
the third house and make it regular; for late Congresses have
not even been dignified Lobbies.

Do I see amongst these great knights of the Lobby my old
friend who wishes a self-respecting government to behave itself
at once. neglect the great considerations of empire no longer,
and rebuild the levees of the mighty Mississippi? I do!
His honest face shines with its wonted fires. He is a little
deaf on one side; but it does not affect the sonorousness of his
elocution, nor make him swerve one hair from his intent. He
fought in the Confederate Army, but he laid down his arms
like a man. He knew when he was whipped. From that day
to this, he has accepted the arrangement of bunting as we tendered it to him upon the end of a pole. He kneels to the judgment of Heaven and the comities of time. Yes, he will take
something, as in former days.

We see him wipe his magnificent brow, and grow slightly
more pronounced in the Southern foreshortenings and inflec-
tions. We see his forefinger extended, and that oath which
has done more service on great occasions than the involuntary
prayer come forth with the rare intensity of a low whisper.

When he sees the alluvial of his country running by the
thousands of tons into the Gulf of Mexico,—the richest soil
under the providence of Heaven, with capacity for several

nations to the square acre,—to build up Cuba and that foreign archipelago which is merely the delta of the Mississippi.

Stop! says he, " are not the West Indies of volcanic formation?"

Volcanic, of course! That's where the wrong and devastation lie. Left to their volcanic selves, they would be barren as the burning marl; but it is *our* alluvial which clothes them green and makes them teem with sugar, indigo, and tobacker. Yes, he will have some Havanny tobacker, though he despises the fatality which produces it.

And my lobby friend, with unfailing resources, spirits, and individualism, unfolds again his olden tale. A few thousand miles of embankment, at a few thousand dollars a mile, will narrow the Mississippi and each of its arteries, and correspondingly deepen them. Hence you save all that you spend for improving rivers; you make every great river navigable the year round; you can build railroads on your levees. And, instead of five million bales of cotton you make fifteen million. Mark this, and wonder at the blindness of human governments! Do you spend the Treasury's money to accomplish such a result? Oh, no! You give merely that useless credit which blesses him that gives and him that takes; you give merely the indorsement of the United States to the bonds of a Levee Company, which relieves the Federal Government from the jealousy of the states in undertaking local work. The Levee Corporation accomplishes its object, collects taxes on all staples raised on the redeemed territory, meets the interest on the bonds, and pays the principal when they fall due in twenty years. Oh, Chiralrickards!

Do you still harp on your state rights, and prefer to be taxed by a construction company instead of by your government? Show me that stock with which your pockets are filled! Whose image and superscription is it? If men would render frankly unto Cæsar the things which are Cæsar's how much less would they have to render unto God!

CHAPTER VI.

Lest we might be discouraged in our day by the presumption that we live in the only dishonest period of the Government, it will be a duty of solace rather than of scandal to show that a percentage of evil has always been present in the public councils and that episodes of impurity and treachery in the administration have been sufficiently frequent to excite the gravest apprehensions and indignations of their day.

In every case, however, the public sentiment in reserve has been strong enough to wash out the stain. Our first scandals referred to speculations in the public lands and the public funds.

The State of Georgia was the first to inaugurate a land swindle in 1789. It sold out to these private companies pre-emption rights to tracts of land ; these companies were called the South Carolina Yazoo, the Virginia Yazoo, and the Tennessee Yazoo ; the whole amount of land disposed of was fifteen and a half millions acres, and the sum agreed to be paid was upwards of two hundred thousand dollars. Subsequently the same lands were sold to other companies because the first purchasers insisted upon making their payments in depreciated Georgia paper. Hence arose the controversy on the celebrated Yazoo claims, so-called.

1798. This year is notable in the chronicles of Congress for the first scandalous breach of decorum that was ever witnessed in that body. It occurred in the lower House during the balloting for managers to conduct the impeachment of Blount, and the chief parties to it were Roger Griswold of Connecticut and Mathew Lyon of Vermont. A number of the

members had collected about the bar of the House, and among
them was Lyon, who in loud tones indulged in abuse of the Connecticut members for their course with reference to a measure
that had just before been under discussion, declaring that he
entertained a serious notion of moving into Connecticut for the
purpose of fighting them on their own ground.   Griswold
retorted by saying "If you come, Mr. Lyon, I suppose you will
wear your wooden sword!" in allusion to Lyon's having been
cashiered and to a rumor that he had been drummed out of the
army while compelled to wear a wooden sword.   At this Lyon
spat in his face, for which he was about to be subjected to bodily
punishment by Griswold when friends interposed and prevented
it.   Immediately the Speaker, who had previously quitted the
chair, resumed it and stated the facts to the House which
resulted in a motion for Lyon's expulsion.   This motion being
referred to a committee of privileges, the latter quickly reported
a resolution for expulsion accompanied by a full statement of
the facts.   But Lyon's Democratic friends obstinately opposing
the resolution it was only by a majority of five votes that the
House proceeded to consider the subject in Committee of the
Whole ; and then, not content with the report already made,
required that the witnesses should again testify.   Lyon in a
speech against the resolution jeopardized his defense by using
a vulgar and indecent expression which became the basis of a
fresh charge.   One of the witnesses who had testified to the
fact that Lyon had been cashiered was Senator Chipman of his
own State.   Lyon stated in his speech, by way of rebuttal, that
he had once chastised Chipman for an insult, which drew from
the latter a full account of the affair, placing Lyon in an unenvi-
able position.   After one ineffectual effort on the part of the
opposition, who were unwilling to lose even one vote, to substitute a reprimand for expulsion, the resolution was lost.   This
unsatisfactory termination of the action of the House, intensify-
ing instead of allaying the resentment of Griswold, he determined himself to punish Lyon.   Upon the occasion of his first
appearance in the House after the decision Lyon was reading

in his seat when Griswold approached and commenced beating
him on the head with a cane. Lyon arose in defense of himself, and a struggle of some minutes duration ensued in which
he rushed to the fire-place and seized the tongs but was felled
to the floor by Griswold who closed with and continued beating
him until they were separated by the friends of the vanquished
Democrat. The House being now called to order, there was a
demand made for the expulsion of both Griswold and Lyon,
but the resolution offered for that purpose was defeated.

Lyon is further notorious as being the first to suffer penalty
under the Sedition Law then recently passed. A principal
charge against him was that he wrote a letter which was published in a Vermont paper, stating that with the President
" every consideration of the public welfare was swallowed up in
a continual grasp for power, an unbounded thirst for ridiculous
pomp, foolish adulation, and selfish avarice," etc. He was convicted and sentenced to four months imprisonment and to pay
a fine of one thousand dollars. During his imprisonment he
was re-elected to Congress, and, after serving out the term of
his sentence he appeared in the House and took his seat, whereupon a resolution for his expulsion was offered, the causes alleged
being " that he had been convicted of being a malicious and
seditious person, of a depraved mind and wicked and diabolical
disposition, guilty of publishing libels against the President,
with design to bring the Government of the United States into
contempt." But this resolution also was defeated, although it
received a bare majority vote, and Lyon kept his seat.

The house, during the session of 1798, refused to pass a
resolution previously adopted in the senate to authorize Thomas
Pinckney to receive certain presents which in accordance with
custom had been tendered him by the courts of Madrid and
London at the close of his missions thither, and which he had
refused to accept because of the constitutional provision relating to presents from foreign powers. The resolution was
rejected on grounds of public policy as was afterwards declared
by unanimous vote of the house.

4

The seat of government was removed to Washington in 1800, but it had been established here only a short time when the building used as the War Office was burned and many valuable papers were destroyed. Within a few months after this occurrence the Treasury building took fire, and although important documents were lost the damage was not so great as in the former case. The violence of party feeling which characterized the times, imputed these occurrences to the design of public officers in seeking to destroy the evidence of their deficiencies.

1804. The Federal Judge of the District Court of New Hampshire was this year tried on an impeachment during the previous Congress for willfully sacrificing the rights of the government in a case tried before him, and for drunkenness and profanity on the bench. He did not appear at the trial before the Senate, but a petition was received from his son representing that the Judge was insane and praying to be heard by counsel. Against some opposition the prayer was granted and testimony was offered tending to prove the fact of his insanity. To this it was answered that his insanity, if it existed, was the result of habitual drunkenness, and the impeachment was sustained.

1804. The impeachment of Judge Chase of the Supreme Court followed closely upon the above and was the work of the Jeffersonians who were in a majority in the house. Chase was a Federalist and had made himself extremely obnoxious to his political opponents by including in his charges to the grand juries of his circuit political dissertations. In one of these he had condemned the action of Congress in repealing a late Judiciary Act, had depreciated the change in the constitution of Maryland dispensing with the property qualification of voters, and had dwelt with some emphasis upon certain proposed changes in state laws which he considered pernicious. His ability made him an object of fear to his opponents hardly less than his obnoxious doctrines subjected him to their hatred, and they determined to make this an instance of popular vengeance.

On motion of John Randolph a committee of investigation was appointed for the purpose of inquiring into his official conduct, but they were compelled to turn back five years into his record before they could discover much against him which would offer a semblance of justification for his impeachment, and they finally concluded to present his action in the Callender and Fries cases as affording the least defensible points in his judicial administration. He was accordingly impeached and preparations were made to prosecute him at the next session. The articles of impeachment were eight in number. In addition to those founded on his conduct in the cases named, two articles were based on his charge to the grand jury referred to. A month was given to the Judge to prepare his defense. It was a remarkable scene when the case came to trial. The Vice-President, Burr, was under indictment for murder and red with the blood of Hamilton, while the man impeached was a signer of the Declaration of Independence, sixteen years a judge, and pure and venerable. Luther Martin, a drunken genius and a Federalist, made a wonderful speech for Chase, and he was acquitted on a majority of the articles while in no case were two-thirds of the votes cast for his conviction. John Randolph played Ben. Butler in this trial and wanted judges made removable by joint resolution. He even opposed paying Chase's witnesses, an act so like Butler's at a later day as to arouse a smile in the reader.

In 1805, Mr. Dallas, father of the subsequent Vice-President, was unofficially charged with having pocketed six thousand five hundred and ninety-eight dollars, for three months services as state paymaster during the whisky insurrection.

In 1806, the Federalists charged Jefferson's administration with voting two million dollars in secret session to bribe France to compel Spain to come to some reasonable arrangement as to the boundaries of Louisiana.

In the same year, 1806, a draft was found amongst the effects of a Kentucky merchant tending to show that Judge Sebastian had been a pensioner of Spain. The same was charged against

General James Wilkinson, Commander-in-Chief of the American Army. About this time Aaron Burr conceived his scheme of fillibustering in the Spanish Colonies, which has led to a very gaseous romance in our history. Burr's whole career shows that he was a sensationalist with little ballast of character or mind. Wilkinson was a military genius without sincerity, and he was court-martialed twice, and vindicated by his talents rather than by the facts. John Randolph was challenged by Wilkinson in 1808, and John Smith, a senator from Ohio, was set apart for expulsion by John Quincy Adams on the charge of complicity with Burr's treason, but a majority only voted to expel.

In 1809, an intricate and prolonged judicial and congressional process arose out of a claim by Edward Livingstone of Louisiana,—who had been a defaulter as Jefferson's District Attorney of New York,—for reclaimed lands known as the Batture in front of New Orleans. Livingstone bought the Batture, conditional upon his recovering it by suit from the city. The court of final resort decided that it was his and he paid ninety thousand dollars for it, but the citizens combined against him and dispossessed him. Jefferson believed that he was an unprincipled speculator, and the militia were paraded and the dikes on the property broken down. Livingstone sued the marshal who had dispossessed him and sued also Mr. Jefferson. The Supreme Court at Washington put Livingstone in possession and after indefatigable exertions he got the property only to find that his title was defective; but he compromised with the other claimants so that the fourth which he obtained netted him a handsome fortune.

We have omitted in this sketch any reference to Albert Gallatin and Mr. Breckenridge, both men of national reputation who were in much responsible for the whisky insurrection in western Pennsylvania. Gallatin was a Swiss who became a United States Senator, Secretary of the Treasury, and Minister to Russia,—one of the most remarkable men we have produced

who lived to be more than four-score and had the greatness to
decline offices greater than he had ever filled.

In 1809, prolonged litigation and scandal arose over the
case of the British Sloop " Active " which had been seized by
her American crew and taken by a Pennsylvania State cruiser.
Connecticut men seized her and Pennsylvanians recaptured
her. A Pennsylvania Judge, despite an injunction from a
Congressional Committee, ordered the prize to be sold. Congress
reversed the decision of the State Court, but Rittenhouse, the
Pennsylvania Treasurer, held as indemnity against his personal
bond the certificates of federal debt in which the prize money
had been invested. His estate was sued by a subsequent State
Treasurer. This led to a conflict between militia acting for
the general government and for the state. The government
triumphed, and punished the resistants.

It was in 1810 that Congress set apart one day in the week
for private bills.

In 1811, the charter of the Bank of the United States expired,
and the offer of a bonus of one million and a quarter failed to
secure a renewal.

In 1812, John Henry, an Irish adventurer, naturalized,
brought on a great scandal by accepting a commission to detach
the New England States from the Union, and then receiving
fifty thousand dollars from President Madison.

In 1813, Clay and Calhoun united in a successful effort to
expel newspaper reporters from the floor, where they had long
been sitting, to the gallery where they could hear nothing.

In 1814 the Yazoo claims were settled by the issue of scrip
to the amount of eight million dollars to the claimants, most
of the money going to a set of sharks who had bought the
claims for a trifle.

In 1815, Dallas's scheme for a National Bank with thirty-
five million dollars capital was adopted. Calhoun carried it
through the house. The next year three hundred and fifty
thousand dollars was voted to the Cumberland Road, the system
of fortifications was provided for and the first public buildings

outside of Washington were resolved upon. Congress also voted itself one thousand five hundred dollars a year per man in place of six dollars a day, and in the same session a preemption right for settlers on the public lands was adopted.

When the books were opened for the Second United States Bank twenty-five million dollars was subscribed, and three million dollars more were taken by Stephen Girard who huckstered it out to other bankers. Branches were established from the present bank in Philadelphia, at Boston, New York, Baltimore, Portsmouth, Providence, Middletown, Washington, Richmond, Charleston, Norfolk, Savannah, Lexington, New Orleans, Cincinnati, Louisville, Chillicothe, Pittsburg, Fayetteville, and Augusta. At that time the public debt was one hundred and five million dollars and the revenue forty-seven million dollars. Jefferson vetoed the bill making the bank pay a bonus of one million five hundred thousand dollars, as well as all dividends upon the public stock which it held for internal improvements. The bank grew corrupt almost immediately, and the State of Ohio refused to pay the tax upon its two branches. This Bank was a source of annoyance, scandal, and corruption until President Jackson finally closed it out. Amos Kendall's biographer summed up the subsequent history of that Bank in 1873:

"Despairing of a recharter from congress, the Bank purchased an act of incorporation from the Pennsylvania Legislature, and still carried on its operations under the name of the Bank of the United States. In common with the other State Banks it stopped payment in 1837, and never resumed. Though declaring its entire individual ability, it discouraged a general return to specie payments to the last, and when the other banks could no longer be restrained it threw off the mask and exposed its insolvency. Its entire capital of thirty-five millions of dollars was dissipated and lost. Such a record as its books exhibited of loans to insolvent political men, evidently without expectation of repayment, of debts due by that class of men charged to profit and loss, of loans to editors and reckless spec-

nlators, and of expenditures for political electioneering and
corrupt purposes, was never before exhibited in a Christian
land. The ambitious author of all this ruin, who had aspired
with the aid of his political allies to govern the government of
the United States, and through his cotton speculations control
the exchanges of the commercial world, and had been carried
on men's shoulders as a sort of demi-god, had resigned the
Presidency of the Bank and retired to a private life, where he
died miserably with the disease which consumed Herod of old."

Mr. Horace Clarke of New York, exposed in the winter of
1872, a plot against him, the principal figure in which was a
Committee Clerk named Cowlam. Mr. Negley, of Pittsburgh,
introduced a resolution in the House, which had been preceded
by alarming telegraphic despatches from Cowlam to Clarke, to
this effect: " Honorable Clarke! I do not know you! Hence
the startling information I give you is the warning counsel of
an honorable friend and the secretary of Benjamin Butler.
An attempt is to be made to pizen you. A dreadful conspiracy
is planned. 'Thrice the brinded cat hath mewed.' Bewair!"

To this, Clarke responded characteristically with an essay
several reams long, breathing an essence of a gentleman, a
statesman, sweet bread and peas.

Another telegraph-despatch rejoined from Cowlam. The
conspiracy was the most dreadful known since the days of Guy
Fawkes, and headed by resolute and extraordinary men. One of
these gigantic freebooters was to rise in Congress and point the
way to the booty, and all the rest were to fill the breach. " Be
warned," says Cowlam, " for my intentions never were sinister,
since I am the secretary of Benjamin Butler."

A lawyer was sent down by the Owl Line, and he called on
Cowlam. For this disinterested savior of the Union Pacific
Road, he saw a youth of a freckled physiognomy, with eyes
which sparkled at the rattle of pennies, and whiskers blown
out from his chops, as if at the vigor of his own windiness.
This was the rescuer of the corporation; and he pointed out,
after much mystery, the dangerous authority who was to have

mounted the barricades.   It was Negley, calmly arranging his
hair at a glass.

The lawyer at once stuck Cowlam's correspondence in the
hands of the immaculate Jim Brooks.   When Negley mounted
the breach, Jim Brooks appeard at the sally-port, and presented
the veracious Cowlam correspondence.   Negley fell into the
moat, Cowlam disappeared by volatile evaporation, and Jim
Brooks slapped his hand over his pocket, and exclaimed:

" The honor of congress has been maintained by me to the
extent of deserving fifty more shares of Mobilier for my dear
little son-in-law! "

An enormous amount of forgery, lobbying, bribery, and litigation has taken place over land claimed under Spanish,
French, and Mexican titles.   Each of these claims has been in
the nature of a romance.   The Bastrop claim was the pretext
of Aaron Burr's descent of the Ohio and Mississippi Rivers.
The Limantour claim, so called from a very noble appearing
old French gentleman named José Yves Limantour who prosecuted it, is described below.

Real Estate valued in California which had continually
increased since the acquisition of that State were among other
causes depressed between 1854 and 1858 by the uncertainty of
land titles resulting from the numerous and fraudulent claims
set up to property that had been purchased in good faith and
long held by its occupants.   Of these claims the most distinguished for audacity and extravagance were those of José Yves
Limantour, by birth a Frenchman.   His claims included four
square leagues of land on the San Francisco Peninsula, embracing about half of the most valuable part of that city, Alcatraz
and Yerba Buena Islands and the Farralores together with lands
in other parts of the state—in all about a hundred square leagues,
and he asserted his right to the same on the ground of a grant
made to him by Governor Micheltorena in payment for merchandise and money advanced by him to the latter ten years
before.   The Board of Land Commissioners created by act of
Congress in 1851 having confirmed his claims, an appeal was

taken to the United States District Court, and the following quotation from the opinion of the Judge rendered in 1858 discloses the enormity of the fraud and the means resorted to for its accomplishment:

" Whether we consider the enormous extent or the extraordinary character of the alleged concessions to Limantour, the official positions and the distinguished antecedents of the principal witnesses who have testified in support of them, or the conclusive and unanswerable proofs by which their falsehood has been exposed—whether we consider the unscrupulous and pertinacious obstinacy with which the claims now before the court have been persisted in—although six others presented to the Board have long since been abandoned—or the large sums extorted from property-owners in this city as the price of the relinquishment of these fraudulent pretentions; or, finally, the conclusive and irresistible proofs by which the perjuries by which they have been attempted to be maintained have been exposed, and their true character demonstrated, it may safely be affirmed that these cases are without a parallel in the judicial history of the country."

Before its conquest by the United States a very considerable portion of the best agricultural lands in California had been granted to individuals by the Mexican Government, and the boundaries of these grants had been loosely described. By the treaty of Guadalupe Hidalgo the United States agreed not to disturb the titles so vested, but the greatest difficulty has been encountered in ascertaining the extent and limitations of such grants. This in part explains the uncertainty of land titles which has occasioned so much confusion and annoyance and which has been the source of a large proportion of the fraud and litigation that has characterized the history of that state. No sooner had the motley crowd of adventurers who had congregated from all parts of the world upon the shores of California, discovered the nature and uncertainty of the title to the lands there than forthwith sprang up from among them a host of claimants and counter-claimants under alleged Spanish and

Mexican grants, bearing aloft in their hands the forged documents, covered by a superabundance of seals, to which they
pointed as evidence of their rights.   About eight hundred claims
were presented to the Board of Commissioners provided for the
emergency, half of which number they confirmed and the other
half they rejected for manifest fraud and informality.   Nineteen thousand one hundred and forty-eight square miles, was
the area of land covered by these claims.   On appeal to the
district courts many of those rejected by the Board were allowed
and some that had received the sanction of the Board were dis-
allowed.   Even now on the docket of the Supreme Court of the
United States this business is well represented, and so far from
being settled it yet affords employment and lucrative pay to our
army of attorneys and clerks.   The General Law Office has done
a goodly share of the labor involved, but it has marked against
it this passage quoted from Tuthill's history of California : " It
was a grievance loudly complained of, that an appeal from the
survey made necessary a journey to Washington to watch proceedings under a subordinate of the Land Office, and many a
disappointed claimant has come home, alleging that the party
which accommodated the clerk with the largest loan won the
decision."

During Pierce's administration the Clerk of the Congressional Committee of claims, Abel R. Corbin, was detected and
exposed in the act of black-mailing some merchants of Boston
under the pretense of saving them taxation.   He was paid one
thousand dollars but the disclosure lost him his clerkship.   A
special report of a blistering nature was made on the case by
Hon. Benjamin P. Stanton.   Corbin had been brought to Washington by Senator Benton, whose organ he had edited at St.
Louis.   After his exposure he removed to New York ; with
means obtained from his first wife, who was much his senior, he
acquired a moderate fortune by speculation.   Years after his
humiliation at Washington he contrived to marry a maiden
sister of President Grant, and it was he who devised the scheme
of selling a house which he owned to the admirers of his brother-

in-law.   The house passed out of Corbin's hands into Grant's and was again sold to one Bowen who was induced to surrender it by the promise of controlling the local offices of the District of Columbia; a new set of admirers again purchased the same dwelling for Gen. Sherman.   Corbin went into a desperate speculation with Fisk, Gould, Smith, and other unscrupulous gamblers, on the memorable "black Friday" of 1869.   Attention was then called to his previous history and I recovered Stanton's report from the Document room and printed it simultaneously in Chicago and New York.

CHAPTER VII.

The custom of making New Year's calls in Washington is of comparatively recent origin. Mr. Madison, who had witnessed the interesting ceremony in the city of New York, in 1790—then the seat of government—inaugurated the custom at the Executive Mansion, when President, Jan. 1st, 1810. Washington Irving was there in January, 1811, and in a letter to Henry Brevoort, describes Mrs. Madison as " a fine, portly, buxom dame, who has a smile and a pleasant word for everybody. Her sisters, Mrs. Cutts and Mrs. Washington, are like the two merry wives of Windsor; but as to Jemmy Madison, ah! poor Jemmy! he is but a withered little apple-John." Francis Jeffrey of the Edinburgh Review, who came out in 1812 to marry Miss Wilkes of New York, said—"Mr. Madison looked like a schoolmaster dressed up for a funeral." When Mr. Madison asked Jeffrey on his presentation—" what is thought of our war in England?"—the latter replied, " it is not thought of at all."

Mr. Madison was small in stature and dressed in the old style, in small clothes and knee-buckles, with powdered hair—was unostentatious in his manners and mode of life—but very hospitable and liberal in his entertainments; with great powers of conversation, full of anecdotes and not averse to a *double entendre*, though of the utmost purity of life. He was a thorough-bred Virginia gentleman, Jeffrey to the contrary notwithstanding.

In August, 1814, the White House was burned by the British, and Mr. Madison removed to the Octagon, the residence of Colonel

John Tayloe on the corner of New York Avenue and Tenth street—now the Bureau of Hydrography. Here he held his New Year's levee, in 1815, and here he signed the Treaty of Ghent, in the month of February of the same year, in the circular room

TAYLOE MANSION—MADISON'S RESIDENCE.

over the entrance-hall. In 1816 and 1817, Mr. Madison occupied the house at the north-west corner of Pennsylvania avenue and Nineteenth street, and here received his guests on the first day of those years.

Mr. Monroe's first New Year's reception was held at the White House in 1818. The first term of Mr. Monroe's administration, from 1817 to 1821, has been pronounced by competent authority, the period of the best society in Washington. Gentlemen of high character and high breeding abounded in both Houses of Congress, and many of the foreign ministers were distinguished for talent, learning, and elegant manners. The Baron Hydé de Neuville represented the French aristocracy of the old *régime*, as Mr. Stratford Canning, now Lord Stratford de Redclyffe, did that of Great Britain.

Mr. Monroe was plain and awkward and frequently at a loss for conversation. His manner was kind and unpretending.

Mrs. Monroe, a Kortwright of New York, was handsome and graceful, but so dignified as to be thought haughty. While in the White House Mrs. Monroe was out of health. Her daughter, Mrs. George Hay of Virginia, attended Madame Campan's famous boarding-school in Paris, and was there the intimate friend of Hortense Beauharnais, the mother of Louis Napoleon. Mrs. Hay was witty and accomplished and a great favorite in society.

In 1822, the Marine Band* performed at the White House on New Year's day, as the custom has been ever since. In 1824, the doors of the White House were thrown open for the first time on the 1st of January to the public. The Intelligencer of the next day congratulates its leaders on the decorous deportment of the people on that occasion.

The winter of 1825 was one of the most brilliant ever known in Washington. It was the period of the exciting election in the House of Representatives, when Mr. Adams, Mr. Clay, and General Jackson were candidates for the Presidency. The Marquis de la Fayette was here as the guest of Congress, and occupied apartments at Brown's Hotel. In the last week of December, 1824, Congress had voted him the munificent sum of $200,000 for his Revolutionary services. On the 1st of January, the reception at the President's was unusually brilliant— for among the guests were the Marquis de la Fayette and his son, George Washington Lafayette, Harrison Gray Otis of Boston, the northern Chesterfield, Governor Gore of Massachusetts, Stephen Van Rensselaer the Patroon, Rufus King, Mr. Lowell and Mr. Graham of Boston, Mr. Edward Langston of Louisiana, Mr. Clay, Mr. Webster, Mr. Calhoun, Mr. Crawford, Mr. Everett, Mr. Wilde of Georgia, Mr. Hayne of South Carolina, General Jackson, and many other distinguished persons, with the ladies of their households—all resident in Washington during that memorable winter and forming a galaxy of talent, beauty, and accomplishment which has never been surpassed in any subsequent period of Washington Society.

---

*The Marine Band of Washington has made music at every great entertainment, levee, funeral, or parade held at the Capital since its foundation. It was formerly esteemed the greatest band on the continent, but has of late years grown rusty and inferior. There are fifty pieces in it, and its leader, a Mr. Scala, receives $75 a month, the men being all enlisted at $21 a month. They live outside the barracks, marry, draw rations, keep shops, and are chiefly foreigners. This band needs overhauling.

A grand entertainment was given on the evening of the 12th of January, 1825, by Congress to the Marquis de La Fayette at Williamson's, now Willard's, hotel. The management of the affair was entrusted to the Hon. Joel R. Poinsett, M. C. from S. C., Secretary of war in Mr. Van Buren's administration. This duty Mr. Poinsett discharged with admirable taste and to the entire satisfaction of Congress and its guests. The company assembled at six P. M., to the number of two hundred. Mr. Gaillard of S. C., President of the Senate, presided at one table—Mr. Clay of Ky., Speaker of the House, at the other. The President of the U. S., James Monroe, sat on one side of Mr. Gaillard, and La Fayette on the other. The latter was supported by Gen. Samuel Smith of Md., a hero of the Revolution, and in the immediate vicinity with Rufus King, Gen. Jackson, John Quincy Adams, Samuel L. Southard, Mr. Calhoun, Senators Chandler of Me., and D'Wolf of R. I., Gens. Dearborn, Scott, Macomb, Bernard, and Jesup—Commodores Bainbridge, Tingley, Stewart, Morris, and other officers of distinction.

The dinner was prepared by M. Joseph Prospere, a celebrated French cook who came from New York for the purpose, and who charged for his services the modest sum of one hundred dollars. It was the most elegant and elaborate entertainment ever given in Washington—many of the dishes being unique and artistically ornamented in a style never witnessed previously in this country.

In the midst of the dinner, an old soldier of the Revolution, arrived at the hotel from the Shenandoah Valley. He was eighty years of age and had served under La Fayette. Mr. Poinsett being informed of his arrival descended to the reception room and thence escorted him to the dining-hall on the floor above and presented him to the Marquis. "General," said the veteran—"you do not remember me. I took you off the field when wounded in the fight at Brandywine." "Is your name John Near," inquired the Marquis. "It is General," replied the veteran. Whereupon the Marquis embraced him in the French fashion and congratulated him on his healthy condition and long life.   John Near also became the guest of Congress and remained at Williamson's a fortnight, feasting to his heart's content upon the good cheer provided him and retiring to bed every night in a comfortable state of inebriation.   When he returned to Virginia, La Fayette presented him the munificent sum of two thousand dollars, with which he bought a farm which is now in the possession of his descendants.

La Fayette at this dinner gave the following toast: "Perpetual union among the States—It has saved us in times of danger, it will save the world."   Mr. Clay gave "Gen. Bolivar the Washington of South America and the Republic of Colombia."

The first private house in Washington thrown open for the reception of visitors on New Year's Day was that of the late Mr. Ogle Tayloe on La Fayette Square, in the year 1830. Here the members of the diplomatic corps were accustomed to present themselves, after their official visit to the President, arrayed in their court dresses and accompanied by their Secretaries and *attachés*.   Many years elapsed before this custom became general.   In 1849 the visitors at the White House proceeded thence to the residence of Mrs. Madison, where they were hospitably entertained.   Mrs. Madison was by far the most popular of all the ladies who have presided at the White House.   Mr. Ogle Tayloe, in his delightful reminiscences, tells us "She never forgot a face or a name—had been very handsome—was graceful and gracious and was loved alike by rich and poor."   Mr. Madison, when a member of Congress, boarded in her father's house in Philadelphia where he fell in love with her, then the widow of Mr. Todd.   Mrs. Madison was ruined by her son Payne Todd, who squandered her estate from which she would have realized at least one hundred thousand dollars.

On New Year's Day, 1828, President John Quincy Adams wrote in the album of Mrs. Ogle Tayloe a poem of eleven stanzas, and of great merit.   He received on New Year's Day and, like his predecessors Mr. Madison and Mr. Monroe, hospitably entertained his guests.   After his retirement from the

Presidency he resided on the corner of Ninth and Sixteenth Streets, where until the close of his life he was accustomed to receive the calls from ladies and gentlemen on the 1st of January. Mr. Adams was stiff and ceremonious in his manners, and though by no means popular, was always an object of respect to the people of Washington. His wife was eminently beloved wherever known.

Forty years ago it was customary among the ladies of Washington to wear for the first time at the New Year's reception at the White House, their new winter bonnets, cloaks, shawls, etc., etc.

General Jackson's receptions, commencing in 1830 and continuing till 1837, were marked by a greater infusion of the *oi polloi* than those of his predecessors. He also provided refreshments, and in 1836, being the recipient of a prodigious cheese from a farmer in Jefferson County, N. Y. ordered it to be cut on New Year's Day and distributed in large slices of a quarter of a pound weight. Many slices of this cheese were trampled under foot on the carpets, and the odor which ascended from it was far from savory.

Mr. Van Buren discontinued the custom of serving refreshments on New Year's Day at the White House, and it has never been revived.

The Winter of 1852, during the administration of Mr. Fillmore, was especially brilliant in Washington. On the 1st of January, the reception at the White House was characterized by the presence of many distinguished persons from every section of the Union. The agitation of the slavery question appeared to have subsided and good-will and fraternity between the North and South were once more the order of the day.

Mr. Fillmore never appeared to better advantage than when receiving his friends. His fine person and graceful manner rendered him conspicuous in this position.

His successor, Gen. Pierce, had also the manners of a gentleman. Mrs. Pierce was saddened by the death of her son, and took little part in the ceremonies of the White House.

Mr. Buchanan's New Year's receptions did not differ from those of his immediate predecessors. Their great charm was the presence of the mistress of his household, Miss Harriet Lane, now Mrs. Johnston of Baltimore, a woman of exquisite loveliness of person and the most charming manners. Who that was ever presented to her can forget the graceful success of her courtesy and her radiant smile of welcome?

During these later years it has gradually become the custom for our private citizens to open their houses on the first day of the year, so that the unusual spectacle to a New Yorker of ladies in the streets on that holiday, is now seldom witnessed. Twenty years ago the streets were filled with carriages on the first of January, bearing ladies in full dress and without bonnets to the President's house and the residences of other members of the Government.

In Mr. Madison's time Washington was a straggling village, without pavements, street lamps, or other signs of civilization. The White House itself was enclosed by a common post and rail fence, while all the other reservations were unenclosed and destitute of trees or any improvement. Even in Mr. Monroe's time carriages were frequently mired on Pennsylvania Avenue in rainy weather. In 1810, the population of Washington was less than that of Georgetown or Alexandria which then each contained eight thousand inhabitants. All those adventurous spirits like Law, Morris, Greenleaf, and others who had made here large investments in real estate, were ruined. Mr. Bush of Philadelphia, writing as late as 1841, said he had long before lost all confidence in Washington property. It was not until the commencement of the Capitol extension in 1851 that the city began to show signs of substantial prosperity and to afford an earnest of its subsequent greatness and strength. In all the past years of its history no improvements equal to those of the year 1872 have been made. At least five hundred elegant houses have been erected by private enterprise—to say nothing of the miles of pavement and drives, constructed by the District Government. A few years more of equal enterprise and

Washington will rank among the most beautiful cities on this continent.

Washington changed character almost entirely after the war. Northern capital moved in and fine architecture prevailed in private buildings. The very form of government was altered, and a Board of Public Works took the paving of streets out of the hands of the local legislature.

The appropriations are now greater than they have ever been in the history of the city,—far greater than when the place was first pitched here. They amount to about $3,000,000 direct this year, and nearly $2,000,000 more for public edifices. The Capitol edifice itself gets a snubbing, the architect being a shy man, who had not learned the art of lobbying and could only state the necessity of repairs at least. But the great new renaissance building for the State, War, and Navy Departments has received a lift which will cover it with stone-cutters as soon as Spring opens; a new statue of General Thomas is ordered, to cost $40,000; and the Farragut statue is taken out of the hands of the artists of the lobby. In two years from this period, there will be six colossal statues in the streets of this city, five of them equestrian, Washington, Jackson, Scott, Grant, Thomas, and Farragut, besides out-of-door statues of Lincoln, Scott, and Washington. The old City Hall has passed wholly into the possession of the United States, and with the proceeds and a diversion of city funds, a new Hotel de Ville will be erected in front of the great new market-house, which has cost $300,000. Several new street-railways are authorized, and the building-permits applied for or granted show an extraordinary advance in construction, much of which is of a villa character in the suburbs. In May, the whole line of the Baltimore & Potomac Road will be opened, as well as the new Metropolitan Branch of the Baltimore & Ohio. And the Municipal Government has spent $8,300,000 in about eighteen months, according to its own report, and its opponents say $14,000,000, assessed upon nearly the full valuation of property.

The enormous aqueduct which runs eighteen miles, through

eleven tunnels and over six bridges, is at last completed and connected with the city, at a total cost of about $6,000,000. Five bridges of the most durable character, probably good for the next quarter of a century, span Rock Creek. One hundred and twenty miles of water-main are now in use in this District, of which twelve miles have been raised or lowered to the new grades; and 530 fire-plugs, 255 public hydrants, and many drinking-fountains carry off the 31,000,000 gallons used every twenty-four hours in this Capital, which is but 20,000,000 less than all Paris gets from its government.

The amount of paving done in the past sixteen months is almost incredible in view of the former slow and conservative progress of the city. Ninety-three miles of brick and concrete sidewalks, and 115 miles of concrete, wood, round-block, graveled, cobblestone, Macadam, or Belgium block street have been laid. Add to this seventy miles of tile-sewer, and eight miles of brick main sewerage through which a buggy can be driven with ease, and the obliteration of the old Tiber Creek and canal by one of the largest sewers in the world, in diameter from 20 to 30 feet, and you will see that old Washington is no more. The landmarks have perished from the eye. And the names of the streets are also to be changed,—those running from north to south to be numbered from First to Sixtieth, instead of First street West, Second street East, etc.; and those running from east to west are to be no longer lettered A, B, C, D, etc., but named, alphabetically, Adams, Benton, Clay, Douglas, etc., on one side, and Anderson, Bainbridge, Chauncey, Decatur, etc., on the other.

The Board of Public Works claims that, between 1802-'72, the Federal Government has spent but $1,321,288 on the streets of the Capital, while the municipality spent upon the same $13,921,767; adding Georgetown's expenditure, $2,000,000 more.

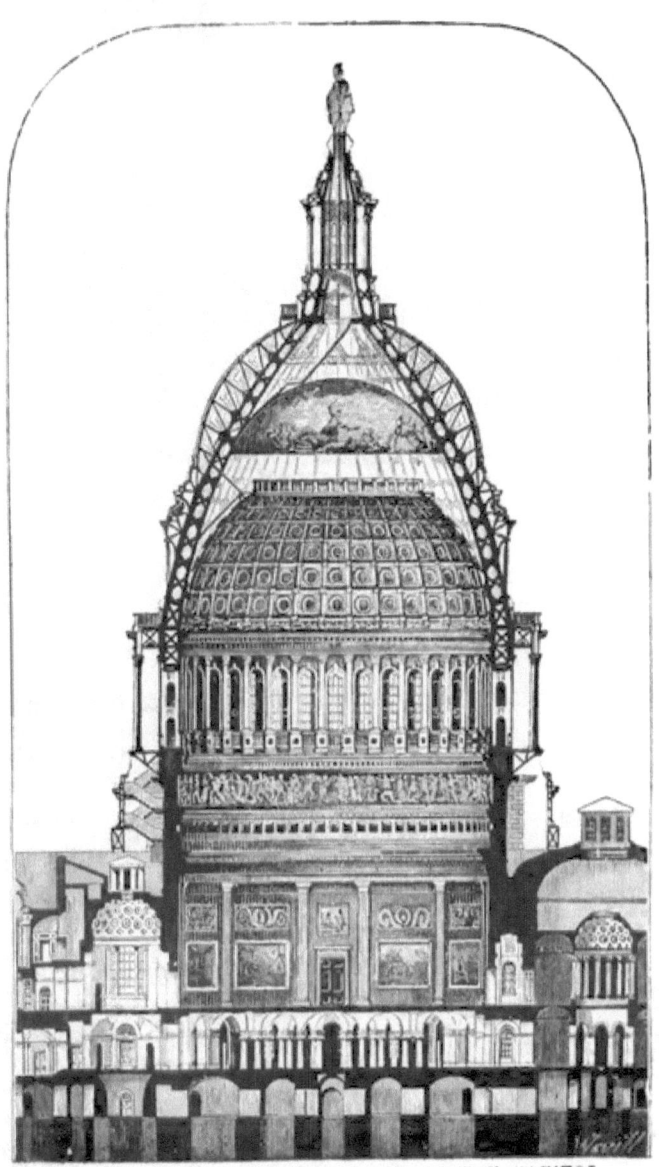

INSIDE SECTION OF THE DOME OF THE CAPITOL,
WASHINGTON.

THE CAPITOL, AS SEEN FROM PENNSYLVANIA AVENUE.

CHAPTER VIII.

THE DOME AND EXTENSIONS OF OUR CAPITOL DESCRIBED.

THE *Dome* of the Capitol, as you know, overhangs the middle of the great building, whose name, in any monarchical country, would be the "Palace of the Legislative Body," as even in this country the White House was originally named the President's Palace, and so described by Washington.

The old Capitol building had three domes upon it; the middle one, standing in the place of the present dome, was constructed of wood, and it stood one hundred and forty-two feet lower than the present. In 1856, it was removed, and the construction of the new dome began, which occupied nine years. It is formed almost entirely of cast iron, resting upon the old Capitol edifice, which, to support so vast additional weight, has been trussed up, buttressed, and strengthened, so that it seems to cower beneath the threatening mass of its superimposed burden.

Let us look at this dome.

Poised over the middle of the long white rectangle of buildings, the great dome rises in two orders: a drum of iron

columns first encircling it, with an open gallery and balustrade
at the top; then an order of tall, slim windows; then a great
series of brackets, holding the plated and ribbed roof, which
ascends, balloon-fashion, to a gallery, within which is a tall
lantern, surrounded with columns, like a cupola, and over this
a bronze figure of Liberty, capped with eagle feathers, holding

STATUE OF LIBERTY.

in her right hand a sheathed sword, in her left a wreath and
shield. She faces east. Her back is to the settled city of the
Capital. Excepting this figure, which is of a rich bronze
color, and the dark-glazed windows, the whole dome is white
as marble. The whole of it, as you see it from the ground, is
made of cast-iron; but it harmonizes well in tint with the
Capitol building, and is of such symmetrical proportions that
it gives you no impression of excessive weight.

It was on the second day of December, 1863, that, at a
signal gun from Fort Stanton, across the eastern branch, the
head and shoulders of the genius of Liberty began to arise
from the ground. As it slowly ascended the exterior of the
dome, gun after gun rang out from the successive forts encircling the city; when it reached the summit of the lantern, and
joined its heretofore beheaded body, all the artillery of the
hills saluted again, and the flags were dipped on every ship

and encampment. Majesty and grace are names for it, and holding at its cloudy height the boldest conception of Liberty, its genius looks calmly into the sunrise, and at night, like a directress of the stars, lives among them, as if in the constellation of her own banner.

Having taken this observation, let us climb to the rotunda. Now look straight up. You are amidst and beneath a vast hollow sphere of iron, weighing 8,009,200 lbs. How much is that? More than four thousand tons; or about the weight of seventy thousand full-grown people; or about equal to a thousand laden coal cars, which, holding four tons apiece, would reach two miles and a-half. Directly over your head is a figure in bronze, weighing 14,985 lbs. If it should fall plumb down, it would mash you as if thirty-seven hogs, weighing four hundred pounds a piece, were dropped on your head from a height of two hundred and eighty-eight feet. This bronze figure is sixteen feet and a-half high, and with its pedestal nineteen feet and a-half. Right over your head, suspended like a canopy, is a sheet of metal and plaster covered with allegorical paintings. This hangs between you and the bronze statue of Liberty, and is a hundred and eighty feet distant. There are, therefore, one hundred and eight feet of the full height of the dome which you cannot see at all within, and in like manner the diameter of the rotunda in which you stand is ninety-seven feet, or eleven feet less than the exterior diameter of the great dome, far above, and thirty-eight feet less than the extreme exterior diameter at the base. The old rotunda erected here by Bulfinch was ninety-six feet high.

This dome differs interiorly at present from most others by being a mere cylinder, closed with a dome, whereas, nearly all famous domes besides are raised upon churches, which are cross-shaped, and project a dome from the abutments of the hollow cross. In these abutments, high up, statues are commonly set, as in St. Peter's, where the four angels are placed there. No merely civil edifice in the world can boast a dome at all approaching these proportions.

The pressure of the iron dome upon its piers and pillars is 13,477 pounds to the square foot. St. Peter's presses nearly 20,000 pounds more to the square foot, and St. Genevieve, at Paris, 46,000 pounds more. It would require to crush the supports of our dome a pressure of 755,280 pounds to the square foot.

The first part of the rotunda, next to the floor, is a series of panels, divided from each other by Grecian pilasters, or *antæ*, which support the first entablature, a bold one, with wreaths of olive interwoven in it.

The decorations of the dome consist of four great *basso-relievos*, over the four exit doors from it, and of eight oil paintings, each containing from twenty to a hundred figures, life-size. These paintings are set in great panels in the wall, under the lower entablature. Four of them are by Colonel Trumbull, Aid-de-Camp to Washington, the "Porte Crayon" of the Revolution, and these are altogether the best historical paintings which the country has yet produced. The other four paintings, with forty years advantage over those of Trumbull, are deteriorations. Three of them represent, respectively, the marriage of Pocahontas, the landing of Columbus, and the discovery of the Mississippi. They are poorer than the average of paintings in the gallery of Versailles, and scarcely rise above the art of house and sign painting. The other picture, Prayer on the Mayflower, has good faces in it, and dignity of expression, but it is dull of color, and without any breadth of light. Trumbull's pictures are conscientious portraits, the work of thirty years' study; they are without any genius, and timid in grouping; but accurate, appropriate, and invaluable. Congress gave him an order for the whole four at once, and wisely. The others ought to be taken down when we can get anything better, and sent into some of the committee rooms.

The *basso-relievos* in the panels, above the paintings, are works of two Italians, pupils of Canova, named Causici and Capellano, who, like a great many other itinerant Italians, have done work about the Capitol. One or two of them, disgusted with the American taste in art, or stricken with the national *benzine*, jumped into the Potomac, and made their lives more romantic than their works. These base reliefs are only of three or four figures each, and are copied from curious old engravings, cotemporary with the events; they are not beautiful, but odd, and make variety amidst our perennial and distressing newness. Between these large reliefs are carved heads of Columbus, Raleigh, La Salle, and Cabot.

These pictures, true and disgraceful both to the national taste, answer in general the purpose of pleasing people. Learned rustics may be seen laboriously criticising them to their sweethearts. The privilege is also accorded to artists and others of exhibiting their models and amateur sketches in the rotunda, whereby all sorts of strange prodigies appear, flattering, at least, to our democratic charity, but very amusing to foreigners.

Above this series of *relievos* and paintings, there is a broad frieze, intended to be painted in imitation of *basso-relievo*. Above this frieze there is another entablature ; these are broken up by tall windows on the outer circumference of the walls of the dome, and at places between the domes can be seen glimpses of galleries and stairways ascending between the inner and outer walls. At last, the interior concave walls of the dome proper made to represent panels of oak foliage, rise in diminishing circles to the amphitheatre in the eye of the dome, which is sixty feet in diameter, and surrounded with a gallery all of iron. Down through the eye of the dome looks the great fresco painting of Brumidi, and you can see people the size of toys walking directly under this fresco, looking now up, now down.

It will cost to finish and paint this dome as it should be done, not less than $250,000. For the painting in the frieze, $20,000 will be required ; to reform the architecture of the dome by reducing the number of the entablatures will cost, probably, $100,000. To paint the iron panels in imitation of oak, as they are cast, will cost $30,000 to $50,000. It was the intention to have buried Washington under the floor of the rotunda ; this failing, to bury Lincoln there, and to open a large galleried place in the floor, through which the visitor could look at the sarcophagus, as is the case with the tomb of Napoleon, under the dome of the *Hotel des Invalides*, in Paris. In either case, the families of the dead objected, and with good taste ; for a rotunda, used for profane and noisy flirting, hob-nobbing, lobbying, and loitering, is no place for a hallowed sepulture. Here the statue of Washington, by Greenough, stood, till removed by barbarous enactment, in all its Roman nakedness, into the adjacent park. Something of the worthiest and most colossal is requisite here—a statue of Public Opinion, say, or an allegory of Destiny, or an effigy of Democracy. So, around the sides of the dome, there are spaces for statues and busts, which ought some day to be filled.

Situated midway between the two houses of Congress, at the middle of the Capitol, and across all the avenues of communica-tion, the rotunda under the dome obtains, as it always will obtain, an important and picturesque place in the history of legislation. There are iron settees around it, where wait for appointments of various sorts, people of all qualities and pur-suits, some to waylay, some to rest, some to see the infinite variety of race or station, or behavior of passing people. Bright paintings encircle it, for height and admissible enterprise are suggested there ; something curiously instructive, some problem to the thought, is everywhere. Danger and power, supposititious accident and vivid carnival, fill up the hours. It is one of the most curious studies in the world, and destined to be the scene of vital conferences, wild collisions, perhaps of solemn ceremo-nials, sometimes of happiness, sometimes of anarchy, sit here, under this high concave ; and, while the feet of the perpetual passengers fill the void with echoes, you may interpret them to the coming of the mob, when legislation is too slow for brutal party rage, or some unflinching Senator may hear from hence the howling of Public Opinion. Here may some brave act the best assassination ; here may be promised the price of eminent treason. Here may some conquering army, mastering the Capitol once more, unfurl their foreign standards, and with

THE DOME AND SPIRAL STAIR CASE IN CONSERVATORY,
AT WASHINGTON.

their enthusiasm or orchestras celebrate the fall of the Republic. So long as the people reign, the Capitol of the United
States will not be distributed between the wings, but concentrated under the dome. The rotunda is western human nature's
.mphitheatre. Here will stroll the chaotic dictator of Democracy, with its hundred hands on the wires of the continent.
.Iany a fair face will do temptation upon patriotism and public
duty in the broad sounding area of assignation, typical as it is
o: the arcana of the earth, where the individual voice but rolls
.into the general echo; the general echo is sometimes articulate,
but the highest shout that all can raise stays a little while, and
expires in stronger silence. The dome, with its hungry, hollow
belly, is government as you find it, familiar with its gluttonies
and processes, its dyspepsias and cramps. The outer dome is
government as the vast mass of citizens behold it—white and
monumental, and crowned with Liberty.

How is this vast height lighted, is the next question. Here
we are in the battery room, which adjoins the dome. The smell
of the acids, ranged in quadruple circles around the place, in glass
jars as big as horse-buckets, has no other effect upon the battery-
tender, he says, than to make him fat. There are here one
hundred and eighty cells set up and filled with sulphuric acid,
after the principle of Smee, constituting altogether the strongest
battery in the world, and which furnishes the power to Mr.
Gardiner's electro-magnetic apparatus, which lights the lantern, the dome and the rotunda, touching up thirteen hundred
gas-burners in a few moments. The whole machinery cost
about thirty thousand dollars. Of itself, this beautiful and
almost miraculous apparatus deserves a newspaper article.
The power is fifty tons, as if a thunder cloud as heavy as a
laden canal boat were concentrated on the point of a needle,
and " fetched " you a dash in the eye. To light up the Capitol
by this machinery, there is an electro-magnetic engine, with
connecting wires to all the burners in the building, and to each
wire a metallic pointer; the gas is turned on by cranks, answer-
ing each to a portion of the Capitol; then the magnetic bolt is

carted up the proper wire; in thirty seconds the darkness is
ablaze. This apparatus occupies one of the old wing domes of
wood, the dome being the battery room, the engine standing next
door. Thus the old building sends light up to the new one; the
little dome holds fire for the great dome. You should see them
turn the great dome from perfect night to perfect day. Stand
under it! A little moon dazes the far up slits of windows; the
concave eye is absolute night; all the sculptures are lost upon
the wall; color and action are gone out of the historic canvases;
the stone floor of the rotunda might be some great cathredal's,
for you can only feel the gliding objects going by, and hear the
dull, commingling echoes of feet and whispers.

At a wink the great hollow sphere is aflame. You can see
the spark-spirit run on tip-toe around the high entablature,
planting its fire-fly foot on every spear of bronze; a blaze
springs up on each; chasing each other hither and thither, the
winged torch-bearing fairies on the several levels race down the
aisles to the remote niches, to lateral halls, to stairways all
variegated with polished marbles, over illuminated sky-lights
armorially painted. Your thought does not leap so instantly;
and people far off in the city see the lantern at the feet of the
statue of Liberty, arise in the sky as if a star had lighted it.
Since the first commandment of God to the earth, light has had
no such messenger. It is nearest to will—it vindicates Moses.

No great building in the world is so lighted, except the
Academy of Music, and some theatres in New York. But
thirty thousand dollars is dear even for a miracle. Matches
are high.

Standing here, at so lofty an altitude, one is apt to suppose
that he has reached the king of human peaks. Not so. St.
Peter's at Rome, is 432 feet high to the lantern, or 144 feet
higher than the tip of this airy Liberty. St. Paul's in London,
is seventy-two feet higher than this.

And the great Capitol itself, down upon which we are looking,
covering 652 square feet, more than three and a half acres, is
one-eighth smaller than St. Peter's Church, and only one-fifth
larger than St. Paul's.

VIEW IN THE CONSERVATORY AT WASHINGTON.
FAN PALMS, ETC.

Yet it is high enough for timid people. The highest part of the Capitol building is nearly two hundred feet below us.

How much money is there in all this Capitol? What did it cost? Upon the aggregate head, I doubt if the congregated consciences of all the architects and builders of the Capitol can reply, exactly. One gentleman, who has been figuring up at it a long time, estimates the cost at $39,000,000. The lowest estimate I have heard at all was $15,000,000. But let us see what is the architect's statement. The entire cost of the old Capitol, down to 1827, was less than $1,800,000. St. Peter's Church, at Rome, cost $49,000,000. The new Court House in New York, is said to have cost $3,000,000. People have talked foolishly about the cost of the public edifices at the seat of government. Here are some precise figures, as Mr. Clark gave them to me. They do not include the furnishing of the buildings, however:

Cost of the library apartments, - - -	$ 780,500
" " " Oil painting by Walker:	
"Storming of Chapultepec," - -	6,000
Five water closets in the House of Representatives, - - - - -	2,178
Annual repairs, - - - -	15,000
Annual repairs for dome, - - -	5,000
Heating old Capitol (centre), - -	15,000
Cost of the new wings of the Capitol, - -	6,433,621
Cost of building the dome, - - -	1,125,000
Total cost of construction of all the public buildings in Washington City, -	27,715,522

It is very pleasant to visit the Capitol in the recess. After Congress adjourns, we begin to know each other. The carpenter and the barber go fishing together. The architect of the Capitol inquires for your family. The Capitol policemen and the officers of the barracks near by stop at your door-step to chat with your baby. It is like living in some college town during the vacation, and very cool, amiable, and agreeable is Capitol Hill in Summer.

At Whitney's I saw, a few days ago, a white bearded old gentleman, of a Northern and business habit and address. He had a brown complexion, a square-ended nose, beveled at the tip, and a hearty down-east manner.

"Don't you know Mr. Fowler, Gath?" said a gentleman near by. "This is Mr. Charles Fowler, who built the dome of the Capitol."

Mr. Fowler was born in Hartford, Connecticut. He is, or was, a member of the former firm of iron founders, Fowler & Beeby, at Read and Centre streets, New York. He was the lowest bidder to cast the patterns for the dome, and that noble piece of iron work, solitary in the world, was set up by him. Perhaps you can best get the spirit of what he had to say in the categorial form in which he gave it.

"What was your contract, Mr. Fowler, when you first undertook to build the dome?"

"Seven cents a pound for all the iron used. The architect, Thomas N. Walter, made the designs, piece by piece. They ran, for example, an inch to eight feet. I was to put up the dome, furnishing all the scaffolds, workmen, and so forth, for seven cents a pound."

"Did they keep their bargain?"

"No. General Franklin was superintending engineer when I first arrived here. He made the contract for the War Department. After I had run the dome up to the top of the first order, or the drum, as you see it there, General Meigs was put in Franklin's place. He cut my contract down, arbitrarily, to six cents a pound. I consulted my lawyers, and they said:

'This cutting down of your contract is a piece of force, having no authority in law. But if you don't submit to it, you will be kept out of your money at ruinous expense. So accept it and come back upon the justice of the government at another time.'

"Therefore I took the six cents, and the work was stopped.

"The yard of the Capitol was littered with iron, Senator Foot and others began to ask:

'Why is the work on the dome suspended?'

VIEW IN THE CONSERVATORY AT WASHINGTON.

BANANAS, ETC.

"They demanded a recontinuance of the work, and had an order made out transferring the work upon the Capitol extension from the War to the Interior Department. This was done to lift out of Cameron's hands the matter of the dome.

"I went to the Secretary of the Interior and demanded my additional cent a pound. It was paid. I demanded also the fifteen thousand dollars which, under the first arrangement, was withheld from my control to insure the finishing of the dome. This was paid over. Then I went to work again."

"On what principle is that dome set up, Mr. Fowler?"

"On this principle: there is a skeleton series of ribs within: they extrude supports for the outer dome: the figure on the top, the government guaranteed to furnish, as it afterwards did, from Clark Mill's designs and castings. The scales on the dome are bolted together. There is no structure in the world more enduring than that dome. You may call it eternal, if you like. It weighs over 5,000 tons. That is, you tell me, only one-ninth the weight of the Victoria tower, on the Parliament buildings, in London. Why, sir, the Rocky Mountains will budge as quickly as that structure. There are some things about it which I don't like, but the Government Superintendent is absolute. For example, the first coat of paint should have been different. I protested. 'Put it on white,' said the chief. Consequently the dome eats up paint by the ton every year, because there is not a good color for a base."

"Does not the dome leak, sir, by reason of the metal plates expanding and contracting? Is it not possible that by the perpetual working to and fro of the plates, rust, fractured rivets and final collapse will take place?"

"Why, the whole dome is of one metal: it expands and contracts like the folding and unfolding of a lily, all moving together. An atmospheric change that will move one piece moves all—scale and bolt. Rust will happen, but to avoid this the building must be kept water-tight and well painted. It is not by mechanical changes that public works are affected, but by sudden and unnecessary political changes. For example: I got

a judgment against the Government in the Court of Claims last
week for twenty-six thousand dollars. They made a contract
with me to put up the wings of the Library, as I had already
finished and delivered the main part of it. The Secretary of
the Interior was suddenly changed, and he abolished my contract whimsically. Therefore, I bring suit, and his little whim
costs the people twenty-six thousand dollars, besides putting me
out of pocket even at that. See, also, the effect of a change
of superintendents, which I have already referred to. I have
a claim of sixty-odd thousand dollars for the increased cost and
delay incurred by me through the substitution of Meigs, for
Franklin. Had they let me go on by the terms of my contract,
I should have had the work done by 1861. They stopped me
arbitrarily; the war came on; iron went up some hundred per
cent; the river was lined with rebel batteries; freights went
up 400 per cent; the price of labor went up almost as badly.
A new man's whim will cost sixty thousand dollars, perhaps,
to the people; if not, it will come out of my pocket.

"I tell you, sir," said the dome-builder, encouraged in his
theme, "whim, freak, change, are responsible for a good deal
of folly and more extravagance here.

"Let me show you how they got a dome in the first place;
for that is an example:

"Mr. Walter, the architect, prepared the plans for a complete
extension of the Capitol—new wings, new dome, and a new
marble front for the middle or freestone building, which was
the old Capitol; and, as he knew very well that Congress would
never vote this money in the most economical way,—that is, in
bulk, or by fixed yearly parcels—he first submitted the wings.

"Next, as Congress was about adjourning at the end of a
session, and they were all very merry at night—ladies on the
floor, everything lively, the dome, splendidly painted, was presented in a picture and adopted at once."

CHAPTER IX.

SOME OF THE ORGANIC EVILS IN OUR CONGRESSIONAL SYSTEM.

THE present chapter will deal in a discursive way with some of the evils in general legislation.

With every Congressman comes a little knot of retainers, often to his own disgust; for he has used them and finished, and now they are quick that he shall fulfil his promises. Promises are ruin-seeds. Nine-tenths of the crime of the state is tied to rash and often needless promises. "Mr. Godtalk," says Stirrup the saddler, "I admire your course, sir, and want to see you re-elected."

"Stirrup," says Godtalk, "why don't you get the post-office? It will be a nice little addition to your income, take no time from your trade, and be an honor amongst your neighbors."

"Mr. Godtalk, I never aspired to office, sir."

"Tut! tut! Stirrup; it's easy as asking. If I'm elected I'll work for you!"

Behold! the first uneasy and interested seed is planted in the good citizen. He becomes henceforward a corrupted man, the "bore" of his Representative, another hanger-on around the Capitol. This loose and almost always needless tendering of promises is the mistake of the politician, and the corruption of the constituent alike. Every promise, loosely made and broken to the hope, returns to plague giver and receiver. We have been promising the darkeys in the South—some of us—a mule and a forty-acre farm. Let us look out that the mule doesn't kick us dead, and the forty-acre farm be our political cemetery. Promise nothing out of the contract of principles. Come to Washington with free hands, and the highway to honor, if it has enemies before, will have no assassins behind ! No sooner had the members of Congress begun to arrive, than the poor promise-bearers followed after. They looked mean, as does every man with an immortal soul, who waits for a favor that he does not deserve. The saddler's fingers were nervous. The citizen's direct look of searchingness, and yet confidence, had a sycophantish, sidewise smile in the bottom of it. The man was clinging by his eyelids to a politician's word of honor, and God help the hold on that support! The constit. uent had already begun to feel revengeful, for his suspicious fears, born of his conscious meanness, had begun to reproach his Representative. Both were disgusted. The politician had dishonored the saddler's hearth with a foolish promise, and made a family malcontent, and traitors to obedient, cheerful citizenship.

There is no time when one sees these personal errors so vividly in their effect upon the State, as at the opening of Congress. The power of the State, as an attraction and an evil, when it enters into competition with the private patrons of the people, is at this time very manifest. You live, perhaps, down in Egypt, or on the Illinois Central Road, and get the paper afar off, and in your heart you honor the State. The news, as it comes from Washington, is vague and great to you. The names of senators are resonant names, which you hold in excellent respect. The Government is the mighty protector of you and yours, a sworded benefactor, a most impartial father, and yet almost your son.

When this Government, by one of its officers—legislator or what not—comes down from its misty remoteness of sun and thunder cloud, like Jupiter to Danae, and singles one of you out for its caresses, the pure worship you have paid it turns to personal lust and jealousy. Therefore, the fewer possessions that the Government holds, the better for it and you. With its clear, attenuated brow and naked buckler, it is our common champion; but with armsfull of public lands, bon-bons of railway subsidies, Christmas gifts of Indian contracts and sinecures, and the whim and capacity to make invidious favoritisms, Government entering the market place is the wickedest debaucher of the people.

A man came to me recently. "You know a good many people in Congress," he said; "I've got a little business I want to see you about after awhile. I'm here in behalf of the Snuffbox tribe of Indians!"

" What do the Snuffboxes want ? "

"Oh! they're despret anxious to get that treaty o' theirn fixed; want to sell their land, you know, being hard-up and desirous of agoing South. It's all just and fair as the Golding Rule. This yer Osage expozay spiled the treaty of the Snuff-boxes. But, as I said before, ourn is clar and just as the Golding Rule."

Not being a street preacher, I replied only in generalities to this gentleman; but in this correspondence may make it plain to you that by the very situation of the Government we have been unjust to the Snuffbox Indians and this corrupt lobbyist together. This was evidently an intention to cozen the Snuffboxes out of three or four millions of rich acres; but why was this man, apparently a good citizen (he had been a soldier) in the job?

Because Government was in the market as patron and employer. The citizen found a short cut to wealth by making a treaty, and quitted his honest livelihood to come to Washington and make marketable the plausibilities of Congressmen. Here he saw a way to spend a year of dishonorable feeling, " smelling," and huckstering for the sake of a lifetime of wealth. We must make an honest man of him by putting Governments out of the market, abolishing the Indian title in lands, and setting the entire government real estate on an equal footing, so that you, John Smith, Tom Walker, and the devil may be made equal purchasers, so far as nature finds you.

The growth of obligations has come to be so much a matter of slavery to the Congressman that he cannot, if he would, evade them. They confront him in the highest places and demand that he keep up the fashion of providing for his friends as he did in the lower walks.

For example, after Mr. Colfax fell into disgrace through the Credit Mobilier Exposure, a leading Senator said to a friend of mine : " The way to Colfax's ruin was already paved. He had deserted his friends."

" How ?"

" Well, he announced after Grant and he were elected, that he would not ask for patronage of any kind but leave it all to General Grant. That was weak, but he did it to appear magnanimous, as if he did not wish to take any of the glory or reward from his colleague on the ticket. Commonplace people thought it hyperfineness. His acquaintances and supporters thought it was timidity or selfishness. General Grant would have understood and respected Colfax better had he come right up and asked that his friends be considered. It was a childish movement on Colfax's part, but he was always juvenile, even in his cunning. You can't make even a Christian statesman out of too good a boy. So Colfax won nothing by his austere virtue and shook all his enemies out of the tree. When he saw his mistake,—and he was the last to see it,—he endorsed everybody's application for office. This was worse than if he had recommended none ; for it carried no weight, being so cheap and common. And so this man broke under his feet the ladder of patronage he had been so industriously building up. He thought there could be a time when he could dispense with his friends. That time never arrives to any but the greatest order of men. The obligations of politics are mutual; the price of fealty is promotion. And it happened opportunely for Colfax's outraged supporters that his time was ripe to rottenness just as he had coolly dispensed with them. They did not dig his grave but they buried him in it."

The mere value of a residence here is esteemed as so much money-right, because you may board with a Senator, lend a horse to a Sergeant-at-Arms, or know a doorkeeper well, and this involves the possible right to demand a favor of the Federal State.

"Do you want five thousand dollars down in a check?" said a man to another once in my hearing. "Here it is. I want somebody in the Senate to propose to take up the bill making seven Judge Advocates. I don't want you to see it pass, because there are seven of us who have fixed all that. It's bound to pass! We only want some one Senator to lift it up. Whom do you know?"

This was in the last hours of the session. Suppose you lived here, and had entertained Senator Enoch, of Hindoocush, with a soft crab lunch; what more easy than to slip up to the doorkeeper, say, "Take this card to Enoch," see Enoch come benevolent through the door, say "Senator, my nephew depends on this bill being raised; vote as you please, only move to lift it; did you enjoy those crabs?" And, presto, there is $5,000 down merely for knowing one man.

So large is the power of the Federal Congress becoming, that to be a doorkeeper, messenger, even a page, is to possess a chance to obtain offices, privileges, and appropriations. I used to see a dull-eyed man in one of the galleries—a doorkeeper. One day there was a huge overthrow of officials, and into a post of great trust this doorkeeper walked. From being a servant, he became an officer of Congress, and in his present place knows matters so valuable, that the regular Secretary of the Senate cannot know them. The choice may have been a superb one, but I instance it only to show the advantage of having the right of acquaintanceship with Congress. Clerkships in the House and Senate, are worth fortunes to some people. Here in the Clerkship of Claims, Mr. Corbin grew wealthy, and yet he never had a vote; but the knowledge of

what was going on, and the right to salute honorable members
familiarly, and to say a good familiar word for some one's
claim—this was his royal road.

Few persons are aware how Congress conducts business, and
one might go to the chambers and read the *Globe* every day for
two years, without growing a great deal wiser. Yet it is by
the defects of the organization of Congress that thievery thrives
—defects inseparable from all human contrivances.

The commercial republic whose soul and courage be not in
sentiment, but in necessity, is open to this criticism, that, while
it has money to spend to keep the empire together, it does not
like to risk its blood for the same purpose.

A Mr. Shannon, of California, who was a member of Congress
during the war, said to me the other day :

" This Congress, and every other that I have seen, is cursed
by demagogues. I can understand a scoundrel, and meet him ;
but a demagogue is an insidious being, who works with treachery upon the instability of periods and localities, and defeats
good legislation, by making somewhere a prejudice. During
the war, when we had been defeated on the Rappahannock, and
everything was going to pieces, Congress sat here in session,
debating how to make a new army. It was proposed, in this
emergency, to have a conscription, and make every man, if
necessary, come out to defend his country ; but when this bill
passed, what did that demagoguing Congress do, though it sat
within a day's march of the enemy ? Why, they set about
passing a commutation bill, which was, in fact, nothing but a
bill to raise revenue. The United States had a right to every
man in it to go to the front if he was needed and take his chances,
but that miserable set of demagogues sat there wrangling as to
whether the draft policy could not be evaded by the payment of
some money."

In this you can see how the commercial republic prefers to
sacrifice but one thing, and that is cash. In peace it will buy
justice, and in war it prefers to buy the nation back, rather than
to fight for it. Here is one of the greatest evils at the Capital,

not that corrupt legislators hot from the stews of caucus, will take money for their vote, but that commercial men of high character, will pay the money in order to save time. When a set of interests in New York want a bill essential to their solvency—a bill perfectly proper in itself to pass Congress, they employ a lawyer and send him on here, with authority to draw money if it be needful; and he generally gets but one instruction, and that is to carry the bill, and, "if these fellows begin to tinker about it, just pay them." It is the country people of the United States who are still its mainstay—the large class who have not been debauched by great profits, and whose devotion to the State is as strong as the family tie itself. If we can stop demagoguing among the poor people, and corruption amongst the enterprising, we shall have solved the main problem; and our reserve forces, which are rapidly gaining strength, —such as intelligence amongst the masses, the dissipation of old illusions—such as the assumption that the plundering of the many is business—and the drafting of good men into politics by a sort of social enforcement—these are our reliances to save the State.

Here, before me, as I write, is the Captain's chart, the manual for the Speaker of the House of Representatives. It consists of 500 odd pages, and superbly bound, and is a piece of government work, pronounced by Colfax to be the best parliamentary manual in the English language.

The contents of this book are: 1. The Constitution, and amendments, of the United States—so well indexed that the Speaker can catch any phrase of it in a couple of winks. 2. Thomas Jefferson's manual of parliamentary practice, which, by law of 1837, governs "in all applicable cases." 3. The standing rules and orders of business in the House of Representatives, 161 in number. 4. Joint rules and orders of the house, 22 in number. 5. Standing rules in the Senate, 53 in number. 6. The whole of the foregoing digested or made compendious and perspicuous by John M. Barclay, Journal Clerk of the House of Representatives. The digest alone,

making 212 large pages. Herein you have the traditional and
self-imposed laws of the National Legislature in the popular
branch, and he who shall study this book well, can be advised
of the most economical, expeditious, and impartial way of
carrying on the federal legislation of the Republic. A very
few members, however, have studied the manual: some have
never looked into ; and a large proportion of those who know
it best, have mastered it for the purpose of taking advantage of it.

Young men and boys have a good deal to do with legislation.

Willie Todd, Speaker Colfax's messenger. Of him I took
occasion to inquire into the person and history of Thaddy Morris, who had been page to Speaker Pennington in 1859, and
virtual Speaker of the House of Representatives. Mr. Pennington was a delightful old gentleman, ignorant of parliamentary practice, and he was elected by a compromise between the
adherents of Sherman and Marshall, of Kentucky. Placed in
his embarrassing chair, he found the great dog-pit of the House
barking, like Cerberus, under him, and he took every ruling,
point, and suggestion from Thaddeus, most gratefully.

Once, it is related, when young Morris had prepared everything snugly for Pennington, outlined the order of business,
prompted him completely, and left the course " straight as the
crow flies," so that a wayfaring man, though a fool, need not go
astray, he said to the Speaker : " Now, go on."

" Now, go on ! " cried Pennington, promptly, to the House ;
at which there was huge laughter.

It was an inspiring thing to see that delicate boy, secreted
in the pinnacle of the nation, like Paul Revere's friend in the
old South Church spire, supplying knowledge to the gray-
beard who had the honor without the skill of governing.
There is many a boy, unseen, at the elbows of statesmen—
little fellows of downy chins—whose heads are as long as a
sum at compound interest.

This is the Senate-house, a room all gold and buff, a belt of
buff gallery running round it ; through the gold of the roof
twenty-one great enameled windows giving light. The floor
hereof is a soft red English carpet : deep golden cornices sur-

round the hall; a blue-faced clock without a sound goes on with time remorselessly. So blackly the people fill all these galleries that it is but here and there a sunbeam falls upon a face, making it warm yellow; the far-ceiling corners of this hall are full of darkness; dark also are the deep-gilt ornamentations in the edge of the ceiling; upon the floor, however, where the chief actors stand, it is clear as open day.

The scenes witnessed in the night sessions are a good deal like the physical manifestations to which you are used in old cross-road churches at what is called "revival time." People speaking against time to exhausted auditors, each auditor, however, getting up steam for his particular turn at exhortation or prayer. The Speaker, whose attention and nervous readiness must be kept up to a high pitch, sits far up in his seat, behind the marble desks of the clerks, gavel in hand, like a man on a wagon-box, keeping in rein two hundred horses at once, and these horses — "fractious," or poorly broken—duck, break up, rear, neigh, or pull the wrong way, or lazily, while his gavel is flourished like a whip-handle without a lash. The disposition to draw blood, and the incapacity to do it, are very clearly expressed in his face, and therefore he brings the House to by a loud "Whoa!" Then he straightens them up with a cautious "Peddy—peddy—whoa! G'lang now!" Directly some stallion bounces off into a ditch, and the Speaker's "Gee, there, Mike!" or "Haw! haw! Tommy!" with dreadful indications of the broken whip-handle, coerce the team into some degree of good behavior.

In the cloak-room, some groups of Congressmen are smoking. Here and there on the floor of the House you see some one surreptitiously pulling at his cigar. Every lobbyist, who by hook or crook can get upon the floor, is traveling about between seats and sofas, with a sly, sidewise look, an express-train tongue, and a vigorous movement of his hand, gesturing on his private interest. Here is a member helping out some such lobbyist, introducing him round, pulling a group of folks into the wash-room or side-lobby, all talking, hearing, suggesting, flying round like folks wrought up to the verge of despair. In the open space before the Speaker a score of anxious people assemble, ready to seize the Speaker's eye and gouge some proposition through it. Now vindictiveness is most alert to beat some hated rival or adverse interest in the dying hours of the session, as it has succeeded so well in doing during the bulk of the season. You can make intense studies wherever you look, as of two such hating and hated enemies watching each other. Here is Bellerophon, the member from Pascagoula, resolved to get his friend Shiftless, of the contested seat, through in the nick of time, for Shiftless has scarcely money enough to embark on the train for his home, and he hopes, by a decisive vote, to save all his back pay, settle his board bills, and have some spending money.

Bellerophon is on the floor, in the area, working his faithfullest. He cries, "Mr. Speaker," in and out of time, feels his skin abraded by repeated failures, and the color, pale or red, rises alternately to his cheeks, while poor Shiftless stands off in pleading silence, saying short pieces of prayer between his need and his hypocrisy, like a man in a steamboat when there is inevitably to be a scuttling. Some distance off, Strike, the unappeasable enemy of Shiftless, lurks, with the light of revenge in his eyeball, and the phrase "I object!" upon his tongue, balanced like a man's revolver at full-cock. So they fight it out. So they stand arrayed—the old immemorial history of friendship, enmity, and hero, celebrated since literature could venture to portray anything. The morning hours advance; nature gives out, and all doze or sleep but these three, and many similar trios like them. At last even interest subsides, and he whose rights are being guarded, feels himself satiety, listlessness, inattention. He sleeps at his desk, while vigilant Friendship, keeping guard in the area with weary legs, cries steadily in all the pauses:

"Mr. Speaker, I believe I have the floor!"

"Mr. Speaker, you recognized me, I am sure, sir!"

Still Malice, with unsmoothable eyes, is ready with his cocked revolver, saying ever:

" I object ! "

Even Friendship wearies in the end, and stopping in some empty perch to rest, feels the leaden weights upon its eyeballs, drive them slowly down. But when the interested one and his champion are quite overcome, still tireless and remorseless the Enemy looks out, bright and prepared, with the uncompromising—" I object ! "

Knowing, as I did, the undertone of motive at the Capitol, I watched the last hours of the session on a Saturday with something of the sentiment of Lord Macaulay when he contemplated the Tower of London :

" They are associated with whatever is darkest in human nature and in human destiny, with the savage triumph of implacable enemies, with the inconstancy, the ingratitude, the cowardice of friends, with all the miseries of fallen greatness and blighted fame."

The same must be said of the latter days of the Senate, in executive session here, when enemies fall afoul of each other and slaughter each other's hopes of place between the decisive instants of triumph. It is the old, old story of Raleigh, Essex, and Sidney.

CHAPTER X.

Dining in Washington is a great element in politics. The lobby man dines the Representative; the Representative dines the Senator; the Senator dines the charming widow, and the charming widow dines her coming man. For reed birds the politician consults Hancock, on the avenue; for oysters, Harvey; and for an ice or a quiet supper, Wormly or Page; but there is no dinner like Welcker's. He possesses an autograph letter from Charles Dickens, saying that he kept the best restaurant in the world. He has given all the expensive and remarkable dinners here for several years; and talking over the subject of his art with him a few days ago, we obtained some notions about food and cooking at Washington.

JNO. WELCKER.

Welcker is said to be a Belgian, but he has resided in New York since boyhood, and he made his appearance in Washington at the beginning of the war as steward of the seventh regiment. He is a youthful, florid, stoutish man, with a hearty address, a ready blush, and a love for the open air and children. Every Summer he goes down the Potomac, shutting his place behind him, and there he fishes and shoots off the entire warm season, wearing an old straw hat and a coat with only one flap on the tail. Nobody suspects that this apparition of Mr. Winkle is the great caterer for the Congressional stomach. Nobody imagines that this rustic is the person whose sauces can please even Mr. Sam. Ward, that distinguished observer for the house of Baring Brothers. Nobody knows—not even the innocent and festive shad—that this Welcker is John Welcker, who came to Washington during our civil broil, drew and quartered for Provost Marshal Fry, fed all the war ministers, and gave that historic period the agreeable flavor of Mushrooms.

In the early days of Washington, entertainments other than family ones were given at the taverns, some of which, as Beale's, stood on Capitol Hill. Afterward Mrs. Wetherill, on Carroll Row, set especial dinners, breakfasts, and suppers to order. In later times Crutchett on Sixth street, Gautier on the Avenue, and Thompson on C street, established restaurants *a la carte*. Gautier sold out to Welcker, who had such success during the war that he bought a large brick dwelling on Fifteenth street, near the Treasury, and at times he has leased several surrounding dwellings, so that he kept a hotel in fact, though without the name. Welcker has a large dining room, eighty feet long by sixteen feet wide, with adjustable screens, adapting it to several small parties, or by their removal to make one large dining room, which will seat one hundred people. Welcker's main lot is one hundred and thirty-three by twenty-five feet.

The character of Welcker's entertainments is eminently select, and his prices approach those of the English *Castle and Falcon*, or of Philippe's in Paris. His breakfasts and dinners *a la carte* are about at New York rates, less than those of the Fourteenth Street Delmonico, and matching the St. James and Hoffman restaurant prices. The most expensive dinners he has ever given have cost $20 a plate. Fine dinners cost from $10 to $12 per plate, and breakfast from $5 to $8 per plate. He has fed between six and seven hundred people per diem, as on the day of Grant's inauguration. His best rooms rent at $8 a day, and consist of a suite of three rooms, but the habitants thereof pay the establishment for food, wine, &c., not less than $50 a day.

Welcker's chief cook is an Italian Swiss, obtained from Martini's, New York,—the same who distinguished himself at Charles Knapp's great entertainment in 1865, the cost of which was $15,000. Welcker supplied the food for Mr. Knapp's last entertainment, in 1867, at the I St. mansion, now occupied by Sir Edward Thornton. There are five cooks in all at Welcker's, and the establishment employs thirty servants. During the past session he has given at least two dinner parties a day, averaging twelve guests at each, and each costing upwards of $100.

The best fish in the waters of Washington is the Spanish mackerel, which ascends the Potomac as high as Wicomico river. They come as late as August, and bring even five dollars a pair when quite fresh.

Brook trout, propagated artificially, Welcker thinks lack flavor. He obtains his from Brooklyn, but says that there are trout in the Virginia streams of the Blue Ridge.

Freezing-boxes, or freezing-houses, such as are established in Fulton Market, New York, do not exist in Washington. These keep fish solid and pure for the entire season. The inventor of them is a Newfoundland man, and he proposes to put them up in Washington for $300 a piece.

Welcker says that the articles in which the District of Columbia excels all other places are celery, asparagus, and lettuce. The potatoes and carrots hereabouts he does not esteem. The beef is inferior to the Virginia mutton, which he thinks is the best in the world—better than the English Southdown. Potomac snipe and canvas-back ducks Welcker thinks the best in the world, and the oysters of Tangier, York river, and Elizabeth river he considers unexcelled by any in the world. The Virginia partridge and the pheasant,—which are the same as the northern quail and the partridge,—Welcker also holds to be of the most delicious description.

Our markets, he says, are dearer than those of New York

and Baltimore, and less variously and fully stocked. The market system here requires organization, being carried on by a multitude of small operators who are too uninformed about prices to institute a competitive system, and hence it often happens that potatoes are sold at one place for $1.50 a bushel, and somewhere near by for only fifty cents a bushel. His market bill will average during the session, $600 a week, and sometimes rises to $300 a day.

The most expensive fisheries on the Potomac rent for about $6,000 a year. Messrs. Knight & Gibson, who have the Long Bridge fishery, opposite Washington, paying $2,000 a year for it, pay also $6,000 for a fishery near Matthias Point, about seventy miles down the Potomac. Knight & Gibson keep a fish stand in the Center market.

The first shad which reach the North come from Savannah, and bring in the month of February as much as $6 a pair. Alexandria is the chief mart for saving and salting shad. Gangs are often brought from Baltimore, Frederick, and Philadelphia to man the shad boats, and five miles of seine are frequently played out. The black bass in the Potomac river were put in at Cumberland several years ago, and have propagated with astonishing fecundity. How much nobler was the experiment of this benefactor of our rivers than the wide spread appetite for destructiveness we see everywhere manifested.

The most expensive dish furnished by Welcker is Philadelphia capon *au sauce Goddard*, stuffed with truffles, named for the celebrated surgeon Goddard of Philadelphia. The best capons come from New Jersey, but good ones are raised in the region of Frederick, Md. The capon is probably the most delicious of domestic fowls, attaining the size of the turkey, but possessing the delicate flesh and flavor of the chicken. Truffles cost eight dollars a quart can, and four dollars and a-half the pint can. They come from France and North Italy, and grow on the roots of certain trees. Truffle dogs and boars are used to discover them, and the boars wear wire muzzles to keep them from eating the precious parasites. Truffles look like small potatoes, except that they are jet black through and through. The capon is boiled and served with white-wine sauce and with sweet breads.

Take next for an example the prices which we receive in the Arlington, which is a small hotel, with a capacity for no more than three hundred and twenty-five persons.

Senator Cameron paid for himself and wife $450 per month, and had but two rooms. Senator Fenton had a parlor, two bedrooms, and an office, and paid $1,000 per month. Mr. S. S. Cox and wife, paid $250 per week, and he gave a buffet supper, for one hundred persons, which cost him $1,500. Mr. W. S. Huntington, gave the Japanese the finest spread ever set in the Arlington Hotel; there were only twenty persons, and he paid $1,000. Dr. Helmbold paid $96 per day, and his bill for two weeks was about $1,600. A parlor, and three bedrooms in the second story of the Arlington, with a small family occupying them, are worth $450 per week, during the season; and one guest here pays for a parlor, bedroom, and bathroom, $300 per month.

At the Delevan House, Albany, Dr. Gautier used to pay $375 per week, and General Darling, with a parlor, three bedrooms, and four persons, paid $400. The hotel at Lake George, had 37,000 on the register last season, in four months; it took in that space of time $294,000, and the net profits were $52,000.

The Fifth Avenue Hotel in New York, rents for $200,000 a year, including the stores beneath it. The St. Nicholas rents for $95,000, although it cost but $425,000. Mr. A. T. Stewart has just rented to William M. Tweed, the Metropolitan Hotel, New York, for $65,000 a year, to put his son, Richard Tweed, into business as a landlord; and the Lelands, who go out, paid $75,000.

The cheapest piece of hotel property, in point of rent, in this country, is the Brevoort House, New York, which rents for $27,500, and has three owners; it is kept on the European plan, excepting the *table d' hote*, which it does not keep up, as it has made its reputation on the best *cuisine* in the world.

One evening in 1870 the Capitol of the nation did itself credit, by heartily welcoming one of the young sons of the Queen of England. The opportunity was a ball given by the British Minister, Thornton, to Prince Arthur, probably with the original motive of making his visit agreeable to the young man, by showing him the pretty girls in their most becoming dresses, and giving him a convenient chance to speak to them, as a young man likes to speak to a fine girl, intimately, and agreeably. Nothing has ever been invented like a dance, to bring the young folks together. The story of Cinderella's slipper turns, upon going to the Prince's ball; and I suppose that, so long as human nature remains what it always has been, Princes' balls will be popular, and Princes the type of all that is noble and exalted. Jones is called the prince of caterers, and Simon the prince of sleeping-car conductors, and if the term be a compliment when it has no reality in it, how really infatuating must be a true Prince, born of the Queen, peer above the highest, with jealous mysteries of blood, and a birthright which will keep respect and inspire superstition, long after its wearer is broken down in character, and ruined in purse. The most decided Republican and Democrat, though he may sneer at Princes and deprecate attention to them, is apt to feel the strange magnetism of the name and the office, for it is an admonition of antique times and government, a word of spell, signifying to the ear at least, the issue of those whose love and nuptials affected a realm, a period, or a world. This Prince is still a Prince, though not a powerful one—a far-off son, with elder brothers between him and a throne,—and perhaps he has had reason to feel the distance at which he stands from favor; therefore, it was gentle in us, who had treated his high-born brother with such opulence of incense and favor, to be no colder towards young Arthur. His father and mother were exceptionally chaste, as affectionate as wife and man in two sensual and selfish lives could be. His mother wrote with her hand, a letter of sympathy to the widow of our most precious President. The office of Prince in our day is reduced to such small political figure, that we could do no harm to monarchy, by showing republican bad manners to this young gentleman. And we owe it to our high place amongst nations to do cheerful hospitality to any Prince or ruler, well-behaved, who comes amongst us with frank confidence in our good will and good breeding.

I write this down, because it is always easy and tempting to sneer at Princes; and when this young man came to the Capital, I had an itching to say something that would make you laugh about him. There is really no reason, however, for any disparagement, because the good sense of our guest and our people, has been displayed during his visit. If any low fellow has said anything coarse in his presence, I have not heard of it. He has been subjected to a round of official dinners and receptions, which I would not have passed through for a hundred dollars a day, and he has kept himself patient and obliging all the time. More than that, he is a young man, and can't help being a Prince. So good luck to him!

Mrs. Thornton, like the first walking lady in a comedy, gathered up her moire antique dress with the satin trail, close to the blue satin panier, and surrounded with Apollos of legation, each looking like a silver-enamelled angel out of a valentine, accomplished the descent of the stairs, treading all the way upon scarlet drugget, and helped by the laurel-entwined balusters.

At the foot was the Prince, dressed in the uniform of the British Rifles,—dark sack coat, double-breasted, buttoned to the throat, and well trimmed and frogged along the lappels; tight, dark-colored pantaloons, with a stripe, strapped over patent leather boots; a steel-sheathed dress sword, at his side; an infantry cap in his hand; a little cartridge box, like a tourist's glass, strapped across his shoulder; and what shone and flashed like a streak of day-light through him, was a huge jewelled star, the insignia of the Garter. This latter, perhaps the symbol of the highest nobility in Christendom, was more observed than the clear skinned, rosy face of the young man, his brown hair, good teeth, and obedient and intelligent eye.

His clothes clung almost as closely to him as his skin, and while he was one of the most plainly-dressed persons conspicuous upon the floor, this fact alone made him somewhat eminent. There was that, besides, which gave him beauty and character beyond the star that threw a hundred sheets of light every way he turned; the fine distinction of ruddy youthfulness, made modest and interesting by being placed in such prominence. If a young man knows how to feel publicity, and yet bear himself well under it, so that there is a nice mingling of self-reliance and sensitiveness, the effect upon a crowd is to get him hearty sympathy—the next thing to admiration.

Arthur gave Mrs. Thornton his arm, and escorted her to the ball room. The Cupids out of the valentines, the Prince's followers, and all the rest of the little suite and embassy joined in behind, making quite a spangled procession, as if the gas fixtures were going to a party in company with the window curtains. As they all came along together, gold ramrod and satin drapery, the band in the gallery struck up, "God save the Queen!" Then the people sitting in cane chairs on both sides of the long hall stood up, and ceased waving their fans. The shoe blacks and darkeys in the street below, looked up at the flaming windows, and said interjections, and danced steps of involuntary jigs, and said out of their malicious little spirits: "Shoo Fly."

Arthur, with Mrs. Thornton still on his arm, walked the whole length of the hall to the carpeted platform, when he turned about, and waited modestly till the music ceased. Then he shook hands with many folks standing round, whom he remembered, or thought he did. Elphinstone, his aid, was covered all over with medals of daring, gained probably, by such victories as this, and he wore the gorgeous uniform of his red-complexioned nation. Picard, another aid, wore the English artillery uniform. They looked well, as Englishmen look—a sort of stiffened-up suggestion of manhood, with indications of skye terrier fringing out.

One of the romances of Washington city was recently enacted

in the Diplomatic Corps.   For nearly thirty years Baron Gerolt
served the interests of Prussia at Washington city, and he lived
long enough to rear native-born American children under the
shadow of the Capitol, one of whom married Mr. Rangabe, the
Greek minister.   Gerolt owed his appointment to this country
to Baron Humboldt, who had been entertained by him while
chargé in Mexico, and who recommended him to the King
of Prussia.   Gerolt was an affable, republican sort of man in
society, fond of the American people, and his social associates
were men like Charles Sumner and others, who inclined him
towards the Federal side in the war of the rebellion.   He probably got considerable credit for original principle during the
war, when he was really subordinate to acquaintances of a
stronger will, who impressed the claims of the North upon him.
It is charged that, at home, he was somewhat tyrannical with
his family, as is the German custom : and that he and his wife
wished to assert too much authority over their children, who
had inhaled the breath of the Western hemisphere.   Whatever
the interior side of his life might have been, Gerolt is remembered enthusiastically by some of the best people in Washington, Republicans and Democrats alike.   He resides at Linz,
near Bonn, in Rhenish Prussia, and is permanently out of the
diplomatic service of North Germany.

The Gerolts, although Germans, are Catholics, and the girls
were strictly brought up under the tuition of the priests at
Georgetown.   Bertha, the youngest daughter of the Baron, now
about twenty-three years of age, and a very rich and handsome
type of the young German girl, fell in love, three or four years
ago, with her father's Secretary of Legation, a tall, handsome,
dashing and somewhat reckless Prussian, and a connection or
relative of Bismarck.   This young Secretary belonged to a fine
old Brandenburg Protestant family, which had decided notions
against forming Catholic alliances.   The young gentleman
would have fallen heir, in time, to large estates in North Prussia ; but these were in some manner, as it is stated, made conditional upon his keeping up the ancestral Lutheran faith.

This young Prussian chap, you may recollect as being the antagonist of one of our ministers, Lawrence of Central America, some two or three years ago, when the two met on what is called the field of honor, exchanged shots, and then patched up the fight without bloodshed. He paid court to Bertha Gerolt, and she was intensely enamored of him. In order to make the nuptials easy on both sides, Gerolt applied to the Catholic Church authorities for an indulgence, or something, warranting the marriage of this hereditary Protestant with his Catholic daughter; but as it was specified that the children issuing from such marriage were to be brought up Protestants, the Roman dignitaries refused. Gerolt, who appears sincerely to have wished to please his child, had also intentions upon the Pope; but while these ecclesiastical efforts were being made, the domestic correspondence between the Secretary and his mother in Germany, and some ensuing letters from Madame, growing warmer and more indignant from time to time, had the effect of racking the poor girl's feelings; and, in the end, the handsome Prussian went home. This is an end to the matter up to the present. Bertha Gerolt refused to accompany either her father or mother to Germany, and has retired to the Georgetown Convent, where, some say, she will take the last veil; and others that she will repent after a while, and reappear in the world.

Opinion is divided in this city as to why Gerolt was remanded to his own country. Some say that he suffered certain indignities at the hands of our State Department. Others allege that he was insufficient particularly about the time that American arms were shipped to France to be used against the Prussians. It is said that, on that occasion, Bismarck asked Mr. Bancroft why our goverment permitted such things; and Bancroft, to make it easy for himself, retorted that there was Baron Gerolt in Washington, and, if he had been attending to his business, the arms would have been detained. Others say that Catacazy drew Gerolt into an intrigue, and got him to work against the late treaty which we made about the Alabama claims. Whatever the facts, the Baron has gone for good, and his admirers here are preparing to forward him an elaborate service of silver, to show that what he did for the country in its crisis is remembered at least by its private citizens.

You have many a pretty girl in the West who would be excited if the prospect were held out to her of marrying the Portuguese Secretary of Legation. Yet a Portuguese person of nearly that description was content to marry a negro girl the other day, at the Capital to which he was accredited. The Peruvian minister's wife was raised here; and the former Russian minister married the pretty daughter of a boarding-house keeper at Georgetown. Yet were any of them happier, or even richer? I doubt it much. One New Year's day I saw a beautiful woman, reared here, who is soon to go to Russia for life, and consort with candle eaters in a cold empire where the flag that was the pride of our babyhood does not float, where the music and the language we love is not spoken, and middle age, and old age, and her children must be given to a people who can never know her like her countrymen. It is strange to see women deluded into these alliances by some high fangled echo of a word, or a fashion-plate. As a rule, these foreigners accredited to the Capital of the United States are either politicians of the third class around the governments of their countries, or courtiers of the third class. An European courtier, reduced to his essentials, is a pleasing politician around his Capital, pressing to be provided for, fed, and rewarded. He has passed through the same straights, shrewnesses, and triumphs as an American politician, held up somebody's coat tail, been somebody's brother-in-law, owed his appointment to the pretty face of a sister, or he has written up the side of some patron, in a pamphlet or newspaper, and crowded all sail to be furnished with an exchequer in other parts. When an American girl, therefore, marries " a member of the foreign legation," she marries merely a politician or a noodle who can speak only bad English, who probably marries her for her money or for his *ennui*, and who is habituated to having mistresses at home.

I am not speaking of anybody, nor of everybody, in the foreign legations at Washington, when I thus produce the comparative light of fact and experience upon them ; but as a general rule, I would not take a turn next door, to see a member of legation.

We know, by observation upon him at home,—that being in a white and gold cocked hat, a sword, a ruffled shirt, and a pair of scarlet and gold trousers, who came up before the President on the first day of the year, and bowed, and left his royal master's condescensions.

It was with such feelings,—while recognizing many reverend and excellent gentlemen among the foreign ministers at a levee, and several persons of talent and pursuit,—that I ran my eye along the gaily attired line,—the romance of the name, and the livery gone from my mind ; while at the head of our State, in plain black, stood the little General who fought bigger battles than any of their Kings, and commanded a nation of men with more destiny than all their combined States possessed antiquity.

The mystery and magic of the foreign service and uniform, are kept alive entirely by our American women. We men do not believe in them. If Miss Jane Smith, or the widow Tompkins, marries Signor Straddlebanjo, she ascends, in the female mind, to the seventh heaven of respect, while eating yet the same pork chops, and taking milk from the same pump and milkman.

Many of these gentlemen have found good wives and comfortable homes among us. You are aware that the famous French Minister, Genet, set this example early, by retreating from the contempt of Washington, and the frown of Jefferson, into the bosom of the Clinton family, and never returned to France at all. That famous old rooster married three times, if I am well informed, in the United States, and some time ago, when I was introduced in New York to a lawyer and city politician named Genet, I said to him musingly :

" Why ! that was the name of the great lettre de marque Frenchman !"

" My grandfather !" replied the politician of Tammany Hall.

When Mr. Johnson shoved his friend, the Adjutant-General, through the tenure-of-office act, he had little idea how he was hastening the marriage ceremony of little Bibbapron. Bibbapron had fixed his engagement day for the first of July, so as to be in New York on the Fourth, and set off some firecrackers, after which he expected to make some good resolutions to regulate family life at Saratoga Springs. But people who are engaged, are always impatient. They are left alone together a good deal, and find waiting to be a sort of dissipation. It is neither pursuit nor possession, neither fish nor flesh. It is the tenderest, most quarrelsome, most tantalized, most disheartened, most forebode-ful period of love. No wonder that Bibbapron, when he heard of the " High Court of Impeachment," the solemnity of the spectacle, and the great learning of the managers and counsel, had but to suggest to Molly what a delightful time it would be to visit Washington, when she embraced himself, and the occasion. The milliner was hurried up. Ma was persuaded that Summer was an unhealthy season in the East. The little marriage ceremony was not held in the church, but in the parlor at home, and the clergyman's fee reduced somewhat in consequence. Bibbapron's papa gave his son a letter to Congressman Starch, and the express train saw the pair tucked in, the last tear shed, and the town of Skyuga fade from the presence of its prettiest girl. It is to tell all the engaged folks how to get to Washington and how to see it, that I reluctantly took Mrs. Bibbapron's diary and copy a few pages from it. They are strictly accurate, for which the other correspondents don't care to use them. Mrs. Bibbapron has a way of italicising every other word in diary, which I don't care to imitate, and she makes a very pretty period with a tear, which, of course, I cannot do. The diary was a present from her younger sister ; it had an almanac in it and blank washing lists, with quotations from the poets under each date. Here it begins :

" April 22, 1868—Dear me, how tired ! I am in Washington, the Capital of the United States. It's not larger than New

York, my husband, Alonzo, says, which I think is a great shame. Government ought to make it bigger right away, or have it somewhere where it would get bigger, itself. The maps are all incorrect about Washington, where it is represented by a great many dots, while all the other towns have only one dot. We went to Willard's Hotel, and, in order to give us a fine view of the city, they put us up in the top story. We went down to breakfast at nine o'clock, and called for oysters, of course. They tasted as if they had been caught in warm water. The fresh shad was quite a bone to pick. My dear husband took a cocktail before breakfast. He says it's quite the thing here. Senator Tatterson joined him, he says. I hope my husband will never be a drunkard!"

N. B.—He says the Senator took *his* straight.

Half-past ten o'clock.—Alonzo, my darling husband, has been to see Congressmen Starch, and brought him into the ladies' parlor. Pa can't abide Congressman Starch, because they differ in politics; but Alonzo's Pa is a Republican, and lent Mr. Starch a horse and wagon to bring up voters. I think it was very generous of the Congressman to ask so particularly about Pa's health. He gave me two tickets for the great trial. He says they are very scarce, and old ones are sold for relics for ever so much money. The managers buy the old ones to paste their photographs on them, and present them to the Historical Societies. Congressman Starch says he lost his best constituent to give me these tickets, but told me to be particular not to tell Pa about it. He says Johnson is the great criminal of the age, and ought to have been impeached before he was born. There is no doubt, he says, that it was Johnson in disguise who murdered Mr. Lincoln, and then bribed Booth with a clerkship to be killed in his place. He says that General Butler offers to prove that Boston Corbett was only Andrew Johnson, who killed Booth to keep him from telling. Poor Booth! He died saying 'Poor Carlotta!' I never sing that song but tears come to my eyes, and I think of my husband. Alonzo will never kill the President. He was brought up a Baptist.

Five o'clock, P. M. I have seen all the great patriots of our country. Mr. Sumner is the greatest of them all, his hair is so exquisite. Mr. Brooks, of New York, who gave him such a beating, was on the floor of the Senate, wearing spectacles. He is a newspaper editor, and drives a pair of cream-colored horses. He must be a dreadful man, but is right good looking. Mr. Sumner forgives him, because he prints his speeches.

I am going too fast, but really, I have so much to do to-day, that I don't know where to begin. We took the horse cars to the Capitol, and went along Pennsylvania Avenue. The National Hotel looks sick, ever since the celebrated disease there. I was surprised to see so many negroes in the car. Congress compels them to ride, in order to carry out the Civil Rights bill. The poor souls look dreadfully as if they wanted to walk some. Dear me! I love to walk since I am married. I can take my husband's arm then and pinch him. It seems to me that we ain't happy unless we pinch those we love!

The Capitol is the grandest, most wonderful building in the whole world. It is all marble, with a splendid dome above it, and a perfect hide-and-seek of aisles, passages, and gorgeous stairways. It looks like a marble quarry in blossom. They wash it every night, and the government officers spit it yellow every day. Alonzo says tobacco is bought by the ream, and charged to "stationery." He says that this is quite right, because when the members have a chaw in their mouths they speak less and save time. I hope my husband will never chew tobacco. Government ought to pass a law against it, and get the women to enforce it. On the top of the Capitol is a statue of Pocahontas, flying a kite; I should think it ought to be Benjamin Franklin, but they have got him inside in marble. It will take millions and millions to furnish the Capitol. I suppose they will have nothing but Axminster carpets and oiled walnut. In the dome of the Capitol there are beautiful pictures. I liked the marriage of Pocahontas the best. She wears her hair plain, and her dress looks like a bolster case. The

Indian women have beautiful figures but their clothes are dowdy. Some of them in this picture wear goose feathers for full dress, and look to have caught cold. But that's what's expected of a bridesmaid. She dresses for a consumption!

We got good seats next to the Diplomatic Gallery. Alonzo pointed out the Russian Minister and his wife to me; we admired them very much till we heard that it was the Minister's Coachman and cook. The foreign Ministers send their servants here when they want their gallery to look genteel. Theodore Tilton was distinguished by his long hair. He has withdrawn the nomination of Chase, and ruined the Chief-Justice. He looks sad about it. Congressman Starch showed us the Chief-Justice, a man like Washington in holy orders. Mr. Starch said he would be impeached soon with all the Judges. The Bench, he says, is rotten. (Why not give them chairs?) He said if it had not been for the Bench, the constitution, which is the cause of all this trouble, would have been done away with long ago. Dear me! an old rotten bench ought not to keep our country in such peril. The Senate Chamber is all buff and gilt, like an envelope on Valentine's day. There is a silver ice pitcher on the table of the President's counsel, which I believe is plated. I wish I could just go down and feel of it. They say that the Government is swindled in everything. Perhaps the coolest swindle is ice pitchers. This is mean. Washington, Webster, and Mr. Starch must be incapable of it. If my husband ever comes to Congress I mean to work him a pair of slippers in red, white, and blue. Then he can't go across the street, like Mr. Alwusbeery to drink between votes, in his stocking feet.

I saw Mrs. Southworth, the great novelist, author of the "Deserted Step-Mother." She lives at Georgetown in a haunted boarding-house. Her health is good, considering what must be her distress of mind, say two hundred pounds without jewelry. Her dress was a black silk, tabs on the mantilla, and angel-sleeves, so as to leave space to swing her beautiful pen. If I could write like Mrs. Southworth, I would keep

Alonzo, my darling husband, sitting at my feet in tears all the time.

Mrs. Swizzlem, the colored authoress of Mrs. Keckley's book, was in the diplomatic gallery with one of Mrs. Lincoln's dresses on, counting through an opera glass the pimples on the face of one of the Senators. She hates his wife, Alonzo says, and means to worry her.

Mr. Thornton, the British Minister, looks very much worried. Congressman Starch says that Senator Chandler is a Fenian, and means to make a dreadful speech at poor Mr. Thornton. Alonzo is afraid it will miss fire, and kill some innocent person. Senator Wade, the next President, looks like Martha Washington. He is a very pious man, beloved by everybody, and would have become a preacher if they had not wanted him so bad for President.

Twelve A. M! Oh, dear! that ever I was married! Be still, my poor soul! I have heard of the wickedness of men—now I know it! Last night I heard something like a wheel-barrow coming up stairs. It seemed to fall around the elbows and upset at all the platforms. It tumbled right up to my room. The wheelbarrow burst right through the door; first came the wheel and then pitched the barrow on top of it. The barrow was Congressman Starch, the wheel was—Alonzo. They joined themselves together again and wheeled forward, right up onto the bed. There were so many legs and so much motion and hallooing that I could not tell my husband from the other. I said, however:

"Merciful Heavens!"

To this replied my husband, in terms like the following:

"Johnsing's gone up. Starchy threw cashting vote. Mime going tee be Conshul-General under Ben Wade—all hunk!"

Said a voice, proceeding, as I conjectured, from the owner of that pair of legs which did not wear Alonzo's trowsers:

"Yesh! bet your Impartial Justice according to zhee laws. Mime going ter be Secretary thinteeryer!"

I rang the bell and wept. The waiters removed the Congressman. My husband snored. I hope the bed was buggy, for he deserved it. In the morning, after a sleepless night, I heard Alonzo cry:

"Miss Bibbapron! Congress water!"

Now I know where this dreadful Congress water gets its name. It's what makes Senators tipsy.

I hope the Impeachment trial will be done soon. Congressman Starch shall never get my vote. Oh! that I should be a bride and bring my husband to Washington!"

WASHINGTON'S WHITE HOUSE AS IT WAS IN PHILADELPHIA, 1790.

CHAPTER XI.

THE WHITE HOUSE AND ITS OCCUPANTS.

The President's residence down to 1800 was of a floating character; now in New York, now in Philadelphia; and the ladies of the Executive branch of the government were very like women in barracks with army officers; sometimes sent into damp dwellings, again like the wives of Methodist preachers, perpetually waiting for ships to come with their clothes and carpets.

Mrs. John Adams, in a volume of letters, edited by the late Minister to England, her grandson, which I have found in the Congressional Library, gives some lively sketches of a President's wife. Writing to her married daughter in the latter part of November, 1790, from Philadelphia, she speaks dolefully of her quarters and those of the ladies of the Cabinet.

"Poor Mrs. Knox, (wife of the first Secretary of War,) is in great tribulation about her furniture. The vessel sailed the day before the storm and had not been heard of on Friday last. I had a great misfortune happen to my best trunk of clothes. The vessel sprung a leak and my trunks got wet a foot high, by which means I have several gowns spoiled; and the one you (Mrs. Smith) worked is the most damaged, and a black satin—the blessed effects of tumbling about the world."

After a while the City of Washington was laid out, and in the first year of this century, Mrs. John Adams started for the great new " Palace " of the President. The whole story is told in a letter to her daughter, Mrs. Smith, written November 21st, 1800. It is notable as being probably the first letter ever written in the White House by its mistress:

" I arrived here Sunday last, and without meeting with any accident worth noticing, except losing ourselves when we left Baltimore, and going eight or nine miles on the Frederick road, by which means we were obliged to go the other eight through woods, where we wandered two hours without finding a guide or the path. Fortunately a straggling black came up with us, and we engaged him as a guide, to extricate us out of our difficulty; but woods are all you see from Baltimore until you reach *the city*, which is so only in name. Here and there is a small cot, without a glass window, interspersed among the forests, through which you travel miles without seeing any human being. *   *   *   *   *   *

" The house is upon a grand and superb scale, requiring about thirty servants to attend and keep the apartments in proper order, and perform the ordinary business of the house and stables—an establishment very well proportioned to the President's salary. The lighting of the apartments from the kitchen to parlor and chambers, is a tax indeed; and the fires we are obliged to keep to secure us from daily agues is another very cheering comfort. To assist us in this great castle, and render less attendance necessary, bells are wholly wanting, not one single one being hung through the whole house, and promises are all you can obtain. This is so great an inconvenience that I know not what to do or how to do. *   *   * If they will put up some bells and let me have wood enough to keep fires, I design to be pleased. Surrounded with forests, can you believe that wood is not to be had, because people cannot be

found to cut and cart it ?   *   *   *   Briesler has had recourse
to coal; but we cannot get grates made and set. We have
indeed come into a new country. You must keep all this to
yourself, and when asked how I like it, say that I write you the
situation is beautiful, which is true.

"The house is made habitable, but there is not a single
apartment finished, and all within-side, except the plastering,
has been done since Briesler (the steward) came. We have .
not the least fence, yard or other convenience without, and the
great unfinished audience-room I make a drying-room of, to
hang up the clothes in. The principal stairs are not up, and
will not be this Winter. Six chambers are made comfortable ;
two are occupied by the President and Mr. Shaw ; two lower
rooms, one for a common parlor, and one for a levee room.
Up stairs there is the oval room, which is designed for the
drawing-room, and has the crimson furniture in it. It is a very
handsome room now, but when completed, it will be beautiful.
If the twelve years in which this place has been considered as
the future seat of Government, had been improved, as they
would have been in New England, very many of the present
inconveniences would have been removed."

Mrs. Adams, writing again November 27th, says that : "Two
articles we are most distressed for ; the one is bells, but the
more important is wood. Yet you cannot see wood for trees.
We have only one cord and a half of wood in this house where
twelve fires are constantly required. It is at a price, indeed ;
from four dollars it has risen to nine!"

Again, Mrs. Adams shows us a picture of distress almost as
bad as a Methodist preacher's wife's experiences :

"The vessel which has my clothes and other matters is not
arrived. The ladies are impatient for a drawing-room. I have
no looking-glasses but "dwarfs" for this house ; nor a twen-
tienth-part lamps enough to light it. Many things were stolen ;
more broken by removal ; among the number my tea china is
more than half missing. Georgetown affords nothing."

Mrs. Adams was a preacher's daughter, married young, and

THE CABINET CHAMBER IN THE WHITE HOUSE, WASHINGTON.

she burst into tears when her husband got his first nomination to anything. They lived together fifty-three years. John was the son of a religious shoemaker, and himself a school-teacher. His conceit was large, his thrift equal to it, and all the Adamses since his day have not degenerated from these standards. They were the original Yankees of the White House, and it is remarkable that every Northern President has saved some of his salary, while the contrary is true of every Southerner but one. They kept the unfinished mansion in a righteous sort of way, drank a good deal of tea, shopped cheap, went to church through mud and snow, and the plasterers told so many stories about what they saw through the cracks that Congress elected Adams out, and demanded a man who should be a little wicked and swear some. Lemonade and oat-cakes were the standard lunch in those times.

Jefferson liked his social glass; he used darkeys to do the chores; he had to pay his own secretary, like everybody else down to Jackson's time, provide his own library, and meet deficits out of his own pocket.* His wife, who had been a widow, like Mrs. Washington, died long before his accession, and he had a house full of daughters and adopted daughters. It was French republican simplicity and camp-meeting courting. Jefferson talked with everybody freely, disliked clergymen, never had an opinion but he ventilated it; but he held more than his own, because he was a great man, without affec-

---

*It is common saying in these days, that it costs a President for the first time more than $25,000 per annum to live in Washington. Mr. Jefferson wrote in 1807: "I find on a review of my affairs here as they will stand on the 3d of March, that I shall be three or four months' salary behindhand. In ordinary cases, this degree of arrearage would not be serious, but on the scale of the establishment here, it amounts to seven or eight thousand dollars, which having to come out of my private funds, will be felt by me sensibly." He then directs his commission merchant to obtain a loan from a Virginia bank, and adds: "I have been under an agony of mortification   *   *   *   Nothing could be more distressing to me than to leave debts here unpaid, if indeed, I should be permitted to depart with them unpaid, of which I am by no means certain." He may have apprehended from tradesmens' rapacity, aided by political hostility, imprisonment for debt.

tations. In those days, atheists, painters, editors, Bohemians, and carpet-baggers of all sorts, foreign and domestic, made free with the White House. The President, red-haired and spindle-shanked, read all the new poems, admired all that was antique and all that was new, but nothing between times. The White House was hung with no red tape. It stood all this loose invasion because there was a real, sincere man in it.

In Mrs. James Madison the present White House found its brilliant mistress, albeit she had been brought up a Quaker, Mistress Dolly Payne, then Mrs. Todd, widow, and at last the wife of Congressman Madison, who had been jilted early in life by Miss Floyd, her townswoman. Madison was well along in years when he married, and Mrs. Madison had to take care of him. He had no children. The place was clear there for outside company, and it is questionable as to whether the house has at any time since been so well administered. Madison was a diminished and watered copy of Washington, and made a good parlor ornament. There was nothing little about him, except a general want of character, compensated for by a good deal of respectability. Mrs. Madison made the big house ring with good cheer; dancing was lively, as in Jefferson's time; the lady was "boss," and, unlike most of her imitators, had the genius for it. The whole cost of the President's house, now perfectly completed, had been $333,307.

After the British burned it, the total cost of rebuilding, and adding two porticoes, $301,496.25. The burning happened so unexpectedly, that one of Mrs. Madison's great dinners was eaten by the British, all smoking as they found it. The lady herself cut out of its frame a cherished portrait of Washington, still preserved in the mansion, and when the President returned, they opened house on the corner of Twentieth street and the avenue, near the "circle," on the way to Georgetown. After Madison died, his widow rented a house opposite the White House, and kept up the only secondary, or ex-Presidential Court, ever held in Washington.

Mr. Monroe's wife was a fairly wealthy lady of New York,

THE BLUE ROOM AT THE WHITE HOUSE, WASHINGTON.

and he came to the Presidency at an era when all parties harmonized. The White House was quite a court in his day, as he had an interesting family, gave great dinners, and looked benevolently through his blue eyes, at all the receptions. He had no brilliant qualities, and therefore had no "nonsense about him." By this time the White House had been all restored and furnished, although the grounds were still a good deal like a brick yard. Let us look at the furniture of it in those days, little changed down to the period of Harriet Lane and Mrs. Lincoln.

James Hoban built both the original and the reconstructed White House. It stands on ground forty-four feet above high water, but the drainage all around it is bad, so that fever and ague may be caught there if you only prepare your mind to get them. A small chest of homœopathic medicines in the house is a sure preventative, whether you take them or not. The building is

THE WHITE HOUSE.

one hundred and seventy feet long and eighty-six deep, built of free-stone over all. There is an Ionic portico in front and rear, opening upon grounds of shade and lawn which are open to the public at all times. The front portico is double, so as to admit folks on foot and carriages also. About one-half of the upper part of this house belongs to the family elected to live in it, and also some of the basement; but the whole of the first or main floor is really public property, and half the second floor is the President's business office. Therefore, ladies, you will own as much of the White House when you come to live in it, as you own of the hotel in which you board.

The great mansion has a wide hall in it, a stairway on one side, leading up to the office-rooms, and at the bottom, or, to be less Cockney, the end of the hall, there is a large oval room, opening out of which are two parlors, left and right; go through the room to the right and you enter the great dining-room; go through the room to the left and you enter the large banqueting-room. Now see the size of these rooms, which you will perceive at once to be home-like as a connected series of meeting-houses:

Hall (entrance), 40 by 50 feet.

Oval room, 40 by 30 feet.

Square parlors (left and right), 30 by 22 feet.

Company dining-room, 40 by 30 feet.

Banqueting (or East) room, 80 by 40 feet.

All these rooms are twenty-two feet high. You will perceive that they are eminently cosy and contracted. The President's private rooms consist of a great barn-like waiting-room, and two or three connecting offices. Let us see how these rooms were furnished in the time of Monroe, Adams, and Jackson; a description which is nearly perfect for to-day. I get these facts from an old book, defunct since 1830, called "Jonathan Elliot's History of the Ten Mile Square." Oval-room, crimson flock paper, with deep gilt border; crimson silk chairs, ditto window curtains; one great piece of pattern carpet interwoven with arms of the United States; tables and chimney-pieces of marble; two huge mirrors and a cut-glass chandelier. Into this oval room the square rooms to left and right open on levee nights, with furniture as follows, distributed also amongst the dining-rooms: Paper of green, yellow, white and blue, respectively sprinkled with gilt stars and bordered with gold; between the two dining-rooms, company and private, the china (not your own, ladies), is stored, and the provender (enough in all con

THE EAST ROOM IN THE WHITE HOUSE, WASHINGTON.

science to pay for) is kept on ice, subject only to the trifling pilferings of the aristocratic steward, who commonly keeps two or three small groceries in the suburbs running. These rooms are plentiful with panelings, mirrors, chandeliers, and a painting or two of not much consequence comes in. There was no gas in these rooms till the time of Polk, and everybody was greasy with candles. It looked like a perpetual secular mass, got up for the masses. The enormous East room had lemon-colored paper with cloth border; four mantels of black marble with Italian black and gold fronts; great grates, all polished; a mirror over each mantel, eight and a half feet high by five feet wide, ponderously framed; five hundred yards of Brussels carpet, colored fawn, blue and yellow with deep red borders; three great cut-glass chandeliers and numerous gilt brackets; curtains of light blue moreen with yellow draperies, a gilded eagle holding up the drapery of each; a cornice of gilded stars all around the room; sofas and chairs of blue damask satin;

INTERIOR EAST ROOM.

under every chandelier a rich round table of black and gold slabs, and in all the piers a table corresponding, with splendid lamps above each; rare French China vases, etc.

Here, you have the White House pretty much as it stands, barring the leaky roof that nobody can mend; a huge hotel, full of the ghosts of dead men and the echoes of political gabble; ringing of nights with the oaths of Jackson, the fiddle of Jefferson, the cooing of John Tyler, the dirges over the corpses of Harrison, Taylor, and Lincoln. If you come to live in it, you know nothing of who else is visitor. Marry a man who keeps a hotel, and you have about all that a President's lady possesses.

John Quincy Adams was arraigned in the campaign of 1828 for having put up a billiard table in the White House. This had been bought by his son and secretary, Charles Francis Adams, out of the latter's private allowance. It was the first billiard table ever set up in the White House. During his administration, the East room, in which his mother had hung clothes to dry, was so gorgeously furnished, that the Jackson people abused him for it on the stump, and in the party newspapers. He was the most perfect host, except Millard Fillmore, and possibly Frank Pierce, that the North ever gave to the White House. Modest, bold, widely experienced, he was the last learned man that has lived in the Executive Mansion, and more learned than any other occupant of it. He was too genteel to be re-elected. He went down to duty as cheerfully as to an apotheosis, and graduated out of the White House into Congress.

"The White House," says James Parton, "has more in common with the marquee of a Commander-in-Chief than the home of a civilized family. Take it, therefore, as it looked under Old Hickory, the archetype of Mr. Johnson. To keep up the Presidential hospitality, he had to draw upon the proceeds of his farm. Before leaving Washington, in 1837, he had to send for six thousand dollars of the proceeds of his cotton crop in order to pay the debts caused by the deficit of the last year's salary. A year previous to that time he had to offer for sale a valuable piece of land in Tennessee, to get three thousand dollars, for which he was in real distress. "Here in Washington," he says, "I have no control of my expenses, and can calculate nothing on my salary."

Earl was the painter Carpenter of Andrew Jackson, and painted his portrait in the White House. Earl used to get orders because he had the ear of Jackson. Everybody in Christendom poured into the White House in those days. Mrs. Eaton was the Mrs. Cobb of the time, and Jackson's most persistent public effort was to make people visit her. He used Martin Van Buren for the tolerably little business of forcing

THE GREEN ROOM IN THE WHITE HOUSE, WASHINGTON.

this lady into society, and finally dismissed all his cabinet and sent his daughter and son home to Tennessee, because they refused to embrace this lady. At the levees everybody ate cheese; when there was no cheese they ate apples, cold smoked sausage, anything provided it had a smell. The place stank with old pipe and smoke; it was redolent with Bourbon whiskey. For the first time the Executive Mansion became a police-office, a caucus-room, a guard-room, a mess-tent. But Jackson's vices were all of a popular sort. He called all his supporters by their first names. General Dale, of Mississippi, met Jackson strolling in the grounds in front of the President's house. (What President walks in the grounds familiarly any more?) "Sam," said the General, "come up and take some whiskey." He shivered his clay pipes, uttering emphatic sentences. He invited his friends to roam at will in the White House. He used to smoke corn-cob pipes, which he whittled and bored with his own hands. He had a collection of pipes greater than has ever been seen in this country outside of a tobacco-shop. There was wine always on his table. He cracked hickory-nuts on a hand-iron upon his knee. The cold-blooded and impenetrable Van Buren he called "Matty," as if Mr. Johnson should address Mr. Seward as "Little Bill." He drove all sorts of odd coaches, had street fights, behaved like the incomprehensibly despotic old patriot that he was; but the people always stood by him, because the people were about as bad as he was. He kept the city in dreadful fear; all his friends were duelists and office-grabbers, desperate with thirst and low origin. Jackson turned 2,000 people out of office in the first year of his reign. Prior to that time only seventy-three removals had been made in nearly half a century. Said one of Jackson's most intimate friends:

"Our republic, henceforth, will be governed by factions, and the struggle will be, who shall get the offices and their emoluments—a struggle embittered by the most base and sordid passions of the human heart."

After the First Andrew had retired from the Presidency, he wrote to a Nashville newspaper in 1840, of Henry Clay:

"How contemptible does this demagogue appear when he descends from his high place in the Senate, and roams over the country retailing slanders against the living and the dead."

Jackson also encouraged Sam Houston to waylay and brutally beat Congressman William Stanberry, of Ohio, for words spoken in debate, saying: "After a few more examples of the same kind, members of Congress will learn to keep civil tongues in their heads." He also pardoned Houston when the latter had been fined by a District of Columbia court for the same act.

When the First Andrew left the White House with a farewell address, the New York *American* said: "Happily it is the last humbug which the mischievous popularity of this illiterate, violent, vain and iron-willed soldier can impose upon a confiding and credulous people." Jackson returned home to Tennessee with just ninety dollars in money, having expended all his salary and all the proceeds of his cotton crop. He was then an even seventy years of age, racked with pains, rheums, and passions, a poor life to pilot by.

Jackson kept two forks beside the plate of every guest, one of steel, another of silver, as he always ate, himself, with a steel fork. I have found in a sketch-book this picture of the White House as he was seen in it at his best:

"A large parlor, scantily furnished, lighted from above by a chandelier; a bright fire in the grate; around the fire four or five ladies sewing, say Mrs. Donelson, Mrs. Andrew Jackson (adopted son's wife), Mrs. Edward Livingstone, &c. Five or six children, from two to seven years of age, playing about the room, regardless of documents and work-baskets. At a distant end of the apartment, General Jackson, seated in an arm chair, wearing a long, loose coat, smoking a long reed pipe, with a red Virginia clay bowl (price four cents). A little behind the President, Edward Livingstone, Secretary of State, reading a despatch from the French minister, and the President waves his pipe absently at the children to make them play less noisily."

Martin Van Buren, the first of the New York politicians,

THE RED ROOM IN THE WHITE HOUSE, WASHINGTON.

and the political heir of Aaron Burr, was boosted into the White House by Jackson, to whom he played parasite for eight years, and who rode with him to inauguration. Van Buren's wife died in 1818; he had four sons; kept the White House clean and decent, but never was heartily beloved. The East Room was one cause of his political death, as Ogle, a Pennsylvania Congressman, described it as a warehouse of luxuries bought with the people's money. Ogle mentioned every ornament and its cost, and the ladies kept all the items going. Had Van Buren been a married man, they would have "skinned" his lady in every dreadful drawing-room in the Union. Happily the poor woman was dead. I forgot to mention, that General Jackson's wife died of joy over his election. She was a very religious woman, very ignorant, and Jackson's friends thought it well that she was never tempted with the White House.

The short month of President Harrison in the White House is chiefly memorable by his death. His was the first funeral ever held in the building. He was sixty-eight years old, a magnified physical portrait of William H. Seward, with something of the bearing of Henry Clay. A full Major-General he had been, and, beloved by almost every one, his graces were nearly meek, except as relieved by the remembrance of his valor. The power of "hard cider," and "log cabin," nick names, while they elected him to the Presidency, also put him under a campaign pressure, which, added to the crowd of office-seekers who ran him down by day and night, quite terminated his life. He took cold seeking the outer air for privacy's sake, and diarrhœa carried him away. His last words were: "I wish the true principles of the government carried out. I ask for nothing more!"

John Tyler was the first President who brought a bride into the White House, as he was the first who buried a wife from its portal. The dead wife he had married in 1813, the new one in 1844. He took the oath of office, owing to Harrison's dying during the recess of Congress, to

7

a District of Columbia Judge. The White House was therefore in a tolerably dull condition all this time, and it improved very little under General Taylor. Two dead Presidents, one dead wife, and a widower's wedding are dismal stock enough for one house in five years. Tyler approaches Johnson in some disagreeable respects. He went back on his party, and never recovered good esteem even among traitors to the country.

President Polk suggests something of Johnson in the place of birth, North Carolina, and in his place of adoption, Tennessee. He was just fifty years old when he took possession of the White House. Mrs. Polk was a daughter of Joel Childress, a merchant of Tennessee, and a Presbyterian, while the President inclined toward the Methodists. She made a good hostess and leaves a good name in the old mansion.

As President Harrison was killed by office-seekers, President Taylor was killed by a Fourth of July,—standing out in the hot sun, after fourteen months' tenure of office. Taylor made more mistakes of etiquette than any other President, not excepting Mr. Johnson, but he had a heart. His war horse followed his rider's body out of the White House gate. In those days Jeff Davis, son-in-law of the President, came familiarly to the White House. Taylor was a good father and a jagged old host. But he always meant well.

Millard Fillmore, his successor, was by odds the handsomest man that ever lived in the building, and also the most elegant. He was the American Louis Philippe. His wife died a few days after the expiration of his term, and also his daughter. Frank Pierce was a winning man, but without any large magnetic graces. He rode horseback every day, unattended, miles into the country; his wife was a perpetual invalid.

We have now come close to the great clash of the rebellion. James Buchanan, the ancient news-carrier between Clay and Jackson, mounting upon the spiral stairs of office-holding, brought for his house-keeper, Hattie Lane, a red-haired, rosy-cheeked, buxom Lancaster county lass, not unused to fair

VIEW IN THE CONSERVATORY, AT THE WHITE HOUSE,
WASHINGTON.

society, and the only drawback to her perfect happiness in the White House was the old uncle himself. He bullied small politicians who had served him at his own table before his niece, but in the sense of outward courtliness, when it suited him, there were few such masters of deportment as old Buck himself. He fell, like all Northern dough-faces, into the hands of rebel thieves like Floyd, and did their bidding till the powder was hot for the match.

Then came Abraham Lincoln with his ambitious wife.

Afterward with Mr. Johnson came his invalid lady, and his daughters, Mrs. Patterson and the widow Stover.

CHAPTER XII.

Some parts of the Federal Government are never noticed here, because they have not associated with politics, and, therefore, never become the subject of party news.

Few persons ever hear of the National Observatory, the only public building here which stands near our meridian of longitude, and where the computations are made by which American sailors grope their way over the main. Few know anything of the Columbia Institution for the Deaf and Dumb, one of those extraordinary enterprises of the Gallaudet family, where deaf mutes are educated for professions, and to be teachers of other institutions. The Coast Survey is also a lost institution to the great mass of Americans, although it is better known abroad than any bureau of our Government.

It is the nearest of all the public ateliers to the Capitol edifice—only one block. A small tin sign set up against the jamb of the open door of a very old brick residence, has been its only advertisement for forty years. This old residence is one of half a dozen stretched along old New Jersey Avenue and on the scarp of Capitol Hill, which are tenanted by the office employees of a service embracing the largest area of labor in the government. Some of the buildings are across the way ; some are in a newer, smaller row on the same Avenue ; one building is a fire-proof safe, big enough for a family to live in ; the main office is in Law's old block, a highly respectable, thread bare, Bleak House sort of pile, which is cracking and groaning through its hollow concavities more and more every year.

If you have any business with the Coast Survey—and it is not to folks in general a "show" department—you might venture to peep into its office door some morning, and there you would see a bare vestibule, a couple of inhospitable naked rooms for clerks, and for the rest a couple of worn and creaking stairs, leading to former bed-chambers. Back passages, also uncarpeted, conduct to some old and would-be stately saloons, where a few steel engraved plates of the coast surveyings hang, as well as photographic pictures of the founders and Superintendents of this beneficent undertaking.

As we wander around these grim and rheumatic old apartments, over the half-faded carpets, amongst the quaint patterns of furniture and plush in former woods, and modes of weaving, and feel the mouldering, dry smell of the rented rooms where science is driven by democracy, we may well experience a sensitiveness as to what a little chance the useful, the diligent, and the conscientious attain amongst us, and how busy are the criticisms of ignorance, calling itself "practicability," upon matters beyond its ken. The meanest committee of Congress has a fire-proof parlor, walnut and leather furniture, a sumptuous clerk and a lackey.

But here is the Coast Survey, suggested by Jefferson, begun by Gallatin, organized by Hassler, perfected by Baché, and recognized by every learned body in this world,—this institution may be said to exist by the oversight of politicians ; it scarcely knows where to lay its head ; it lives like the poor scholar, up back-attics, and in neglected dormitories ; it steadily refuses to be regulated by politicians, and it only gets its regular appropriation because of the ignorance of the caucus Congressmen, who are afraid to be voted asses if they denounce it.

One of the most interesting personages of the Coast Survey is Mathiot, the electrotyper, who has been at his business for the Government about a third of a century.

He is a Marylander, a quiet, spectacled, grave man, below the medium size, and he discovered the art of separating the engraved plates of coast survey charts from the metallic impressions taken of them—these impressions being used to print from, while the original plate is deposited in the fire-proof magazine. This discovery has saved ours and other governments tens of thousands of dollars, but it is needless to say that Mathiot never got any recompense, and perhaps little recognition for it. He is one of those ancient, slow, dutiful men, such as grow up and ripen, and are happy under benignant governments. Some years ago he went down the river on the memorable excursion which killed a part of Tyler's Cabinet, and when the gun called the "Peacemaker" burst, Mathiot heard the gunmakers discuss the causes. They agreed that all the vibrations of the metal were caught in the acute angle where the breech was pealed down to the barrel—tons of pressure concentrated upon a spot. Mathiot got to thinking this over, as it applied to the substance he should interpose between his plates. He had tried wax, and many other mediums, but the problem seemed to be something which should receive and deaden the whole force of electrotyping,—not make the plates cohere, nor yet deface the original plate. After much groping he hit upon alcohol and iodine. This, transferred by galvanism, makes a thin coating between the plate and the metal copy, of the scarcely conceivable thinness of 1,400 of the billionth part of an inch. Then, by filing off the edges of the two plates, the copy comes off absolutely perfect. Prior to that discovery the costly plates were crushed and defaced in the press, and were good for nothing after a few hundred impressions. But by the Mathiot process a dozen printing plates could be produced from one engraving.

It is the pleasantest sight in this bureau, to see the plates separated, and the tin burnished silver faces of the large and delicate charts come perfect from their delicate embrace, every line, figure, fluting and hair clearly defined, and the microscope showing no difference whatever. They have not touched, yet they have imparted and received the whole story. It makes the dogma of the Immaculate Conception credible.

To reduce the original drawings of charts to plate and standard size, the camera is used. The sheets are printed on a hand press, the ink being rolled over frequently. There is no line engraving in the world superior to these charts.

By the establishment of the Coast Survey the sea is made as sure and as familiar as the land. Almost every port in the Union has derived benefit from this organization.

A Judge of the Supreme Court was telling me, a few days ago, about some inordinate fees which counsel had received, within his knowledge. For example: David Dudley Field received $300,000 from the Erie Railroad. William M. Stewart was paid $25,000 cash by the Gould-Curry silver mine, and so many feet of the ore, which altogether netted him $200,000. Jeremiah S. Black received $60,000 from the New Alexander mine, and a few months ago he sued them for $75,000 in addition, and received judgment. Wm. M. Evarts has been paid $25,000 for defending Andrew Johnson, and his annual income is $125,000. He recently charged $5,000 for one speech, which occupied eighty minutes. The Justice who gave this information decried the high charges which lawyers everywhere receive in one day, making no apology for extorting $100, where, ten years ago, $5 and $10 were deemed good fees.

A few days ago I had the pleasure of passing through the document and folding-rooms of the Capitol, which are under the custody of the Doorkeeper of the House. If you understand by the Doorkeeper of Congress, a person who stands on guard at the entrance thereof, you greatly err; for the doorkeeper has more than one hundred employees, and is literally a person in authority, saying to one person go and he goeth, and to another come and he cometh. The chief subject of superintendence with the doorkeeper is that of the printed bills, acts, memorials, petitions, reports, etc., of Congress, which are filed, preserved, and distributed in a series of rooms called the document room, and he also has all the printed matter of Congress

wrapped up and mailed, after it has been franked. The Chief
Doorkeeper's salary is $2,650, and his Chief of Folding Room
and Chief of Document Room receive each $2,500. The fold-
ing-rooms lie in the cellars and clefts of the old Capitol building, and comprise twenty-six rooms, some of which are below
the surface of the ground, and are packed with layers of books
twelve deep, the fall of a pile of which would crush a man
to death. About 260,000 copies of the Agricultural Report
alone are printed every year, and these will probably weigh two
pounds a-piece, or 260 tons. Each member of Congress has
about 1,000 copies of this book, for distribution, and all these
copies are put up and warehoused in the folding-room, subject
to the member's frank, and when they are to be mailed they
are packed in strong canvas bags, of the capacity of two bush-
els of grain measure. Sometimes 200 of these heavy bags are
sent of a single night to the Post-office, to take their turn on
the much-abused mail train. The boys who put up speeches
and books for the mail are paid by the quantity of work done,
and good hands can make nearly $50 a month. It is a busy
scene in the depths of the old Capitol building, to see wagons
come filled with documents, long rows of boys sealing envelopes, and others working with twine, and the custodians and
directors of the work are generally free to admit that there is
much unnecessary printing done, and that many of the books
printed are stored away and forgotten, in the vaults of the
mighty labyrinth.

The document-room occupies what was once the Post Office
for the House of Representatives, and a part of the lobby and
galleries of that celebrated old hall, now many years deserted
for the new wing, where subsequent to the year 1818, the popular body of the Legislature assembled under the Speakership
of Henry Clay, James K. Polk, John Bell, Philip Barbour,
Andrew Stevenson, Robert C. Winthrop, Howell Cobb, and
Linn Boyd. Here upwards of two millions of copies of bills
and documents are annually received, distributed, and filed, for
nearly the whole of the vast business of Congress is done by

aid of printing,—the bills, acts, etc., being on the desk for every member at the moment of debating them. The usual number of copies of a bill printed is 750, and, if five amendments should be proposed, this would make 3,750 copies. If, therefore, each Congress should pass or consider 1,000 bills, each having five amendments, there would be 15,000,000 copies issued. About 20,000 copies of the laws of the United States are printed every year at a cost of several thousand dollars, and the sum of $689,000 was expended last year in all sorts of Congressional literature. The documents of Congress go back to the first Congress, and a manuscript index to them is kept, but the repository for them is neither fire-proof nor of sufficient capacity, so that they are in danger of combustion or hopeless confusion. The Capitol edifice is already too small for the multifarious offices and uses required of it, and we shall soon be compelled to meet the question of a general enlargement of the whole affair or a relinquishment of much of the work which has been imposed upon the legislative body.

We shall have to expect differences of opinion on such questions as concern the gravity and self-knowledge of the whole Federal Republic.

Take this case : The Commissioner of the Land Office, Joseph Wilson, is a man of wide reading and wonderful industry, and every year he prepares a very voluminous report upon the condition of the public domain, not only returning the statement of the new surveys, the quantity of land sold, and such technical tables as belong to his duty, but he also composes and throws together in an admirable way, the latest problems of empire and extension, the history of gold, and many miscellaneous statements of the highest interest. In addition to this he has handsomely measured and executed in his office, by accomplished German map-makers, such charts as will illustrate his report. One of these maps in particular, intended to show, upon Mercator's projection, the past, the present, and the prospective routes to, and possessions of, the Pacific, is entirely unique and admirable, and it is, perhaps, twelve feet square.

The question at once arises in the mind of every Congressman, " Shall we accept and print that report and have the expensive maps appended to it engraved ?"

Here are two arguments at once ; and where would you, if a Congressman, stand upon the question ?

1. Pro. : It was good of the Commissioner to do so much good work, and he ought to be encouraged in it. He is justly proud of his valuable map, and it will do much good to scatter it broadcast with the report. The nation rejoices to see itself in the light of its rivals, and to see the century in the light of the past. Few officials care to do overwork, and Wilson's reports are as readable as they are important.

2. Contra : The Commissioner's reports are too long, and undertake too much schoolmastership. His big map will cost $200,000 to engrave it. The Republic is not a high school, and a Land Commissioner is not a Professor of History. If we print this report it will be putting a premium on extra and unnecessary printing, and if we circulate the map the private map-makers will find their trade gone.

Where do you stand on this question ?

Yet, this is one of the innumerable topics coming up to require to be voted upon, and this one was discussed last session in all varieties of ways. Charles Sumner thought the Federal State ought to waste no expense to understand and properly represent itself, both before its own citizens and the world. Mr. Anthony thought economy and a due restriction of Federal endeavors inclined us to reject the map.

I think that I should have voted with Anthony and against Sumner, and on this ground: Under our institutions the Government has no business to try to do too much for us. If it content itself with giving us a fair chance, the people of themselves will write treatises and engrave maps. particularly upon special topics. An international copyright law, which will cost the Government nothing, will at once raise authorship to a profession here, and out of authorship will come maps, facts, excursions, discoveries, and books, all the more valuable that

the people were rational enough to do them without law. Too
much help at the centre makes helplessness in the extremities.
Mr. Wilson's maps ought to be deposited in the Library of Congress, and any map-maker should be allowed to take copies of
them at his own expense. Help the Library, Mr. Sumner!
and give us a copyright law, and national instruction from
American sources will ensue.

"Are you a revenue detective?" said I to a man of my acquaintance.

"No, not exactly. I had been studying up whiskey frauds,
and I told Mr. Boutwell, who is an old friend of mine, that I
believed that I could recover some millions of money lost during the years 1866, 1867, 1868."

"You see," continued Mr. Martin, "that during those years
of Johnson's administration the revenue derived from whiskey
was only about $15,000,000 a year, although five times as
much whiskey was distilled then as now, and although the tax,
which is now 50 cents a gallon, was then $2 a gallon. Now,
the revenue from whiskey obtained during the first year of
Grant's administration has been $72,000,000, and I believe
that $200,000,000 can be recovered from the distilleries and
the defaulting revenue officials at civil suit. My investigations
have been confined to New York, where I am confident that I
can recover $50,000,000."

"What was the nature of those frauds?"

"It is my belief that in nine-tenths of the cases the government officials were the corrupters of the distillers. Those corrupt officials escaped summary expulsion by the operations of
the Tenure-of-Office law, for, even when Johnson was willing to
turn out a perjured collector or assessor, that willingness was
interpreted by the Senate to be a political prejudice, and the
rascal always kept his place by proving that he was an anti-
Johnson man. The distillers have almost invariably admitted
to me that they would have made more money, with less wear
and tear of conscience, had they paid the whole tax and traded
on the square"

" Explain how the frauds were committed generally."

" Well, the act of fraud was generally perpetrated in this manner: The law compels every distillery to have two receiving tubs, into which the high wines or whiskey is run, and no liquor is to be run into those tubs after dark. The revenue officer is supposed to come to the distillery and watch the whiskey drawn from the tubs into barrels, at which time he takes note of the number of gallons, and collects the tax. I have found distilleries of the largest capacity to return fifteen or twenty barrels a day, whereas a thousand, fifteen hundred, or two thousand barrels was probably the actual quantity manufactured. The fraud was, of course, perpetrated by collusion with the revenue officers, and in this way: An underground pipe extended from the bottom of the receiving tubs to a neighboring building rented by the distiller and called a rectifying room. If the underground pipe was suspected or found to be awkward, some boards were loosened in the roof above, and a hose or pipe dropped into the whiskey, which was then pumped by a hand pump or a steam engine into the rectifying room, where it was secretly barreled. Now, we come to that part of the fraud by which it was made next to impossible to trace the illegal whiskey into the hands of the buyer. The distiller would go to a whiskey dealer or speculator and conclude a mock purchase from him of, say, two thousand barrels of whiskey. When the illegal whiskey from the rectifying room was sold and shipped, therefore, the distiller's books showed that he has purchased two thousand barrels of crude whiskey of a certain party, and rectified it merely ; while a detective, tracing up this whiskey, would find the books of the pseudo seller to correspond with those of the distiller ; everything, therefore, seemed to be fair and square, and the detectives were baffled. But, I am able to show, even where I cannot prove such a sale to have been a false one, that the government has a right to damages because, in almost every case this mock sale is marked down at a price below the tax, and this of itself the law supposes to be *primâ facie* evidence of evasion."

" But, Mr. Martin, were there not door-keepers placed upon all the distilleries ? "

" Certainly ; but they, like the gaugers, and all the rest up to collectors, were put upon salary, and found it convenient to slip away whenever necessary. I am prepared to show that as much as $15,000 a week was paid for months and months by some single distilleries, and from that down to $100 and $500 a week, as blackmail. In many cases the first instalments of these enormous subsidies were paid as flat blackmail. Let me give you an example : A distiller, in one case which I investigated, was a matter-of-fact German, who was mentally incapable of keeping himself informed upon the intricate system of laws affecting the distilleries, which were constantly being amended, repaired, or repealed by Congress. The character of legislation upon this subject is of itself a snare and a pitfall to the simple man. Well, my old German distiller, knowing little of some new turn in the law, was waited upon one day by a revenue officer, who told him that he was operating illegally, and that his place must be forthwith closed up.

" ' Why,' says my simple-minded man, ' I had no intention of violating the regulations. If you close me up now you will ruin me. Here I have stored away an immense quantity of grain and other material. Is there no way of avoiding this seizure ? '

" ' I don't know,' says the revenue man, dubiously, ' I have only one set of orders. But you may keep on until to-morrow, when I will see the Collector. I won't close you up to-day.'

" The next day back comes the revenue man, with a serious face, and says :

" ' We have talked this matter over at the office, and we don't want to shut you up. We think that you are a good man, and that you mean to do right. I am instructed to say that $5,000 will fix this matter for the present.'

" The distiller sees no way of escape. Time is precious to him. So he gives his check for five thousand dollars drawn to ' cash.' Thus begins a series of blackmailings, and there is no

going back, because the distiller's offence is a State's Prison
one. At last weary of these repeated exactions, he agrees
with the revenue officer to pay a fixed salary every week.

" Take another case: A man has put up a distillery; he
finds the tax on whiskey is two dollars a gallon, and yet that
he can buy it in the market for a dollar and a quarter, so he
goes to the Collector.

" ' I have spent a hundred thousand on my distillery,' he
says, ' and I propose to go into the busines; but, if I pay the
tax and sell at the market rates, I do not see how I can make
anything.'

" Well,' answers the Collector, ' you must do as others do.
I will send a man to you to-morrow, who will tell you how to
act.'

" The next day a man goes down and debauches the distiller
with a statement of how others do. Thus a mighty net-work
of villainy covers the whole trade. The distillers get to look
upon the government officials as a class of blackmailers, and,
as I have said, at least a quarter of a million dollars has been
lost to the Treasury. The distillers put upon their guard, effect
an organization for mutual defense, and send their attorneys to
Washington. In the pursuit of these discoveries, I have been
opposed by the majority of the revenue officers in New York
most bitterly. But I believe that the distillers, as a class, have
been seduced into dishonesty, and, instead of sending them to
jail, I am in favor of beginning a series of civil suits to recover
the money lost during the years I have named.

At this point Mr. Martin gathered himself up like a box-ter-
rapin, and refused to make whiskey frauds any more mysterious.

Washington City is the paradise of blank-book and bill-head
makers. There are about half-a-dozen firms of this sort on
Pennsylvania Avenue, which keep up an ornamental shop front,
sell an envelope or a bottle of ink twice a week, and for the
rest exist, or rather prosper, upon government contracts. The
fattest take these worthies have is the Interior Department,
whose Secretary makes his stationery contracts blind-folded.

A couple of ex-Commissioners of Patents seem to have seconded him to the extent of ordering about ten thousand dollars in stationery every month, and when, some time ago, Hon. Elisha Foote took charge of the office, and found that a thousand dollars a month would be an extravagant outlay for this material, the combined cohorts of Browning, the stationers, the Patent agents, and the corrupt clerks of the Patent Office in collusion with the swindlers, charged home upon him.

The subject-matter of this collusion was the merry contract of Dempsey and O'Toole, a pair of gentlemen whose losses in the lost cause of J. Davis & Co., naturally made them objects of sympathy. They were awarded the contract for stationery and printing for the entire Interior Department, being the lowest bidders, according to the extraordinary description of bidding in vogue in Washington. This manner of bidding is something like this; the stationer sees that among a large number of articles there are needed gold pens, steel pens, expensive bound books, and envelopes. He makes a mental guess that not more than twenty-five gold pens will be needed by the whole department; therefore, he offers to furnish these at seven cents each, the price of the same being, perhaps, three dollars each. But steel pens, he guesses, will be required to the amount of a hundred thousand; the price of these he sets at five times their value. So with the few expensive ledgers. These he bids for at half their value, while he charges 300 per cent. profit upon common envelopes, the demand for which is enormous. By taking the average of an audacious bid like this it will be found in the aggregate lower than an honest contract; for the department is unable to specify precisely the amount of each article it may wish to use, and the stationer expects to regulate this use by collusion with parties inside the office.

When Mr. Elisha Foote, the Commissioner of Patents, came to his office, he found that under this fraudulent contract he was burdened with useless stationery at enormous rates. Bond paper, worth two cents a sheet, charged eight cents, lay in the vaults of the Patent Office, enough to last twenty years. Nevertheless, the contractors demanded to furnish $24,000 worth more at the same extravagant rate, and claimed that a verbal contract to that effect had been made with A. M. Stout, ex Commissioner. Mr. Foote then, to test the honesty of the contract, ordered three hundred gold pens at the low rate annexed in the schedule; at this the stationers raised the cry that Commissioner Foote was profligately buying gold pens for all his clerks. Small paper-covered entry-books, as big as a boy's "copy-book," worth twenty-five cents, were charged twenty-five dollars! Fifty thousand strips of paste-board, three inches square, worth a mill apiece, were charged four cents apiece. A bill was exhibited, paid by one of Mr. Foote's predecessors, for twenty-eight thousand Patent Office heads and forms whereas only eleven thousand had been delivered. Interrogated upon this, the stationers, appearing by Richard Merrick, their counsel, alleged that they had been permitted to collect in advance and use the government funds in their business. Asked why the additional heads were not forthcoming, they accused Mr. Foote of taking away the printing plate.

In brief, Mr. Foote refused to pay the bill of $24,000 without an investigation. This was ordered to take place before three patent-officers, B. F. James, of Illinois, Norris Peters, of Delaware, and E. W. W. Griffin of the District of Columbia. This report is one of the most extraordinary pieces of white-washing in the history of Washington audacity.

"The terms and conditions of the contract proper," says this commission, "exclude, necessarily, any inquiry into its character or of the prices stipulated to be paid, unless fraud is shown."

"And we are also of the opinion that bills presented to the Patent Office, accepted and paid, are also an estoppel on the part of the office as to the character of goods purchased and the prices paid therefor. Such purchases may be considered a matter of contract," etc.,   *   *   "other matters that *refer to the interests of the Office*, in which Dempsey & O'Toole have not by any testimony been implicated, and which in their nature should not be made public by the commission, will form the subject of a separate report."

Meantime Secretary Browning, with unseemly haste, twice ordered Commissioner Foote to cash this bill. The Commissioner said he would go to jail first. Arrangements were then made to take him in front, flank, and rear, by threat, innendo, and storm, and while the stout old gentleman was wondering whether it was wise or possible to be honest in any public place, Congress happily came to his relief, despite the objections of the Democrats, and forbade the bill to be paid without investigation.

This case is convincing that the whole business of contracting for stationery at Washington is unprincipled, that waste and profligacy of stationery is universal, and that the Patent Office is full of people in collusion with outside scoundrels.

Here comes the manuscript of the Secretary of State, and it is set up by sworn compositors, who dare not disclose it. Here most generally by observance, but not at present by breach, comes the first draft of the President's message, and all its accompanying papers. The long reports of Committees of Congress upon every conceivable question, are put into type here. In a word, no where else is any printing done for the general Government except the debates of Congress, which are given out by contract, and the bonds and notes of the United States, which are printed in the Treasury Department. In this building even the money orders are printed and stamped, which go through the post-office like so many drafts. So are the lithographic plates prepared here to illustrate the large reports of explorations.

In 1860, Cornelius Wendell, a celebrated typographical and political jobber, sold this establishment to the United States for $135,000, and it is now the very largest printing office in the world.

Among the public printers have been Gales and Seaton, Jonathan Elliott, Armstrong of Tennessee, Duff Green, Blair and Rives, Cornelius Wendell, and John D. Defrees, who has held the position since 1861.

If there is anything that is pretty, it is to see a pretty girl on an Adams' press, feeding the monster so daintily.

Here is a double row of them—Una and the lion reduced to machinery—presses and girls, the press looking up as if it would like to " chaw" the girl up, if it could only get loose from the floor, and the girl dropping a pair of black eyes into the cold heart of the press, all warm now with friction, ashamed of its grimy mouth, burning to slip its belt and trample the paper to ribbons, and turn bondage into bliss. She, meantime, touches it with her little foot, thrills it with the gliding of her garment, poises over it on one white little finger the plain gold ring of some more Christian engagement, and black with jealousy, the press plunges into its slavery again, dishevelled with ink; dripping varnish, cold and keen of teeth, the imp goes on, and the beautiful tyrant only smiles.

The government printing-office involves a yearly expense of from one million and a-half dollars to over two millions, and this does not include the printing of the debates of Congress, which is done by contract at the Globe office, and which costs seven dollars a column to report them, and six dollars (I believe) a copy per session for the Globe, in which they are printed.

The five successive stages of this building are busy in scenes and suggestions worthy of our attention, but the limits of your pages and your patience demand more substantial matter.

Government printers get a trifle better prices than are paid elsewhere in the country. Steady work will give one $1500 a year in this manufactory. The work girls get from nine to twelve dollars a week. The printers are almost always in excess, however.

The great Bullock press cost $25,490. In one year new type added cost $18,804 ; printing ink, $19,717 ; coal, seven hundred tons ; new machinery, $5,000.

In the bindery, four thousand Russian leather skins were

used, seven hundred and sixty packs of gold leaf (costing nearly $7,000), nearly five thousand dollars worth of twine, and as much of glue.

The Executive Departments, with the Courts, required in 1867 about $757,000 worth of printing, while the House of Representatives ran up a bill of $454,000, and the Senate $186,000. In addition to this, Acts of Congress warranted about $233,000 additional of work done for miscellaneous objects. Mr. Seward was a dainty hand with the types, and would have no bindings but the best. His bill in one year was about $32,000. The Supreme Courts and its satellite courts take less than half as much, or nearly $15,000. The Congressional printer himself has a little bill of $700, but the Attorney-General is most modest of all, not reaching the figure of $600, nor does the new Department of Education consume more. The Agricultural Department, with its huge reports, passes $32,000. The monstrous appetite of the Treasury leads everything, with nearly $300,000, and the War Department follows it with $148,000. Next come the Post Office, Navy and Interior Departments, ranging from $78,000 to $52,000.

No enlightened Government in this age can do without public documents, but the whole system of distributing them should be changed. There are, perhaps, 3,000 odd counties in the United States. Let Government content itself with presenting a copy of every public work to these, and let it sell the rest to the people at cost price.

Of the agricultural report the extraordinary number of 220,000 copies have been ordered for last year alone, at a cost of $180,000, or about eighty-five cents a copy. This cost is enough to pay the President, Vice-President, all the Cabinet officers, the Speaker of the House, and two-thirds of the first-class foreign ministers. In these reports there are 450,000 pounds of paper, or 225 tons, enough to take 225 double-horse wagons to pull them. Now, put these 225 tons into the mail bags, franked by Congressmen to corner grocers and gin-mill proprietors, and you get some notion of the reason why the Post-Office Department was not self-sustaining.

One evil suggests and supports another. The swindles of the world are linked together, and the devil's forlorn expedients against the nation are " omnibussed."

At this very moment there are 800,000 copies of the reports for various years lying in the vaults of the Patent Office building, being the quantity annually printed in excess of the demands even of extravagance. These copies represent $80,000 of the people's money invested in waste paper, mildewing, rotting, the spoil of paste-rats and truss makers. The new Commissioner of Patents, Mr. Foote, when he took his seat some time ago, was not aware of this decaying mass of agricultural knowledge, manuring the ground instead of the yeoman intellect. The Patent Office is self-supporting, but that is no reason why it should print more books than it wants. The bill for engraving plates of models for the Patent Office last year, was $85,000. This is not mis-spent, but the excess of books was profligacy.

The usual number of copies printed of any public document is 1,550, or about the average circulation of books printed by private publishing houses. Out of this number more than one-half are bound up, the rest being distributed in sheets by gift, mail, or otherwise.

It is the current belief in Washington that the Patent Office department of the Government is not without corruption, but the agents and lawyers whose offices lie in its environs, and who are at the mercy of its examiners, are chary to speak, much of their bread and butter being bound up in the good-will of the directory. A partial awarding of patents, in the interest of money instead of merit, involves unjust millions of dollars, besides discouraging inventors, and making them doubt the righteousness of the Government. With a corrupt Patent Office, infinite law-suits arise, and yet it is probable that money is freely used within the precincts of that building, the claims of inventors who are willing to pay being considered in many gross cases

beyond those of the needy. So is there preference among the
patent agents—those who solicit patents—some being understood to have the ears of the office at their disposal, others
failing to secure patents which are afterwards willingly granted
to cotemporaries. One of the oldest patent lawyers in the city
said to me a few days ago:

" The Patent Office has been more or less corrupt for fifteen
years! Yes, twenty! When I used to be an anti-slavery man,
in the years of Pierce and Buchanan, my clients were given to
understand that they would be wise to apply for patents by
some other agent. Recently, I have known the changing of
the agent to get the patent promptly. The office ought to be
thoroughly overhauled. It has become so that examiners
expect to serve a brief term and go out rich."

Mrs. Foote, the wife of the Commissioner, is an inventor,
whose patents have been profitable. She has invented a skate
without straps, and several other things.

Thaddeus Hyatt, once incarcerated in the District Jail for a
complicity which he affected to have with John Brown's raid,
is now a successful inventor, his patents for glass-lights in pavements netting him a very large income.

About fifty thousand patents have been issued in the United
States in thirty years, the receipts for which in fees have been
nearly two millions and a half of dollars, while the British
Government has granted only about forty thousand patents in
250 years. This shows the extraordinary mental activity of
the American mind in mechanics, and the Patent Office building, which has cost the government no money, is the best monument to American shrewdness and suggestiveness in the world.
Amongst nearly a hundred thousand models stored in the splendid galleries of that institution, one may wander in hopeless
bewilderment, feeling that every model, however small, is the
work of some patient year, lifetime, and often of many life-
times, so that the entire contribution, if achieved by one mind,
would have extended far into a human conception of an eternity
of labor.

The best patent lawyers in the United States are Judge Curtis and Mr. Whiting of Boston, Messrs. Gafford and Keller of New York, George Harding of Philadelphia, and Mr. Latrobe of Baltimore.

The most successful firm of patent agents is represented by the newspaper called the *Scientific American*, which began upwards of twenty-two years ago. One of its partners is one of the ancient enemies of Bennett, who classified them as " Old Moses Beach and those other sons of Beaches," proprietors of the New York *Sun*. The other partners are Munn and Wales. Their income is fifty thousand dollars a year to each partner, and they obtain one-third of all the patents issued, which are chiefly, however, what are classified as " cheap patents," on small and simple inventions. The *Scientific American* was started by an inventor, Rufus Porter, who sold out to the present owners. They refused to insert in it the cards of other patent agents, and it being the only paper of its class, the inventors at large transact their business through its proprietors. It was lately edited by Mr. McFarland, and under his management was altogether the best paper for inventors in the world. The Commissioners of Patents include some good names, chief of whom was Attorney General Holt, others being Ellsworth and Bishop of Connecticut, Burke of New Hampshire, Ewbank of New York, Hooper of Vermont, Mason of Iowa, and Theaker of Ohio.

The Patent Office building is generally adjudged to be the most imposing of all the national edifices of the Capital. To my mind the Post Office is a better adaptation. The former was the work of the present architect of the Capital, Edward Clark, and its three porticoes cost $75,000 apiece. The four grand galleries, or model rooms, are unlike and magnificent. It is related here that inventors who spend many years among these models commonly go crazy.

These divers operations, possessing little affinity, are all to be transacted by one head. The Bureau of Pensions dispenses nearly nineteen millions of dollars a year ; the Land Office gives away from seven to ten millions of acres of land; three hundred thousand Indians are dealt with by the Indian Bureau; seventeen thousand patents are applied for to the Commissioner; all the Pacific railways are superintended and subsidized; the public buildings and property in the United States in the District of Columbia and all the territories are administered; two millions of dollars are paid to the United States Courts: the whole of this immense and various business is transacted by one man. The Secretaryship of the Interior is therefore one of the very strongest positions in the government. So manifold became its duties that sometime ago the Agricultural Bureau was endowed with a special head, reporting directly to Congress, and moved out of the o'ercrowded Patent Office. Now the Indian Bureau demands to be also brought nearer to the executive head of the Government, or made independent, so that its Commissioner can have his legitimate influence with Congress. The Patent Office building is packed with Clerks, who also occupy the whole or parts of adjacent buildings, and it is demanded that a Department of the Interior be built on the Judiciary square, in the rear of the city hall, with the earnings of the Patent Office.

MOUNT VERNON.

CHAPTER XIII.

A PICTURE OF MT. VERNON IN 1789.

On a Tuesday morning, the 14th of April, 1789, a venerable old gentleman, with fine eyes, an amiable countenance, and long, white locks, rode into the lawn of Mount Vernon, coming from Alexandria. Two gentlemen of the latter town accompanied him. It was between 10 and 11 o'clock. A negro man sallied out to take the nags, and the old gentleman, entering the mansion, was received by Mrs. Washington.

"Why, Mr. Thompson," said the good lady, "where are you from, and how are your people?"

"From New York, Madame," answered the old man. "I come to Mount Vernon on a good errand, for the country at least. The General has been elected President of the United States under the new Constitution, and I am the bearer of the happy tidings in a letter from John Langdon, the President of the Senate."

The General was out visiting his farm, however, and the guests were entertained for two or three hours, as we take care of our visitors in the country nowadays. A glass of the General's favorite Madeira, imported in the cask, was probably not the worst provision made for them, and the cheerful gossip of Mrs. Washington, who had known Mr. Thompson, and visited his house in Philadelphia, helped to enliven the time. This grave and respectable old man was the link between the new Government at New York, and the new Magistrate at Mount Vernon. Charles Thompson had been the Secretary through all its eventful career of the Continental Congress which had directed the cause of the Colonies from desultory revolt to Independence and to Union, and now he had ridden over the long and difficult roads to apprise the first President of the Republic of the wishes of his countrymen. At 1 o'clock, General Washington rode into the lawn of Mount Vernon, in appearance what Custis, his adopted son, has described:

An old gentleman, riding alone, in plain drab clothes, a broad-brimmed white hat, a hickory switch in his hand, and carrying an umbrella with a long staff, which is attached to his saddle-bow. The umbrella was used to shelter him from the sun, for his skin was tender and easily affected by its rays.

Washington greeted Mr. Thompson with grave cordiality, as was his wont, inquiring for his family, and divining already the object of his visit, broke the seal of John Langdon's official letter. Dinner followed, and, while the visitors retired to converse or stroll about the grounds, the President-elect wrote a letter to the President of the Senate, and sent it forthwith to the Post-Office at Alexandria by a servant. The letter was as follows:

"MOUNT VERNON, April 14th, 1789.

"SIR:—I had the honor to receive your official communication, by the hand of Mr. Secretary Thompson, about 1 o'clock this day. Having concluded to obey the important and flattering call of my country, and having been impressed with the idea of the expediency of my being with Congress at as early a period as possible, I propose to commence my journey on Thursday morning, which will be the day after to-morrow."

This done, the rest of the day passed in conferences between

8

Washington and his wife, in the preparation of his baggage for the not-unexpected journey, while meantime the distinguished guest was amused by the young official household in the library and grounds.

At Mount Vernon was one of the brilliant Bohemians of his time, David Humphreys, colonel, poet, biographer, translator of plays, foreign traveler, courtier, and delightful fellow generally, with locks like Hyperion, a "killing" countenance, and no fortune to speak of; so he had become a permanent guest of his old General. To him Thompson was turned over for hospitality, and we may suppose them mixing the grog, discussing France and the pleasures of the Palais Royale, and guessing the names in the new Cabinet with the staid Secretary, Tobias Lear, a New Englander, like Humphreys; while, perhaps, the latter recited his tolerably bad rhymes:

> "By broad Potomack's azure tide,
> Where Vernon's mount, in sylvan pride,
>   Displays its beauties far,
> Great Washington, to peaceful shades,
> Where no unhallowed wish invades,
>   Retired from fields of war."

The estate of Washington in this pleasant springtime of the year, was well adapted, with its deep shade and broad, peaceful landscapes, to be the home of the most honored American. Amidst the long grass of its lawn stood the mansion of Mount Vernon, such as we behold it now, when it has ceased to become a home, and has become a shrine,—a low-roofed, painted straight edifice, with a high piazza on the river-front, which covers the two stories; and the whole is built of wood, cut in blocks to imitate stone. The light columns which uphold the porch are also of wood, sanded. There are dormer windows in all the four sloping sides of the roof, and a cupola full of wasps' nests, surmounts the whole, from which you can see the long reaches of the river. The house and immediate out-buildings could be built, at the present price of lumber and labor, for about thirty thousand dollars. But nobody would now

build such a house. Instead of the high, hollow portico covering the whole front of the building, we would now put a low
veranda, and upper balconies. Instead of imitating stone,
we would carve the wood into pleasing designs, or use stone
outright. The interior of the mansion is pleasantly habitable
to this day, but the naked, white-washed walls look very blank.
The rooms are generally low of ceiling, and we would think it
a hardship to live in the room where the Hero of the American
hemisphere died. Neither gas, nor water-pipes, nor stoves, nor
wall-paper, nor a kitchen under the mutual roof,—but simply a
library, a drawing-room, with a carved marble-mantel, and an
old, rusty, fine harpsichord; a hall through the house,—a
reaching up for grandeur with feeble implements; some plain
bed-chambers, and a few relics of the great man;—this is
Mount Vernon as an abandoned home. The house is now
above a century and a quarter old, and good for another century,
if pieced up and restored from time to time. Back of it a pair
of covered walks reach to the clean negro-quarters, between
which is seen a rear lawn, with garden-walls on the sides; and
across the lawn passes the road to Alexandria and Fredericksburg, so often ridden by the General. The gardens are of a
showy, imposing sort. He inherited this house from his half-
brother, and lived in it for fifty years, not counting seven years
during the Revolution, when he was absent.

Washington, the son of a second wife, had been married to
a widow fifteen years when he was put at the head of the Colonial armies. He belonged to a military and commercial family; rather New Englanders in thrift and enterprise than like
the baronial planters round about them. But he was a man
who grew in every quality, except pecuniary liberality, and no
book-keeper in Connecticut watched his accounts with more
closeness, although he was very rich and childless. He was
the most perfect fruit of virtuous mediocrity, and the highest
exemplar of a disciplined life which the scrupulous, the prudent, and the brave can study. Every triumph he had was a
genuine one, if not a difficult one. Guizot, the best student of

his larger life, who had in his eye of neighborhood the careers of all the great men of that quarter of a century, including Bonaparte, Talleyrand, and Wellington, said that Washington's power came from his confidence in his own views, and his resoluteness in acting upon them; and that no great man was ever tried by all tests and came out so perfectly. Jefferson said that he was the only man in the United States who possessed the confidence of all, and that his executive talents were superior to those of any man in the world. He had wonderful power in influencing men by honorable sentiments, and he never gave a man an office to quiet him or gain him over. His character was a little picturesque, but he was as plain as Lincoln in the parts which he himself prescribed.

In that day Mount Vernon had all the fame it still retains. Engravings of it were common in Europe and America, and it was a place of resort for the curious and the eminent, the stranger and the politician, because its proprietor stood first amongst the private gentlemen of the world. His battles and his wisdom, his Republican principles, and the purity of his character, recommended him to men as the living model of all that Rousseau had delineated—a great unselfish citizen. The time had come when the vague, poetic, and earnest aspirations of humanity inclined towards this stamp of man. Europe did not contain his like. The mighty writers there had filled the people with a scorn for kings, while yet they had not created one citizen-hero. Distance led them to enchantment with the name and person of Washington; and this was he, at home amongst his slaves, with his busy, knitting housewife, on the high, sequestered shores of the Potomac. He was aware of his fame, for every mail expressed it in the eulogies of authors, journalists, statesmen, and even princes. The gravity of public thoughts and things had deepened the shadows of a life by temperament reflective, almost austere; and this planter and farmer had grown judicial in his calmness and equipoise, so that he was already a Magistrate in intellect, and his election did not, probably, so much as ruffle his feelings.

His mansion was a museum, illustrative of the ordinary culture and tastes of a planter of his period. In his parlor, doubtless, were these effigies which he had ordered from France thirty years before.

"A bust of Alexander the Great ; another of Julius Cæsar ; another of Charles XII. of Sweden ; another of the Duke of Marlborough, of Prince Eugene of Savoy ; and a sixth of Frederick the Great, King of Prussia.

"These are not to exceed fifteen inches in height, nor ten in width.

"Two wild beasts, not to exceed twelve inches in height, nor eighteen inches in length.

"Sundry small ornaments for chimney-piece."—(Washington's directions to his foreign factor.)

There had been exemplars of Washington at a younger period, when the military art was his delight. During the long war of the Revolution, his estate had escaped pillage, and what had since been collected were mainly the gifts of friends, or the reward of arms and eminence. But it appears from what remains to us, that Mount Vernon was supplied with all the comforts and many of the luxuries of his time,—a period when foreign art and literature were at a high standard, and skill and science had begun to look for their patrons below Palaces and Ministers of State, to the firesides of the prosperous middle-class. The social revolution had already transpired in America and in Europe. Commerce, education, and accumulated wealth had insensibly triumphed over ranks and reverences. The Democratic age had not fairly dawned, but the men lived who were to lead it, and at the head of the middle class of conservative Republicans in America stood the men of homesteads, broad lands, and large crops, like Washington. They were yet to have a few years of semi-supremacy ; but a fiercer wave of equality was gathering in the distance, which should spare Mount Vernon alone amongst family shrines.

Washington was rich, but not the richest of the planters. At least two Presidents were to succeed him, better burdened

with money and lands.   He was, however, always above the fear
of poverty, excepting the possible calamities of war ; and the
personal supervision of as many acres, servitors, and interests
would be thought onerous in our time.   Yet he was ever seeking, later in life, to increase the revenues of his farms, to lease,
or to colonize them.

His property was chiefly in stock, slaves, and land, but the
land was already showing signs of giving out, and he made
reference more than once to Pennsylvania and Maryland,
" Where their wheat is better than ours can be, till we get into
the same good management."

Probably no account of his estate can be found so reliable as
that of the President himself, written to Arthur Young, a celebrated English authority on agricultural matters, just at the
close of his first term of office :

" No estate in United America," said Washington, " is more
pleasantly situated than this. It lies in a high, dry, and healthy
country, three hundred miles by water from the sea, and, as
you will see by the plan, on one of the finest rivers in the
world.   Its margin is washed by more than ten miles of tide-
water ; from the bed of which, and the innumerable coves, in-
lets, and small marshes, with which it abounds, an inexhaustible
fund of rich mud may be drawn, as a manure, either to be used
separately or in a compost, according to the judgment of the
farmer.   It is situated in a latitude between the extremes of
heat and cold, and is the same distance by land and water,
with good roads and the best navigation, to and from the
Federal City, Alexandria, and Georgetown ; distant from the
first, twelve ; from the second nine ; and from the last, sixteen
miles.   The Federal City, in the year 1800, will become the
seat of the General Government of the United States.   It is
increasing fast in buildings, and rising into consequence ; and
will, I have no doubt, from the advantages given to it by
nature, and its proximity to a rich interior country, and the
Western territory, become the emporium of the United
States."

" The soil of the tract of which I am speaking is a good loam, more inclined, however, to clay than sand. From use, and I might add, abuse, it is become more and more consolidated, and, of course, heavier to work. The greater part is a grayish clay ; some part is dark mould ; a very little is inclined to sand ; and scarcely any to stone."

" A husbandman's wish would not lay the farms more level than they are ; and yet some of the fields, but in no great degree, are washed into gullies, from which all of them have not yet recovered."

" This river, which encompasses the land the distance above mentioned, is well supplied with various kinds of fish at all seasons of the year ; and in the spring, with the greatest profusion of shad, herring, bass, carp, perch, sturgeon, &c. Several valuable fisheries appertain to the State ; the whole shore, in short, is one entire fishery."

" There are, as you will perceive by the plan, four farms besides that at the mansion-house ; these four contain 3,260 acres of cultivated land, to which some hundreds more adjoining, as may be seen, might be added, if a greater should be required."

Again, he wrote to a foreign factor, to whom he shipped his tobacco, pretty much as Horace Greeley might write :

" I am possessed of several plantations on this river (Potomac), and the fine lands of Shenandoah, and should be glad if you would ingeniously tell me what prices I might expect you to render for tobacco made thereon, of the same seed as that of the estates, and managed in every respect in the same manner as the best tobaccos on James and York Rivers are."

It was the custom of the Virginian planters, living upon tide-water, with the coasts deeply indented everywhere, to ship their crops direct from their estates to Bristol or London. Washington wrote : " The best Potomac harbor (Piscataway) is within sight of my door. It has this great advantage, besides good anchorage and lying safe from the winds, that it is out of the way of the worm, which is very hurtful to shipping a little lower down, and lies in a very plentiful part of the country."

The manner of putting crops. aboard ship was generally by the use of scows, which could come up the shallow streams. Thus, he wrote :

" So soon as Mr. Lund Washington returns from Frederick, I shall cause my wheat to be delivered at your landing, on Four Miles Run Creek, if flats can get to it conveniently."

A few passages from the correspondence of Washington will make plain his mode of life and his business habits. He was always minute in his instructions to his superintendent, as thus, when closing up a notification to build roads :

" At all times they must proceed in the manner which has been directed formerly ; and, in making the new roads from the Ferry to the Mill, and from the Tumbling Dam across the Neck, till it communicate with the Alexandria road, as has been pointed out on the spot."

This shows that, though a planter, he was always a man of affairs, having personal cognizance of all belonging to him.

Again :

" When the brick work is executed at the Ferry Barn, Gunner and Davis must repair to Doque Run, and make bricks there, at the place and in the manner which have been directed, that I may have no salmon bricks in that building.

" Oyster shells should be bought wherever they are offered for sale, if good, and on reasonable terms."

As a landlord and creditor, Washington was exacting but not harsh. The year he was elected President, he wrote as to the collection of rents and debts :

" Little is expected from the justice of those who have been long indulged."

To his wife, grandchildren, and his own nephews and nieces, he was provident, but still never lavish. In the same year as above he wrote to certain needy ones :

" You will use your best endeavors to obtain the means for support of G. and L. Washington, who, I expect, will board, till something further can be decided on, with Dr. Ceaik, who must be requested to see that they are decently and properly provided with clothes from Mr. Porter's store. He will give them a credit on my becoming answerable to him for the payment. And, as I know of no resource that H. has for supplies but from me, Fanny will, from time to time, as occasion may require, have such things got for her, on my account, as she shall judge necessary."

These paragraphs convey to us, as fully as the twelve volumes of Sparks, the tone of the first Magistrate in affairs of private life. His estate, like that of many Virginians, labored under disadvantages from the unthrifty agriculture of slaves, and the sort of improvidence which large estates seem to necessitate. Seven years after the period at which this chapter begins, he said :

" From what I have said, that the present prices of land in Pennsylvania are higher than they are in Maryland or Virginia, although they are not of superior quality, two reasons have already been assigned : First, that in the settled part of it, the land is divided into smaller farms, and is more improved ; and, secondly, it is in a greater degree than any other the receptacle of emigrants, who receive their first impressions in Philadelphia, and rarely look beyond the limits of the State. But besides these, two other causes, not a little operative, may be added, namely: that until Congress passed general laws relative to naturalization and citizenship, foreigners found it easier to obtain the privileges annexed to them in Pennsylvania than elsewhere : and because there are laws there for the gradual abolition of slavery, which neither of the two states above-mentioned have at present, but which nothing is more certain than that they must have, and at a period not remote."

Unfortunately the first President failed to give his active support to emancipation, and those laws were delayed for seventy years.

The neighbors of Washington were, in some cases, of even greater social consideration than himself. Of the adjoining State he said :

" Within full view of Mount Vernon, separated therefrom by water only, is one of the most beautiful seats on the river for sale, but of greater magnitude than you seem to have contemplated. It is called Belvoir, and belonged to George William Fairfax, who, were he living, would now be Baron of Cameron, as his younger brother in this country (George William dying without issue) at present is, though he does not take upon himself the title."

The land of the neighborhood, at the time we have indicated, sold at a good price, for he says at Fairfax :

" A year or two ago, the price he fixed on the land, as I have been well informed, was thirty-three dollars and a third per acre."

In the lifetime of Washington, the slow and henceforth steady decay of Virginia lands began. His own cherished fields steadily declined after his death, and will not now, probably, bring as much per acre as when he died. His chief crops were wheat and tobacco, and these were very large,—so large that vessels sometimes came up the Potomac, took the tobacco and flour directly from his own wharf, a little below his deer-park, in front of his mansion, and carried them to England or the West Indies. So noted were these products for their quality, and so faithfully were they put up, that any flour bearing the brand of " George Washington, Mount Vernon," was said to have been exempted from the customary inspection in the British West India ports. Such was the home of Washington, where he spent the days of his private life, and his domestic enjoyments were of a dutiful rather than of an enthusiastic sort.

His mother lived until he was fifty-seven years old, but his father died when he was eleven. His wife was rich, but not accomplished, and he set free 124 slaves at his death. He always rose to the needs of history, and, if his household seems to lack pathetic and feminine features, that is, perhaps, because he was never out of the public regard, because he had no children, and also, possibly, because he was unfortunate in all his early loves. There are half-a-dozen cases on record of his direct rejection by ladies to whom he proposed.

Bishop Meade, the devout and careful chronicler of Virginia, received the following note from one of the family of Fauntleroy:

" My grandfather (who was called Colonel William Faunt Le Roy) was twice married. By the first wife he had one daughter (Elizabeth), who became the wife of Mr. Adams of James River, after having refused her hand to General George Washington."

On this the Bishop remarked: " It would seem from the foregoing, and from what may be read in my notice of Mr. Edward Ambler and his wife, and from what Mr. Irving and other writers have conjectured concerning Miss Grymes of Middlesex, and perhaps one other lady in the land, that General Washington, in his earlier days, was not a favorite with the ladies. If the family tradition respecting his repeated rejections be true,—for which I would not vouch,—it may be accounted for in several ways. He may have been too modest and diffident a young man to interest the ladies, or he was too poor at that time ; or he had not received a college or university education in England or Virginia ; or, as is most probable, God had reserved him for greater things,—was training him up in the camp for the defense of his country. An early marriage might have been injurious to his future usefulness."

Much of his life was passed in camps, and in lonely surveys, and he made himself by acceptance, instead of choice, a rigid historical being. He was worth, during all his married life, about $100,000 sterling, not counting his slaves as merchandise, and it paid him not above 3 or 4 per cent in money, or about $20,000 per annum.

In this quiet, almost elegant home, he received many princes, exiles, and refined travelers, lured so far by the report of his deeds and character. He disappointed not one of whom we have any record, and his neighbors, as well as those remote, forgot his austerities in his integrity. We could have placed no more composed and godlike character at the fountain of our young State; and his image, growing grander as the stream has expanded, is reflected yet in every ripple of the river. We have grown more Democratic since his time, and we often wish that Washington had been more pliable, popular, and affable; but it is to be remembered that he was a Republican, and not a Democrat. As one of his federalistic observers has said of his day:

"Democracy, as a theory, was not as yet. The habits and manners of the people were, indeed, essentially Democratic in their simplicity and equality of condition, but this might exist under any form of Government. Their Governments were then purely Republican. They had gone but a short way into those philosophical ideas which characterized the subsequent and real revolution in France. The great State papers of American liberty were all predicated on the abuse of chartered, not abstract rights." (Note—Gibbs' Life of Wolcott.)

As an original suggestor, Washington was wise, without genius. His designs were all bounded by law, the rights of others, and the intelligent prejudices of his time. He told Coke, the Methodist, that he was inimical to slavery. The better elements of our age were all intelligent, and growing in him. But the mighty whirlwind raised by Rousseau, and by Jefferson, blew upon the country, and we are what we are, while Washington and Lafayette, soldier and pupil, stand the only consistent great figures of the two hemispheres,—the last Republicans of the school of Milton and Hampden. Such as he was, there he lived, and the vestiges of the breaking up of the past are all round his honored mansion,—the key of the Bastile; his surveyor's tripod, which first measured the streams beyond the Alleghanies, and, at last, the forts which the North planted against Virginia slavery.

The life of Washington at Mount Vernon, subsequent to the War, had been lived with that rigid method which he prescribed for himself at an early age. Temperate, yet not disdaining the beverage of a gentleman of that time, and dividing the day between clerical and out-of-door duties, he had escaped other diseases than those incident to camp-life, and he was not fond of the prolonged convivialities of the table. His breakfast hour was seven o'clock in summer, and eight in winter, and he dined at three. He always ate heartily, but he was no epicure. His usual beverage was small-beer or cider and Madeira wine. He took tea and toast, or a little well-baked bread early in the evening, conversed with or read to his family, when there were no guests, and usually, whether there was company or not, retired for the night at about nine o'clock.

He loved Mount Vernon, and had never expressed a desire to change its retirement for the concerns of a denser society ; but the wish seems to have been fixed in his heart at an early period, to see the banks of the Potomac become the seat of a great city. Annapolis, Baltimore, and Fredericksburg, were each a stout day's journey from his estate, and Georgetown and Alexandria, were his post-office and market places. It had now been fifteen years since he had considered the subject of breaking his allegiance to his King and England, and fully half the time had been spent away from his estate.

During more than seven years of the war, Washington had visited his pleasant home upon the Potomac but once, and then only for three days and nights. Mrs. Washington spent the winter in camp with her husband, but generally returned to Mount Vernon during his campaigns.

From this mansion he had departed to take part in the first Continental Congress, as one of the four delegates from Virginia, when, in the language of a diligent historian, on Wednesday morning, the 31st of August, 1774, two men approaching Mount Vernon on horseback, came to accompany him. One of them was a slender man, very plainly dressed in a suit of minister's

gray, and about 40 years of age. The other was his senior in
years, likewise of slender form, and a face remarkable for its
expression of unclouded intelligence. He was more carefully
dressed, more polished in manners, and much more fluent in
conversation than his companion. They reached Mount Vernon
at 7 o'clock, and after an exchange of salutations with Washington and his family, and partaking of breakfast, the three
retired to the library, and were soon deeply absorbed in the
discussion of the novel questions then agitating the people of
the Colonies.   The two travelers were Patrick Henry and
Edmund Pendleton. A third, " the silver-tongued Cicero" of
Virginia, Richard Henry Lee, was expected with them, but he
had been detained at Chantilly, his seat in Westmoreland.

All day long these eminent Virginians were in council ; and,
early the next morning, they set out for Philadelphia on horseback, to meet the patriots from other Colonies, there. Will
Lee, Washington's huntsman and favorite body-servant, was
the only attendant upon Washington. They crossed the Potomac at the falls, (now Georgetown,) and rode far on toward
Baltimore before the twilight. On the 4th of September, the
day before the opening of the Congress, they breakfasted at
Christina Ferry, (now Wilmington,) and dined at Chester ; and
that night Washington, according to his diary, " lodged at Dr.
Shippen's in Philadelphia, after supping at the New Tavern."
At that house of public entertainment, he had lodged nearly
two years before, while on his way to New York, to place young
Custis, his wife's son, in King's (now Columbia) College.
With that journey in 1774, began the glorious period of this
Virginia planter's career. Even at that date, he drew upon
himself the admiration of the best of his contemporaries, and
John Adams—now elected Vice-President with him—wrote to
Elbridge Gerry—subsequently to be Vice-President with Presi-
dent Madison—this warm compliment in his favor :

" There is something charming to me in the conduct of Washington. A gentleman of one of the first fortunes upon the
continent, leaving his delicious retirement, his family and friends,

sacrificing his ease, and hazarding all in the cause of his country! His views are noble and disinterested. He declared, when he accepted the mighty trust, that he would lay before us an exact account of his expenses, and not accept a shilling for pay."

The history of the war which speedily followed that first Congress is mainly the career of Washington. He was a persevering, a prudent, and a magnanimous captain, and his character grew round and lustrous as the independence of the country advanced. Foreign nobles, countries, and officers did him reverence, and his behavior was always modest, grave, and yet cheerful, so that he neither made enemies nor provoked severe analysis; and he set the example of obedience to the civil powers, so that his army graduated in the love of law, and their transition to citizens became as natural as his own to the First Magistracy. If he had not the military genius of Bonaparte, he had not also the love of blood and of violence in the same arbitrary degree. As has been well said, " war was to him only a means, always kept subordinate to the main and final object,— the success of the cause, the independence of the country." As a captain, he was subject to none of the petty and irritable jealousies so common with conquerors ; and he saw, without chagrin and ill humor, the successes of his inferiors in command. Still more, he supplied them largely with the means and opportunity of gaining them. Only once was he tempted with the anonymous proffer of a crown, and he rebuked it; and the fomentor of the single conspiracy against him wrote in remorse, " you are, in my eyes, the great and good man."

When the armies disbanded, and he had bidden adieu to his companions and staff at New York, and delivered up his commission at Annapolis, he made one or two of those long journeys of which he was so fond, and which acquainted him so well with the needs and capacities of the future State, and then he sought the society of his wife and the congenial pursuits of agriculture. But one of his fame and large acquaintance could no more be permitted to dwell in solitude. For some time, indeed, after his return to Mount Vernon, Washington was in a manner locked up by the ice and snow of an uncommonly rigorous winter, so that social intercourse was interrupted, and he could not even pay a visit of duty and affection to his aged mother at Fredericksburg. But it was enough for him at present that he was at length at home at Mount Vernon. Yet the habitudes of the camp still haunted him; he could hardly realize that he was free from military duties; on waking in the morning, he almost expected to hear the drum going its stirring rounds and beating the *reveille*.

As spring advanced, however, Mount Vernon, as had been anticipated, began to attract numerous visitors. They were received in the frank, unpretending style Washington had determined upon. It was said to be pleasant to behold how easily and contentedly he subsided from the authoritative Commander-in-Chief of armies, into the quiet country gentleman. There was nothing awkward or violent in the transition. Mrs. Washington, too, who had presided with quiet dignity at headquarters, and cheered the wintry gloom of Valley Forge with her presence, presided with equal amenity and grace at the simple board of Mount Vernon. She had a cheerful good sense, that always made her an agreeable companion, and was an excellent manager. She had been remarked for an inveterate habit of knitting. It had been acquired, or at least fostered, in the wintry encampments of the Revolution, where she used to set an example to her lady visitors by diligently applying her needles, knitting stockings for the destitute soldiery. While Washington was waited upon by scholars, inventors, suggestors, and people with projects of material, moral, and intellectual improvements,—and the two hundred folio volumes of his writings and correspondence attest how engaged he was for the five years between the peace and the Presidency,—his wife was busied with the care of her orphan grandchildren.

There was another female dear to the newly-elected President, and he kept her in filial remembrance at the very moment of his greatest promotion. It was growing late in the evening of

the day on which our chapter opens, when Washington mounted
his horse, and, followed by his man Billy, rode off into the
woods of Virginia with speed. His destination was Fredericksburg, nearly forty miles away, with two ferries between,—one
at the Occoquan, the other at the Rappahannock. His purpose
was to see his old mother, now over eighty years of age, and
drawing near the grave. It had been long since he had visited
her, but he could not feel equal to the responsibilities of his great
office until he should receive her blessing. Few candidates for
the Presidency in our day would leave a warm mansion, filled
with congratulating friends, to ride all night through the chilly
April mists, to say adieu to a very old woman. But thus piously
the administration of Washington began. He passed old Po-
hick Church, of which he was a Vestryman,—soon to tumble
to ruins,—crossed the roaring Occoquan, and by its deep and
picturesque gorge, where passed the waters of the future bloody
Bull Run, and, by night, he saw the old churches of Acquia
and Potomac rise against the sky ; he saw the decaying sea-
port of Dumfries. In the morning, he was at Fredericksburg,
and his mother was in his arms. Marches, perils, victories,
honors, powers, surrendered to that piteous look of helpless
love, too deep for pride to show through its tears. And the
President of the new State was to her a new-born babe again,
—no dearer, no greater. He was just in time, for she had but
the short season of summer to live, and, like many dying
mothers, life seemed upheld, at four-score and five, by waiting
love, till he should come. History is ceremonious as to what
passed between them, but the parting was solemn and touching, like the event.

"You will see me no more," she said, " my great age and
disease warn me that I shall not be long in this world. But
go, George, to fulfil the destiny which Heaven appears to as-
sign you. Go, my son, and may Heaven's and your mother's
blessing be with you always."

Passing from that dear, pathetic presence, the President
elect, perhaps, did not hear the plaudits of the people in the

streets of Fredericksburg.   He rode all day by the road he had
come, and reached Mount Vernon before evening, having exhibited his power of endurance at the age of 57, by riding
eighty miles in twenty-four hours.

His good wife had made all ready ; the equipage and baggage were at the door next morning ; and, leaving Mrs.
Washington and most of the household behind, he set out for
New York at 10 o'clock on Thursday, the 16th of April,
accompanied by Thompson and Humphreys.   The new State
was waiting anxiously for its Magistrate.

CHAPTER XIV.

CURIOSITIES OF THE GREAT BUREAUX OF THE GOVERNMENT.

Few readers have ever pushed into the queer nooks and queerer documents around the Capitol which exhibit the multifold operations of a modern government.

Let us run over some items of what is called the Legislative, Executive, and Judicial Appropriation Bill, selecting the Bill of 1871 which was passed by a relatively honest Congress.

CONGRESS.

Do you know what it costs to pay the Senators' salaries and mileage per annum? Four hundred thousand dollars! Cheap at half the money! Do you know what it costs the House for the same? One million! But halt! The officers, clerks, and messengers of the Senate get, besides, $180,000; and the same officers of the House get about $200,000. The police, who patrol the Capitol, and sit around the little parks enclosing it, cost $43,000. The stationery and newspapers of the Senate cost about $14,000, and for the House $37,000. The little pages, who run around the floor, cost in the House $7,600, and in the Senate $8,000. What does the Senate want with so many pages, when the more numerous body requires so few?

It costs the Senate $46,000 for packing-boxes, folding documents, furniture, fuel, gas, and furniture-wagons. It costs the House, for wagons and cartage, $16,000. The Committee clerks of the House cost $33,000, and of the Senate $25,000.

The Secretary of the Senate and Clerk of the House get $4,320 each, and the Librarian of Congress gets $4,000. All the clerks of the Library of Congress, taken together, require $26,000 a year; and the library is allowed only $12,500 per annum to buy books, purchase files of periodicals and newspapers, and exchange public documents with foreign Governments.

Public printing costs an enormous sum, and the appropriations almost always fall short. Still, it is questionable whether, on the whole, we do not dignify ourselves, and confer benefit on the country by maintaining, as we undoubtedly do, the most perfect printing establishment in the world, not excepting Napoleon's printing house in Paris as it used to be maintained. For the present year, there will be appropriated for the public printing, $655,000 for composition and press work; $709,000 for paper to print upon; $552,000 for binding books, and $75,000 for engraving and map-printing.

Coming to Executive appropriations, we find that two policemen, two night-watchmen, a door-keeper, and an assistant door-keeper, at the White House cost unitedly $8,000. The President's Private Secretary gets $3,500; his assistant $2,500; two of the President's clerks $2,300 each; the White House steward, who buys the grub and gets up the dinners, $2,000; and the messenger $1,200.

At the State Department, it costs $12,000 to publish the laws in pamphlet forms; and for proof-reading, packing the laws and documents off to our Consuls, and such, we spend $47,000 annually. The eternal Mexican Commission costs us $28,700 a year, and our Commissioner gets $4,700, and the umpire, who lives out of town and is seldom called on, $3,000. The Spanish Commission costs us $15,000. The High Joint business at Geneva was provided for by a special appropriation of $250,000. They drink over there nothing less than chambertin.

At the Treasury Department are required for the Secretary, his assistants and immediate clerks, $384,000. What is a char-woman? There are here provided for, ninety char-women, at $180 a year each. These are, indeed, *scrub* wages. The

Architect's office, presided over by the great Inigo Jones Mullett, costs about $27,000. This bill provides that, from the contingent expense appropriation of $100,000, no part shall be expended for clerical hire. The Comptrollers of the Treasury cost, unitedly, $11,500. The office of the Commissioner of Customs at Washington costs $37,000. The Auditors' offices cost as follows : First Auditor, $58,000 ; Second, $384,000 ; Third, $289,000 ; Fourth, $83,000 ; Fifth, $60,000 ; and the Special Auditor of the Treasury for the Post-Office Department requires $267,000. Uncle Spinner, the Treasurer, demands for his office $189,000. The office of the Register of the Treasury requires $85,000 besides additional compensation at the discretion of the Secretary. The office of the Comptroller of Currency absorbs $117,000. The Commissioner of Internal Revenue demands merely for office assistance,—including Commissioner's salary of $6,000,—$364,000. His dies, paper, and stamps cost $400,000. To pay throughout the country the different Collectors, Assessors, Supervisors, Detectives, and Storekeepers, the Revenue Bureau demands $4,700,000. To punish violators of the Internal Revenue laws, $30,000 are appropriated. The Lighthouse Board costs, to keep up the Washington Office, $14,000. The Bureau of Statistics costs $65,000. The stationery of the Treasury costs $45,000 ; its postage, newspapers, seals, brooms, pails, lye, sponge, etc., $65,000 ; its furniture, $25,000 ; its gas, fuel, and drinking water, $40,000. Besides, the Secretary is allowed $45,000 for temporary clerks.

Perhaps you were not aware that we have an Independent Treasurer in this country. We have. His office is in New York, and he gets $8,000 a year personally, while his clerks receive $140,000. The office of the Assistant Treasurer at Boston costs $33,000, at San Francisco $21,000, at Philadelphia $36,000, at St. Louis $16,000, at New Orleans $14,000, at Charleston, S. C., $10,000, and at Baltimore $24,000. The Treasury's Depositaries require, to pay salaries, $10,000 at Cincinnati, at Louisville $6,000, at Pittsburgh $4,000, and at Santa Fé $5,000. It costs $6,000 to pay Special Agents to

examine these Depositaries. Then you come to the matter of
Mints.   The chief officers of the Philadelphia Mint require
$38,000 per annum, the workmen $125,000, and for incidental
and contingent expenses, besides, $35,000,—in all about $200,-
000.   The Mint at San Francisco costs $290,000, to pay sala-
ries and wages next year; at Carson City $90,000, at Denver
$30,000, at Charlotte, N. C., $4,500, (provided the Mint be not
abolished this year, as it will probably be.)   The Assay office
in New York costs $118,000, and at Boise City $12,000.   On
the whole, we pay a good deal of money in the way of salaries,
considering we see so little coin floating around.   If these
Mint-men cannot diffuse hard money more, there ought to be
some curtailment of their appropriations.

Arizona costs us for salaries $14,000 a year, and there is a
proposition also to pay its noble Legislature—that Legislature
which fell upon the Apaches like Joal's band and slew them—
$20,000, including their mileage.   We pay Colorado, out of
the National Treasury, $14,000, and nothing is said about
mileage or paying the Legislature.   We pay Dakota $54,000
for officers, and $20,000 for its Legislature.   Idaho gets $15,-
000, and $20,000 for the Legislature.   Montana, New Mexico,
Utah, Washington, Wyoming, get nothing for their Legislatures,
but cost us for officials $15,000 apiece, and the District of Co-
lumbia costs the Federal Government, for salaries, $28,000.

The office of the Secretary of the Interior costs, for clerks
immediately around his person, $47,000 ; for watchmen, $21,-
000 ; for stationery and packing, $16,000 ; and for rents and
repairs, $26,000.   The Land Office costs, for clerks, $53,000 ;
for maps, telegraphs, etc., $244,000.   The Indian Office costs,
for salaries, $30,000, and for incidentals, $5,000.   The Pension
Office costs the extraordinary sum of $344,000, besides addi-
tional clerks to the amount of $92,000.   This office also uses
$75,000 for stationery, engraving, printing, &c.   The Patent
Office costs, for salaries $319,000, besides, for extra clerks and
laborers, $147,000.   The stationery, &c., here cost $90,000,
and for photo-lithographing, $40,000.   The Bureau of Education,

an excrescence upon the Government, of no earthly account except as an auxiliary to take common-schools from the States and counties where they belong, and run them nationally,—this costs $27,000.

Now we come to the Surveyor-General's office: In Minnesota it costs $6,300, and in Kansas $2,000; in California $14,000, and in most of the other States about $30,000. The interesting Department of Agriculture, whose ornament—the bleached Capron—has been imported into Japan as a curiosity, costs, for salaries alone, $75,000, for statistics and fodder for the annual report, $15,000, to scatter seeds around and put them in bags, $45,000. These seeds make Vice-Presidents and Senators when properly distributed. The Experimental Garden of the Agricultural Department costs $10,000, the stationery and the books on bugs, $23,000; besides, there is a gorgeous report on the education of oysters, and the intellectual needs of pumpkins, for which a monster appropriation has to be made annually.

The salaries of the Post-Office Department in Washington City alone cost above $400,000, and the building demands for stationery, besides, $50,000. In this particular bill, Postmasters are not considered.

The War Department takes $47,000 for salaries; $46,000 are appropriated for examinations, and for copying from the Rebel archives, the Adjutant-General demands $100,000 per annum; the Quartermaster-General, $18,000; the Postmaster-General, $70,000; the Commissary-General, $42,000; the Surgeon-General, $25,000; the Chief Engineer, $29,000; the Chief of Ordinance, $25,000; the office of Military Justice, $5,000; the Signal Office, $2,800; and the Inspector-General, $1,600. These salaries are merely for clerks and stationery in the Washington Offices, and do not apply to salaries throughout the military service. The War Department, besides, requires for rents and repairs, $44,000.

To run the central office of the Navy Department, where Secretary Robeson sits at the table with an oar in his hand, crying " Heave ho !" the clerks get $36,000, and *billet-doux* are written to the extent of $5,000. Then the Bureaux have their particular clerks. The Yards and Docks Bureau requires $16,000 ; that of Equipment, $12,000 ; of Navigation, $6,000 ; of Ordnance, $10,000 ; of Construction and Repair, $113,000 ; of Steam Engineering, $8,000 ; of Provisions and Clothing, $15,000 ; of Medicine, $5,000, &c.

THE JUDICIARY.

And now we come to the Judicial part of our Government,— a third and co-ordinate part of the whole ; and what does it cost ? To pay the whole Bench demands $72,000 a year, ex- clusive of nine Circuit Judges, who cost $54,000 altogether. To pay the District Judges, and some retired Judges, costs $193,000, and the Court of the District of Columbia costs $20,000. The total salaries of all the District Attorneys of the United States is put down at $19,000, and of the Marshals also, $19,000. The Marshals and Attorneys get fees besides. The District Attorneys get 2 1-2 per cent. on all the money they recover for the country, and the District Attorney's office in New York City is said to be worth $30,000 a year. The Court of Claims, at Washington costs about $35,000, and $400,000 is appropriated to pay its judgments. This extraor- dinary clause—the only piece of light reading in the bill—is put at the end of the Court of Claims appropriation :

Provided, That no part of this $400,000 shall be paid in satisfaction of any judgment rendered in favor of George Chor- penning, growing out of any claim for carrying the mail.

The Department of Justice requires $73,000. The Solicitor- General gets $7,500, which is only $500 less than the Attor- ney-General. Each of the Assistant Attorneys-General gets $5,000, and the Solicitor of Internal Revenue $5,000. The Solicitor of the Treasury costs, for himself and clerks, $22,000 ;

three Commissioners for codifying the laws of the United States cost $18,000 ; the British Claim Commission, meeting in Washington city at present, costs $49,000.

The above, perhaps, dull reading, is an analysis of one of the large appropriation bills, and will give you some idea of what it costs merely for clerks, stationery, office service, and printing in the departments at Washington. Since that day back pay has been voted by Congress, and all the larger salaries increased.

The greatest office of the Government, outside of Washington, is the New York Custom House.

Consider that it employs nearly one-tenth as many men as constitute the regular army of the United States ! That it is the toll-gateway for the greater part of all the foreign cargoes which are poured amongst our forty millions of people ! That it is not only the most fruitful source of revenue which we possess, but also the most fruitful source of corruption ! Ten per cent. a head, levied upon its employees,—as was done every year down to the present,—will make a purse sufficient to carry an election in the largest community in the Union. Senator Morton, of Indiana, if I am properly informed, had no trouble in the world to get $15,000 from this hive of pensioners to help him lose the State of Indiana at an election in 1870. Out of this great den of revenue comes the cash which is mysteriously dispensed amongst us in the critical periods of partisan appeal. This Custom House has always been wielded for party purposes, and it is said never to have had an efficient chief. Its director is called the Collector of the Port of New York. He nominally receives $6,400 a year, his Assistant Collector $5,000, his Auditor $7,000, and his Cashier $5,000. His seven deputies receive $3,000 a piece. Under him are employed an immense number of persons, as for example, 247 inspectors of one particular class, whose aggregate wages are $380,000 ; 120 night watchmen, getting altogether about $130,000 ; 100 store-keepers, who cost him, in gross, $150,000 ; 60 examiners, and several hundred clerks. Few of the salaries fall as low as $600, and the average salary passes $1,000. Mr. Allison, the Register of the Treasury, alleges, in his newest report, that one set of items show a bill of expenditures at the New York Custom House of nearly $1,800,000. Mr. Boutwell sets down the revenue derived from all the customs in the year 1870, at $195,000,000, which was ten millions more than the gross receipts of the internal revenue system. If we go back to the year 1869, we shall be able to see more distinctly what a great part the New York Custom House plays in our finance and our politics. According to the statistics of that year, the value of all goods now imported into the United States is $414,000,000 per annum. Only $42,000,000 worth are entered free, and $160,000,000 are sent to bonded warehouses before their duties are paid. The gross custom duties received on this $414,000,000 reach the heavy figure of $180,000,000, or nearly 40 per cent. of the value. The New York port enters $270,000,000 of goods per annum paying duty, and $27,000,000 of goods duty free. Of the dutiable goods, $120,000,000 worth go to New York bonded warehouses, or three-fourths of the warehoused goods in the country. Last year there entered the port of New York, subject to the Custom House restrictions, 5,218 vessels, with a tonnage of 3,200,000 tons, and with crews amounting to 110,000 men. This is equal, therefore, to the head-quarters of one of the largest navies in the earth.

Speaking of navies suggests the great old Marine Barrack of Washington city, which few visitors ever enter.

The marines are under the direction of the Secretary of the Navy, and they may be described as the military of the ships. They stand guard at the gangways, magazine, forecastle, navy yards, and navy arsenals; are the boarding party in the ultimate collision of vessels, and in time of action they must fight the after-division of guns. The service, although a useful one, is generally considered a fancy one, and it is in request. Candidates are examined for it in our day, but there are no Marine cadetships at West Point, and to be between the years of 20 and 25, to have a fair collegiate education and physical strength, are sufficient endowments. Appointees are put under drill, and one of the marine officers is now preparing a book upon the manipulation of the corps.

There are in all ninety-two officers of the Marine Corps, counting the general staff; the file numbers 2,500 men. Privates, who formerly received $16 a month, now get $13 only, and there is much grumbling over the reduction, and desertions are more frequent. A corporal only receives the pay of a private. Two promotions from the rank are recorded. The uniform of the corps is dark blue jacket and light blue trowsers, with white pipe-clay cross-belts, and, for dress, the conical short hat, with red fringe pompon. Sailors are seldom enlisted in the corps; they will not " set up " well, have a swagger incompatible with the noble stiffness of a true marine, and are averse to the service besides. The old black high stock forced upon the marines, to give them the quality of ramrodness, is now abandoned.

Promotion to the head of the Marine Corps is made by selection, and not by seniority.

A cosy part of the Navy Department is the Judge Advocate's room. Around it are a series of those old-fashioned naval pictures which one finds scattered through the Navy Department, executed in abundant blue, framed in dingy gilt, forgotten as to their authors, and as to their date immemorial. Doubtless they were the work of some old clerk, whose amateur, self-learned skill with the pencil got him relief from fuller duties; perhaps the work of some old salt, officer or seaman, who so whiled away his lazy hours while out of commission; possibly wrought by some decayed or embryo artist whom a past secretary has salaried to illustrate our naval career. All through the department, these unclaimed, unhonored canvasses lie, with portraits of distinguished " salts " set between; here Bainbridge, there McDonough, yonder Hull. It is not improbable that many of them are ascribed excellent for technical merits, which strike a sailor more than art; but there they are, forgotten as their episodes, useless to the world of action as are the old swords, scimeters, hari-karis, forbidden to our officials, which repose in the museum of the Patent Office.

"Judge Bolles," said I, "does anybody know what these old ship-scenes represent?"

"These in my room," said the Judge, from the depths of his leather-cushioned office-chair, "tell the whole story of the fight between the Guerriere and the Constitution. Here they are sailing for the action. Yonder they haul to, and the Guerriere opens at long distance. In the third picture, the Constitution being within pistol shot, delivered her first terrible broadside. In the next the Guerriere strikes. The last picture represents the hulk of the Guerriere, and the Constitution turns on her heel, sailing away in victory.

Beside the Smithsonian Institute upon this flat, and on the site of what has been called the "Experimental Government Farm," a fine new building has arisen, 170 feet long by about 60 feet deep, made of pressed brick, with brown-stone dressings, built in the modern French style, with steep slate roof and gilt balustrades and galleries. This building is to be occupied within a month, and the Agricultural Department carried out of the vaults of the Patent Office; then the thirty-five acres allotted to the new department will be supplied with an orchard-house, an orangery, a cold grapery, and houses for medicinal and textile plants. The building is one of the simplest and purest, in a modern sense, in Washington, the design of a Baltimore architect. It cost $100,000. The Agricultural Department *in toto* costs about $150,000 a year, of which nearly one-sixth goes to the distribution of seeds. In the new building the happiest being will be our enthusiast, Townsend Glover, the naturalist, him to whom your farmers apply for a knowledge of what birds eat the pippin apples, and what worm gets into the beet-root. Glover is a Brazilian by the accident of birth, a Yorkshire Englishman by parentage, a German by education, American by adoption and enthusiasm. He is a singular-looking man, short, thick, near-sighted, peculiar, an Admirable Crichton in the practical arts. Agriculture has been his fanaticism for forty years. He paints, models in plaster, engraves, composes, analyzes, and invents with about equal facility. His passion is to be the founder of an index museum to all the products of the American Continent, from cotton to coal oil, from pitch pine to wine. Heretofore he has had only two little rooms in the dingy basement of the Patent Office; hereafter he is to have a handsome museum-room in the new building, 103 by 52 feet, and 27 feet high. His objects, already largely perfected, are to methodize, by models and specimens, the natural history, diseases, parasites and remedies of every individual product in America. For example: A man wants to move to Nevada. What are the products of Nevada? Glover has a series of cases devoted to that State, models of all its fruits, berries, prepared specimens of its birds, illustrations of its cereals, *flors*, grasses, trees. A small pamphlet conveys the same information; the man knows what to expect of Nevada. A man forwards a blue bird; is it tolerable or destructive, to be encouraged or banned? Glover forwards the names of fruits, etc., which the blue bird eats. He will show you, in living, working condition, the whole lifetime of a cocoon: the processes of Sea Island cotton, from the pod to the manufacture; the economical history of the common goat; the processes of hemp from the field to the hangman. Every mail brings to him a hawk, a strange species of fish, a blasted potato, a peculiar grass, which poisons the cow. He is the most dogged naturalist in the world, probably; a wrestler with the continent. He is a bachelor, married to his pursuit, one of those odd beings hidden away in the recesses of government, whose work is in itself its own fame and fortune.

A curious subject, to the inquisitive reader, was debated before Congress in 1871. It was the revision of the laws pertaining to the mint and coinage of the United States.

This measure originated with a quiet and indefatigable bachelor official of the Treasury Department. Mr. John J. Knox, the Deputy Comptroller of the Currency. He has spent almost his whole life in the atmosphere of banks, and, receiving a salary of only $2,500 in a city where it costs $3,500 to live, he has made use of all his leisure time to put himself into association with the former, as well as the present, practical men of the mints of the United States.

You know what the United States Mint is—an institution ordained by Congress in 1792, while the Capital of the United States was yet at Philadelphia. The fine body of organizing men who were setting the nation right at that time, resolved upon giving their image and superscription to the world upon their hard money. The first Director of the Mint was the renowned David Rittenhouse, astronomer and mechanic, who made watches, orreries, telescopes, and mathematical instruments, and who went heartily to work in the new institution, devising machinery, organizing a clerical force, and otherwise establishing so handsome an institution, that, when the Capital was removed to Washington, the mint was permitted to remain in the city of the Quakers. Rittenhouse was succeeded by such strong men as De Saussure, Boudinot, and the two Doctors Patterson, father and son. These kept the mint up to a good standard of efficiency, but much of its machinery remains modeled upon the same pattern as the early days. This mint is a staid, unattractive building, on Chestnut street, and it enjoyed the remarkable distinction of keeping a permanent set of officers down to the year 1861, when, for the first time, as we grieve to say, the new Republican administration put its hand upon the Directorship of this most responsible concern, and made its management a part of the political patronage which curses the country.

From that mint, as the necessities of the country demanded —or rather the covetousness of localities—branch mints sprang up in Georgia, North Carolina, and Alabama, and an assay office was established at New York city. After the discovery of gold on the Pacific coast, a more needful mint was given to San Francisco, where really the larger part of the coinage of the country is now done. After a time the greed of localities, and the growth of jobbery, gave a mint to Carson City, Nevada; one to Dallas City, Oregon; another to Denver, Colorado; and, finally, an extra assay office to Boisé City, Idaho. Thus the business of coining money, instead of being confined to one establishment, as in almost every other government, has got to be very nearly a State matter in the United States.

According to the report of Architect Mullet, we have twelve pieces of Mint and assay property, which, altogether, have cost, or will cost, between four million and five millions of dollars. The New Orleans Mint, which has cost $620,000, is a dead loss, and of no use whatever. The Carson City Mint, which was put up to tickle the Nevada silver mining interests, cost nearly $300,000. The Mint at Charlotte, North Carolina, cost upward of $100,000, and at Dahlonega, Georgia, $70,000. The old California Mint cost $300,000, and the new mint will cost more than $2,000,000. The assay office at New York cost upward of $700,000. Mr. Mullett's Mint at San Francisco appears to be architecturally an adaptation of the Patent Office at Washington, with the front of the mint at Philadelphia appended, and there are two large smoke chimneys in the centre, which give the whole thing the appearance of a steamboat ready to go right off through the Golden Gate. The edifice is to be 221 by 164 feet in dimensions.

As the mint edifices have been scattered, so have the regulations about the coinage fallen behind the well-organized system of other nations, and the final capture of the mint by the politicians has proved to be a serious matter. The Philadelphia Mint has continued to retain a traditional supremacy, its chief officer being "the Director" in name of the whole mint system of the country, while the executive officers at the places are called Superintendents merely. Yet the mint at Philadelphia has latterly come to be, in great part, a mill for making nickel pennies, and engraving medals from the "Great Father" to his Indian braves, and other Generals. In 1873 the bill just referred to, passed, and hereafter the Commissioner of the Mint will reside in Washington city at the Treasury building.

Another quaint bureau of the Treasury Department is the Detectives', headed by Colonel Whitely.

The position which Colonel Whitely maintains is more important than any secret police agent holds in the Union. He is charged with all the manifold and intricate offences against the currency and the Treasury, including counterfeiting, defalcation, whiskey, and tobacco frauds, the use of false stamps, etc. His headquarters are in Washington, and his main branch office is on Bleecker street, New York. His force is distributed through the Union, and the area of his personal superintendence is circumscribed only by our national boundaries.

He is a tall, wiry, rather debilitated-looking young man, with a long, pale, youthful face, light eyes, and dark hair, a shy manner, without any worldliness in it, and a sober, modest, nearly clerical, black dress. He neither drinks nor smokes, and is as much of a Puritan as Mr. Boutwell. Whitely has been very successful and systematic in his operations, and he has a fair knowledge of the civilization of professional thieves, their jargon and methods, and their haunts and associates. With some youthful confidence and self-esteem, he is still thoughtful, persevering, and adroit, and, armed with the enormous moral and material power of the Federal State, and its great system of marshals and attorneys, he is not subject to the restraints of cross-jurisdiction and State laws, which impede the pursuit and capture of local criminals. He occupies the whole field, and is free from the jealous annoyances of police rivalry.

If one could penetrate the Treasury building, and see the strange and motley character of the lesser clerks, he would find meat for wonder. In it, filling weary benches, are ex-Governors, ex-Congressmen, soldiers of rank, the sisters of generals like Richardson, decayed clergymen by the score, some authors, many *bon vivants*, and, they do say, young girls with dangerous attractions for public atmospheres or public individuals. The population of the Treasury building is that of a good-sized town, between three and five thousand. It is, and will be till war comes again, the great position of public life, no sinecure, demanding profound statesmanship at its head. The destinies of the people lie bound up in it. It can overbalance all private sagacity if it be weakly administered, and if corruptly or partisanly, it will be our debaucher or tyrant.

Next to the Capitol itself, the spot most consecrated to our marvels here is the old theater where Mr. Lincoln was murdered. The rash design, ascribed to Stanton, of leveling it to the ground, has happily not been approved, and in essentials of situation and exterior it is the same object. But all around it the zeal of housebuilding is at work to make the spot unrecognizable to the half-buried ghost of Booth. The alley of his bad escape is there and also the stable where he hid his nag, but

FORD'S THEATRE.

the open areas and naked lots which lay around the old theatre and the hulks of dwellings are filled with brick walls and plaster-beds. A new Masonic temple faces the neck of the alley; the theatre itself is preserved only in its bare walls and these are freshly roughcasted, the doors and windows changed; the boxes and galleries are torn out. Strong floors girded of iron and vaulted with brick replace at different heights the open canopy of the theatre, and iron stairways climb from floor to floor, guarded on every platform by one-armed soldiers standing to their crutches. The murder of the President still tenants the building like some lost trace of a skeleton hid away, or a spectre vaguely seen, but for the rest it is an association merely, and every day the incident grows less vivid and the narrative of it more wayward. But added to the martyrdom of the father of the people, the contests of the building are now of the aggregate reminder of the bruises, wounds, and agonies of the entire struggle for the Union. It is the Army Medical Museum, the depository of the names and casualties of every stricken soldier and the perpetual miniature of that vast field of war whose campaigns of beneficence followed in the footsteps of its heroes, and death and mercy went hand in hand.

Here are 16,000 volumes of hospital registers, 47,000 burial records, 250,000 names of white and 20,000 names of colored soldiers who died in the hospitals. Here are the names and cases of 210,027 men besides, discharged from the army disabled. Here are names and statements of 133,957 wounded men brought to the hospital, and the particulars of 28,438 operations performed with the knife. In one year—so methodized and perfect are the rolls and registers collected in this fire-proof building—49,212 cases of men, widows and orphans demanding pensions have been settled in this edifice. If you look through the lower floors you will see a hundred clerks searching out these histories, cataloguing them, classifying them, bringing the history of the private soldier down to the reach of the most peremptory curiosity, and assisting " to heal the broken-hearted and set at liberty them that are bruised."

It is this museum which is at once the saddest memorial of the common soldier and the noblest monument to the army surgeon. It contains a complete history of the surgery of the war, illustrated by casts, models, photographs, engravings, and preparations. There are here nine hundred medical pathological preparations, and two thousand eight hundred microscopical preparations. There is no similar army medical collection in the world, and from Baron Larrey down to Nelcton and Joubert the published reports of this collection have delighted and surprised the *savans* of the world. Scarcely a leading surgeon in Europe but has written praises and sent them here.

Let us see what this museum has to show us. It is a long, cool room, the whole length of the theatre. Show-cases extend lengthwise down it. Models of hospitals and skeletons of war-horses stand at top and bottom. The yellow standard of the hospital planted with the blue colors of the regiment and the tricolor of the nation is fixed in midground. Two splendid human skeletons, at full length, guard the head of the room. The walls are covered with large photographs, some of them two yards square, of the great hospitals of the war, those superb edifices which are now nearly all broken up. Near by are photographs of the great army surgeons of all nations, Larrey, De Genette, O'Meara, and others of our own service. A table is full of books of photographs of surgical operations, where, spent, and unshaven, the camera has been turned upon the amputated man's freshly severed stump and made his sufferings vivid forever. So are the healed and scarcely less cruelly suggestive wounds photographed with views of men in the various transitions between the cutting of the bullet and the final convalescence. Photographs of amputating tables all prepared and the victim stretched out insensible almost make you smell the fumes of chloroform on the doctor's bloody sponge. Stereoscopes are set near by, wherein you may examine the field of battle with the corpses yet unburied and see the bleached bones of the Wilderness as the camera discovered them to make their profanation eternal. So may you see the decks of battle-ships, where they are carrying the splintered and shot-riven below, and the cockpits where they seek to save the remainder of the carcass.

Continuing on we come to great cases of artificial limbs, bandages, slings, lint, and crutches. Some of these latter are actual crutches made of forked boughs, whereon wounded men hobbled unassisted to camp. After this are models of every sort of ambulance, stretcher, dissecting table, hospital bed, and the interiors of miniature hospitals, clean and sweet-scented as their originals.

Then follows a long array of human skulls, some perforated by bullets, some staven in by cannon-balls, some fractured by blows from sabres, some eaten with syphilis. Afterward follows the vast collection of preparations, dissected parts of men corrupt with decompositions, abnormal by neglect or the results of wounds, or swollen or attenuated with camp diseases and unwholesome food. Following these by hundreds are models in plaster or wax, of preparations too perishable to keep. Then come collections of parasites, deposits, impassable articles of food found in the liver and stomach's of the dead, strange instances which fell from drinking filthy water, and tokens of monstrous disease or indigestion beyond the reach of the dissecting knife. Bones in catacombs come after, splintered, broken, ill-set, amputated away from the man—whole jaws, noses, eyes, ears, shoulder blades, the leg from the hip-joint to the toe. Here is that cartilage of Wilkes Booth, broken by the ball of Boston Corbett. Here is a view of Sickle's leg, amputated on the field of Gettysburgh. Next are valuable cases of most minute microscopic preparations, a library of books, reports, experiments, suggestions made by the medical wisdom of the doctors of the war, and by this time the eye, running along so much that thrills it, wearies of even the fascinations of death and refuses to explore these painful wonders further.

In this museum, the war will live as long as its moral and political influence. This collection is worthier than the proudest victory won even for freedom. It is the infiltrating genius of mercy, unable to prevent the blow but claiming the victim when he is stricken. And not less extraordinary than this ocular demonstration are the figures deduced from the rolls of the surgeons, shedding light upon the natural history of man at large.

From skulls to books is an easy step.

Right off the Rotunda, that amphitheatre of politics, the Congressional library lies, its windows facing the pit of the city of Washington. Opposite the main door, behind a high table, piled full of books, sits, or stands the Librarian—a dark-skinned, black-haired man, perpetually at work with a pen, cataloguing, or, with a catalogue, directing; and his self-imposed labors are probably greater than his duties. He was never known to be in doubt about any volume, and probably never known to waste any time in mere book gossip. His

CENTRAL ROOM, CONGRESSIONAL LIBRARY,
CAPITOL, WASHINGTON.

place is one for which he has personal ambition, and he indicated his choice beforehand by minute and extensive conversance with bibliography. His nights are the Government's, like his days; for he has resolved, of his own will and motive, to catalogue this large library by subjects and by authors, and not merely to catalogue its books by titles, but by contents, so that when one is interested in a subject, he can be apprised even of exceptional references to it.

Thomas Jefferson, the author of the Government, as we understand it, was also the author of the library, and in the first year of this century \$3,000 was appropriated to buy books, only 2,000 volumes of which were collected, when the British burnt the Capitol. In 1814, Jefferson again appeared in the guise of Phœnix, and offered to replace the perished library with his own, consisting of 7,500 well-selected volumes. The usual hue and cry of Federal partisans was raised, but that small majority of common sense patriots which comes to the rescue at opportune times carried the measure, and nearly \$24,000 was appropriated to make the purchase. It was not until 1825 that the library obtained good housing in the central Capitol, and by small yearly appropriations it had grown to be 55,000 books in 1851, when fire destroyed three-fourths of it, sparing many of Jefferson's books. Cut down to 20,000 volumes, its great days seemed to have passed. Congress cheerfully voted within three years \$157,000 to build a fire-proof library room, and to buy new books, but only 70,000 volumes had been accumulated up to the period of the war, when there providentially appeared an old man who had devoted sixty years of his beautiful and dutiful life to saving from the ravages of time and waste, a library of American history for just such an exigency. This was Peter Force, now an inhabitant of his grave for nearly two years. He is, *par excellence*, the founder of the " New Library of the United States."

Peter Force was the greatest New Jerseyman, and the earliest collector of American books and antiquities. A printer in New York; a resident of the Capital City half a century;

Mayor of Washington; editor of the American Historical documents, and founder of the American Bibliography, his rank
in our literary civilization was more eminent than Sloane's in
English.   There is nothing more interesting and peculiar than
to follow this grand and ardent old man through the garrets
and attics of old colonial homes, from Maine to Mexico, discovering in chests and rubbish heaps, the precious footprints
of our history, raising from the brink of extinction some paper,
autograph letter, or a pamphlet which, from its mouldy pages
threw the phosphorescent spark upon some mistaken fame or
injured cause, and kept for man the memory of an expiring
episode to guide or to beguile him.   His venerable presence
haunted the frequent auction sales of all the towns and cities,
and his hand interposed between the frivolous plunderer and
the hammer, to guard many cherished data for the State.
He touched with his wand many young men, and they, like
him, went groping into the garrets of the past to add to his
collections, and at last, from every side, books, pamphlets, and
letters were forwarded to him from gainful people, who put
upon his sinking shoulders the duties that elsewhere are undertaken by the State.   He labored to the end, this Noah of our
literature, bridging over the gap of oblivion with his providence, and his house, at Tenth and D streets, was a veritable
ark, containing the seeds of our past species.   Offers from all
sides were made to him to sell, but he relinquished his library
only to the United States, and then pined for its society, and
died like the last man of the former generations.

In all his life, but one great pain came to Peter Force.   Secretary of State, Marcy, refused to accept his second series of
American archives, probably in some pique of the politician's
spirit, and Force declined to explain or to resume.   The work
ceased.   It can never be done so well by any survivor.   This
is an episode of the old, interminable war between power and
art—place and pride of scholarship—fought over by Johnson
and Chesterfield, Chatterton and Walpole, Motley and Seward,
Force and Marcy.

The Congressional Library is about 180 feet long, by 34 feet wide—a gallery, bent twice, so as to form a hall and two alcoves, the hall itself 91 feet long, and the height of all the three uniformly 38 feet. The hall contains the Librarian's desk and a few baize tables: one of the wings or alcoves is exclusively for Congressmen, the other affords reading space for perhaps fifty people. The floor is marble; the ceiling is of decorated iron, with skylights; all the shelving is iron. The architecture of the room is pleasing, and the prevailing tints are cream-color, bronze, and gold.

Like Georgetown College and the Smithsonian Institute, the Soldiers' Home of Washington is a contribution from outside

SOLDIERS' HOME.

parties. Gen Winfield Scott extorted the money with which the land was purchased from the city of Mexico on account of the violation of a municipal obligation affecting the truce. A very eligible site was chosen on the high ridge of hills about four miles from the city, and this may be considered the Central Park of Washington. A few cents a month is subtracted from the pay of soldiers to support the institution, which has been so well managed that in 1868 the fund was about $800,-000. Some of the ex-volunteer generals in Congress, who had no very magnanimous appreciation of the regular army, endeavored to have this fund divided amongst the loosely managed volunteer asylums throughout the country. To prevent such spoliation, the beautiful estate of Harewood, belonging to W. W. Corcoran, was purchased in 1872, thus expanding the grounds to a truly ample and noble park. About the same time a statue of General Scott, the benefactor, was ordered from Launt Thompson of New York, which work was being

modeled while the great equestrian statue of General Scott
which the Government had ordered was being cast in Philadelphia. This accounts for two statues of a hero of Mexico at
the Capital. During the fierce times of the war Mr. Lincoln
made his summer home at one of the cottages on the lawn of
this institution, and it is a matter of tradition and general belief that one evening as he rode out he was shot at upon the
road, but whether by assassins or mere highwaymen was not
known. This led to his being accompanied by a small guard
at the close of the war. From the upper windows of the
central tower of the Soldiers' Home, a panorama can be seen
much wider and more varied than that from the dome of the
Capitol, including a back view of the Maryland country toward the Patuxent. Right under the eye is a very old church,
Rock Creek, one of the old parishes of Maryland before the
District was surveyed. This church was erected in 1719, rebuilt in 1775, and remodeled as we now see it, in 1868. Strong,
hoary oaks surround it, and the old grave-yard is full of the
tombs of people who lived at Washington and in the surrounding country anterior to, and contemporary with, the founding of
the Federal town. A large and neat soldiers' cemetery lies
between Rock Creek church and the Soldiers' Home. In Summer the drives in this region are enchanting, and one of the
few roads in the vicinity of Washington which is passable in
Winter and Spring for pleasure teams is that leading from
Silver Springs toward Sandy Spring. Sandy Spring is one of
the boarding-house settlements for Washingtonians. Silver
Springs is the estate of Francis P. Blair, Andrew Johnson's
official editor, who is still living in a hale old age. Between
Silver Springs and the Soldiers' Home are the villas of Alexander H. Shepherd, Mathew G. Emery, and other prominent
citizens of Washington.

We will conclude this chapter with some sketch of the
Smithsonian Institute :

The will of James Smithson, like that of Stephen Girard,
Mr. Rush, and many others, did not express with sufficient

directness or coherence what he wished the United States to do with his money. Some members, as John Randolph, were opposed to receiving it on the ground, probably not wide of the mark, that a great nation was not a distributing reservoir for idosyncratic philanthropists. To add to this Mr. Smithson offended some of the more aristocratic members by his illegitimate descent. His original name had been, James Lewis Macie; his father had been the Duke of Northumberland and his mother the niece of the Duke of Somerset. He was a scientific man of much industry and good professional acquaintance. His death occurred at Geneva, Italy, in 1829. He is

SMITHSONIAN INSTITUTE.

said never to have visited the United States, nor to have had any friends residing here. His bequest was announced to Congress by President Jackson in 1835. The money, which amounted to above $515,000, in gold, was obtained by Richard Rush and brought to the country in 1838. This money was lent to the United States Government by Levi Woodbury, Secretary of the Treasury, and was invested in Arkansas State bonds at par. Some of this money was squandered by Senator Sevier, of that State, and his harpies, and the whole amount was lost and the bonds repudiated. Congress debated what to do with the bequest for several years, and between John Quincy Adams and Robert Dale Owen, an agreement was completed

by which the present Smithsonian Institute was organized in
April, 1846. Professor Joseph Henry, of Princeton College,
New Jersey, was made the Secretary, or really the Regent, and
Superintendent of the whole concern. This Secretary was the
first official in Washington after the President who appropriated to himself a residence in one of the public buildings. A
large reservation of 52 acres was selected on the knoll between
the Tiber and the Potomac, nearly in the centre of the city.
The architect was Mr. Renforth, of Washington, and he designed an edifice of mediæval character, a sort of battlemented
abbey, of Seneca redstone, with towers, chapels, etc., 426 feet
long by about 60 feet wide. This building cost $325,000, and
when it burned down in the war period it was again rebuilt so
that its erection and maintenance were said in 1869 to have
involved an outlay of $450,000. As has been well said, the
Smithsonian can be indefinitely extended, and there is architectural reason why it should be, to eke out its shallow depth,
in almost any mediæval military style.

Although a handsome object in the landscape of the city,
contrasting well with the large classical offices of the Government, it is by no means a favorite with those around it. The
interior of the building has an unsatisfying and inhospitable
look, much of it being closed from the public and given up to
mere inhabitancy, while the grounds around it, which, until
recently, were separated from Pennsylvania Avenue by a
nasty, exuding creek, were patrolled by lewd and offensive
vagrants, who often committed outrages upon citizens ventur-
ing to cross from one part of the city to another after dark.
The efficiency of the Smithsonian has been much disputed,
although it has assisted several scientific expeditions and
helped in the publication of technical treatises. It maintains
a very perfect correspondence with foreign learned societies
and publishes an annual report, which is said to be a little
more dry than the report of its associate, the Agricultural Department. Its uses are nondescript, and the average inquirer
will give it up when he asks precisely what they are, and receives in response a whole essay, which he cannot recollect.

CHAPTER XV.

MY PURSUIT OF CRÉDIT MOBILIER.

ALL previous sensations of a civil character in the history of the nation were eclipsed in the years 1872-73 by the disclosures which take the general name of Crédit Mobilier. My connection, as one seeking information, with this celebrated scandal, may not improperly make the narrative of this chapter.

It was in September, the tenth of the month, that I received by telegraph a commission to proceed to the State of Arkansas, and unravel some local mutiny there, and while making some preliminary readings, a second communication, from another source, asked me to visit Philadelphia and New York. It became necessary, therefore, to undertake the second commission with immediate despatch in order to improve the opportunity for the first and more distant one. The remainder of this chapter is my report of Commission No. 2, as published in the *Chicago Tribune*.

The most uneasy and serious scandal which we have yet had has undesignedly grown out of the lawsuit of Henry S. M‘Comb, of Wilmington, Del., to compel the delivery to him of certain shares of stock in the Crédit Mobilier. The suit is taking place in Philadelphia, which staid and respectable Quaker City is the only part of the country uninformed about this *cause célèbre*. The case in its context, has been charged to implicate two Speakers of the House of Representatives, half-a-dozen Congressmen, and other dignitaries. "Our Correspondent" in Washington was not, therefore, surprised to receive a telegraphic despatch, as follows: "Please go to Philadelphia and investigate impartially the Crédit Mobilier affair.—HORACE WHITE."

The diary of this pursuit, as far as the first day's prosecution is concerned, will show a novice how many things have to be done within a given time to answer one newspaper requirement.

At early daylight (September 12) I reached Philadelphia, investigated the docket at the Supreme Court Office there, saw the counsel for the plaintiff, telegraphed the plaintiff in New York for a meeting, after ascertaining his whereabouts; traced the Crédit Mobilier back to its origin, interviewed members of the Legislature contemporaneous with the passage of the act, and, in ten hours, was on my way to New York, reading, as I traveled, the long report of the Crédit Mobilier suit with the Commonwealth of Pennsylvania, in "Smith's Pennsylvania State Reports," volume 17.

In half an hour after I reached New York, I was in conversation with the plaintiff and other authorities, and that night sat up to "catch the manners living as they rise," by jotting down the matter most easily forgotten.

At the early hour at which I began to perambulate Philadelphia, I knew of but two attorneys nearly certain to be in their offices, the diligent and alert Henry R. Edmunds, one of my old schoolmates, now full of learning and business, and covered with venerable red hair; and the gristly and tough Joseph A. Pile, who works all night amongst the Pandects, and labors all day over Roman and Quaker law. Sure enough, there they were.

"Gentlemen, do you know anything of the suit of Henry S. M·Comb, who spells the Mick without a c, the c having dropped out by reason of the distant period when it got in—against the Crédit Mobilier of America?"

"Why, no. There's nothing in the *Ledger* or the *Franklin*

Almanac about it. We've read everything this morning but the obituary poetry and the editorials, which we preserve to the end of the year, for the solace of old age and the repose of children."

" The Crédit Mobilier," said the Hon. Joseph Pile, " is all the while here engaged in mysterious suits. They are often equity suits, before Masters in Chancery, or before the Supreme Court of the State, and everything about them is hushed up. Nothing much is published, and we are all in the dark. The State sued the Crédit Mobilier for taxes, and this involved appeals and two trials. But we have seen no mention of any such case as M·Comb *vs.* The Crédit Mobilier."

Here the Hon. H. R. Edmunds produced a large volume of the Acts of the Legislature of 1859, and he said:

" Gath, this is the beginning of the Crédit Mobilier. It was snaked through the Legislature fourteen years ago, under the name of the Pennsylvania Fiscal Agency."

I took the book and made this note from it:

The Fiscal Agency began November 1, 1859, W. F. Packer being Governor of the State. The " Pennsylvania Fiscal Agency " was incorporated, with the following Commissioners, or Directors: Samuel Reeves, Ellis Lewis, Garrick Mallory, Duff Green, David R. Porter, Jacob Zeigler, Charles M. Hall, Hon. R. Kneass, Robert J. Ross, William T. Dougherty, Isaac Hugus, C. M. Reed, William Workman, Asa Packer, Jesse Lazear, C. S. Kauffman, C. L. Ward, and Henry M. Fuller.

The act of incorporation was of the most general and discursive character, and covered all operations under the sun, banking, opening of offices in foreign lands, funding State debts, assuming the responsibility for corporation debts, guaranteeing bonds, etc. It provides that the general offices shall be in Philadelphia, and that a certain proportion of the Directors shall be citizens of Pennsylvania. This act is in six clauses, and it provides that the corporation shall consist of 50,000 shares of $100 each, and that when 5,000 shares are subscribed, and 5 per cent. thereon paid, the shareholders may elect five directors and begin business. The Fiscal Agency, therefore, contemplated a capital of $5,000,000, but required only $25,000 to be put up in the first place, and all facilities were given for watering the stock, etc. The State was to be entitled to a tax of one-half a mill on capital stock for each 1 per cent. of dividends.

And this little charter, said our correspondent, brought to life one year before the election of President Lincoln, is the foundation of the stupendous Crédit Mobilier, which, as an *alias* of the Union Pacific Railroad Company, robbed the generous Age and Nation which endowed it, and bribed the Congress of the people!

"It had to stand a suit two years ago," said Mr. Pile, "for taxes due the State under the charter, amounting to above half a million of dollars. All tax-suits of this sort are tried in Dauphin, the county of the State Capital. The Company, then under the *alias* of the Crédit Mobilier, beat the State, reversed the decision of Judge Pearson, and paid nothing. You will find the suit here in Volume 67, Pennsylvania State Reports."

"And here," said Mr. Edmunds, is the continuation of the Fiscal Agency in a report only five years old. It put off its old apparel and took a disguise."

Our correspondent then copied the original act by which the State gave the Fiscal Agency extended powers to veil the operations of the Union Pacific Railroad Ring:

"Laws of Pennsylvania, 1867, page 291, Act No. 278.

"A further supplement to the act to incorporate the Pennsylvania Fiscal Agency, approved November 1, 1859, empowering said Company, now known as the Crédit Mobilier of America, to provide for the completion of certain contracts.

"Section 1. Be it enacted by the Senate and House of Representatives of the Commonwealth of Pennsylvania, in General Assembly met, and it is hereby enacted by the authority of the same, That, in every case where the Crédit Mobilier of America—a body corporate established by the laws of the Commonwealth—has heretofore agreed, or shall hereafter agree, to aid any contractor with a railroad company, by advancing money to such contractor, or by guaranteeing the execution of a contract, for the building, construction, or equipment of a railroad, or for material or rolling-stock, it shall be lawful for the said Crédit Mobilier of America to take such measures as will tend to secure the full and faithful performance of the contract; and the said Crédit Mobilier of America, may to that end, appoint its own officers, agent, or superintendent, to execute the contract in place of the contractor so aided or guaranteed,—saving, nevertheless, to all parties, their just rights under the contracts, according to their true intent and meaning.

("Signed,")

"JOHN P. GLASS, Speaker, H. R.,"

"LOUIS W. HALL, Speaker, Senate."

"Approved, the 28th day of February, A. D. 1867."

"JOHN W. GEARY, Governor."

"You will find out here," said my informant, "that nothing ever leaks out about the Crédit Mobilier. Ben. Brewster is their attorney, and the papers are taken out of court, so that nobody can get at them. I don't believe that any considerable portion of the Bar knows anything about the suit of M'Comb vs. The Crédit Mobilier."

Our correspondent now set out to find somebody familiar with the Legislature at the period of the passing of the Fiscal Agency Act, so as to understand how this doppelganger corporation came into the world. All inquiry was answered by the name of Colonel A. R. McClure, as the person who had, at the time specified, been an attendant or member of the State Legislature.

Colonel McClure, a little grayer and redder in these campaign-times than of old, being full of patriotism and public speaking, said as follows :

"The Fiscal Agency began in the vagary of old Duff Green,

Tyler's editor, who was a visionary man ; and the Legislature humored him by the presentation of the charter he solicited. He came to Harrisburg in the fall of 1859, without a cent, and being a kindly old bore, whose name and years were venerable, he wormed the charter from the members by personal solicitation.   We all supposed that he wanted to assume the consolidation and care of our State debt, which is divided up in parcels, and scattered around in many forms.   The charter got from Duff Green into the hands of Charles M. Hall, who sold it to the Crédit Mobilier people,—some say to their proxy, George Francis Train.   Hall is a creature of Simon Cameron, and was made Postmaster of Philadelphia under Johnson, and rejected."

" Is that the way, Colonel McClure, that charters are bought and sold in this State ?"

"Precisely.   No business man thinks of applying for a charter, and hazarding blackmail.   He goes into the street, and buys some of the many charters which have been issued to charter-jobbers, and cover all forms of corporate enterprise, from raising wrecks to funding the debts of nations.   If we are fortunate we shall get a General Incorporation Act passed in the next State Constitution, and so dispense with the present peddling in nondescript charters."

" Will you please tell me whether you know any of the names of the ' Commissioners ' or incorporators under the first charter,—that of 1859 ?"

" That is not vital," said Colonel McClure, " as none of these men are retained in the Crédit Mobilier.   However, Samuel J. Reeves is a wealthy iron-man of this city ; Ellis Lewis was Chief-Justice of the State ; Garrick Mallory was a great lawyer here ; David R. Porter was the father of Horace Porter, Grant's Secretary ; Jacob Zeigler was Clerk of the House ; Horn R. Kneass was a city politician ; Robert J. Ross is a banker at Harrisburg ; W. T. Dougherty is the brother of another banker there ; Isaac Hugus was a Democratic State Senator and Cameron man ; C. M. Reed lived at Erie ; Asa

Packer is the Lehigh millionaire ; Jesse Lazear was Congressman from Greene County ; C. S. Kauffman was in the Legislature from Lancaster ; Henry M. Fuller was a Native American Congressman ; and C. L. Ward, an operator of Towanda, is dead. The names in the Crédit Mobilier are mainly ' blinds,' set up to stand for other people. The Fiscal Agency was a chimera ; the Crédit Mobilier entered the skin of it as the devils possessed the crazy man."

" Have you read the exposure of the Congressmen in the suit of M'Comb against the Crédit Mobilier ?"

" Yes. It's true. The only names that surprise me there are Dawes and Boutwell, because both are too shrewd. My experience in legislative things and corporations teaches me that the continuous legislation required to accomplish all the purposes of the Union Pacific Railroad, could not have been attained without bribery in the highest seats. Only the influence of the highest leaders could have passed such rapacious acts through Congress, and no men of reputation would have pressed them upon their colleagues except by pecuniary interest. The letters of Ames are recognized as perfectly valid, and M'Comb's reputation in the middle States is that of a gentleman who will not lie. The people implicated, who have been quaking over the probability of these exposures, must be relieved that they have come." *

Our correspondent now visited the office of the Clerk of the Supreme Court, in the venerable State House row. It was a

---

* The New York Sun published the Crédit Mobilier exposure in the month of August, 1872, having, it is said, purchased a copy, surreptitiously taken from the Commissioner's office. The vital part of the abstracts published were some letters of Oakes Ames to Henry S. M'Comb, saying that he had " placed Crédit Mobilier Stock in Congress where it would do the most good," and stating the number of shares allotted to each of certain States. A memorandum taken by M'Comb from Ames's pocket-book indicated that the Congressmen implicated were Dawes, Eliot, Blaine, Boutwell, Kelley, Schofield, Fowler, Patterson, Garfield, H. Wilson, Bingham, Colfax, and Brooks.

10

little old hole, and two white-haired old parchment men were moving around the dockets, exceedingly impertinent as to the case we were looking for. As we approached the Crédit Mobilier, everybody's spectacles seemed to take a jump, and all the venerable ears flapped like a puppet's when you pull a string. There was a smell of old sheepskins, and an impression of obsolete styles of stenography all over the place. Everybody looked like aged phonographic characters in motion.

Our correspondent got behind the docket-desk, and over-hauled the ponderous manuscript tomes. After looking without reward for a while, he took up an equity docket, and, on page 313, found the long-expected case of M'Comb vs. The Crédit Mobilier."

It is set down for the January term of 1869, number 19 in order. About the whole of one of the great folio pages is covered with the successive dispositions of the case, as it is now continued, now put over, now referred, and again postponed. The last entries show that, on the 20th of April, 1872, J. E. Gowan, for plaintiff, had the time extended for closing plaintiff's testimony 90 days from date ; and that a further extension of 60 days had also been granted. The case, therefore will go over the Presidential election, as both set of litigants are Grant people. He polls the undivided vote of the Crédit Mobilier, who think Greeley will not be a " Safe President " for such operations as theirs.

The defendants enumerated in this suit are as follows : Sidney Dillon, John B. Alley, Roland G. Hazard, Charles McGhrisky,* Oliver W. Barnes,* Thomas Rowland, Paul Pohl, jr.,* Oakes Ames, Charles H. Neilson, Thomas C. Durant, James M. S. Williams, Benedict Stewart,* John Duff, Charles M. Hall, and H. G. Fant.

The five names to which the asterisk is affixed are stool-pigeons, put on by Ames & Co. For instance, Thomas Rowland is a shovel-maker and compeer of Ames in the same business, and a quiet country-side man in a hamlet near Philadelphia. The names of McGhrisky, Barnes, Rowland, Pohl, and Neilson were afterwards indicated to me by M'Comb as of no potency or presence in the inside affairs of the Crédit Mobilier. Another suit had been in process from October 3, 1868, a period of four years, and another commentary upon the endless career of Chancery proceedings. Involving only $300,000, here were four years' work put upon this single piece of litigation. Verily, one might say, in a paraphrase of Mr. Lincoln: "Even so; if every dollar taken by the swindler must be replaced with another taken by the lawyer, still we must cry: 'The judgments of the Lord are good and righteous altogether.'"

There have been, at various times, employed by Colonel M'Comb, as plaintiff in this case, such counsel as William Strong, now Judge Strong, of the United States Supreme Bench, Jeremiah S. Black, and James E. Gowan. It is at present managed by S. G. Thompson, son of the Pennsylvania Chief-Justice Thompson, as associate of the Hon. Jeremiah S. Black. The defence is entrusted to Robert McMurtrie, who stands at the head of the Philadelphia Bar, as successor to John O'Brien, James Ottarson, and other less lawyers in the same case. This would seem to show that Dillon, Alley, Ames & Co. mean to contest strenuously the claims of M'Comb.

It appeared that the Court had appointed A. W. Norris to take testimony in this proceeding in equity; and searching out Norris's whereabouts, I found that he occupied the office of S. G. Thompson, the plaintiff's counsel. The next step was to see whether Norris, or Thompson, or both, would satisfy a laudable curiosity, and give me the testimony to consume, assimilate, and exhale.

Behold our correspondent, therefore on the way to the office of Thompson with a p.

There are periods in life when the p in Thompson's name appears to be an insurmountable barrier. Such was the present. The mind of the correspondent, in its anxious, not to say precipitate condition, transferred to the p all that might be

obdurate in mankind, and in Thompson individually, and fond-
ly imagined that, if he had spelled the name in smooth, flowing fashion, Thomson,—with no thump to the pronunciation
of the same,—he could have been a man of genial inclination, and those conversational talents which are conducive to a
great deal of newspaper information unconsciously. Mentally
assured that the *p* in Thompson's name would not permit him to
be an obliging man, I took the precaution of stopping at the
telegraph office and sending a message to Wilmington, Del.,
to inquire the whereabouts of Thompson's client, Colonel
M'Comb.

Arriving at Mr. Thompson's office, I recognized in him an
acquaintance not far from my own age, and then I despaired.
The newspaper profession, abused as it is, is the only one where
a man never puts on airs over being the repository of anything.
He sheddeth and imparteth like the gentle dew of Heaven
upon the place beneath, even if a person of the same age
should occupy the place. The only thing in which he is perfectly at home is instruction. But your lawyer delights in
magnifying his mission, and the extent of the confidence reposed in him. In Thompson's manner there was a deep and
bibliological mystery, associated with a covert and gentlemanly
sense of delight that he had come to be an authority. At first,
the social animal, beaming and gladsome (I say gladsome,
because nobody ever knew a lawyer to be really glad), Thompson in a minute divined my errand, and asserted the counsel.
What a dulcet sound to the young and ardent lawyer lies in
that word, Counsel. Behold him, referring to his grandfather
in a subdued tone, but with more or less apparent solemnity,
as "my client." Observe him step in advance of the prisoner at the dock, saying: "'Sh! 'Ronor, I appear as counsel
for the prisoner!" Nothing in life becomes him like these
occasions, and, in the presence of a newspaper man, Thompson
was now all counsel.

"I think I know your purpose," he said; "it is the Crédit

Mobilier case. I am in an embarassing position as to that. I am—ahem!—I am counsel for Colonel M'Comb."

"Yes. But like Captain Cuttle when Sol Gills left his last will and testament, I say where's the testament,—the testimony?"

"A part of it has got out. Col. M'Comb has written to me to ask how it did leak out. Do you know a man named Gibson?"

"Yes. Gibson is the industrious mouse. He published eleven columns of this testimony in the New York *Sun*, as well as the Ames letter and memoranda."

"There is a person of that name," said Mr. Thompson; I suspect I know how the letters got out. A man came to me with a letter from Judge Black. Perhaps I don't know. I think I do."

There was great and impressive mystery at this point. Mr. Thompson fell to examining a copy of the New York *Sun* in my possession. He read it all over as if he had never before beheld it. He smiled a counsellor-kind of smile at times, as if he had recognized something. The counsellor finally told me the trial had been long because all equity proceedings are so; that, when Judge Strong had charge of it, he could not take any step without consulting with Judge Black; and that Colonel M'Comb had refused to leave the Ames letters, in their original, with the testimony, but had copies made. He said that the Ames letters were in existence; that the implication of public men appeared not yet to be exhausted; and that I could see the testimony with an order from M'Comb. As I left the office, Mr. Thompson said:

"If you printed the testimony and letters, and all the people in the country read them, it wouldn't change a vote?"

"Perhaps not. But it is a horrible admission to make about one's countrymen. Nothing changes votes in this Christian age, but money and patronage; is it so?"

I made up my mind that the part of the testimony already published, had first met the eye of Jerry Black, and that he

had let it out to a reporter, who got access to the manuscript,
and hastily copied or imitated such parts as he wanted. It
also occurred to me, if any of the immaculate men referred to
in that list of the bribed, had, all the while, been conscious
that Jerry Black was aware of the purchase and sale, and that
young lawyers had also found it out, and that the area of exposure was inevitably widening toward explosion, how disturbed
at times must have been their sleep! The sleep of the distinguished hypocrite, what agony it must be of nights! To
know that, in the hands of remorseless men there is a secret;
that all time and occasion press nearer and nearer to its
revealment; that come it must, and that it must be met.
Such is the modern Eugene Aram in high places. But then
"it wouldn't change a vote!" Yes, it will. Not this year,
perhaps, but the next or the next, and it will change history,
too, and men's conception of man, and the man's happiness,
and the children's heritage of honor. Politics may apologize
for bribery, but the dead corpse will be apparent the longer it
is kept. No political party in the world can reason away the
conclusion that, if a trusted statesman sold his vote and influence, the public faith, and the public law, and all the while
played the outward part of piety and honor, he did a thing of
infamy, and lived a lie, and his face will be turned to the wall.

Finding that the Colonel, the plaintiff, was not in Wilmington, but in New York City, I telegraphed to No. 20 Nassau
street, and, in half an hour, got an answer, giving me his
address, and saying he would see me. I bought the State
Report with the long Crédit Mobilier case in it, to read on the
way, and was soon in the midst of a mass of villany. What
things people will do to make money! Half the world, it
would appear from the law-book, ought to be in the penitentiary. Here is a charter begged by a poor old man for a visionary end, or, perhaps, to serve some scheme of rapacity never
developed, which, stamped with mendicancy at its birth, goes
through the stews of politics and commerce, and becomes at
last the bawd of men to whom this country has been generous,

selecting them to lay a path between the coasts of the Continent, and liberally advancing them money and credit to perform the work with conscientious celerity, and make their lives useful and their names renowned. With the spirit of Joseph's brethren, they hasten to put the heir in the pit, and institute therefor a bastard corporation, parasitical in its nature, which shall eat the life of its wholesome brother, and divert the revenues and gifts of a highway whose achievement the world admires, into a mere "fence," or receiving-shop for stolen goods. Having succeeded in this, beyond the usual fate of roguery, they next turn about and swindle the Commonwealth, which gave them the bastard charter, out of above half a million of taxes. Such was the purport of the long report I read on the way to New York City. Prosperous we are indeed, but at what moral cost? Will the world believe that, while we were waging a warfare with the slavery of the whole body, we were making the patriotism in whose name we fought, a cover for such crimes as the Crédit Mobilier?

The Pacific Railway exists; but the corner-stone of the masons thereof was plunder.

At 9 o'clock I walked into the great commercial, social, and gamester's market in New York, the Fifth Avenue Hotel, and soon afterward the handsome Colonel Harry M'Comb walked in.

He had been a poor boy, native and now citizen of Wilmington, Del. Handsome and prepossessing from his childhood up, he was prosperous enough, when the war began, to become a merchant in supplies, and distinguished himself by the energy and resolution with which he competed with men of greater capital, and wider reputation. He is said to be the richest man in Delaware, the Duponts probably "excepted," and his business at home, in Wilmington, is the tanning of leather. With an orthodox education, and the best social connections in a quiet and virtuous community, he superadds to the dashing contractor and merchant, the semi-Southern tone and spirit of genial address, magnanimous personal impulses, the touch of

honor, and the carriage of a man of the world, yet heedful of
his reputation.   Nature designed him for a large part in life ;
he is the equal of any to whom he speaks, and courteous to all.
In New York he takes a rank relatively as high as at home.
Invincible, imposing, cool, agreeable, he is the least provincial
and the most exalted of men of his class.   He is portly, careful of dress, loud in nothing, with *bonhommie*, natural intelligence, and ease.

"Our correspondent" at once made known the object of his
errand, and the conversation which followed is here set down.
An interview such as follows, often does injustice to a public
man by the unavoidable misplacing of the order of questions
and answers, so that statements often appear climatic, and
things take context of themselves, and give impressions which
the just order of the dialogue would not show.   The subjoined
is believed to be a fair and candid relation of this interview:

"Colonel M'Comb," said our correspondent, my errand is to
get from you the impartial truth as to the revelations of late
made concerning the sums of Crédit Mobilier stock allotted to
members of Congress about the year 1868.   You have seen the
published extracts and the printed memorandum made by you
upon the back of a letter from Oakes Ames, in which memorandum 2,000 or 3,000 shares, respectively, are set down to
these persons: Blaine, Colfax, Boutwell, Garfield, Kelley, Bingham, Senators Patterson, of New Hampshire, Fowler and Henry
Wilson ; Schofield and Kelley, the deceased member Eliot, and
Henry L. Dawes.   I wish to know if this is a hoax or a reality.   I also wish permission, as so much has been said already,
to see the testimony."

Colonel M'Comb: "I have given my testimony before the
Commissioner to take it by appointment of the Court.   The
letters from Oakes Ames are in my possession, and copies of
them have been taken in the testimony.   But I was surprised
to see the letters and several columns of the testimony printed
here in the public papers, and disclaim any agency in that revelation.   It would not be proper for me to give you an order to

see the testimony, unless Mr. McMurtrie, counsel for the defense concurred."

"But why permit these terrible excerpts to go broadcast, if they are not parts of the testimony, to do injury to eminent and innocent people?

Colonel M'Comb: "They are parts of the testimony, and that is the reason why I can have no hand in anticipating their inevitable publicity. Somebody in your profession has had access to the Commissioner's manuscript, and taken that part of the evidence, sometimes copied it with haste, and often without accuracy, and again attempted to condense it. He has, besides, copied injurious parts without the link between. But what is printed is substantially there. I endeavored to keep the names of those gentlemen back, but Mr. Oakes Ames was perfectly indifferent to the exposure of his friends. He is about to retire from Congressional life, and will take no step to cover anybody's nakedness.

"How did you seek to avoid this disclosure?"

Colonel M'Comb: "In the first place, I tried to have the proceedings before a private Board of Referees or Commissioners, to be named by the Court, both parties to the suit consenting. They had all along been saying that my suit was merely a blackmail operation; and, when I brought it to trial, and expressed my willingness to put it in arbitration, Ames, Alley, Dillon, and the rest, cried: 'Oh! he will never dare to put it in open Court; he has no case, and shows that he has none by making it a private trial!' I was thus forced to bring open suit in the State Courts of Equity. I laid my papers of all sorts, which bore reference to this suit, before my counsel, Judge Black. He read them over, and said: 'M'Comb, these men will never dare to let this case come to trial with these reputations involved in it.' But they did, and fought and defied it at every step. Finally I came to a spot where, in the cross-examination, these letters of Oakes Ames were vital to my cause, and I again notified Alley and the rest, that I should be compelled to put them in. Ames knew all about their contents, but he did not move one step. I produced them after repeated taunts to do so, and a transcript of them has come to light, as could not, probably, be avoided.   I have no hesitation in saying that, had I been assisted by gentlemen as Ames was, I should have made every sacrifice rather than betray them, as he has permitted the course of this suit to do. With all of those gentlemen we stand upon terms of fair fellowship, and most of them are our party friends."

" There is no politics in this suit, then ?"

Colonel M'Comb: "None whatever! I told the editor of your paper, at the Brevoort House, last July, that I could not support Greeley ; that Grant was not my first choice, but that I could not be convinced to vote for Greeley.   The suit in which I am plaintiff began before General Grant had fairly got into his office.   It is for a direct and considerable money-loss which Oakes Ames obliged me to make by his bad faith,—a loss which is not merely in stock not delivered, but stock which I took from my own share to keep a contract with a friend. The letters of Ames belong to this suit, showing that he professed to divert my stock to Legislative uses, and act as the trustee for those Congressmen to whom he presented it ; and the memorandum on the back of one of these letters shows that just the amount he took from me he put to the account of the persons thereon named. The names he read to me from a memorandum book, and I wrote them down in the office as he dictated them. They remain as they were put on that letter, many seasons ago, and 1 repeat that, if I had not got those letters in at the time I put them in, they would not have been in order subsequently."

" How came you to lose your own stock through Ames' confiscating yours ?"

Colonel M'Comb: "It happened in this wise: Hamilton G. Fant asked me to take up for him, when I came to New York, $25,000 worth of Crédit Mobilier shares.   I gave the order for it, and told Crane, the secretary, to draw on him for the money. They said they did not know much about Fant, and preferred my check. I got a power of attorney from Fant to make the purchase, but the power of attorney was bad in form, and Crane, the Secretary of the Crédit Mobilier, made out a new and correct power of attorney,—which is a link of evidence in my suit. I got a certified check of my own, and paid for the stock. This check was mislaid in the office; and when, after some time, it was discovered that Fant had not paid for his stock, the Company drew a draft upon him for the amount. His circumstances had meantime changed, and the draft came back protested. The Company now notified me that they expected me to pay the draft, and this led to a search for the certified check, which came to light. At this period I was called away, and was absent some time—some three or four months—attending to matters in a distant quarter. But I had promised Mr. King, of Massachusetts, to deliver to him $25,000 worth of stock, and expected to give him Fant's stock. Oakes Ames, however, would not deliver to me Fant's stock, and, in excuse, showed me in the registry-book that he had disbursed the $25,000 amongst the members of Congress aforesaid. I was, therefore, forced to take of my own Crédit Mobilier stock $25,000 worth at the original valuation, and deliver it to King. My suit is for this stock, and the dividends which it produced. Whether Oakes Ames kept it, or paid dividends in bonds or money out of it to others, is not my business to inquire. I want what is mine."

"How does Fant's name appear in your suit added to the list of defendants?"

Colonel M'Comb: "They had arranged at one time to get Fant on their side, to rout me in the suit, and I put him in with the rest."

"Are not some of the names of the defendants used as mere blinds?"

Colonel M'Comb: "Yes. Rowland, Pohl, and several others are of no note in the Crédit Mobilier."

"Who got the charter for the Crédit Mobilier?"

"George Francis Train got it for Durant, who paid him $50,000 for it."

" Why do the Ames party dislike Durant ? "

Colonel M'Comb : "They were jealous of him, and have been slandering him for several years, saying that he is dishonest; that he made away with bonds, earnings, etc. At one time, I was induced to believe these things ; but I found Durant had more brains and more honesty than their party."

" Is the testimony of Ames, Alley, and others, in the suit of the State of Pennsylvania for taxes, reliable ? "

Colonel M'Comb : " No, it is all false. They swore they made no dividends, when Ames' letters to me assert just the contrary."

" Colonel M'Comb, what does this line mean in the memoranda as published : ' Painter (Rep.) for Quigley, 3,000 ? ' I know who Painter is, and suppose the ' Rep.' means reporter. Who is Quigley ? "

Colonel M'Comb : " Quigley is a townsman of mine, in Wilmington, Del. That has been erroneously copied from my memoranda in the *Sun*. The reporter who took it down for that paper must have been nervous, and he has made several mistakes. The names of Painter and Quigley belong to another memorandum. They are interested with me in the canal property between Washington and Alexandria, a piece of property owned and controlled by myself, Ames, Quigley, and some others. The figures 3,000 at the end of each name do not signify shares in the Crédit Mobilier, but dollars' worth of stock. If you look at the published memoranda you will see that no word occurs after these figures. It is true that $3,000, at the rate of profit obtained by the stockholders, would come to about $18,000. Therefore, the $25,000 worth of stock which Oakes Ames says he held as trustee for the Congressmen named would be worth many times its face. I held my suit for this stock in the Crédit Mobilier to be far above $300,000. That represents, as near as may be, the whole of the divided sum, provided Ames paid it to them, set down in that memorandum to the Congressmen implicated. I feel distressed at the publicity given to this thing, on account of their reputations, and the annoyance it gives to these gentlemen; but I have done all in my power to get what is due me without taking this step."

"Will you give me an order upon your counsel, S. G. Thompson, to look at the testimony taken before the Commissioner, A. W. Harris?"

Colonel M'Comb: "I will, if you get a similar order, or the consent of Robert C. McMurtrie, the counsel for the other side. But I do not want to be a party to any political designs which may be based upon the testimony, and my position as plaintiff is too delicate to take the advance in throwing that testimony open to the reporters. The fact is, Mr. McMurtrie, defendant's counsel, is now in possession of all the testimony; he borrowed it some time ago, and keeps it under the excuse of wishing to read it carefully."

" Where is Oakes Ames?"

Colonel M'Comb: "He is coming to this city to-morrow. If he denies those letters, I shall feel myself at liberty to let you see them: and, if you can get an authorized denial from him that he wrote them, I will give you an order on Thompson to look at the manuscript."

Colonel M'Comb then said: "What use do you propose to make of all this matter you have been gathering up in Philadelphia and New York?"

Correspondent: "Print it all to satisfy the wholesome inquisitiveness of the period, pin the responsibility where it belongs, and let people unfairly implicated explain their way out. The matter is certainly the greatest of all Congressional scandals. If Golladay, Whittemore, and such poor shoats are to be expelled for selling West Point Cadetships for a few hundred dollars, don't you think Speakers of the House, Senators, and such magnates ought to be brought to the bar of public opinion for abetting a swindle like the Crédit Mobilier, pushing private mortgage ahead of the Government's first mortgage, and otherwise prefering the claims of a corporation to the rights of their country and the tax-payers?"

Colonel M'Comb: "Well, I have no responsibility in this personal part of the suit; and I tell you now that, if my object was merely scandal, I could produce a letter not yet printed or proffered in the testimony, which would extend the area of implication, draw in other names of persons not suspected of collusion in any gainful matter, and make the present unfortunate disclosure secondary only."

"Has Oakes Ames no feeling for his colleagues in Congress?"

Colonel M'Comb: "No. Selfishness is implanted in Ames on the widest scale. He has the hide of a bull. If he had the sentiment of honor he would do anything,—leave the country, —rather than put the past services of his friends to the test."

"What were the circumstances under which you took that memorandum? Please repeat it."

Colonel M'Comb: "Why, I took it from Ames himself, he reading from a memorandum which he took from his pocket, to account to me for the stock he would not furnish, and, by accident, I made the memorandum at that moment on the back of one of Ames' own letters to me,—the same which has got into the testimony. That is how the thing leaked out. The letter was coerced from me in the course of litigation, and being discovered, the memorandum was made public with it."

"Then the weakness of the evidence is in the fact that you alone wrote the memorandum, and nobody can get the stock-register to confirm your memorandum. At the same time, the very incompleteness of this evidence at law will be moral proof to thousands of men. It lacks the lawyer's arrangement, but what is missing in evidence carries most conviction."

Colonel M'Comb: "Ames might have made a false entry of the names of the Congressmen, or he might have dictated entries of names not on the register. I had no suspicion of such possibilities at the time. We were on fairly amicable terms, members of the same Company, and he read straight on, giving me time to copy the list."

"It seems to me, Colonel, that you are employing a formidable array of counsel for a very doubtful consequence. What do Ames, Allen, Dillon & Co. care for the Crédit Mobilier charter now, having worn it out, and having no responsibility within the State of Pennsylvania longer? The Crédit Mobilier has about wound up, has it not?"

Colonel M'Comb: "No. It is still worth three millions of dollars at least, and its charter is worth preserving."

" Are you still a stock-holder?"

Colonel M'Comb: "Yes. I possess six [or sixty, correspondent not certain] shares, and my suit is not to get in, but to get my proportion of what I have paid for."

" Is Oakes Ames worth anything?"

Colonel M'Comb: "Yes. Three or four millions."

While a part of the above conversation was taking place, two gentlemen sat beside Colonel M'Comb and our correspondent, viz: H. D. Newcomb, President of the Louisville and Nashville Railroad, and Josiah Bardwell, an owner of Crédit Mobilier stock.

Colonel Newcomb informed me that Mr. Bardwell invested $50,000 in the Crédit Mobilier, and that his net drawings thereon had amounted to $360,000. Mr. Bardwell is a stout, brown-whiskered gentleman, and he said, pleasantly:

" Gath, you ought to go and talk to Oakes Ames to-morrow. He will talk freely. He don't care."

" How much do you infer," said Mr. Bardwell to ' our correspondent,' " were the proceeds or profits of Crédit Mobilier investments?"

Applying the information derived only a moment before on the other side, our correspondent answered:

" About six or seven for one,—say on an investment of $50,-000, about $360,000 net !"

This shot seemed to tickle Mr. Bardwell, and he laughed in a serio-comic way.

" Well," said he," provided that is true, we took a good deal of risk."

" Yes," said another," I wish I had some of that risk. The

stock and the dividends I don't mind, but I am quite put out that I didn't get some of the risk."

Here there was a general laugh.

Colonel Newcomb said, directly,—no other person at the moment present:

"What surprises me most is, that the newspaper profession, with all its acuteness, did not discover this matter long ago,—four years ago,—it being an old subject of conversation amongst railway men and operators. You will observe that Speaker Blaine denies that he ever received or owned any stock or money in the Crédit Mobilier. My understanding is, that no stock was given, but that the dividends were in the bonds given to the Railroad Company, which in turn became the dividends, etc., of the Crédit Mobilier. A man set down as having an interest would merely be presented with bonds at periods when dividends came to be declared, and some of the earliest of such dividends would clear off his stock of indebtedness."

It was now near midnight, and the company separated. Colonel M'Comb said, before going to bed:

"I have talked more to-night on this subject than I have yet allowed myself to do. Three New York newspaper men have been to see me to-day, and I have refused to speak, being already annoyed at the publication of my garbled parts of evidence, and at the appearance of Ames' letters. There, for example, is the letter of Crane, the Secretary of the Crédit Mobilier, which is omitted. I did not want anything published, and the omissions and the publications are equally annoying. I have told you this to satisfy you that I am merely going straight on to get my dues in a business suit, and am no politician at any time. I shall vote for General Grant, and could never vote for Greeley anyway."

"Why?"

"He is too much of a whirligig. Good-night."

Wondering if Greeley were more of a whirligig than the Crédit Mobilier, which began with Duff Green, passed along to George Francis Train, fell as a family chattel into the hands of

Tom Durant, was gobbled up by Oakes Ames, Sidney Dillon, and John B. Alley, and has finally become a bombshell in Congress, exploding the caucus, our correspondent also retired to his room, made his notes, and composed himself to rest, congratulating himself that he had deserved well of his country.

The above was the first letter published confirmatory of the disclosure from a principal.

CHAPTER XVI.

CREDIT MOBILIER BROUGHT TO BAY.

PERHAPS nothing in American history will bear comparison with the Crédit Mobilier as a drama in which all the human emotions have been played upon from farce to tragedy. The subject is of the grandest area, and the conspiracy within it close and criminal as in any scheme of treason aimed at a great empire. Look at the dates, and see what they imply:

In the Summer of 1862, a Pacific Railroad was empowered by Congress. In 1869 the road was built, and cars were running from New York to San Francisco. In 1872, ten years after the Government exercised its generosity, the chief builders and capitalists of the enterprise appeared like common criminals at the bar of public opinion, and the highest heads in Congress were dragged down for complicity in their crime. Two separate investigations were held in the House of Representatives, and one in the United States Senate. Two members of Congress, Oakes Ames and James Brooks, and one Senator, James W. Patterson, were reported back for expulsion. But public opinion was so far from satisfied, and Congress so wholly demoralized by apprehensions of other exposures, that neither House took definite action, and Congress adjourned under a cloud, and the entire country, which had just passed through a presidential election, was overcast with doubt, shame, and indignation. The two members marked for expulsion died in little more than two months and within a few days of each other. It is true that one of them was a sufferer from bodily disease, and the other was an old man, but the public superstition connected in their obituary the tragedy and its context, and not all the funeral pomp could clear the stigma from the dead, nor obtain a revocation of public sentiment in favor of the score or more men who had been members and Senators, and had abused the magnificent dowry of the nation. Almost while the funeral services of Brooks and Ames were being said, the United States Government was filing complaint and bill in equity at Hartford, Connecticut, May 26, 1873, in the Circuit Court of the United States, against "The Union Pacific Railroad Company and others," of which a newspaper despatch said:

"This marks the opening of the great legal struggle between the Government on one side and two of the greatest and most extraordinary corporations ever created on the other, and will, beyond doubt, occupy some of the attention of the Courts for ten, perhaps twenty, years to come. It is, unquestionably, the most gigantic litigation on record, and the printed complaint and exhibits appended thereto, twenty-five in number, make a book of 134 printed pages.

"The total sum to be accounted for will, if a verdict be given against all the defendants, be probably not less than $25,000,000, and interests in the litigation may be transmitted, in all likelihood, to the second generations of the posterity of some of the parties defendant."

An examination of this bill shows that it makes defendants not only about one hundred rich individuals but also the following corporations: the Union Pacific Railroad Company, a corporation created by acts of Congress of the United States, whose principal office for business is located at Boston, in the State of Massachusetts, and its President, Horace F. Clark, of the city, county and State of New York; the Crédit Mobilier of America, a corporation created by the Legislature of the State of Pennsylvania, and located in Philadelphia, in said State, and its President,

Sidney Dillon, of the city, county, and State of New York;
the Wyoming Coal and Mining Company, a corporation organized under the general statutes of the State of Nebraska; the
Atlantic and Pacific Telegraph Company, a corporation
organized under the general statutes of the State of New
York, and its President, John Duff, of Boston, in the State
of Massachusetts; the Pullman Palace Car Company, a corporation transacting business in Chicago, in the State of
Illinois, and its President, George M. Pullman, of Chicago;
and the Omaha Bridge Transfer Company, a corporation
transacting business at Omaha, in the State of Nebraska.

Amongst the individual defendants are ex-Congressman
Henry M. Boyer, and Helen Boyer, his wife; William Tracy,
the executor of Congressman Brooks, deceased; General G.
M. Dodge, and Anne M. Dodge, his wife; the widow of ex-
Senator Grimes; and very many ex-Congressmen and hitherto
respectable citizens.

The United States attorneys claim in one paragraph of this
bill that the following extraordinary state of morals and
finance prevails in the Union Pacific Railroad Company:

"The Union Pacific Railroad Company is insolvent. The
cost of the railroad and telegraph line was considerably less
than one-half the sum represented by the aggregate of stock
and other pretended liabilities of the company outstanding.
The largest part of the stock and bonds of the company before
mentioned was issued, in the name of the company, by its
managers, not in the interest of the company, but to enrich
themselves in a manner and for purposes unauthorized by law.
A large majority of the stock now habitually voted upon as of
right, in electing officers and controlling the affairs of the
company, is stock issued in a manner not authorized by law,
and which was never paid for, in cash or in any other thing of
equivalent value to the company. A large part of its income
is used habitually in paying its managers high interest and
commissions on loans, and in paying interest on bonds issued
unnecessarily, without lawful motive or adequate consideration.

"The earnings have not been sufficient to pay accruing interest on its floating debt and on the several classes of bonds issued by the company. Ten millions of dollars of its income bonds, so-called, will be due in September, 1874; but no fund has been provided or is accumulating for either new ties and rails or payment of said income bonds. Interest on United States bonds issued to the company is allowed to accumulate without payment, as before stated. The company is insolvent, and obliged to depend on temporary loans to save its obligations and promises from dishonor. Its principal managers treat it as depending on their personal credit to save it from bankruptcy, and make profit by loaning it money for high interest and commission."

The Wilson Committee of Congress showed that the Crédit Mobilier conspirators made at least twenty-four millions of money beyond a liberal profit by contracting with themselves, not only to build the road, but to rob it in every possible manner after it should go into operation. The rapacity and wealth of the conspirators, and the general demoralization of American commercial and political society at the time, involved a wholesale purchase of engineers, examiners, Congressmen, newspapers, cabinet officers, state governors, and judges. Society stood back appalled, unwilling, but compelled to believe the disclosures, and there can be no doubt that Republican Government lost the faith of many thousand men and women.

Let us look at the two railway companies which interlink midway from the one highway to the Pacific.

The Central Pacific Company at the West End sprung out of the needs of California, and the yearning of all the people and capitalists there to have quick and reliable connection with the bulk of their countrymen in the East. The Union Pacific Road, on the contrary, did not aim to give relief to a rising nation of people, by affording them an outlet to civilization, but it was simply a tie which should bind the Central Pacific to the country east of the Missouri. This intervening country was without large towns, and, indeed, without any population to speak of, except the few herders of cattle, and some isolated band of miners. The Union Pacific Road, therefore, did not promise to become, in a short time, a profitable highway to its devisors. It tumbled into the hands of certain lobbyists and Congressmen, who were much more concerned to make something out of its construction than to build it up into a property, and wait, like the Central Pacific people, for the business to increase, the country to fill up, the mines to grow profitable, and the freights and passenger-travel to yield their legitimate award. The Union Pacific Railroad did not break ground until the 5th of November, 1865,—nearly two years after the Central Pacific had resolutely driven the spade, and looked with courage, almost beyond hope, at the steep sides of the Sierra Nevadas. To build the Union Pacific Road was a much lighter task than to lay the Central Pacific. On the former lines the long level plains and steppes afforded such easy accommodations for railway builders that it is a matter of history how even six miles a day of track were laid when the work had been fully undertaken. The Union Pacific Company laid but forty miles of track up to January, 1866 ; but, in that interval, and after it, the incorporators of the road found out an opportunity to make money more easily than by patient processes.

When the Crédit Mobilier, so called, had been created, to receive the proceeds of the Government bonds, and sieve the same into the railroad through the pockets of the manipulators of the Mobilier, they warmed up, and were able to lay 305 miles of road in one year, 235 in the next year, and finally, to complete the road, for the whole 1,085 miles, by the 10th of May, 1869. The Union Pacific Road retains to the present day 1,032 miles of road lying between Ogden and Omaha. It received a vast subsidy in land from Congress, besides such a stupendous bonded aid that, by the testimony of experts, it was able to lay the whole line within the amount in cash realized from the sale of its bonds, put a large fortune in the hands of everybody who belonged to the Crédit Mobilier, and receive, besides, the whole of its land-grant, as a clear margin of profit.

The scandals which accompanied the building of this road are, perhaps, forgotten by many of the old generation, and are scarcely known to tens of thousands of the new generation which has arisen since the Pacific was opened. The traveller over the line at this day will observe that, whenever a rich piece of level ground is attained, the road begins to snake around like a great brook which draws water from every spring ; and sometimes the eye is bewildered to see what appears to be another railroad, parallel with that on which he travels ; but the information is soon afforded that it is the same piece of road he had gone over half an hour before. If he asks why it should be so crooked, the answer will be : "That was a part of the job." The Union Pacific Company let out the building of the road to its own contractors, under the name of the Crédit Mobilier ; and they had no desire to make a short line where it was easy laying track, because they received so much per mile in bonds from the United States, and whenever they could build the road for less per mile than the bonded aid, they went winding round and round, like a circle, and put the overplus in their pockets.

"But," you will ask, "was the Government so blind that it could not see that a swindle was being perpetrated upon it in describing three sides of a square to get the distance of the fourth side ?"

"Yes," will be the answer ; "but the road will be examined by persons selected at the suggestion of the Company, and these were induced to report that everything was correct."

All the above is literally true, as any man knows who has crossed the plains. The time between Omaha and Ogden could be greatly decreased had this railroad been laid on the thrifty principle of a responsible organization and honest engineering. Begun as a job, the Union Pacific Railroad soon failed to be of interest to those who had prostituted the Govern-

ment Charity, after it was opened.   While the Central Pacific
Road, of which it is the receiver, is a splendid piece of property, with its stock jealously kept in the hands of its original
conceivers, the Union Pacific has several times changed owner-
ship, President after President going out ; and the scandal of
its management was so notorious that the Tammany Hall
Judges thought it would "come down" easily and pay them
black-mail. So Judge Barnard put it into the hands of a
receiver in New York, and had its safe broken open with cold-
chisels and gun-powder.

At Saratoga, during the trial of Judge Barnard, Horace F.
Clark, an associate of this road, was put upon the stand, and
asked to give testimony concerning the Crédit Mobilier. He
declined to say anything about it, asserting that all he knew
was hearsay and not evidence, and refused to bring the books
of the corporation, which are now in the city of Boston, within
the jurisdiction of the State of New York. Hence the mystery
involving the Crédit Mobilier,—which we may call, for short,
the ring of Union Pacific Directors and stockholders, who get
the bonds, put the road down cheaply, and filch the remainder
of the aid Government gives them,—and the difficulty of getting at any of the facts, although the people know that one of
the most monstrous and impudent swindles ever perpetrated
upon a magnanimous Nation was the act of that Union Directory, of which Oliver Ames was President and Oakes Ames the
Congressional Agent.   It will ever be a subject of scandal to
an inquiring posterity that Schuyler Colfax, as well as his
successor, James G. Blaine, kept at the head of the Pacific
Railroad Committee in the House of Representatives, this
Oakes Ames. He was a large, heavy-set, secretive shovel-
maker, from the Taunton District of Massachusetts, who kept
his pocket full of free passes over this railroad, and dealt them
out judiciously to whoever might be able to do him either good
or injury.   A member of Congress, and as such obligated to
protect the State in its property in the Pacific Railways, Oakes
Ames was, all the while, a member of the Crédit Mobilier, and

a brother of the President of the road. He never made a proposition concerning this road which did not become the law or the observance by act of Congress. He carried through Congress a scandalous proposition by which the Government abandoned its first mortgage of this highway, and allowed the private mortgage bonds of the Railroad Company to take precedence, and crowded the Government with a second mortgage. He was able, with the help of the most eminent men in the Republican party, to collect from the United States the gross sum for carrying the mails over this road, while, at the same time, he never paid the interest on the Government bonds as it accrued. In short, the Union Pacific Railroad first begged a loan from the United States of from sixteen to sixty thousand dollars a mile, and then robbed it of the interest on the loan, forced the loan itself back to a contingent place, and pasted it over with another, and a private loan of its own, and then swindled it out of the whole gross sums for the mail service.

During the time that these robberies were taking place, and the Crédit Mobilier could be daily heard to chuckle as it received Government bonds, a great deal of wild and florid gammon was poured out upon the country. Our attention was called to the giant pines of California, whenever we proposed to look down to the ties, and see where our money had gone. If we presumed to ask when the road, under good management, might pay for itself, we were directed to spend no time upon such mercenary amusement, but to look, instead, on the splendor of Yo Semite Valley, and the wonderful apricots in the region of Los Angeles. There was so much drumming, and fifing, and fuss, and palaver, kept up about this glorious achievement (which was the easiest achievement ever undertaken by civilized man, when he had the money in his hands to do it with), that the imagination of the country was carried away from the solid business which belonged to the undertaking, and now, after many years of mystery, a private law-suit

11

in a secondary city proves that murder must out at last, and that what is so ugly can never be wholly concealed.

The Crédit Mobilier, it appears, built nearly the whole of the Union Pacific Railroad, or 1,038½ miles, which was a little more than the Union Pacific now retains. It really built 1,035 miles, but sold to the Central Pacific subsequently all that portion of the road between Ogden and Promontory, and now owns less, by 6½ miles of rails, than the Crédit Mobilier, its stool-pigeon, built. For this 1,038½ miles of road the Crédit Mobilier got United States bonds, amounting to more than $27,250,000, besides 12,080,000 acres of land. Upon this land were issued 7 per cent. land-grant bonds, to the amount of $10,400,000. The capital stock of the Crédit Mobilier, meantime, was 37,000 shares, at a par value of $100. Exactly how designing and successful this transaction was, has come out in the letter of Oakes Ames to H. S. M'Comb. According to Ames' own admission in this letter, the Crédit Mobilier paid less than $25,700 a mile to build the highway, or, in gross, $25,900,000. The letters from Oakes Ames are valid and undoubted ; they are written by him, and appear in his handwriting ; they were indited in the due course of business, and are now about four years and a half old. They show the secrecy, the Jesuitry, and the ingratitude of the corporation which could receive such an amount of help, and abuse the Government's confidence ; and they show, more than all, that it was a member of Congress who wrote these letters, and he implicated, in all secrecy and seriousness, men whom the country has delighted to honor.

The country owes nothing perhaps to Henry S. M'Comb, who was one of the Crédit Mobilier men, for having been the means of showing up their system of plunder. It seems that M'Comb was a fellow capitalist with Thomas C. Durant and joined Durant's faction when the Mobilier people got to cheating each other. Durant had been a physician in the western part of Massachusetts, but he had too much worldly enterprise for professional life, and took to railroad contracting. He observed the drift of opinion to be in favor of a railway to the Pacific, and put himself forward in the project, but being a reckless speculator, without conscience toward his creditors, his country, his friends, or his friend's wife, he had no sooner become Vice-President of the Union Pacific railroad, than he sent George Francis Train to Pennsylvania to buy him one of those floating charters by which our modern legislatures empower gamblers to cheat mankind. The name of Crédit Mobilier was derived from a stock gambling corporation which existed in Paris during the reign of Napoleon III. Had the Pennsylvania legislature possessed anybody of general reading, and been particular about honesty, it would have suspected a corporation with such a title. Durant got his charter at such a time as to show that he meditated a swindle from the beginning. He gathered around him a set of loose law-defying contractors, men of means and vigor and associated these with him in the Crédit Mobilier. Then the company moved to New York so as to get out of observation in Pennsylvania, and when one of Durant's clerks by the name of Hoxie, a man without means, had been given by the Union Pacific Company a contract to build 246 miles of road, Hoxie transferred the same to Durant, and Durant to the Crédit Mobilier. At this time the whole Union Pacific Company had paid up but $218,-000. The object of getting the Crédit Mobilier charter was to protect themselves individually as partners for debts. As the Crédit Mobilier, they turned around and bought the $218,000 worth of stock aforesaid. The Union Pacific stock was then watered one thousand per cent., and thus the Crédit Mobilier ate up the Union Pacific Company. The Hoxie contract at $50,000 per mile was now fulfilled in a cheap way, at a cost of $27,500 per mile, including equipment. About 350 miles of road were built in this way, of which 58 miles alone netted the Crédit Mobilier more than a million and a third dollars " without any consideration whatever." August 16, 1867, the Oakes Ames contract was made for 66.7 miles, at from $42,000 to $96,000 a mile, the Government meantime paying $96,000, in

all about $48,000,000. The Crédit Mobilier now handed over
to Ames the absolute disposition of the Union Pacific railroad.
Ames associated with himself an ex-Congressman from Massachusetts named John B. Alley, and Messrs. Bushnell, Dillon,
M'Comb, Durant and Bates, the core of the Crédit Mobilier.
The chief Engineer, Granville M. Dodge, was bribed with one
hundred shares of Crédit Mobilier stock, placed in the name of,
his wife. The profit under this contract was nearly $80,000,-
000, in stock, cash, bonds, &c. In the same way the Davis contract was made, on the same terms as the Ames contract, for
125 miles. The committee of investigation, headed by Hon.
Jeremiah M. Wilson, reported on the above contract as follows:

Your committee present the following summary of cost of this road to
the railroad company and to the contractors, as appears by the books:

Cost to railroad company.

Hoxie contract, - - - - - - - - -	$12,974,416.24
Ames contract, - - - - - - - - -	57,140,102.94
Davis contract, - - - - - - - - -	23,431,768.10
Total, - - - - - - - - -	93,546,287.28

Cost to contractors.

Hoxie contract, - - - - -	$7,806,183.33	
Ames contract, - - - -	27,285,141.99	
Davis contract,	15,629,633.62	
	50,720,958.94	
		42,825,328.34
To this should be added amount paid Crédit Mobilier on account of fifty-eight miles, - - - - -		1,104,000.00
Total profit on construction, - - - -		43,925,328.34

It was while Oakes Ames was in the enjoyment of these
contracts, that he was a member of Congress, and to smooth
his path there, he gave stock in the Crédit Mobilier Company
in small sums to a large number of members, and outside
people. His method was to hold the stock in their names,
privately, but himself trustee, and known as such within the
Mobilier Company. It was this very stock which led to a law-

suit in the courts of Pennsylvania, by Henry S. M'Comb. Ames and his clique had fallen out with Durant, and his clique and the latter were discontented to see so much plunder falling to their opponents. M'Comb affected to believe that Ames had never paid the Crédit Mobilier in question to Congressmen, or to put the proceeds in his own pocket. He therefore laid damages at a very considerable amount, and found it necessary to sustain his case, that he should put in the *Transcript* some private letters which Ames had written to him. These letters involved the reputation of Congressmen.

It appears that Ames, being of a dull unsensitive nature, paid little heed to the consequences of such publications, and his coterie, of which the head was John B. Alley, supported him. An attempt was made, however, to get the originals out of M'Comb's hands, and make way with them. It appears that with rare delicacy M'Comb had merely put in copies and omitted altogether the memorandum of names of Congressmen.

Here is the letter of Ames' counsel:

M'Comb vs. C. Mobilier.

PHILADELPHIA, May 21, 1872.

DEAR SIR: On Thursday, the 23d, you have appointed to close the cross-examination of Mr. M'Comb, and to proceed with your evidence.

Allow me to remind you of promises made by your client at the prior meetings, many months since, to furnish or produce the papers or documents from copies of which he spoke, or referred to, or memoranda taken from them. Some at least were to be sent me next day; none have been sent. He stated the other day that they had been withheld for a purpose. I must ask that you will require him to produce at the meeting on Thursday, if you desire me to cross-examine, the following:

Letters from Oakes Ames in reference to the distribution of 343 shares as gifts to members of Congress:

His books showing the original entries and dividends, or sums, stated to have been received as dividends—April, 1866; July, 1866; September, 1866; December, 1866; and January, 1868.

I would also like to have a copy of Mr. Ames' letter, April 13, 1867 (exhibit No. 2, A. W. N.)

Very truly

(Signed)   R. C. McMURTRIE.

To JAS. E. GOWEN, Esq.

But M'Comb made McMurtrie take copies in his presence, and copy one letter at a time. The manner of McMurtrie when he saw such letters did exist, was that of a man deceived by his own clients.

Ames said to M'Comb, when asked if he did not value the reputation of his friends:

"I don't care whether you put the letters in as evidence or not. Everybody knows that Congressmen are bribed."

After these letters became evidence, it was inevitable that they should appear in print. They did appear in some mysterious way and made great scandal. After a long and most awkward silence, suspicious denials of their validity appeared from Ames and other parties. Ames argued that he had never sold or presented a share of stock to any member of Congress, —a piece of unblushing falsehood, as he has himself shown under oath. The denials of the others were made under a mistaken idea that the thing would blow over after the political campaign, and that meantime it would pass as mere vituperation of the canvass. The names of Grant and Wilson, it was thought, would prove all-protecting;

> Ulysses! name that charms our fears,
>   That bids our sorrows cease;
> 'Tis music in the sinner's ears,
>   'Tis life, and health, and peace!

After the election was done and Congress met, the word *Mobilier* was raised again, and the quickened consciences of some of the members showed in their troubled talk, and walk, and countenances. A Democrat was now known to be in the case, and the Poland Investigating Committee met with closed doors. The news leaked through the cracks and keyholes. A savage speech made by James Brooks against M'Comb on the floor contemporaneously with a screed of evidence from John B. Alley under oath in the darkened Committee-room, only whetted the public interest. A cry arose for "Open doors! Less white-wash and more fumigation!"

Then the sick men who groped their way about the Capital

City would have been the pitied of men and angels but for that speech of Brooks' against the Government witness, which had closed the gates of mercy. The fatal truth, half told, came forth at last from the lips of Oakes Ames. That shovel-iron statue spoke like the sire of Fredolin, cursing his posterity.

It may be asked why James Brooks was put forward by the Crédit Mobilier people to make a speech against McComb. The fact was that Brooks, under the guise of an aristocratic and strictly honorable member of the opposition, had been robbing the Union Pacific Company all the while. He had secured from Andrew Johnson as a Democrat the appointment of Government Director of the Union Pacific railroad and in that position was not allowed to be a stockholder, or interested in any way in the corporation. But with a vicious and dishonest nature he used his power all the more to extort from the confederates stock in both the Union Pacific and Crédit Mobilier Companies, and the very bonds of the United States which he was appointed to protect. Public guilt was never less undoubtedly shown in any government. With his honors, riches, and age all to protect, it may be imagined that Brooks was more apprehensive than any living man of the consequences of an investigation. He was so nervous about the matter that he betook himself to the old newspaper mode of silencing an enemy by ruining his character. This he attempted to do before Congress came together by concerted attacks upon M'Comb, comparing him to Jim Fisk and Judge Barnard. When the Investigating Committee met with closed doors the guilty man heard almost immediately that his villainy had been put in evidence. He could not stand and wait; for he knew that now his only escape was in loud and brawling defiance. He claimed, therefore, the privilege of a personal explanation, and delivered a personal attack upon M'Comb too ingenious to be honest and too cowardly not to provoke response. M'Comb's friends at once demanded the opening of the doors in equity to a witness so grossly, and as they claimed so unjustly, maligned by a member pleading his privileges. There was an agonizing

time in Congress when the proposition was made to open the
doors and men of both parties struggled hard to keep them
close. But a paralysis had fallen upon the body. They saw
the full galleries and knew that all the country was looking in,
and although the Committee itself protested that a secret examination would be the best, it was ordained that the public
should know all about the matter.

Induced to believe that Mr. Oakes Ames would shield himself and them, several of the members sent him word or intimated in person that they wished him to exonerate them as far
as possible. For some days he seemed to desire to do so, but
being an old man, of a bluff, ingenuous nature, he finally grew
ashamed of duplicity and enraged at the evident disposition to
make him a principal and a perjurer besides. He and Mr.
Alley therefore changed face upon their dupes and friends
and corrected their statements. Mr. Colfax, Vice-President
of the United States, and Mr. Patterson, U. S. Senator from
New Hampshire, were ruined in the sequel after an agonizing
effort to perplex or compound Mr. Ames. Mr. Kelley, Mr.
Schofield, Mr. Garfield, Mr. Allison, Mr. James Wilson, commonly called "The Singed Cat" of Iowa, and one or two
others were scathed a good deal by the evidence. The Committee reported in favor of the expulsion of Brooks and Ames
from the House, and the Senate followed up the report by entertaining another investigation, whereby Senator Patterson was
named for expulsion. These proceedings did not satisfy the
public and an effort was made in the House to censure Messrs.
Kelley, Garfield, Samuel Hooper, and even Speaker Blaine.
Against the latter, Mr. Job Stevenson of Ohio hurled a bitter
piece of invective, and Mr. Speer of Pennsylvania debated the
complicity of two of the others. The whole subject was disposed of by censuring Ames and Brooks, both of whom died
of the shock and other ills in little above two months. Mr.
Patterson left the Senate by the expiration of his term, seeking
in vain afterward to have his transaction and character vindicated. Mr. Colfax went out of office morally ruined and men-

tally wrecked. He had maintained a semblance of purity and frankness for so many years of general consideration that the knowledge of his corruptibility and his painful exhibition of falsehood under oath gave the country a blow.

Some scenes in this investigation may be sketched rapidly just as they were taken in my note book at the time.

The Committee-room where the half-dozen gentlemen who had been appointed to seek out the why and wherefore of the railroad bribery met for one hour or more every forenoon is at the foot of a long flight of dark stairs which lead from the Rotunda to the floor usually called the crypt, or cellar. At the foot of these stairs, a lighted corridor, whose cheerful appearance does not deprive it of a certain dungeon-like look,—probably the effect of the consciousness of the heavy weight supported above, and of the broad and solid walls, and piers, and window-sills in view,—leads to the Committee-room.

Within the Committee-room the atmosphere and air immediately change for the better. A good grate-fire burns under a symmetrical, old fashioned mantel of white marble, above which is a mirror of the largest proportions. Opposite the mirror is a book-case filled with law-calf-bindings ; and down the floor, lengthwise between the fire and books, runs a baize table surrounded with arm-chairs. Nearest the door half-a-dozen newspaper-writers are seated around the end of this table.

At the other end is the Chairman of the investigation, Judge Luke Poland, of Vermont. Merrick and Niblack, the two Democrats, sit to the left hand of Judge Poland, and on his right is Mr. McCrary, of Iowa. These seem to be the chief members of the Committee who are paying any attention to the proceedings. McCrary, Merrick, and Poland do all the questioning.

Next to Niblack sits Henry S. M'Comb, and sometimes Judge Black and Lawyer Smithers occupy a place at his side. Mr. Smith, the official reporter, sits on the opposite side. Next to McCrary, facing M'Comb, are the two inseparable companions, Ames and Alley, the Massachusetts Dromios.

Around the chamber are half-a-dozen or dozen reporters and idlers. The Court proceeds in the most informal, but in the quietest way, and progress is made slowly.

Judge Poland looks like a French Marquis. He is a tall, aristocratic-looking old gentleman, with full white hair, and full white side-whiskers combed forward. His nose is straight and long, and his profile handsome; but, when he turns his full face, he seems to carry a mouth full of tobacco, and speaks with a sense of apprehension that some of it may spill. His method is courteous nearly to a fault, and slow to irritation; but, as there is nothing of the demagogue or sensationalist about him and as he is what he appears to be, a kind and generous old gentleman, all look with confidence to his return of the facts in their spirit. Alley began by talking down everybody, and was interrupted at no time, except when he was slavering Ames all over with praises, when Niblack said:

"Mr. Alley, how many monuments do you want to have erected to Mr. Ames?"

Persons coming into the Committee-room for the first time are wont to say:

"Who is that fine-looking man across the table?"

"Henry S. M'Comb!"

"*That* M'Comb! Why, I expected, from what Brooks said, to see a monster."

Yes, a man in the o'er ripe prime of life, alert, rosy, cordial, perceptive, and so unusually handsome as to imply a social importance chiefly, whereas there is an engine at work all the while within the man, and half-a-dozen different fly-wheels. Not a fully educated man, he compensates for it by native graces, and the acquaintance since boyhood with people of culture at home, and men of power throughout the country. In the social, intellectual, and material scale, M'Comb is the superior of anybody who has lost time seeking to impeach him.

Oakes Ames is a very large man, of the type of a Yorkshire

manufacturer, gnarled, spectacled, with great, bent shoulders, a slow walk, and prodigious limbs and feet. He will probably weigh 280 pounds, and he looks to be 6 feet 2 or 3. He has strong, coarse, brownish hair, and bristly beard around the long, sternwheeled shaft of his jaws. His forehead is low, and the nose seems to be half of the face. The eyes behind the spectacles are small, and of a slow, searching look. Ames came to Congress with the soul of a commercial traveler, and, if expelled from it, would feel no particular inconvenience or loss of self-esteem. The shovel which his trip-hammer beats into shape is scarcely harder, and, as the man grows old, he rusts, but is too rugged to decay. A monument to Oakes Ames ought to be made of scrap-iron, and John B. Alley would be the solitary mourner over it, and, unless watched, *he* would peddle away the monument piece-meal.

Ames made small bones of telling the most of what he remembered about Congressmen, and, but for Alley, he would probably have remembered considerably more.

Alley sat by his side all the while, lifting or lowering his brows suggestively, as Ames helplessly looked around at him for counsel. He was thirteen years the junior of Ames, who was nearly 70 years of age.

Alley was a shoemaker in boyhood, and he is now the proprietor of the best house in Lynn. He is proud of his money, and holds to it with the desperation of a cannibal husbanding his last corpse. He is a short, demure, white-headed man, and has an endless tongue, which testifies all manner of hearsay, and covers time with space, to the exclusion of information, and to the prejudice of more modest and less doubtful evidence.

Alley has enormously profited by Ames's contracts, and he appears in Ames's letters as the incorrigible opponent to every dividend to outsiders. He was the chief adviser to Ames's course toward M'Comb, and he is really on the spot at present as the principal and counsel of Ames. He may say, with Sir Giles Overreach:

"In being out of office, I am out of danger;
Where, if I were a Justice, besides the trouble,
I might, or out of wilfulness or error,
Run myself finely into a premunire,
And so become a prey to the informer.
No, I'll have none of it; 'tis enough I keep
Greedy at my devotion. So he serve
My purposes, let him hang, or damn, I care not!
Friendship is but a word, I must have all men
Sellers, and I the only purchaser!"

We have no remark to make upon Senator Patterson—who is a good sort of commonplace man—described by Senator Nye as "a little college professor," except to remark that New Hampshire is the jobbingest State in the Union, and this city is overrun with its spawn. They are claim agents, "counsellors," strikers, land rats, and water rats.

At the latter part of the week the meek-faced Boyer of the town of Norristown, where Hartranft hails from, might have been seen moving around the hotels. He and Brooks belonged together to the Union Pacific Railroad Committee, and both are implicated, Boyer as trustee, and mayhap thereby hangs a tale.

Does the Democratic party wonder why it possesses no confidence? Here are a Democratic editor at the metropolis and a Pennsylvania Democrat, both Congressmen, tied up in national securities, and of course the intimidated creatures of the Administration side. During the last campaign, when the Greeley journals were pushing the Crédit Mobilier scandal, Brooks was running around the Fifth Avenue Hotel nightly saying "M'Comb's character is bad on the street!" He kept up this senile speech, and alleged that the Crédit Mobilier talk was not righteous ammunition for the canvass, thereby doing his part to cripple the candidates. Greeley is in his grave, but Brooks lives. What a commentary is this on the value of life!

A fat man, square everywhere below the head and outside of the heart, and named Bushnell, came before the committee last week to say that his children's children would honor him for building the Pacific railway. The correspondent had no difficulty in putting this person down as one of the "stalls" for Ames and Alley.

Unless we are incorrectly posted, this very person gave his check for two hundred shares Crédit Mobilier ($20,000) on a bank where he had no funds, and he palavered the check along, saying he would attend to it, arrange it, &c., until he had actually collected all the stock, bonds, and cash dividends for two years, just as if the check had been paid. The reason was that he was necessary to Ames, Alley, and Dillon. Moreover, as gossip in the committee-room says, $112,000 worth of Government certificates and $400,000 worth of first mortgage bonds, (partly charged to one Shaw, according to the notable book-keeping of the Crédit Mobilier,) which were traced into Bushnell's hands years ago, are yet unaccounted for by him. This man, nevertheless, says that Congressmen ought to have moral pluck and admit their Crédit Mobilier, and he says that $50,000 worth of his stock in the Crédit Mobilier was recently thrown out of bank on account of the present investigation. Which bank? The same he gave the $20,000 check upon?

Bushnell struck us as a blower. When we heard him talk we wondered whether his monument—they all expect monuments and "children's children"—had not better be constructed on the pneumatic principle, of wind.

For the half dozen or eight members of Congress who, in a moment of weakness or temptation, accepted this Crédit Mobilier stock from Oakes Ames, there would be no severe expressions from anybody except for their precipitate denials. Mr. Schofield merits no sympathy on the ground of meekness; for during the campaign he was stigmatizing this and other charges as a "Greeley lie." Mr. Colfax's situation is most pitiable of all; for he denied outright that he had any stock, denounced correspondents for merely intimating as much, and yet, by the testimony, seems to have done the sinister service for the

Crédit Mobilier of "blocking the game" of an investigation and inciting even the pernicious Ames to exclaim:

"In Colfax's case don't you think the investment paid?"

And then that idiotic explanation read before the committee by Mr. Colfax; that assumption of childishness; that touch of the immaculate conception when he still professed not to know what the Mobilier was; that shallow beseeching of somebody to cross-examine him! The man disarms us by his littleness. Go, Schuyler Colfax and let us forget thee! This stage of public life is too large for such puppetry as thine.

Mr. Dawes has a robust explanation, which acquits him of anything mean except his evasive denial. Mr. Blaine was too sagacious to sell out his prospects so cheaply. Of two or three other members, Ames took advantage and turned their poverty into a public temptation nearly disastrous to their reputations. Mr. Kelley is one of these men; but in view of Ames' testimony that he is still the latter's debtor for $1,000, how unnecessary was this explanation of Mr. Kelley:

"I have never owned a share of stock in the Crédit Mobilier of America, nor has any member of my family, either directly or by the intervention of a trustee or agent."

Well did Hamlet say that playing on such stops was easy as lying.

In General Garfield's case Mr. Ames seems to have taken advantage of a man in distress, and to have secured a loan by an entangling investment. As soon as Garfield discovered the cheat he returned the money.

Mr. James Wilson of Iowa, who has been doing a good deal of something in this city since he left Congress, and who was so touchy as to his honor that he made a great speech once in the House, saying that he had never received any imputation but one, and who proved his peace of mind by persecuting newspaper writers, this friend of Billy McGarrahan, has been the subject of inquiry in this case, and we suggest that he now accept one of those three Cabinet positions which the President offered him. He would seem to need some such extension of confidence!

Mr. Allison has made himself mysterious by a denial. When Peter denies his Crédit Mobilier the cock crows thrice for dividends!

Henry Wilson has been the victim of a wedding gift. At the fine old gentleman's silver wedding, the anniversary of honorable domestic years, the Ames gang strode in and put Crédit Mobilier stock on the plate. To defame a well-spent life by such a testimonial proves the brutality of this crowd. Why did they not put their hands in their pockets and subscribe any honest currency which they might have possessed? As it was, they might as well have given another man's gold watch to the old couple.

The youthful Painter, who has been hanging on the verge of the newspaper profession for ten years or more, affecting to know how to spell, and proving that he affects it only to job, appears in this case as a striker for Crédit Mobilier stock. He not only got twenty shares, but, says Ames, "was in a high dudgeon that he did not get fifty." He had failed to strike Durant for this amount, and appears to have got it out of Ames only by proffering his malignant services to defame M'Comb.

The three persons who appear to constitute the central directory of the mortal remains of the Crédit Mobilier are Messrs. Ames, Alley, and Brooks. Mr. Brooks' speech in Congress against M'Comb has reacted upon himself. We leave him to deal with the evidence which has developed since his speech, and if it be brought home to him that, as a Government director, he took interest in the Union Pacific railroad, and as a Democrat demanded stock to "take care of the Democratic side," he should receive that generosity he meted out to M'Comb. On cowardice and cruelty sympathy is thrown away!

Mr. Alley has labored very hard here to prove himself a parsimonious toady and an example of grasping contemptibility. To look at him and hear him talk is a surfeit. He has voluntarily put himself beside the principal in this matter, and his screed upon M'Comb was that of a vulgar slanderer whose ignorance could not estimate the effect of a coarse action.

As to Mr. Bingham, who met the charge with that old-fashioned shaking of the head and jabber about a licentious press, reading meanwhile a piece of blunt acknowledgment, he fell over his own ingenuity directly ; for he wished it made a part of the record that he had introduced a bill in Congress obligating the Company to protect the national interest. A correspondent promptly forwarded a question as to whether the said security for the Government's interest was not appended to Bingham's bill in the Senate and returned to the House in the form of an amendment ? Mr. B. slunk a perceptible slink and confessed the soft impeachment.

Mr. Bingham then qualified his rhetorical allusion to "a licentious press," by saying that he meant by it only the editor, who attributed to him $20,000 worth of profits in the Crédit Mobilier.

Let us see.

The dividends in Crédit Mobilier were eleven hundred per cent. prior to 1870. If Mr. Bingham got but $6,500 he ought to bring Oakes Ames to account, for the man Bushnell says that any member who had the stock promised to him ought to demand it.

Go, John A. Bingham, and take Bushnell's principals at their word. They sold you for a Chinaman and gave you but one-third of what you were entitled to.

We looked at Bingham giving his testimony before that meek and courteous chairman, old Judge Poland, and recalled the time when Bingham himself, conducting the McGarrahan investigation, tyrannized over witnesses in the interest of the Micks and O'Shilleys. Poland, mavourneen ! Thou art nothing less than a gentleman of the old school.

In our judgment Messrs. Dawes and Garfield came off victoriously in this matter. The miserable Ames, who seems to have been a public money lender, took advantage of Garfield when in need of money to tie him up in Crédit Mobilier. Of Mr. Dawes he took advantage when the latter wanted to buy some Cedar Rapids stock.

Ames richly deserved expulsion, and without it all this investigation would have been for naught. The following railway jobs he conducted successfully through Congress, and some of them were accompanied with better endowments than the Union Pacific: namely, Sioux City, Iowa Falls and Sioux City, Cedar Rapids, Union Pacific, and finally that magnificently endowed Eastern Division of The Union Pacific. He came to Congress to job in railways, and gave all his time to it.

Mr. Glenni W. Scofield's statement has a measley and hardly convalescent look. When a man says he "does not remember receiving any dividends" and does not remember what his attitude was on legislation affecting the Union Pacific railroad, we regard him in the words of the same poet we have quoted, as follows:

> "With sadness that is calm, not gloom,
>   We learn to think upon him;
> With meekness that is gratefulness
>   On Oakes Ames who hath won him.
> Who suffered once those dividends
>   To public shame to blind him,
> But gently led the blind along
>   Where Jerry Black could find him."

The ugly fact has come out, that Jacob Harlan received $10,000 from Thomas C. Durant, that chief of sinners and gallants, to elect himself Senator from Iowa. And mark! Harlan had been the Secretary of the Interior during the time that the Union Pacific wanted work done in that department. If we are to believe the gossip on the street, Mr. Harlan got from this interest not merely $10,000, but $30,000.

But where is the Rev. Dr. Newman, who wrote the circular letter and had it lithographed with the caption: "Dear Sir and Brother," and asked the suffrages and lobby devotion of all the Methodist preachers in Iowa for Harlan? Did he get none of the Crédit Mobilier, or was his portion passed through his countenance and melted to brass to swell the cadence of the chimes? If we were a Senator we would hoist the reverend lobbyists, at any rate, out of our wing.

James Brooks would have received plenty of sympathy had he respected another man's character. When a man plays it fine he must have some of the *naïveté* of an artist to give dignity to his misses. Mr. Brooks has changed his flag-ship two or three times during the action. Once we heard him appeal to the Deity in a rather blasphemous way to say that he had never had a share's worth of interest in the Crédit Mobilier or Union Pacific.

On the whole we sum him up to be a *parvenu*, who has made most of his money in this sort of way, and has dissipated his nerve. His political positions have generally been those of a pompous dough-face, extenuating the rebellion, while filching from the Union. He subscribed $10,000 to the Union Pacific Railroad, and has drawn $300,000 from it, including his commission as the salesman of the Pacific Railroad telegraph line. He is reputed to exist now as a director in the Union Pacific by the use of the shares he received as dividends on Crédit Mobilier. He opposed the Union Pacific road until he was "let in," when he became its oilman, and greased the Democratic side, or professed to do so.

It was an awful picture to see this sickly man examining Tom Durant as to the high patriotic necessity of the Union Pacific Railroad, while feebly requesting old Judge Poland to lug in Jeems, Lazarus, and Fagin to prove M·Comb not a credible witness. Death and reputation seemed at work in our friend, and Durant so sympathized with him that he said :

"By Jupiter! I must let up on that man. I don't want any male corpses laid at my door-post untimely."

Durant did let up, covered Brooks' tracks as much as he dared, and proved himself the magnanimous materialistic Bohemian that he is.

No two confessions were alike. Henry Wilson sentimentalized his error over by expressing his notion of the vileness of imputations. He called his Maker and himself face to face in his closet, and attempted to butter Oakes Ames over with humble praise.

Henry Wilson, beware of the fate of Schuyler Colfax! Hypocrisy in the Vice-President is a garment of gauze. The oft iteration of poverty as an excuse for simony becomes at last disgusting. This country calls on no man to be an ass in order to serve it with spirit; and to perceive and apprehend a case of bribery bottomed on public robbery is the duty of a Senator.

When a man has been ten or fifteen years in continuous public life, and still affects not to know what the Crédit Mobilier is, we set him down as a fraud. If he does not know, away with him for stupidity; and if he does not know any more, while mysteriously receiving the dividends, we classify him with Cowper, of whom the poet said :

> " That while in darkness he remained,
>   Unconscious of the guiding,
> All things provided came without
>   The sweet sense of providing."

Poverty is not a plea in rebuttal of a direct charge of peculation, for it may be the concomitant of profligacy. To talk about the deceased members of one's family in a whining way, and offer to sell out one's goods for thirty-five hundred dollars, seem to us to be overrating the credulities of men. Mr. Wilson bought that Crédit Mobilier stock in January, 1868, and parted with it at the close of the same year. Now, between these dates above, four hundred per cent. dividends were declared.

Mr. Wilson says that if ten thousand dollars were due him, he would not touch a cent. of it. Where does this leave Messrs. Bingham and Hooper? Ah! Messieurs in Congress, " thus conscience doth make cowards of us all."

We heard Wm. D. Kelley's long-winded harangue, delivered with all the resonance of an unending tune in a negro meeting-house, with compassion not wholly unmixed with wonder.

A person who pretends to be the great statesman of the period, and to know whys and wherefores, from the Sutro tunnel up to sublimated potash, and to be still so stupid that he did not know the difference between a loan and a purchase,

is a candidate for the asylum. Where is the shame of these
people, to sit in the presence of such satirists upon human
nature as Ames and Alley, and tell these forgetful reminiscences? Mr. Kelley makes a great point that two thousand
dollars could not buy him. We do not know about that! The
picture he drew to the point of satiety about his renewals,
protests, mortgages, etc., did not reduce the timeliness of any
two thousand dollars. He certainly made himself appear
a sufficiently impecunious victim of Oakes Ames. Said Mr.
Kelley: "For largely more than a quarter of a century I have
advocated the Pacific Railway."

Let us see.

We acquired California in 1847, twenty-five years ago. Did
Mr. Kelley start the project of a Pacific road before we had
any population or right on that coast? These touches of
rhetorical egotism are entirely unmeaning. Mr. Kelley is
neither a saint or a hero, and we prefer to let him slip with
the apology that "Oakes Ames did tempt me and I did eat."

While Congressmen wriggle and writhe and say that it was
noble-minded to own Crédit Mobilier stock, read the letters of
Oakes Ames! He expresses his opinion of these men, and
shows why he wanted them in the contracting company. With
the stock in their pockets they were his. And here is a singular passage in one of his letters:

"In view of Washburne's move to investigate us I go for
one bond dividend in full. I understand that the opposition
to it comes from John B. Alley."

Now, why did Alley object? Because he had parted with
his stock!

He had sold 250 shares Crédit Mobilier at 8200 per share to
Peter Butler of Boston, December 5, 1867. He had expected
to pick up more stock for less money, but he found in New
York that nobody would sell. He therefore availed himself of
his position as trustee to resist a dividend. Durant, knowing
Alley's rapacious motive, proposed to buy him up, which he
did, as the following receipt will show. Alley thus got 250

shares of stock, and of course he changed tactics and received a dividend:

(Copy.)

T. C. Durant having sold to me a call to take from him within ten days from this date two hundred and fifty shares of stock of the Crédit Mobilier of America, in case I do not avail myself of that privilege I promise to return to said Durant the memorandum conveying said privilege on his return to me of this paper.

(Signed), JOHN B. ALLEY.

New York, December 12, 1867.

THE MANNER OF RENDERING TESTIMONY.

Our opinion of the committee conducting this investigation is enhanced by its behavior during the last week. Incisive questions were proposed by McCrary and Niblack. Judge Poland, whose error is slowness, and who examined these speculators as if they were of the blood royal, also addressed some pertinent inquiries to the witnesses. The question asked by McCrary of Kelley as to the tone of the letters of Oakes Ames, was of the sort which should have been put among these proceedings more frequently. Mr. Merrick has preserved watchful and discriminating behavior during all this investigation, which probably accounted for Bingham's blustering way of reading his evidence to Merrick, as if the latter had intentions on him.

There have been too many statements made in these proceedings—written statements, not in the form of legitimate testimony, and artfully contrived to evade admissions. On some of these there has been no cross-examination whatever. Colonel M'Comb stood up and answered orally, and took no advantage of the lax rules of evidence accorded here. A flagrant case of libel, in the form of testimony, not wholly unlike forswearing—to call it by no graver name—was that of John B. Alley. His evidence was prepared by R. C. McMurtrie of Philadelphia, a lawyer always resident in the Quaker City. Mr. Alley said that he had prepared his testimony, and submitted it to a distinguished New England jurist, who had told him that to omit a word or a line of it would be to his prejudice.

"Who is that New England jurist?" was asked by Judge Merrick.

After a pause Alley replied:

"Mr. McMurtrie."

As Alley was under oath when he said that his adviser was a distinguished New England jurist, and as he named McMurtrie, never a New Englander, where is Alley's veracity? And four-fifths of the said testimony was mere slander, such as such a creature could pour out on M'Comb.

P. S.—SATURDAY'S TESTIMONY.

"Very eloquently said, Mr. Wilson!" remarked Judge Niblack satirically, after James Wilson had quoted several thousand words laudatory of the Union Pacific road, and its construction "amidst bands of hostile Indians."

Everybody who has passed over the Union Pacific road knows that no Indians are to be seen, and that the construction is over gently rising slopes and acclivities nearly as adaptable to track-laying as the level prairies. The only startling thing about the road is its crookedness, after reaching the three hundreth mile, where Durant ceased building and Ames began. The new crowd, commencing their career with consistent rapacity, made the road serpentine, and often bent it back on itself at level and fertile places to get more land and more bonds.

Wilson's testimony, as we understood it, made him claim a great deal of credit for saving the Government half the charge of mail transportation over the Union Pacific railroad, whereas the original bill saved the Government the whole charge.

Mr. Wilson said that he had made $3,000 on his stock, the full salary of a member of Congress for about eight months, or all the working time of Congress for a whole year. He did not remember any dividends, and the manner of the sale looked very awkward. Mr. Wilson is now in this city, seeking to locate railroad lands about one hundred miles off the line of the Burlington and Missouri railroad. Judge Poland pertinently asked whether Wilson sold his stock to qualify himself to be a Government director of the Union Pacific Railroad, which he is at present. This evidence was full of solicitude for the Government twenty years hence. The quantity of singe about this cat amounts to a sheepskin.

Boyer, the young chap from Norristown, was in Congress just four years, between 1865–69, and got 100 shares of Crédit Mobilier (25 being for *Mrs.* Boyer). He was on the Pacific Railroad committee with Brooks, and at 1100 per cent. increase, his profits were $110,000. The New York *Nation* says the profits were 1500 per cent., making, if true, $150,000 profit. Pretty good for the young fellow by the name of Boyer! The Norristowners will have a little family legend on this sudden wealth for many generations. This was mere plunder from the Treasury and the public lands of the United States. Yet " he had the right to do it."

Mr. Colfax came with counsel, and again and again sought to break the rampart of the old man's confession.

" You've got the stock, and you know it," said Ames, " So what's the use of getting around it ?"

" How could I own it and not be aware of it ?" said Colfax, " Why didn't people tell me ?"

" Why," said Ames, " nobody ever told me I owned my own hat !"

The fact was that the Vice-President had taken a quantity of the Mobilier Stock, drawn the dividend, and put them in bank, so that the bank-book, the cheques paid by the Sergeant-at-Arms, and the testimony of Oakes Ames made a complete, serried, and simultaneous narrative. It was irrefutable. It broke down the dignity of his office. It was crushing.

To a young man concealed on a committee-room sofa, enter Oakes and John B. Alley, diligently toadied by two newspaper-reporters.

Ames grunts, and fills a whole leather sofa. Alley takes a

chair, grunts, and stows away his coat-tails, to save them from wear and tear.

Alley : "Oh, dear ! Ames, I knew that great heart of yours would get you into trouble. I knew that great heart of yours would be our ruin. I told you that your generosity was too abundant, and your impulses too noble. Didn't I tell you so ? I want these gentlemen to hear it said."

Ames : "Oh, Alley ! I can't remember everything you remind me of. I believe you did say something of that description."

Alley : "You hear him admit it, gentlemen. Ah ! Mr. Ames has a foolish, noble heart. He wants to be doing good, even when it is dangerous to do so. That scoundrel M'Comb now gloats in his distress. Mr. Ames is a persecuted hero, and, as I have often said before, deserves a monument as high as the shaft on Bunker Hill."

Here enters an old whining Virginia Railroad man.

Old Whiney : "Meister Ames, I called to see if you wasn't going to help me out with your subscription to the Catoctin & Occoquan Railroad."

Ames (very gruff) : "No. Pretty time to ask me for a subscription. Go to M'Comb. He's got plenty of money. He is ruining me. I believe he's a friend of yours ?"

Old Whiney : "No, Mr. Ames, I don't think highly of Mr. M'Comb. He refused to help me with my enterprise."

Ames : "What's that ? M'Comb's a d—d scoundrel, is he ? Alley, remember that !"

Alley : "Yes, Mr. Ames, I believed, by looking at Whiney's intelligent head, that such must be his opinion. He says that M'Comb is a scoundrel, gentlemen " (to the reporters).

Ames : "Whiney, come around and see me to-night. Maybe I can let you have ten thousand or so in your enterprise. But remember to remark to your friends that, in your opinion, M'Comb is a scoundrel."

We need not prolong these little sketches. After a very long examination, conducted with all frankness by both the

Poland Committee and the Wilson Committee, the former reported Brooks and Ames for expulsion, but made no recommendation in the cases of the other members, whose statements they declared to be painfully contradictory. A great debate ensued, lasting more than two days, and heard by enormous audiences in the galleries and on the floors. The corrupt interest triumphed, and Brooks and Ames were merely censured. An attempt was made to censure also Messrs. Hooper of Massachusetts, Kelley of Pennsylvania, Garfield of Ohio, Bingham of Ohio, Dawes, Butler, and others. However, Congress, satisfied that the people lacked the interest and indignation to make it any penalty, not only laid the whole matter on the table, but, as if to show that corruption was the organic law of the land and of the American Congressman, immediately turned about and increased the pay of a member nearly one-third, and made the provisions of the act apply to the Congress just expiring. This most scandalous action was worthy of a body of men which has become diseased and corrupt by the advantages of war, and has wholly lost its own self-respect and the confidence of the country.

CHAPTER XVII.

June 15th, 1800, the public offices were opened at Washington, and Congress assembled there for the first time, November 22d. The laws of Virginia and Maryland were extended over the portions ceded by those States, which constituted respectively the counties of Alexandria and Washington, both of which had jurisdiction on the intermediate Potomac river. A court of three judges, with U. S. Circuit Court powers, was provided for, and also an orphans' court.

February 11th, 1800, while a snow storm raged without, and intense partisan activity and bitterness went on within, the House of Representatives proceeded to ballot for the successor of John Adams. One member was carried to the Hall in a litter, and the ballot-box brought to his side. Express-riders were kept in relay from Washington to Richmond, and one Session of Congress continued for thirty-one hours. Jefferson and Burr were both in the city. On the thirty-sixth ballot, February 17th, Jefferson was elected.

Washington was first so called explicitly by the three commissioners—Johnson, Stuart, and Carroll—in a letter addressed to Major L' Enfant, from Georgetown, September 9th, 1791.

Under the first board of commissioners—Johnson, Carroll, and Stuart—who kept in office until 1794, there were sold 6,227 Washington lots, for $541,384. The next board—Scott,

Carroll, and Thornton—sold 83 lots for $50,217. The third board—Scott, White, and Thornton—sold 101 lots for $41,081. About $117,000 failed to be collected. In 1802 the board was dissolved, and the office of Superintendent created, and Thomas Monroe appointed. He served until 1817, and sold 288 lots for $51,652. Colonel Samuel Lane succeeded Monroe, and sold 69 lots for $21,128.

The early commissioners held themselves accountable to nobody but the President, and their returns were short $126,-000, as late as 1825. Mr. Monroe was also reported derelict, and Lane failed to satisfy a committee of the Eighteenth Congress. The next Superintendent was Joseph Elgan, who had better business habits than his predecessors, and under him both the Capitol and President's house were fully restored. In 1825 there remained unsold 3,406 lots belonging to the United States.

Under the commissioners in the first eleven years of the city, the total expenditures were $900,857, of which $670,000 were gifts and cash receipts. The President's house had then cost $240,000 and the Capitol $880,000. The first Treasury and War Office cost nearly $90,000; and two bridges over Rock Creek, and one over the Tiber, $8,000. Two wharves at Rock Creek, and on the Eastern branch, had cost $11,000. The total expenditure for salaries, maps, office-rent, etc., had been $90,-000, on the part of the Commissioners.

By the report of the Commissioners for the city, presented in the early months of Jefferson's administration, we find that soon after the 15th of May, 1801, there were 191 brick houses finished, 408 wooden houses, and altogether 95 brick houses unfinished, and 41 wooden houses unfinished.

The town of Carrollsburg has been mentioned as preceding the City of Washington, on a part of the site. Carrollsburg was situated between the Eastern branch and St. James's creek. Its streets, which were parallel with the river, in the order of recession from it, were Short, North, Union, Middle, and St. James; crosswise, they were called, going down-stream, No. 1, 2, 3, etc., to 8.

The most notable purchases of lots at the early sales—October, 1791—December, 1794—were:

Tobias Lea, whose purchases amounted to £572;

Peter Charles l'Enfant, who paid but £25 upon his lot, and the remaining £198 was settled by the City of Washington;

Wm. Augustine Washington, £225;

Samuel Blodgett, who bought nearly to the amount of £2,000;

Daniel Carroll of Duddington, who paid £555 for a shipping seat, near the mouth of the Eastern branch;

David Burns, who picked up, for £350, two of the most valuable lots now to be found, right opposite the Treasury;

James Hoban, architect of the President's house, who purchased to the amount of £900, on City Hall Hill, and Capitol Hill;

Thomas Sim Lee, who bought on the flats below the President's, at low rates, and in small parcels;

George Washington, who gave £515 for four lots, on deep water, Eastern branch, one square behind Buzzards' point, and £400 for two lots between the subsequent Observatory and Rock Creek;

James Greenleaf, the greatest of all purchasers, who bought to the amount of more than £140,000, or about 6,000 lots, nearly all at Greenleaf point, and on the Eastern branch;

William Thornton, designer of the Capitol, who paid £200 for his lot opposite Observatory hill.

Greenleaf paid about £25,000 on his lots, and they passed over to Morris & Nicholson who died insolvent. This was the Robert Morris, the financier of the Revolution.

The ground where the U. S. Treasury stands, was the property of Thomas Davidson, who purchased it from the Commissioners, between October, 1792, and January, 1794. In time it came again into the hands of the United States.

Where the Post-office building now stands, was Blodgett's Hotel, where the Thirteenth Congress met at President Madison's call, September 19, 1817.

On Pennsylvania Avenue, opposite the Metropolitan Hotel,

formerly stood the *National Intelligencer* office when Cockburn destroyed its type and presses.

Between January, 1795, and January, 1800, we find these notable purchases:

George Washington, who bought the lot on Capitol Hill, where the two residences belonging to his widow remained;

Walter Stewart, paying $17,823; Solomon Etting and Thomas Corcoran.

Between 1800 and 1821, we find the following purchasers: Daniel Carroll, of Duddington; Charles W. Goldsborough, Jonathan Elliott, Richard Cutts, who bought nearly $14,000 worth of property outlying the White House reservation.

Much has been said about the cupidity of the rich proprietors of land on the site of Washington, but John Law, a distinguished citizen who had come to the place in 1800, charged in the year 1820, that the city was made too vast by the politicians in order to gratify their own cupidity, and tempt as many farm holders to give up half their property as possible. "To compel this the principal public buildings were widely separated; no central points were designated at which improvements might commence, and gradually diverge, and therefore sufficient money was thrown away by men of enterprise on remote situations capriciously selected, to have founded a very respectable town in the beginning. The squares were also injudiciously subdivided into merely building lots, and improvidently sold to get money for public buildings, instead of being parceled out with space for shrubbery and gardens. Hence," said Mr. Law, "a loose and disconnected population was scattered over the city, and instead of a flourishing town the stranger who visited us, saw for years a number of detached villages, having no common interest, and furnishing little mutual support, hardly sustaining a market, and divided by great public reservations."

William Wirt, who went to school at Georgetown during th revolutionary war, says that he always understood that town

had taken its name from George Beall, who lived there, and
whose daughter married the chief of the Magruders, (Wirt
says McGregors) fugitives from Culloden to the borders of the
future American Capital.

A dispassionate English traveler (Weld), who visited the
site in 1796, relates that Georgetown contained about 250
houses, and Alexandria double the number, and that there were
in Washington five thousand denizens, including artificers who
formed by far the largest part of that number. The greatest
number of houses at any one place was at Greenleaf's point,
which divided public opinion, as to its eligibility for trade, with
the shores of the deeper waters of the Eastern branch. "Numbers of strangers," says this guarded authority, " are continually
passing and repassing through a place which affords such an
extensive field for speculation." If the houses already built had
been placed together, a very respectable town would have appeared upon the landscape, but some were building near Georgetown, some around the Capitol, some adjacent to the President's
House, and the solitary unofficial construction of imposing
appearance was a brick hotel, ornamented with stone, on the
site of the present General Post-Office, "large, just roofed in,
and anything but beautiful." The private houses were all
plain buildings, and most of them built upon a speculation and
still empty. The President's House had been " rushed up,"
was nearly done, and was undoubtedly the handsomest building in the country, while the Capitol was but a little way above
its foundations. No other public building had been begun, and
although the published regulations required all houses to be of
brick or stone, numbers of wooden habitations had been built,
despite the caution that they might not be allowed to stand.
"Notwithstanding all that has been done at the city and the
large sums of money which have been expended, there are
numbers of people in the United States living to the north of
the Potomac, particularly in Philadelphia, who are still very
adverse to the removal of the seat of government thither and
are doing all in their power to check the progress of the build-

ings in the city, and to prevent the Congress from meeting there at the appointed time."

The first account in book form of the District of Columbia, was written by Washington's Aide, Colonel Tobias Leon; the second book was soon afterward published as far from Washington as the city of Paris, by Dr. Warden, and it gives some interesting particulars of early times at the little seat of republican government. From this book* we learn that Mr. Villard, afterwards a victim of the Scioto Company, first established the military depot at Greenleaf's point, which was full of Greenleaf's tumbling houses; that Blodgett's hotel cost $36,000, besides the freestone which the Government gave him, and it was built by lottery. It was bought by the Government in 1810, for $10,000. Dr. Franklin, a native of the West Indies, applied $3,000 to fit it up for a Patent Office and museum; that the Great Falls locks took 100 workmen two years to build them; they are 100 feet long, 12 broad, and 18 deep. The canal at the point is 1 mile long, 6 feet deep, 25 feet wide, and descends 75 feet by five locks. Relics of these old locks remain (1873) on the farm of Caleb Cushing, on the Virginia side of the Great Falls. The subsequent Chesapeake and Ohio Canal, is quite a different affair.

Dr. Warden says that in Madison's administration, "Nearly one-half the population is of Irish origin. The laboring class is chiefly Irish, and many of them have no acquaintance with the English language. * * *

The President's house resembled Leinster house in Dublin. * * *

The (old) Patent Office was constructed according to the plans of J. Hoban, Esq., who gained a prize for that of the President's house. * * *

Mr. Law, brother of Lord Ellenborough, had proposed to

---

* The title of this book is: A Chirographical and Statistical description of the District of Columbia, the seat of the General Government of the United States: Paris: Smith, Publisher, Rue Montmorency, 1816. By D. B. Warden, Ex-Consul. It is dedicated to Mrs. Custis.

establish packet-boats to run between the Tiber creek and the Navy Yard on the cross-town canal.   *   *   *

The first Long bridge cost $96,000, and was opposed by the Goergetowners, as injurious to their ferry."

Thus for the communicative Warden who proceeds with many other matters of interest. He tells us that "Benjamin King, English, was the first mechanical director of the Navy Yard, at a salary of $2,000 a year, and that frigates built there cost, originally, from $70,000 to $220,000."   *   *   *

Two academies were established as early as 1806; of the first, Rev. Robert Elliot was the principal—a native of Ireland and educated at Glasgow University.

At Georgetown there was a female boarding-school, kept by Madam Du Chevray, a native of France.   *   *   *

The leading country seats were Parrot's and Peters's.   *   *

Toxhall's cannon foundry stood one mile above Georgetown, the proprietor being an Englishman whose machinery was made by one Glasgow, a Scotchman. It employed 30 workmen, chiefly emigrants. "A cannon was lately cast at this foundry, throwing a 100 pound ball, to which was given the name of Columbiad."

The Georgetown bridges are described by Warden thus : One is of three arches, and is 135 feet long and 36 feet broad ; the other is 650 yards further up stream, and is supported by piles ; it is 280 feet long and 18 wide. A daily packet boat ran between Alexandria and Georgetown. So muddy was the latter place, that strangers described Georgetown as houses without streets ; Washington, streets without houses.

Robert Sutcliff, a Quaker merchant of Sheffield, who visited Washington, in Jefferson's second term, and published a book, describes the watchmen of Alexandria blowing horns all night as they made their rounds, the excellence of Gadsby's inn, and the plentiful Quakers in Virginia and Maryland. He had for friends "T. M., of Sandy Springs—who was employed (1805) to fill up the deep channel of the Patowmack, on the south side of Mason's island, in order to turn the stream of that river to the side next to Georgetown," and Dr. Thornton and General Mason. He wrote hopefully of everything.

Francis Ashbury wrote, March 12, 1815: " I behold the ruins of the Capitol and the President's house; the Navy Yard, we burned ourselves. Oh, war! war!" Here are some of his diary notes, previously: " We crossed over into Maryland at Georgetown. Surely the roads are bad!" " O, the clay! O, the insolvent' roads. Obliged to wait an hour at Georgetown ferry. At Montgomery Court House, I found a decent, attentive congregation, in a house as well contrived and fitted for religious worship as any I have seen" (1801).

Tom. Moore, the poet, at the age of 25, came to Washington in the Summer of 1804, and " spent near a week with Mr. and Mrs. Merry, the family of the English minister. They presented him at the levee of President Jefferson, whom he found sitting with General Dearborn, and one or two others, and in his usually homely costume, comprising slippers and Connemara stockings, in which Mr. Merry had been received by him—much to that formal minister's horror —when waiting upon him in full dress to deliver his credentials." Moore wrote a great deal of ridicule for the few days he spent at the Federal seat, and addressed his mother from Baltimore, saying the roads and the stage he took northward from the Capital were " of the most infamous description." Moore gave in a note to his Epistle to Thomas Hume, his prosaic idea of the city in 1804:

" Most of the public buildings have been utterly suspended. The hotel is already a ruin ; a great part of the roof has fallen in, and the rooms are left to be occupied gratuitously by the miserable Scotch and Irish emigrants. The President's house, a very noble structure, is by no means suited to the philosophical humility of its present possesor, who inhabits but a corner of the mansion himself, and abandons the rest to a state of uncleanly desolation. This grand edifice is encircled by a very rude paling, through which a common rustic stile introduces the visitor to the first man in America. The private buildings exhibit the same characteristic display of arrogant speculation and premature ruin."

The following are some of Moore's oft-quoted rhymes upon the Capital at that date:

> . "While yet upon Columbia's rising brow
>   The showy smile of young presumption plays,
>   * * 'tis heartless speculative ill,
>   All youth's transgressions with all ages chill."

> "Even here already patriots learn to steal
>   Their private perquisites from public weal,
>   And guardians of the conntry's sacred fire,
>   Like Afric's priests, let out the flame for hire."

> "In fancy, now, beneath the twilight gloom,
>   Come, let me lead thee o'er the second Rome
>   Where tribunes rule, where dusky Davi bow,
>   And what was Goose creek once is Tiber now;
>   This embryo Capital, where fancy sees
>   Squares in morasses, obelisks in trees
>   Which second-sighted seers, even now adorn
>   With shrines unbuilt and heroes yet unborn."

Moore then pays his respects to the mighty river, and landscape gracing a race

> "Of weak barbarians swarming o'er its breast
>   Like vermin gendered on the lion's crest."

The poet at this distance has grown relatively small as his impatient opinion of a city just begun. Goose creek *is* Tiber now, occupying a rank not inferior in North America to the Tiber over the ancient world.

The roads in the State of Maryland leading to Washington, says Isaac Weld, writing in 1795, " are worse than in any State in the Union; indeed, so very bad are they that on going from Elton to the Susquehanna ferry, the driver had frequently to call to the passengers in the stage to lean out of the carriage, first at one side, then at the other, to prevent it from oversetting in the deep ruts." He also describes the " execrable roads from the Susquehanna to Baltimore, the unpaved streets of Baltimore itself nearly impassible with water and stiff, yellow clay, and the road thence to Washington, where a sulky will sink up to the very boxes;" and adds: " General Washington, a short time before was stopped in the same place where I was engulfed, his carriage sinking so deep in the mud that it was found necessary to send to a neighboring house for ropes and poles to extricate it."

Weld shows the sizes of the other cities of America, in 1796, to be as follows :

" Lancaster, the largest of the interior towns, contained 900 houses in 1796 ; Newport, R. I., 1,000 ; no other town between Boston and New York, above 500 ; Albany, 1,100 ; Trenton, 200 ; Harrisburg, 300 ; New York City 40,000 people ; Baltimore 16,000 people ; Wilmington, Del., 600 houses ; Philadelphia, 50,000 people."

The wharf at the foot of 17th Street, mouth of the Tiber, was provided for as long ago as 1806. A warehouse to contain 600 hogsheads of tobacco was a feature of the city 40 years ago, on square 801, Eastern Branch, as it is shown in old views of the city.

We derive from the Commissioners' reports, in Adams's administration, the reason of the early failure of Greenleaf, Nicholson, and Morris, the greatest purchasers of land and the ablest speculators on the site.

This first report of the Commissioners says :

" No sales took place deserving attention until the 23d December, 1793, when a contract was made with Robert Morris and James Greenleaf, for the sale of six thousand lots, averaging five thousand two hundred and sixty-five square feet each, at the rate of eighty dollars per lot, payable in seven equal annual installments, without interest, commencing the first of May, 1794, and with condition of building twenty brick houses annually, two stories high and covering twelve hundred square feet each, and with the further condition that they should not sell any lots previous to the first of January, 1796, but on condition of erecting on every third lot one such house within four years from the time of sale. This contract was afterwards modified by an agreement of 24th April, 1794, by which the payment of eighty thousand dollars, and the erecting the first-mentioned houses, should rest on the joint bond of the said Morris and Greenleaf, and of John Nicholson ; and that one thousand lots should be conveyed to the said Morris and Greenleaf D, which was accordingly done."

" Notwithstanding the favorable prospect which this transaction for a time, afforded," say they to the President, " the scene soon changed. The purchasers not only failed to pay the installment which became due in May, 1795, but early in that year discontinued the buildings which they had commenced under their contract, and on which very little progress has since been made."

It was therefore determined to solicit the patronage of Congress, which was done in the year 1796, by a memorial from the Commissioners stating the affairs of the Federal Seat, in as clear a light as circumstances would then admit, and suggesting the propriety of authorizing a loan, bottomed on the city property, and guaranteed by Congress, if that property should prove deficient. Congress approved of the measure, and authorized a loan under their guarantee, to the amount of three hundred thousand dollars. It is needless to detail the fruitless attempts which were made to fill this loan with actual specie. The only loan which could be obtained was two hundred thousand dollars, in United States Six per cent. stock, at par, from the state of Maryland, and for which the Commissioners were obliged, in addition to the guarantee of Congress, to give bonds in their individual capacities, agreeably to the resolutions of the assembly of that State, passed in the years 1796 and 1797."

A line of stages was first established between Baltimore and Philadelphia only in 1782, and corporate roads had no existence before 1804. Hence, when Washington laid the cornerstone of the Capitol, September 18, 1793, and when John Adams passed through Baltimore to occupy the magistrate's house, June 15, 1800, the surroundings of the city were sylvan to the eye only. Steamers ascended to the city in Madison's administration ; the Chesapeake and Ohio canal, began in 1828, was opened to Hancock in 1839, at a cost of above eleven and a half millions of dollars. Finally the Washington branch of the Baltimore and Ohio railroad was opened for travel August 25, 1835. It was not until 1851 that stages to the West were wholly suspended, and another competing railway to the North was not to be had until 1872, when the Baltimore and Potomac railway was opened. Direct steam communication with upper Maryland is now (1873) about to be given to the District of Columbia by the Metropolitan branch railway, and to this day little packet steamers carry mails and passengers up to the locks of the Potomac four miles an hour.

On the Fourth of July, 1800—Independence Day—Oliver Wolcott, Jr., then Comptroller of the Treasury, wrote thus to his wife, about the ancestral people of Washington and Georgetown :

" There are but few houses at any one place, and most of them small, miserable huts, which present an awful contrast to the public buildings. The people are poor, and so far as I can judge, they live, like fishes, by eating each other. All the ground for several miles around the city being, in the opinion of the people, too valuable to be cultivated, remains unfenced. There are but few enclosures, even for gardens, and these are in bad order. You may look in almost any direction, over an extent of ground nearly as large as the City of New York, without seeing a fence, or any object, except brick-kilns and temporary huts for laborers. Mr. Law and a few other gentlemen, live in great splendor ; but most of the inhabitants are low people whose appearance indicates vice and intemperance, or negroes."

" All the lands which I have described are valued, by the superficial foot, at fourteen to twenty-five cents. There appears to be a confident expectation that this place will soon exceed any city in the world. Mr. Thornton, one of the Commissioners, spoke of 160,000 people, as a matter of course, in a few years. No stranger can be here a day, and converse with the proprietors, without conceiving himself in the company of crazy people. Their ignorance of the rest of the world, and their delusions with respect to their own prospects, are without parallel. Immense sums have been squandered in buildings which are but partly finished, in situations which are not, and never will be, the scenes of business ; while the parts near the public buildings are almost wholly unimproved.

" I had no conception, till I came here, of the folly and infatuation of the people who have directed the settlements. Though five times as much money has been expended as was necessary, and though the private buildings are in number sufficient for all who will have occasion to reside here, yet there is nothing convenient, and nothing plenty but provisions. There is no industry, society, or business. With great trouble and expense, much mischief has been done which it will be almost impossible to remedy."

Charles William Janson, an Englishman, who had been bitten in American speculations, thus describes the place about 1804 :

" The entrances, or avenues as they are pompously called, are the worst roads I passed in the country, and I appeal to every citizen who has been unlucky enough to travel the stages North and South leading to the city, for the truth of the assertion. I particularly allude to the mail stage road from Bladensburg to Washington, and thence to Alexandria. In the Winter season, during the sitting of Congress, every turn of your wagon wheel is for miles attended with danger. The roads are never repaired ; deep ruts, rocks, and stumps of trees every minute impede your progress."

" Arrived at the city, you are struck with its grotesque appearance. In one view from the Capitol Hill the eye fixes upon a row of uniform houses, ten or twelve in number, while it faintly discovers the adjacent tenements to be miserable wooden structures."

" Of the hotel so vauntingly promised to rival the large inns of England, the walls and roof remain, but not a window."

" The frigate which brought the Sunisian Embassy grounded on the rocks below the city and the barbarians were obliged to be landed in boats."

Janson then tells how the fever of speculation raged in Europe over the great city.

" In London £500 sterling was, at one time, asked for a sixth-part of a single lot, many of the prime of which were originally purchased for £20 at three years' credit."

The same plain author, in his book (1806) shows that Washington was blamed for the choice of the site:

" The Republican party insinuated that Washington had pitched on a spot for the seat of government near his estate of Vernon, in order to enhance its value. This choice, I believe, was directed to one object only—the Capitol is built in the centre of the United States."

" It can never become a place of commerce, however, while Baltimore lies on one side and Alexandria on the other."

" Washington himself wrote as to the lotteries to build parts of the city: 'the whole Washington lottery business has turned out a bed of thorns rather than roses.' "

Janson goes on to say that:

" Strangers after viewing the offices of State, are apt to inquire for the city, while they are in its very centre."

" Many English artists, enchanted with the description given by interested writers, left their employ in order to exert their abilities in finishing this scene of contemplated magnificence."

" Tippling shops and houses of rendezvous for sailors and their doxies, with a number of the lowest order of traders, constitute the Navy Yard, the only flourishing part of the town." Six frigates in ordinary, one in commission, and a small vessel of war were just launched at the time of his visit:

" A long range of houses, called the twenty buildings at

Greenleaf's Point, begun by Nicholson and others, first-rate speculators, are covered in, unfinished, and are dropping piecemeal." So they are to-day.

" I never heard," said he, " of more than Pennsylvania and New Jersey Avenues in 1805, except after some houses had been uniformly built, in one of which lived Mr. Jefferson's printer, John Harrison Smith ; a few more of inferior note, with some public houses, and here and there a grog shop. This boasted Avenue is as much a wilderness as Kentucky, with this advantage, that the soil is good for nothing. Some half starved cattle browsing among the bushes present a melancholy spectacle to a stranger. Quails and other birds are constantly shot within a hundred yards of the Capitol during the sitting of the houses of Congress."

" Mr. Green and the Virginia company of comedians were nearly starved in the small place called a theatre, in the Pennsylvania Avenue, during the only season it was occupied, and were obliged to go off to Richmond during the very height of the sitting of Congress."

John Davis, a school master, who resided in America from 1798 to 1802 has given like amusing testimony :

" *Washington*," he says, " on my second visit to it, wore a very dreary aspect. The multitude had gone to their homes, and the inhabitants of the place were few. There were no objects to catch the eye, but a forlorn pilgrim forcing his way through the grass that overruns the streets, or a cow ruminating on a bank, from whose neck depended a bell, that the animal might be found the more readily in the woods."

Extracts from the reports of the early Commissioners present some interesting facts :

" The city owned an island of free-stone of immense value (at Acquia Creek).

*   *   *   *   *   *   *

Mr. A. White (1796) was of the opinion that filling up some gulleys or ravines near the Capitol and paving the Pennsylvania Avenue from thence to the President's house was all that was necessary to be done to the streets except clearing them of stumps and grubs, etc.

* * * * * * *

A sale of water property of 3,500 feet front brought $16 a foot prior to 1796.

* * * * * * *

The first engraved plans of the city and territory cost $870, the first bridge over the Tiber $788, the first bridge at James's Creek $342, and the first wharf (on the Eastern Branch) $1,017 ; the first bridge over Rock Creek cost $12,700.

* * * * * * *

The Lottery Commissioners to build a canal in 1802 were Notley Young, Daniel Carroll, Lewis Deblois, George Walker, Wm. Mayne, Duncanson, Thomas Law, and James Barry.

As early as 1803 Mr. Bacon of Massachusetts moved resolutions to re-cede the district to the States which had given it. After two days' debate they were lost,—66 to 26.

In 1816, there were but 750 assessable persons in Washington, whose houses, land, and slaves were valued at $2,391,357. Georgetown had 645 such persons better possessed in proportion and Alexandria with 782 taxables was worth $3,259,901. In the whole ten miles square, there were but 3,000 tax-payers. The population of all the Maryland side of the District, had been about 17,000 when the British invaded it.

The only water used in the city for years was well-water, and to this day the Capital is supplied from the springs on Tiber Creek. The source of Tiber Creek was estimated by Ellicott to be 236 feet above tide-water, or 158 feet higher than the base of the Capitol at the distance of two miles; he designed at one time, to use Rock Creek for the source of permanent supply of the city. The highest ground in Washington within the city boundary is back of Massachusetts Avenue and is about 103 feet above low tide. The base of the observatory is above six feet higher than the base of the Capitol, which is 89½ feet above low tide. Lafayette Square is about 15 feet above low-tide water.

The Great Falls are only 108 feet above tide-water, and can be relied upon for a supply of 86,000,000 gallons per diem. Andrew Ellicott first suggested the Great Falls as the source of the city's water-supply; and sixty years afterward, Lieutenant Meigs confirmed his judgment.

If this country had no Niagara, the Great Falls of the Potomac would be one of its most celebrated ornaments. It is astonishing to know how few people of Washington have ever visited it. The road to the spot leads over the gentle level of the great aqueduct, and is a charming succession of sights, prospects, and lonesome stretches; but the road is unfortunately unpaved, and, therefore, in wet weather, is hardly passable. A slow but agreeable way of getting to the Falls is by a quaint little steamer, which runs up the canal, carrying mails and passengers to Point of Rocks, every alternate day. The

THE GREAT FALLS OF THE POTOMAC.

locks on this canal are among the most magnificent in the world; and the entire trip to Harper's Ferry, which consumes all the hours of daylight, is one of the most agreeable in our landscapes. It passes the Little and the Great Falls, the great arch over Cabin John Run, the Seneca quarries, the battle-fields of Ball's Bluff and Monocacy, and along the whole line of that haunted stream which seems to echo forever those deep and olden tones: "All quiet on the Potomac."

There are eleven tunnels on the Washington aqueduct and six bridges; the bridge over Cabin John now is a stupendous arch 220 feet span and 100 feet high. The reservoir covers eighty acres.

The Great Falls itself is something of a canal-village. There is a large and commodious house for the Canal Company, and a storehouse and some shanties put up to accommodate laborers on the aqueduct. The canal and the creek must be crossed to get to the Falls, which are situated a quarter of a mile from the village. The Fall itself can be beheld from the rocky precipices which inclose it, in all the solemnity of nature and loneliness. A series of strong and heady rapids fleck the wide river as it comes narrowing down to a series of strewn rocks, some of them of formidable size. Between some of the greatest of these, the river tumbles in elbow-form, and, proceeding a few feet farther, dashes again into a dark gorge, surrounded with naked steeps, along which the firs and forest-trees are revealed in the back-ground, hemming in the lonesome pool with stern and befitting foliages. Back of the Great Falls, on the Maryland side, are the villages of Offutt's Cross-Roads and Rockville, as well as a gold-mine which has produced several fine nuggets. On the Virginia side are the towns of Drainesville and Leesburg, and the beautiful Difficult Creek, which formed a feature in the War of Secession.

Washington City, without reference to its associate towns in the District of Columbia, remained nearly stationery in population between 1800 and 1810, with about 8,000 inhabitants. The British did the place no permanent injury but rather reinsured it to be the immovable seat of government, and by 1820 Washington was enumerated at above 13,000 people. It missed 20,000 at 1830, and even at 1840 was a place of little above 23,000 people, but by 1850, it numbered one soul more than 40,000 and in 1860 contained above 60,000. In ten years more there were 110,000 residents at the Capital, and all the rest of the old District, including the discarded Virginia portion, could not now add to the city above 40,000 more than it possesses.

The message of General Henry D. Cooke, May 28th, 1873, showed that $856,597 had been collected of taxes and $619,000 due. In the nineteen months preceding, the cash receipts had been $10,007,676 and the expenditures $9,913,716. The funded debt was $9,016,891 and the bonds of the corporation were held at 97 cents on the dollar. There had been 1216 buildings erected in the city during the year 1872, valued at $3,209,250, and there had been 2,833 transfers of property.

The bridge which precedes No. 3 over Rock Creek was a plank structure and that in turn was replaced by a bridge made of the refuse materials of the public buildings.

When Hoban rebuilt the President's house the main portico was omitted until about 1831. About the same time a stable was proposed for the President. Mr. Bulfinch proceeded in 1830 to plant the Avenue with forest trees. In 1871 the architect, Mullet, diverted an appropriation into a new stable for President Grant, which caused some animadversion.

There were eighteen burying grounds in Washington in 1846 and but one modern cemetery, Glenwood. In 1873 there are half a dozen cemeteries besides national ones.

One of President Harrison's first acts was to institute a commission of inquiry into what was feared to be a needless and extravagant expenditure of money upon the public works in the City of Washington.

The only Presidents of the United States who are known to have bought property in Washington are General Washington, John Quincy Adams, and General Grant. Mr. Adams erected a commodious mansion still standing near Lafayette Square. General Grant disposed of his house, before he became President, to his successsor at the head of the army, General Sherman.

The Treasury building was destroyed by fire in Jackson's administration, and he is said to have commanded Mills, the architect, to erect the new one in its present site, thereby concealing the White House from the Avenue. Mr. Mills was making strict measurements with instruments when Jackson, restive of delay, put down his walking stick and said : " Right here I want the corner stone !" Jackson also ordered a public clock, the location of which had been a matter of debate, to be put up on the Treasury water-closet, and Mr. Mullet told me he took it down from that spot while building the extensions.

Seneca stone was used about the Capital at a very early period, and in 1828 there is a charge of $3,740 for it. Mr. Lee, the proprietor, charged fifteen dollars a ton, delivered. The stone was used for flagging and steps.

The bill to build an aqueduct to carry the canal over the Potomac at Georgetown, was pressed in 1832, and met with much opposition from Georgetown, whose people alleged that the piers would ruin their harbor.

Oldish, castellated, with queer, feudal-looking round towers, stands Georgetown College on the heights above the Potomac, with a deep funeral vale winding below, and the sprawling, shining, islet-sprinkled river brawling away right opposite.

Georgetown College is the largest Jesuit college in the country. The oldest part was built 1789, the main edifice in 1791. It was founded by John Carroll, first Archbishop of Baltimore, who renounced his interest in the Duddington and other estates when he became a priest in 1771. He was educated at Bohemia, Md., and St. Omer, Flanders. He gathered together the Catholics of Montgomery County and adjacent parts, while still in his youth, proceeded to Canada with Dr. Franklin, and Charles Carroll, his relative, to make an alliance for the Revolutionary Colonies, led a devout and beautiful life, and died Dec. 3, 1815, at Baltimore. In this College lived, for more than forty years after her husband's tragic death, the widow of Stephen Decatur, and his portrait hangs in the College. All the Carrolls of Duddington are buried there. The institution possesses a large estate.

Washington City has never propelled a satellite or accessory town, nor have any of the older villages in its vicinity grown by receiving sustenance from it, Baltimore only excepted. Bladensburg declined at the beginning of the revolution by the flight of the Scotch factor and agents who carried on its commerce. Alexandria, about 1798, was quite flourishing, but the capture of American vessels by the French in the West Indies, occasioned many failures. In 1803, the yellow fever broke out there. The town in 1803 had but two or three ships in the trade with Great Britain.

As early as 1809 a company was incorporated to cut a canal
through the city of Washington to extend from the deep navigation of the Eastern Branch, to the Potomac River, taking
chiefly the course of the Tiber. No benefit was derived from
this inefficient company, and in 1831 the city corporation purchased the right and interest of the Canal Company, in order
to introduce the business of the Chesapeake and Ohio canal into
the city. The lock connecting this Corporation canal with the
Chesapeake and Ohio, was placed at the foot of 17th street,
beside the Van Ness mansion, where the old stone lock-house
is standing yet, in dilapidation and loneliness. Just below
this lock, a large basin was formed at the outlet of the Tiber.
A small island called Goose-Egg Island stood in this basin, and
both canal and basin were walled with stone throughout the
whole course. The Corporation Canal cost $225,000, and
between 1836 and 1838 it was of some utility as far up as the
market at Seventh street. Being a sewer and a stench, it has
been filled up by the present Board of Public Works, and
henceforward will show no trace upon the landscape of Washington. The Chesapeake and Ohio Canal has been of little use
below Georgetown for several years. Above Georgetown for
184 miles to Cumberland it is in active and useful operation,
and probably will continue to be so with posterity. The average
movement of freight by the Potomac Canal is now about 850,000
tonnage, bringing a net revenue of upwards of $200,000. The
toll per ton of coal from Cumberland to Georgetown has generally been 46 cents, and on grain $1.80 per ton. The canal
has a debt of about $3,500,000. It costs in all, to deliver coal
to vessel at Georgetown from the coal-field, $2.13½ per ton,—
wharfage standing at 35 cents.

The Washington Navy Yard was provided for in 1804 under
the encouragement of Mr. Jefferson. Benjamin H. Latrobe,
architect of the Capitol, designed its arched gateway. Within
the yard are about 28 acres of ground surrounded by a strong
brick wall; an exquisite object on this wall is the sentry-box
at one corner, which is built of brick in the style of the feudal

turret. This was put up during the war, when it became necessary to guard enlisted seamen with carefulness. Here were built some of the best old vessels in the Navy such as the ships *Wasp* and *Argus*, the brig *Viper*, the *Columbus*, of 74 guns, the frigates *Essex*, *Potomac*, *Brandywine*, and *Columbia*, the schooners *Shark* and *Grampus*, and the sloop of war *St. Louis*.

The corner stone of the old City Hall, now the United States and District Court building, was laid August 22, 1820. Within it was deposited the following:

"This corner-stone of the City Hall, designed by George Hodfield, architect, was laid on the 22d day of August, A. D. 1820, A. L. 5820, and in the forty-fifth year of the independence of the United States of America, by Wm. Hewitt, R. W. G. M. of the Grand Lodge of Freemasons of the District of Columbia; James Munroe, President of the United States; Samuel N. Smallwood, mayor of the city of Washington."

And on the reverse side of the plate:

"Commissioners for erecting City Hall—Samuel N. Smallwood, mayor; R. C. Weightman, William Prout, Thomas Carberry, John P. Ingle."

The orator of the day was John Law, Esq. Many notable trials occurred in this building, amongst which were those of Daniel G. Sickles, for the murder of Philip Barton Key, and of John Surratt for the murder of Abraham Lincoln. In 1873 the United States Government gave the District $75,000 for its interest in this old freestone edifice, when it was determined to begin at once the construction of new municipal buildings on Market square. Mr. Law remarked at the laying of the corner-stone, that Washington then claimed 14,000 souls, and $6,000,000 capital, and the corporation revenue was $40,000. Thirty miles of streets had been opened and improved, and some turnpike roads and bridges opened. The Government had lent the town $100,000 in 1798, and $12,000 in 1800, both of which sums had been fully repaid with interest.

The old market houses of the Federal City were destroyed in 1870-72, and the present elegant edifices built in their stead.

The longitude of the Capitol was determined in 1823, by William Lambert, to be 76° 55′ 30″.54 west from Greenwich. General Washington had designed the meridian of the Capital to be the first meridian of the United States, and instructed Andrew Ellicott to record 0° 0′ longitude and 38° 53′ north latitude, in the original plan of the city. In 1809, Lambert, above referred to, a Virginian, memorialized Congress to take the longitude, and a committee reported in favor of the plan, but it lapsed until 1811, when Secretary of State Monroe gave it a good, if a diffident, word, and endorsed Mr. Lambert's patriotism. The indefatigable astronomer addressed as many of the assembled Congressmen as would hear him, and in 1812, Dr. Samuel L. Mitchell, of New York, reported in favor of a National Observatory. Not until March 3d, 1821, did the proposition meet with its deserts. Different observations were made by Andrew Ellicott, Abraham Bradley, and Seth Pease; but, in 1821, Lambert, commissioned as astronomer, resigned his station of inferior clerk in the Pension Office, took lodgings on Capitol Hill, and borrowed his instruments from the Coast Surveying authorities of that time. He had a transit instrument,

NATIONAL OBSERVATORY, ON OBSERVATORY HILL.

a circle of reflections, an astronomical clock, and a chronometer. William Elliot, a teacher of algebra and mathematics assisted him. A large platform was erected to facilitate the work. The latitude was declared to be 38° 52′ 45″. Lambert made a copious report to Congress, and advocated a National Observatory. He may be named among the great clerks—and there are many noble men in all departments of the Government—who have risen to eminence from a desk in the departments.

In 1825, President J. Q. Adams advocated a National Observatory, and met with ridicule, and it was not until

1836 that Williams College became the pioneer observatory of the land. Finally both the Government and the Georgetown College built observatories. The longitude of the National Observatory on Braddock's hill is 77° 3' 2.4".

The third session of the 13th Congress, called by President Madison, to convene on the 19th of September, 1814, met in Blodget's old hotel, which Dr. William Thornton had, meantime, made habitable, and turned a part of it into a repository of arts, models, and inventions, and he had succeeded, as well, in saving it from the torch of the British incendiary by whom it was doomed. At this time Dr. Thornton was a clerk, at $1,500 a year, in the State Department.

Morse's Geography for 1812 describes Blodget's hotel ; it was 60 feet by 120 and about 50 feet high, with three stories ; it was built of brick, with a freestone basement. The old jail of that day was 10 feet by 26, and two stories high, with low ceilings. The marine barrack, 300 feet long, and the War and State buildings, 120 feet front, were occupied. The yearly exports of the whole district were upwards of one million per annum. Georgetown had four churches and Washington three market houses. In 1810 a turnpike was incorporated by Congress from Mason's causeway to Alexandria.

The turnpike company between Georgetown and Fredericktown was incorporated by the Maryland legislature, in 1812.

The old poor-house of Washington stood on the elevated ground to the north of the old Post and Patent Offices. Not a vestige remains of those old buildings, where strangers from all parts of the Union, coming to prosecute claims and grievances and seek redress from the Government, often found their last hospitality on this earth.

The old asylum of Georgetown still stands, and is a quaint, Flemish-looking structure of brick.

The Treasury building was originally built between 1794 and 1799, and in 1801 a fire swept part of it off. The British burned it in 1814, and it again began to arise three years later, and was not finished until 1823. Ten years later, on March 29, 1833, it was destroyed by fire again, and now its

13

architectural history, as we see it, began. In 1835, Robert Mills, of South Carolina, was appointed to supervise it, and in four years he raised that façade of columns which was the glory of his period, [and the exceeding annoyance of Mr. Mullet, a subsequent architect, who said that [it resembled a box of cigars, escaped as they stood on end in a long row. The old State Department long stood at right angles to Mills's façade, where the north end of the Treasury extension now is. Mills's Treasury was finished in 1839.

In 1855 the arrived potentate in classical architecture, Thomas N. Walters, planned the extension of the Treasury. Instead of Virginia freestone, granite from Dix Island, Maine, was to be employed for these three great parts of the edifice remaining. Mr. A. B. Young, who is still a resident of the Capital City, living between the Treasury gate and the Potomac, on Fifteenth street, was the architect following Mills, and he superintended the work and drawings for six or eight years. Next in immediate supervision came Mr. Rogers, architect of the Astor House hotel, New York City. Mr. Mullet, of Cincinnati, a native of England, but a resident of the United States since childhood, completed the work, and in his headquar-

TREASURY BUILDING.

ters, in the basement of this Treasury, he subsequently made the designs for the majority of the great Post-Offices, Custom Houses, Marine Hospitals, U. S. Courts, etc., in the country. The south wing of the Treasury was completed in 1860 ; the west wing in 1864 ; and the north wing in 1869. This is the most costly of all our public buildings, considering its extent. It is 560 feet, by nearly 273, including the porticoes and steps. Its cost was more than half that of the far nobler Capitol. Mr. Mills long lived on New Jersey Avenue, Capitol Hill, in a celebrated brick dwelling, with a peaked roof and sky-light.

Wevill— N.Y.

NEW BUILDING FOR DEPARTMENTS OF STATE, ARMY, AND NAVY.

The State Department at Washington was originally in a private dwelling and then on the site of the present Treasury. It was removed to an Orphan Asylum at the foot of Meridian Hill during the rebellion, and in 1872 the plans of A. B. Mullet were accepted for an edifice of granite to cost from six millions to eight millions of dollars and to accommodate at once the Departments of War, the Navy, and the State. The building was forthwith begun and will be finished about 1876. It is in the style of classical *renaissance*, the basement of Richmond granite and the superstructure of Maine granite. While superintending its construction Mr. Mullet was also erecting thirty-five other government buildings in various parts of the country.

UNITED STATES POST-OFFICE.

The General Post-Office is said to have cost, in round numbers, one million and a half. Its controlling masters were Meigs, Walters, and Edward Clark. It was commenced about the close of Pierce's administration, and at the outbreak of the civil war was finished only on the E street or rear wing where the chimneys stand and the rest was a Commissary storehouse. The architecture of the exterior is due to Mills, the correction and completion of the remaining two-thirds to Walters and Clark. The edifice was wholly occupied in 1866.

The Post-Office extension was constructed of Kennebec, Me., and Woodstock, Md., granite at about 43 cents the cubic foot. The marble walls were of Lee and Baltimore granite; the monolithic columns and their trimmings from Carrara, Italy, at $1,500 per column. Nearly all the work was done by the day. Captain Meigs superintended the work and Edward Clark, assistant superintendent, received $3 per diem.

The office of Indian affairs was created by the Act of July 9, 1832; the Treasury was given a Solicitor in May, 1830; the Post-Office obtained an Auditor in the Treasury in 1836. The Attorney-General of the United States was created Sept. 24, 1789. The General Land Office was created April 25, 1872, and made a section of the Treasury Department.

In 1836, the records and models in the Patent Office were destroyed by fire, on the 15th of December. The following

PATENT OFFICE—SOUTH FRONT.

March, Congress made legislation compelling the recording of all patents and drawings, and models were in all proper cases demanded anew. The Patent Office goes back to 1790, and between 1793 and 1836 the Secretary of State issued patents subject to the revision of the Attorney-General. Above 9,000 patents had been issued up to 1836, but the loose regulation led to many infringements and much litigation. William Elliott, writing in 1837 of the destruction of the archives of the Patent Office, said: " There lie the ashes of the records of more than 10,000 inventions with their beautiful models and drawings. There lie also, smouldering in the same heap of ruins, the elegant, classical correspondence of Dr. Thornton with the most of the ingenious and scientific men of this country and of Europe for upwards of 23 years."

The Patent Office was the conception of two surveyors and engineers of Washington City who lived in the Jacksonian period, Messrs. Elliot and Town, the former of an English family notable in Washington for giving hints and doing conscientious work. According to a legend amongst the architects of the city the plan was Town's, but as he left the firm the plan was usually named and accepted as Elliot's. The site of the building had previously been a nursery for trees and plants. In 1836, Robert Mills was made architect and he built the sand-stone portion on the F street side of Acquia Creek " free-stone." In 1851 Mr. Walters came to Washington, with the reputation of Girard College upon him, bringing Mr. Edward Clark as his assistant. Secretary of the Interior, Seward, had become dissatisfied with Mr. Mills's work and he dismissed that gentleman, to the great ado of the period, and Mr. Clark was appointed to straighten out Mills's beginnings and make the windows face each other and the rooms assume some rectangular form. The Seventh street side was the first marble part added, and the whole edifice was done in 1867. It cost $2,200,-000. The marble came from Cockeysville, Md.

The second edifice of the State Department was occupied in 1836, and it remained until the close of the civil war, but the great pile of the Treasury obliterated it.

Columbian College was commenced by Rev. Mr. Rice in 1819 and chartered in 1821, the buildings erected and the institution opened speedily and its prosperity was exceptional until 1826, when its officers ran it in debt to the extent of $135,000. Then followed a pinching period, wherein the debts were mainly paid off, but the College lost its popularity. The Baptists have generally controlled it.

The present building of the Columbian Law School was the original Trinity Episcopal Church, third in the city in point of time, and was consecrated May 11, 1829. The Third Trinity Church was designed by Renwick, architect of the Smithsonian Institute, and opened in 1857. This church is what is called "low" or ultra Protestant, and it was taken possession of by the Government during the war.

Old Christ Episcopal Church points up its four little pinnacles near the Marine barracks. It was built about 1806 and the Society had been in existence since 1795. Jefferson and Madison were regular attendants of this church, and the Marines from the barracks formerly marched every Sunday to its ministrations. The Congressional burying ground, otherwise Washington Parish Cemetery, belongs to this plain, crude little cottage-windowed edifice, which was the progenitor of nine other parishes in Washington City.

The First Baptist Church, at I and 19th streets, was begun in 1803, and finished in 1809. In 1810 the Second Baptist Church was constituted near the Navy Yard.

The Convent of the Visitation at Georgetown, was founded by Archbishop Neale, in 1798. The sisters of the order elect a mother superior every third year, eligible for only two consecutive terms.

The Academy of the Visitation was established at Georgetown, about 1808.

St. Patrick's Church, destroyed in 1873, was built in 1810; St. Peters, Capitol Hill, in 1821; St. Matthew's Church, in 1839.

The First Presbyterian Church, N Street, in the rear of Willard's, was composed of persons who had belonged to the Associate Reformed Church, in Philadelphia, and removed with the Capital. It received a pastor in 1803, and the congregation first worshiped in the Treasury building. The Second Church followed, on Capitol Hill, and the Third, in New York Avenue, was instituted in 1820. At the latter Mr. Lincoln worshiped.

The Methodist Church, in Georgetown, was built in 1806; the Navy Yard Methodist Church in 1810; the Foundry in 1815.

St. John's Episcopal Church was built from the gratuitously presented designs, and under the eye, of B. H. Latrobe. Originally it was a Greek cross, afterward enlarged to the Roman form, and endowed with a tower. It was consecrated by Bishop Kemp, December 27, 1816.

The old Unitarian Church, on Louisiana Avenue, was designed by Bulfinch, and was provided with a bell of 900 pounds weight, cast by Mr. Revere, in Massachusetts.

The Penitentiary of the district was established at Greenleaf's Point after 1830.

It was 120 feet by 50, with 160 cells, surrounded by a wall 300 feet square and 22 feet high. Charles Bulfinch designed it.

The present jail was erected in 1841, near by its predecessor. A new jail is going up (1873) at the Eastern Branch.

The Washington Arsenal was re-built in 1815, from the designs of Colonel George Bomford. Another structure, by Major W. Wade, succeeded this.

In 1831 there were nine banks, in the ten miles square: Bank of Washington, $479,000 capital stock; Metropolis, $500,000; Patriotic, $250,000; Farmers' and Mechanics', $486,000; Union of Georgetown, $478,000; Alexandria, $500,000; Potomac (Alexandria), $500,000; Mechanics' (Alexandria), $372,000; Farmers' (Alexandria), $310,000.

The debt of Washington City was about $800,000 in 1837.

To the Chesapeake and Ohio Canal the State of Maryland subscribed $5,000,000; the United States, $1,000,000; Washington City, $1,000,000; Georgetown, Alexandria, and the State of Virginia, $250,000 each. Ground was broken July 4, 1828.

The greatest freshet on the Potomac, of which there is any available record, occurred in 1852, raising the river at Chain Bridge 43 feet; at Aqueduct Bridge, 10 feet; and at the Arsenal 4 feet 9 inches. The flow of the Potomac river was gauged in 1863, above Great Falls, and found to be 1,176,000,-000 imperial gallons for twenty-four hours, exclusive of the supply required for the district. The canal has an available fall, above Georgetown, of 34 feet, equal to **11,000** horse power.

At the time of the Mexican war the leading hotels stood as follows, starting at the Capitol gate and going west:

Gadsby's, Pennsylvania Avenue and Third street.

Temperance Hotel, } Third street, behind Gadsby's.
St. Charles Hotel, }

United States, } Both on Pa. Avenue, between 3d and 4½.
Veranda, }

Exchange, C street, between 4½ and 6.

Coleman's, Pa. Avenue, between 4½ and 6.

Brown's, Pa. Avenue, between 6 and 7.

Fuller's, Pa. Avenue and 14 st.

European, Pa. Avenue, between 14 and 15 street.

During the Thirtieth Congress, the following notable men resided as indicated:

Geo. M. Dallas, at Mrs. Gadsby's, President's Square.

John C. Calhoun, Mrs. Read's, C Street, between 4½ and 6.

Lewis Cass, Tyler's Hotel.

John M. Clayton, Young's, Capitol Hill, N. J. Av.

Jefferson Davis, Mrs. Owen's, Capitol Hill.

Stephen H. Douglas, Willard's Hotel.

A. H. Sevren, Hill's, Capitol Hill.

Daniel Webster, Pa. Av., near 6th St.

John Q. Adams, F street, bet. 13 and 14.

Abraham Lincoln, Mrs. Sprigg's, Capitol Hill.

At the time of the rebellion the leading hotels were as follows:

At Georgetown, the City Hotel and Lang's Hotel.

On Pennsylvania Avenue, Willard's, Owen's, Brown's, National, Kirkwood, Henry Clay, Victoria.

On Capitol Hill, Whitney's, Caspar's House.

North of the Avenue, Hendon House, F Street; Pennsylvania House, C Street.

The National Hotel was the first building in Washington, of

large dimensions, for public accommodation, a few rods from Brown's, or the Metropolitan. Brown's was the first to establish a bridal-chamber, and here Kossuth's compatriots went to bed with their boots and hats on, after getting very drunk at the National. Clay died at the National, and Buchanan took the mysterious sickness there. At Brown's, James B. Clay, Henry Clay's son, was struck in the face by General Cullom, of Tennessee, and a bloodless duel ensued at Bladensburg, in 1858.

WILLARD'S HOTEL.

The brothers Willard, of Vermont, had the largest house in the city when the war began, and they made a very advantageous lease of it. In their house the Peace Convention of 1861 was held. That hall has been turned by Mr. Cake, the new proprietor, into a reading and music room, which will probably be the *place recherché*, as the young men with pale neckties put it, for soft and non-percussion theatricals.

The present proprietor of Willard's belongs to the race of family magistrates, dignified, industrious, and agreeable as a Bishop. It is a great moral advance, if no more, to see the

old, tawdry horse-racing race of inn-keepers disappear, and
public men and their families, and patriotic folks who visit the
Capitol, receive the entertainment of quieter and more demure
and responsible hosts. Persons familiar with Washington
hotels will be interested to hear that the new Willard's has a
grand marble and walnut office, a billiard-room where the bar
formerly stood, a ladies *café* over the office, where used to be
" Camp Sykes " (a lumber room), and the long and gawky
sitting-room has been dissected, and half of it made a ladies'
promenade.

The Arlington Hotel, on Vermont Avenue, is celebrated
over the country for the elegance of its apartments, and the
experience of its proprietors. The hotel was built by W. W.
Corcoran, Esq., and leased to Revesel and Sons, of Lake
George, for $40,000 a year. The waiters wear a uniform, and
like all the four large houses of Washington, it contains an
elevator.

THE EBBITT HOUSE.

The Ebbitt House is one of the largest and decidedly the
best-looking establishment, architecturally, at the Capital. It
arose during the war, and became celebrated as the favorite
headquarters of army and navy officers, and was extended from
time to time to meet the demands upon its popularity, until in
1872, it was wholly reformed and reconstructed. It is now a

very elegant mansion, six stories high and of a bright, cheerful color, which lightens the spirits of the guests ; from every window canopies of canvass depend to cool the interior through the Summer ; for this house, unlike several in Washington, is kept open the whole year round. The taste of the proprietor, Caleb C. Willard, Esq., is displayed in the elegant French pavilions, and broken lines of the roof, and in the series of classical window mouldings, which liken the establishment to the purer class of the public edifices. The new dining-room is made to include two entire stories in height, and the lofty ceiling is beautifully frescoed, while the windows are given nearly the loftiness of the hall, thus bathing the apartment in the exquisite light of this latitude. Beneath the dining-room is the historic line of offices known over the whole country as " Newspaper row." The newspaper correspondents had pitched upon this block before a hotel was devised, on account of its immediate proximity to the telegraph offices, the Treasury, all the lines of city communication, and as it was centrally situated to the White House and the great departments. When the Ebbitt House was rebuilt the proprietor reserved the basement stage for newspaper offices, and for the length of the whole block, lights can be seen shining at every night in the week, where these indefatigable correspondents, representing the active press of the whole country, hang out their signs and feed the telegraph instruments. On notable occasions, Newspaper Row is illuminated by its landlord. The Ebbitt House contains the largest rotunda and office in Washington ; it has an elevator and 300 rooms. and there is not a prettier piece of architecture in Washington than its ladies' portico and rich bay window at the angle of the building. In this house have put up nearly all the eminent sailors and soldiers of the country : Rogers, Farragut, Worden, Canby, Thomas, Porter, Winslow, Boggs, Case, Drayton, and the rest. The Ebbitt House set the example of making a deduction for army and navy officers at the close of the war. It is the newest hotel production at the national Capitol.

Speaking of the army and navy hotel, suggests the capture of Washington in 1814, and the military history of the city.

Washington had few military traditions, prior to the late civil war. Observatory hill was the camping and landing-ground of Braddock, Washington, and a part of the British army, April 11–14, 1775, and as Washington was at this time only 23 years of age, he may have paid especial attention for the first time to the beauty of the situation. A neck below Observatory hill was often designated by Peter Force, as Braddock's landing place. This hill was also designed to be the site of a fort, when the city was planned, and a brigade of militia encamped upon it, August 23, 1814. During the Revolution, troops were almost constantly crossing Alexandria and Georgetown ferries. Fort Washington, on the Potomac, was originally Fort Warburton, and at the time of the war of 1812, it was merely a water battery, with a block house on the hill above it, to protect it from being taken in the rear. This fort was built after the British war, and strengthened in 1861, when Fort Foote was also laid out by Major Alexander. Traces of breastworks exist at Whitestone point where the British vessels, retiring from Washington, were cannonaded.

Here is a quaint item :

July 10, 1814. General Wilkinson, temporarily suspended from command of the army, made a tour of the city in company with General John Mason, of Mason's Island, and Charles Carroll, of Bellevue, to inform them of his plan, in the last resort, to repel a British surprise. It was as follows : Two redoubts, one in the fork of the Tiber and Potomac, the other on the height north of the Avenue called "Davidson's orchard ;" also the fortification of the Capitol and the President's house, in this way : Of the Capitol, by ravelins, to connect the two disconnected blocks (wings) and round towers of stone up the angles, with loop-holes to defend the extension-ends of the blocks ; the windows to be barricaded with loop-holes for musketry, and the lower floor of the Capitol, as well as the ravelins, to be sufficiently furnished with artillery, and the preparation of the President's house for the reception of musketry ; competent garrisons for the several posts to be detailed and held in readiness to occupy them, should it become necessary, and suitable munitions of war to be previously deposited in each. It was also practicable to arrange for the defense of the Navy Yard.

"Had these obvious, economical precautions been adopted," says Wilkinson, "the rival ministers, Monroe and Armstrong, would not have been exposed to the humiliation of advising General Winder, when he reached the Capital, to rally and form his troops on the heights in the rear of Georgetown."

The total strength of the United States soldiery, of various sorts, at the battle of Bladensburg, according to William Elliott, was 8,049, of which 1,100 were regular infantry, seamen, and marines, and 540 Virginia, Columbia, Maryland, and regular dragoons. The whole number of regulars, including seamen, was 1,240. The Americans had 20 pieces of field artillery. The entire British force, August 17, 1814, was 3,500, without artillery.

This is sufficient to show that there were enough men on the American side to have defended the city, and to blame the Administration, was probably to put the disgrace upon sacrificial shoulders. This is further attested by the miserably disproportionate loss of life on the American side, as estimated by the importance of the object to defend and the number of the defenders—only ten men were killed and thirty wounded. Lossing says twenty-six were killed and fifty-one wounded. It was not believed by good observers on the field of battle, that the British brought up above 1,500 men. Their loss was nearly 500 killed and wounded.*

The following buildings were destroyed by the British in 1814—the unfinished Capitol, the President's house, two build-

---

*General Wilkinson's estimate is 64 killed and 249 wounded, on the British side, and 10 horses killed and 8 wounded. On the American side, 8 men killed, 13 marines wounded.

ings containing public offices, and the fort at Greenleaf's point, Mr. Sewell's house on Capitol Hill, Mr. Carroll's hotel on Capitol Hill, General Washington's house and Mr. Frost's house, on the same elevation ; work-shops in the Navy Yard ; a sloop of war and public stores ; Fort Washington, and two bridges over the Eastern Branch. The British soldiers and the runaway negroes who attended them, plundered a few houses, amongst them Mr. A. McCormick's, Mr. D. Rapine's, and Mr. Elliott's. The types and presses of Gales & Seaton were cast out of the window.

The Potomac was first crossed in the rebellion on the night of May 23, 1861,* in three columns at the Georgetown Aqueduct, the Long Bridge, and by water to Alexandria. The three columns were commanded respectively by Major Wood, Major Heintzelman, and Colonel Ellsworth. The first defences were laid out by General Mansfield, and Captain H. G. Wright next day at Forts Corcoran, Runyon, and Ellsworth.

For seven weeks the work of defining and throwing up works went on, until the three forts named were built, and also Forts Bennett, Haggerty, and Albany. Fort Runyon exceeded any of the subsequent works. After the disaster of Bull Run, the works in Virginia were immediately connected, strengthened, and extended. By the beginning of the year 1862, there were 48 forts in all, 23 south of the Potomac, 14 (and three batteries) between the Potomac and the Eastern Branch, and 11 forts beyond the branch. The greater portion were enclosed works of earth, but several were lunettes with stockaded gorges. In October, 1862, Mr. Stanton, Secretary of War, took the responsibility of ordering new works, and he appointed a commission consisting of Generals Potter, Meigs, Barry, Barnard, and Cullum, to report upon those already completed. They reported 53 forts and 22 batteries with 643 guns and 75 mortars mounted, and demanding 25,000 infantry for garrisons, and

---

* The hills of Maryland opposite Alexandria were filled with troops, and the gunboat *Pawnee* had been lying for weeks in the channel, when on the 24th of May that outpost of the rebellion was captured.

9,000 artillery men.   Enormously increased works were built
in the early part of 1863, and three beautiful " semi-permanent
field works" were those of Fort Whipple, Fort C. F. Smith, and
Fort Foote.*   The whole system of works was strengthened
in 1864, and in July of that year, Early advanced within sight
of them and retired.

The aggregate length of good military roads for the defences
of Washington was 32 miles ; the circuit of defences was at
least 37 miles.   The Long Bridge was reconstructed by the
enemy in 1861, and the railroad bridge beside it was built by
the Engineers also in 1864.

"The stone piers of the Aqueduct are works of the highest
class of engineering, resting on bed rock 20 to 30 feet below
the surface of the river."

The hired labor force on the forts was at its greatest in 1863,
—1,500 men, wagons trains of 25 to 44 horse teams were used.
The disbursements for hired labor and material, were all made
by James Evelett, and amounted to more than one million of
dollars.   No compensation was paid land owners for injury,
although a church, many dwellings, and many orchards were
demolished.

At the close of the war in 1865, Washington was surrounded
by 68 inclosed forts and batteries having an aggregate perim-
eter of 13 miles, and a circuit of 37 miles, with 807 mounted
guns, and 98 mortars and implements in all for 1521 guns.
Compared with the Torres Vedras, constructed by Wellington
from the Tagus to the sea, which cost £200,000, the works of
Washington cost $1,436,000, and exceeded the former in length
of circuit.   The whole line from the Chickahominy Pine
Works in 1865 was 32½ miles long.

The highest fort around Washington was Gains, 403 feet
above mean tide.   At forts Reno, Totten, and Lincoln, the
heights are respectively 440, 330, and 230 feet above the tide.
From Fort Meigs to Fort Stanton, the ridge is about 300 feet
high ; the Theological Seminary back of Alexandria has an
elevation of 400 feet above the Potomac.

---

* Fort Foote is still occupied (1872).

The geology of Washington is peculiar: at the head of tide water, it stands amongst the vertically stratified metamorphic rocks which, varying in composition from hard grains to soft mica slate, yield unequally to degrading action, and thus produce the bold headlands and deeply excavated valley in which the land terminates at the margins of the Potomac. Overlying these rocks is a series of nearly horizontal beds which form the various distinctive earth masses around Georgetown, Washington, and Alexandria. These peculiar sands and clays, with their fossil woods, belong to the older part of the Atlantic cretaceous formation. The underlying metamorphic rocks, are only exposed on Rock Creek, which took its name from them. Northwest of the city may be seen the material eroded over the sandstone of red Seneca, where the river once flowed 400 feet higher than now.

Few things even in our notable time have come up with more suddenness than Washington City since the abolition of slavery.

At the close of the contest for a division of the country, it was inevitable that there should have been such an agitation for a change of the seat of government as followed the burning of the young city by the British in 1814. After sixty-five years of preparation Washington seemed to be still unfinished in any part. The Capitol was not done; the President's mansion was out of repair; the streets were generally unpaved, and the social chaos following the war, had made old and new elements dissatisfied with their associations, and despondent about the site.

Nothing seemed so necessary to Washington as a good frightening, and that it received through an authority sufficiently amusing at the present distance.

A red-bearded, crippled, Quilpish looking man of St. Louis, Missouri,—by name Mr. L. Q. Reavis,—with a certain sense of resistance about him and an uncertain sense of reformation, took it into his head that St. Louis had been slighted and ought to be the Capital of the Government. He had a simple nature, a love of circulation and public consideration, and some hopes of authorship. Perfectly honest, always approachable, always approaching, loose and continuous in argument, striking high for eminent attention, and carrying acquaintance by the assiduity with which he cultivated it, Mr. Reavis tested to extremities the power of the unit of citizenship to upset the Capital City and drag it away. His ingenuities were all in the noblest nature of destructiveness. He had very little to propose in the way of reconstruction, and was indifferent whether the public edifice should be carried away piecemeal or abandoned to the unworthy people on the Potomac. But it happened at the moment that the strength of the dominant party in the West, the fever of change, the opening of the Pacific railroad and other lines to the extreme frontier, and perhaps more than all the rising agitation on the subject of free trade which the Western free traders hoped to settle in their favor by getting Congress amongst them, gave a noisy and it was thought a favorable celebrity to Mr. Reavis's scheme. Mr. Horace Greeley favored the removal in the New York *Tribune*, and a convention or two were held at St. Louis. The conservative sense, reverence and thrift of the nation prevailed, however, and Congress settled the question by voting a large sum of money to begin a grand State Department at Washington which should cost several millions. The city itself at its own expense put on a new apparel, and the national appropriations of 1872-3 were unusually generous and even excessive.

After the peace of 1865 a little timid building began about the city, led by A. R. Shepherd, a native of the District who had made some accumulations while the armies and hospitals centred here, by conducting plumbing and gas fitting on a large scale. He put up several Philadelphia rows of brick houses adjacent to the old Duddington house of the Carrolls and also erected the first business edifice of consequence on the lower side of the Avenue. His architect was Mr. Cluss, a German, whose domestic architecture has given Washington a style of its own. He designed the central market house, the Franklin, Jefferson, Wallack and other public schools, and the dwellings of

Jeffreys, Hutchinson, and other new arrivals.   Walter S. West, a Virginia architect, showed his skill in the transformation of the old Crawford property on Highland place and in the elevation of the residences of Mr. Schenck and Senator Stewart. Ploughman and Starkweather of Philadelphia designed the Freedman's bank, the Young Men's Christian Association Halls, and the quaint row of dwellings which are occupied by Speaker Blaine, Fernando Wood, Senator Buckingham, and Thomas Swann.   The Howard University and the large modern mansion of George Taylor on Vermont Avenue, were designed by Mr. Searle of Rochester, N. Y.   Vernon Row, an elegant business block on the Avenue, was the plan of architect Fraser. Mr. A. Grant of Wisconsin, designed the block of lofty brick on East Capitol street.   A Baltimore architect planned the little opera house near the central market and the Arlington hotel.   Marshal Brown's and Mr. Thompson's brown stone houses on I street were by F. G. Myers, a German.   Edward Clark designed Merrell's and Edmunds' neat houses on Massachusetts Avenue.   Prominent builders in this new period are Robert I. Fleming of Va., W. H. Baldwin, Entwistle and Barron, and Edmonstone.

It has been mentioned in another chapter that the territorial government expended from ten millions to fourteen millions in 1872; three new bridges were thrown across Rock Creek; three large market houses were partly finished; a new city hall was designed; a reform school was begun; new railroads and depots were added; new school houses built and the entire system of street paving, sewerage, parks, suburban roads, and street railways reformed and made metropolitan.   Destiny seems to be against the city in the matter of commerce and manufactures.   Factories do not flourish here; the great glass works near the observatory which were so long successful have fallen into decay, but rural gardening has taken the start and it is to be hoped that some day Washington will be fed from the fields within sight of its hills.

In 1871, when the project for the removal of the Capital was rife in the Western country, two members of Congress, John Coburn, of Indiana, and Philetus Sawyer presented a minority report in favor of the scheme. Their energies came to naught, but we are indebted to them for extracting from the Treasury Department a very complete statement of the cost of Washington City and of the District to the taxpayers of the United States. These have amounted in gross to above forty-five and one-half millions of dollars in three quarters of a century. To make this grand total every possible appropriation and investment in the District was brought out, inclusive of several uncompleted edifices, some of which will not be wholly built until about 1876. By that time we may safely assume that the expenditures of the Federal Government in the district will have been hard upon sixty millions of dollars.

CHAPTER XVIII.

1861. Jan. 4. Mrs. Robert Anderson passes through Washington to join her husband in Fort Sumpter. Returns Jan. 9, and stops at Willard's Hotel.

1861. Jan. 5. The South Carolina Commissioners leave the city. Cockades of both zones blossom in hundreds of hat-bands. Captain Charles P. Stone organizes the militia and troops in the district. Fourteen Senators, amongst them Jefferson Davis, caucus in Washington, to form themselves into a directory, and take control of the South.

1861. Jan. 12. The Gulf State Congressmen and Senators begin to withdraw from Congress.

Jan. 21st. Jefferson Davis withdraws.

February 4th. Slidell and Benjamin withdraw.

1861. Feb. 4. The Peace Convention meets at Willard's Hall, on F st., John Tyler presiding ; adjourns March 1st.

1861. Feb. 23. President Lincoln, accompanied by Ward Lamon and Norman Judd, arrive at the Washington depot, at daylight, and are received by Elihu Washburne ; he goes to Willard's Hotel, where Mr. Seward meets him.

On the 27th, the Mayor and Council wait on the President-elect.

1861. March 4th. Mr. Lincoln and Mr. Buchanan, in a carriage. with Senators Pearse and Baker, proceed to the Capitol, flanked by troops on the parallel streets. Chief-Justice Taney administers the oath.

1861. March 5. Three Confederate Commissioners arrive, and stop at Willard's.

1861. April —. Mayor James G. Barrett arrested.

1861. April 13. The Virginia Commissioners meet the President.

1861. April 18. The Cassius M. Clay battalion organized at Willard's Hall, and given arms to patrol the city. The Capitol and Treasury guarded by howitzers. Five volunteer companies from Pennsylvania and forty regulars arrive at the depot, in all 530 men. They are quartered in the House of Representatives ; the same evening Harper's Ferry armory destroyed.

1861. April 19. The Massachusetts Sixth arrives.

1861. April 20. Seizure of telegraph despatches, followed by the weeding of the disloyal out of the Departments.

1861. April 21. Robert E. Lee leaves Arlington House for Richmond, to offer his services to the State of Virginia.

1861. April 25. Arrival of the Seventh New York Regiment ; two other regiments arrive next day.

1861. May. All the public buildings filled with troops and the Glacis converted into bakeries.

1861. May 1. Lieut. Tompkins raids through Fairfax Court House.

1861. May 11. Washington severed from the North by the burning of bridges north of Baltimore.

1861. May 18. A Confederate flag seen on the Virginia heights.

1861. May 25. Colonel Ellsworth's body embalmed at the Navy Yard.

1861. June 16. Confederate soldiers seen at Chain Bridge and High Point ; Vienna and Falls Church occupied.

1861. July 4. A special session of Congress is held.

1861. July 9. One hundred and sixty-one millions appropriated to carry on the war.

1861. July 15. McDowell's army advances.

1861. July 21. All the horses and vehicles in the District of Columbia seized to bring in the wounded. Hospitals improvised.

1861. July 25. McClellan makes headquarters in Washington, at the head of 50,000 infantry and thirty pieces of cannon, the city fortified, and the army recruited and reorganized.

1861. October 1st. The Potomac blockaded for nearly six months after this date.

1861. October 15. The city circumvallated by earthworks; seventy thousand men armed and disciplined; the Potomac picketed from Liverpool Point to Williamsport; great reviews in September and October, opposite Washington.

1861. October 17. The Confederates again fall back to Centreville.

1861. Oct. 25. General Baker's dead body brought from Ball's Bluff to Washington.

1861. Dec. 20. Fight at Drainsville, near Washington.

1862. Street railroad laid on Pennsylvania Avenue.

1862. March 10. McClellan advances to Manassas and Warrenton Junction.

1862. April 1st. McClellan descends the Potomac, leaving 18,000 men in garrison, and 20,000 in Virginia around Manassas.

1862. June 28. General Pope takes command of the forces before Washington, and takes the field July 29th.

1862. Sept. 1st. Battle of Chantilly, and return of the army to the fortifications of Washington.

1862. Sept. 4th. The Confederates cross the Potomac 40 miles above Washington.

1862. Sept. 7th. The Army of the Potomac, 87,000 strong, moves north of Washington. Battle of Antietam.

1862. Dec. 31st. Burnside recalled to Washington, from before Fredericksburg, and removed from his command.

1863. Jan. 1. President Lincoln proclaims emancipation from Washington.

1863. Washington Fire Department organized ; it consisted in 1873, of five steamers, six hose carriages and two trucks, a fire-alarm telegraph and twenty-eight horses. Annual expense $80,000.

1863. Mar. 8. John S. Mosby dashes into Fairfax and captures Colonel Stoughton ; the Confederate draft enforced in counties opposite Washington.

1863. June 16. Hooker's army, defeated at Chancellorsville, falls back to Fairfax.

1864. July 6. The Sixth Corps, under General Ricketts, passes through Washington northward.

1864. July 9th. The battle of Monocacy, for the defence of the city, with a Federal loss of 2,000.

1864. July 12th. Battle at Silver Springs, with a loss of 600 men on each side ; Early re-crosses the Potomac.

1865. April 10. President Lincoln returns to Washington from Richmond ; the city illuminated.

1865. April 14. General Grant arrives.

1865. April 15. Death of Mr. Lincoln, at the house of Mr. Peterson, opposite Ford's theatre.

1865. May. Grand review, for two days, of the armies of Grant and Sherman.

1865. July 7. Mrs. Surratt, Payne (or Powell), Harold, and Atzerodt hanged in the yard of the old penitentiary, Greenleaf's Point.

1865. Nov. 10. Henry Wirz, the Andersonville jailer, hanged, in the rear of the house where Calhoun died, and which was called " The old Capitol."

1865. Dec. Only 35 votes are cast in favor of negro suffrage in the District ; 7,369 against.

1866. June 3. Calvary Baptist Church dedicated ; burned December 15th, 1867.

1867. March 7th. President Johnson vetoes the District of Columbia suffrage bill, but it is passed over the veto by more than two-thirds of each House

1869.   December 24.   Death of Edwin M. Stanton, at his home, on Franklin square.

1869.   Completion of the Howard University for freedmen.

1871.   Feb. 20, 21.   Grand Carnival and Masquerade on the completion of the wood pavement on Pennsylvania Avenue from the Treasury to the Capitol ; the same day the President signs the bill making a Territorial Government for the District of Columbia, with a Governor and Council, a House of Delegates and a Delegate in Congress.

1872.   Opening of the Baltimore and Potomac, and Washington, Alexandria and Fredericksburg Railroads.

1872–3.   Complete rehabilitation and reformation of the city, at a cost to the taxpayers of eight millions, and to the Government of four millions.   Commencement of the new State Department.

1873.   May 12.   Salmon P. Chase interred at the Oak Hill Cemetery, Georgetown.   Services in the Capital.

1873.   May 26.   Opening of the Metropolitan branch railroad to Point of Rocks.

1873.   Sept.   The sum of fifteen millions five hundred thousand dollars in gold, awarded to the government of the United States, to pay to its citizens for losses incurred by the depredations of the Alabama and other Anglo-Confederate vessels, was paid into the Treasury of the United States.

1874.   March 11.   Charles Sumner of Massachusetts, died suddenly.

1875.   Nov.   Vice-President Wilson stricken with apoplexy, and after lingering a few days, died.

1876.   March.   General Babcock, the President's private secretary, on trial and acquitted, for complicity in the whiskey frauds.

CHAPTER XIX.

If we ever have a literature in America, much of it must illustrate the government and collateral society at the national capital. Many agreeable pens have been at work jotting down the materials for this work, and it would be an oversight in our book to say nothing of the old families and the new in the city by the Potomac.

It is already hard to realize with precision and picturesqueness the state of social life and living which existed in the early days of our Capital. The city has found it necessary in the course of improvement to take out of the landscape many familiar forms and vistas which will belong to the biographer, novelist, and poet of that great period in letters which must be approaching.

Amongst the local landmarks of the District of Columbia which have been recently obliterated in the leveling processes of the new corporation, are the mound and stone to mark the centre of the ten miles square, set up by Andrew Ellicott, in 1791. Gen. Babcock said he thought it was merely the base of a derrick to hoist things to the Washington Monument.

The other landmark was the Van Ness Mausoleum, in which was buried David Burns, the Scotch farmer who owned the ground on which the most popular part of Washington stands. This fine old relic (see cut below) was taken down in the latter part of 1872, to give room for a new alley. It stood between

14

the Church of the Ascension and an Orphan Asylum, on H
street near Ninth,—the ground for both of which was presented
by Mrs. Van Ness, or Marcia Burns, daughter of the Scotch
farmer aforesaid.

As to this family there is a quaint tale which may be worth
telling:

David Burns was a farmer at the river-side behind the President's Mansion, who had been fortunate enough, under the law
of primogeniture prevailing in the Province of Maryland, to
inherit his father's property, to the exclusion of his kin. He
was a positive old fellow, and annoyed Washington very much
when the President sought to "locate the Capital City upon
his farm." "The obstinate Mr. Burns," as Washington called
him, will be the subject of portraiture often in the future, stick-
ling for the largest equity and conditions, and paying little
relative respect to the opinion of the General, whom he once
declared to be of eminence chiefly on the score of having married the rich widow Custis.

Burns had a daughter, as well, whose prospective wealth in
Washington City-lots was to make another man historic. This
was Marcia Burns, a fairly-educated, fair-looking, clear-headed
young woman, the only child of the crusty David. When the
Congressmen settled on the agueish site of the new city, and
found the distances too magnificent for patience, they sought
relief from poor lodgings by visiting the Carrolls, Calverts,
Taylors, Laws, Peters, Lloyds, Keys, and others; and immediately there was a courteous contest for the hand and fortune
of Davy Burns' child. The Congressmen filled the long, low,
one-story-and-garret farm-house of nights, and the most assiduous and good-looking of them all was John P. Van Ness, of
New York. They all besieged Miss Marcia Burns, and she
followed the rule of choosing trumps when in doubt. She
beamed upon the handsome Dutch member.

John P. Van Ness was now past 30, and the son of a celebrated New York anti-Federalist and Revolutionary officer, Judge
Peter Van Ness. His father was a supporter of Aaron Burr

against the Livingston and Clinton interest; and William P. Van Ness, his brother, "that talented man, of dark and indignant spirit," as Jabez Hammond says, was Burr's second in the duel with Hamilton, and afterwards secreted Burr in the family home of Kinderhook, where subsequently Irving wrote a part of his Knickerbocker's History, and Martin Van Buren raised cabbages and smiled on Nature.

The elder Van Ness sent Aaron Burr, recently United States Senator, to sound the young woman Burns, and ascertain the degree of her worldly wisdom and her father's worldly prospects. Burr, always plastic in match-makings, reported in an exalted strain upon Miss Marcia's strength of mind and probabilities, and thus Columbia County, New York, and the District of Columbia, united their leading families.

The groom had been educated at Columbia College, New York, and was of such equal spirits, that, till death, he retained all his popularity in Washington, and "filled all the high offices that the citizens of Washington had the power to bestow upon him." His bride was equal to her alliance, and kept a tender memory in Washington long after her obstinate father was laid in the Cave of Macpelah.

MARCIA BURNS.   VAN NESS.

For a little time the bridal party inhabited old Burns's cottage, still standing at the foot of Seventeenth street. Next, Mr. Van Ness built a two-story brick house on the corner of Twelfth and D streets. The city lots selling well, and money being unstinted, Van Ness next erected, right beside old Burns's cottage, a great brick mansion, still perfect, and inhabited now by Thomas Green, the son-in-law of the elder Ritchie, the celebrated Richmond editor. This great house was designed

by the architect Latrobe, and it cost about $50,000, upwards
of half a century ago.   The country-place of the bridal couple
was meantime the "Globe," situated in Virginia, not many
miles from Washington, where they possessed 1,500 acres, part
of which is now owned by Caleb Cushing.   In 1865 the mansion on "The Globe" burned down.

VAN NESS MANSION, AND DAVY BURNS'S COTTAGE.

It is customary to refer to **Burns** as a common old fellow,
but he appears to have used the first moneys derived from the
sale of his land and lots to educate his daughter in a manner
to fit her for the exalted company expected on the site of his
farm.   Seven or eight years elapsed between this good fortune
and her marriage.

A copy of the funeral discourse of Rev. William Hawley,
(Nicholas Callan's copy), rector of St. John's Church, delivered on the occasion of the death of Mrs. Van Ness, 1832, is in
possession of W. H. Philip, Esq.   Parts of this discourse say
as follows :

" She survived her only child, Mrs. Ann E. Middleton.
Born on the spot on which she expired, the whole of Mrs. Van
Ness's life had been passed in witnessing the beginning, the
rise, and progress of this flourishing metropolis.   She was
placed by her parents in the family of Luther Martin, Esq., of

Baltimore, who was then at the height of his fame as the most distinguished jurist and advocate in the State of Maryland, and with his daughters and family she had the best opportunity of education and society.* At the age of twenty she was married to the 'present worthy mayor of our Capital.'

"In early life," continues the clergyman, "she had great sprightliness of mind and amiableness of disposition. The sedateness of her manner gave her dignity, and the genuine piety of her heart became her rule of life, when her daughter had been born and educated. This daughter returned from boarding-school at the time the splendid dwelling on Mansion square was prepared for the reception of the family. Leaving the cottage which stands at hand, and under whose humble roof she had been born and nurtured, Mrs. Van Ness witnessed the subsequent marriage of her daughter. But in November, 1822, the bride who had been but a few months before 'attired in nuptial dress, adorned with jewels and surrounded with gay attendants,' plighted her vows, was consigned, with her infant, to the grave.

"From this period Mrs. Van Ness seemed to have bid the world and all its gaieties farewell. She endowed an orphan asylum with $4,000 in real property, left it by will $1,000—the legacy an old friend, widow of Governor Blount, of North

---

* Luther Martin married a daughter of Col. Cresap, of Maryland, long the reputed slayer of the family of Logan, the Indian chief. Martin was a shiftless genius, who had been born at New Brunswick, New Jersey, in 1744, and removed, in 1762, to the little Eastern shore Maryland, part of Queenstown, where he studied law and taught school until 1770. He was a protégé of Judge Samuel Chase, and in 1778 became Attorney-General of Maryland, distinguishing himself by prosecuting tories. In 1804 he defended Judge Chase, in the unfinished capital, Burr presiding, in a speech pronounced " wonderful " at the period. In 1807 he defended Aaron Burr, at Richmond, and lost his popularity in Maryland for years. Intemperance grew upon him, and he became, at last, a guest of Burr's banished years, and died in 1826. Chief Justice Taney describes him as a rambling talker, with slovenly rhetoric, using vulgarisms, but fair 'and weighty in argument, and wearing ruffles at the wrist, richly edged with lace, but dabbled and soiled, and with rich clothes unbrushed, and intoxication often paramount.

Carolina,—and labored with Congress for its further endowment of $10,000. She attended the church and Sunday School in this church constantly, and sought out orphans with a mother's yearning. The old cottage house in which she was born and in which her beloved parents ended their days, was an object of her deep veneration and regard. In this humble dwelling, over whose venerable roof wave the branches of trees planted by her dear parents, she had selected a secluded apartment, with appropriate arrangements for solemn meditation, to which she often retired, and spent hours in quiet solitude and holy communion. Her sickness was long and painful. A few days before the end she celebrated the sacrament with a few of her Christian friends around her bed. She bade all the several members of the family an affectionate farewell, and on parting with her dear husband, while he kneeled by her dying bed, she said, with her hand upon his head : ' Heaven bless and protect you ; never mind me.' "

The funeral took place Monday, September 10, at 4 P. M. The mahogany coffin was covered with black velvet, and ornamented with a silver plate, on which was engraved her name, the day of her birth, marriage, and death. A leaden coffin was inside the wooden one. Another plate, the gift of citizens who had held a meeting of condolence at the " Western Town House," referred to her piety, charity, and worth, and it was fastened on the coffin, " a little below the former." It told the story thus : " Born 9th May, 1782. Married 9th May, 1802. Died 9th Sept. 1832."

The Mausoleum had been erected some years previously. Her hearse and family carriage (coach and four) were dressed in mourning. Little female orphans, in divided ranks, marched to the bier and strewed it with branches of the weeping willow.

A poem in the *Globe*, by H. G., (Horatio Greenough ?), said :

> " Mid rank and wealth and worldly pride,
> From every snare she turned aside.
>   *   *   *   *   *   *

"She sought the low, the humble shed,
Where gaunt disease and famine tread.
And from that time in youthful pride,
She stood Van Ness's blooming bride,
No day her blameless head o'er past,
But saw her dearer than the last."

After Van Ness had been a Bank President, Militia Commander, and what not, he died several years after his wife. He had provided a tomb, unrivaled in the New World, a copy of a temple of Vesta, where the Burns and the Van Ness alliance should be monument-

VAN NESS MAUSOLEUM.

ally inurned. This tomb was constructed of stone, and was an open dome, with stone pillars, and a deep vault beneath it, eight feet in depth, with three tiers of cells, six cells to the tier. Mr. Edward Clark, architect of the Capitol, told Col. W. H. Philip, who recently removed and 'set up the Mausoleum, that it was one of the few tombs strictly monumental in the country, and that the material in it, and the fashioning of them, would cost, at the present time, $34,000. They took the structure down, and have re-built it precisely as it was, in Oak Hill Cemetery, Georgetown. Underneath it they found seven bodies. viz. :

1. David Burns.—a few bones, and a skull and teeth, and the relics of an old-fashioned winding-sheet, which wrapped the defunct around and around, as if afraid he might get out of it, as out of some other bad bargain. The undertaker of the latter part of the nineteenth century looked at this winding-sheet as if he were stumped at last. It was too much for him.

2. Mrs. Burns, wife of David. On this lady history is silent.

3. Gen. Van Ness. A fine old body, who sued the Government of the United States for violating its agreement with the original proprietors of Washington in the matter of selling to private purchasers lots near the Mall. He was beaten, although he had Roger B. Taney for counsel. He gave an annual entertainment to Congress, and his six horses, headless, are said to gallop around the Van Ness mansion annually, on the anniversary of his death.

4. Marcia Van Ness, heiress of Washington. Mrs. Van Ness's portrait is at the Orphan Asylum, and at Colonel Philip's residence ; a sweet, thin Scotch face, with gleaming, dewy eyes, crowned with a lace cap.

5. Mrs. Ann E. Middleton, only child of John P. and Marcia Van Ness ; married Arthur Middleton, son of a signer of the Declaration of Independence ; she died in childbirth, and Middleton married for his second wife a daughter of General Bentevolia, of Rome.

6. General Montgomery, a relative of the family.

7. Gov. Cornelius P. Van Ness, ex-Collector of the Port of New York, Chief Justice and Governor of Vermont, and for nine years Minister to Spain. He was the father of Mrs. Judge Roosevelt, of New York City, and of Lady Ouseley, wife of Sir William Ouseley, Secretary of the British Legation, who was married at the Van Ness mansion.

The square on which the Mausoleum stood sold for $160,000 not many years ago, and the proceeds went to the Bentevolia alliance.

The heirs of John P. Van Ness were three, in equal parts :

1. One-third to Mrs. Philip, whose son is W. H. Philip, Esq., of Washington City.

2. One-third to Gov. C. P. Van Ness.

3. One-third to the heirs of Judge W. P. Van Ness, Burr's friend.

Of this celebrated estate there are still many lots in the possession of the heirs of the above.

General Van Ness lived down to the period of the Mexican war, attaining the ripe age of seventy-six. He became the first President of the Bank of the Metropolis in 1814. Several portraits are extant of him. In one he is represented as wearing a powdered wig and toupee with very light, fine, brown hair and side-whiskers, with a short forehead, and strong perceptive brows, very full and memory-keeping, a fine, aquiline nose, straight lip and chin, and small mouth and a fine, hazel, open eye with brown lashes and eyebrows. A handsomer man, a woman, nor a novel reader never looked upon. There is a luscious, Dutch look about that portrait Gilbert Stuart painted of Van Ness which does not fail to account for his success with Miss Burns. He left no will and never made one. The toast after his death was, "well fed, well bred, well read: we never shall look upon his like again!"

William P. Van Ness, brother of the Mayor, was also a striking-looking man of larger intellectual development than General Van Ness, but of less pleasing expression; he enjoyed a larger area of career than the Mayor. The Van Nesses were said to be descended from Ayrd Van Ness of West Vriesland, Lieutenant Admiral of Holland.

Amongst the episodes of the old Van Ness mansion is the story of Ann G. Wightt, well known in her day as "sister Gertrude."

She was a cousin of Mrs. Marcia Van Ness, and of a Maryland family. A young and beautiful child, she was sent to school at Georgetown Convent, and while her parents were absent in Europe she became enamoured of the ideal convent life and took the veil. She is said to have risen to such consideration that she was talked of as Lady Superioress. When about thirty years of age she slipped on the dress of one of the monks or fathers, and one evening, left the Convent by stealth and was driven to the Van Ness mansion, where she claimed the protection and hospitality of John Van Ness on the score of cousinship. A day or two after she arrived, two priests called at the house and demanded to talk with her. She

answered them from the head of the stairs that under no circumstances would she return to the Convent.   It was never
known why she had taken flight, but she became the reverse
of a recluse and was a gay and brilliant woman in society, but
she never married.   Amongst her intimate acquaintances at a
later period was Isis Iturbide, a daughter of the Emperor of
Mexico, who left Miss Wightt a legacy of $10,000, and the lat-
ter had the sagacity and perseverance to go to the city of Mexico and obtain the money while the other Iturbides got little or
nothing.   She was notable for her splendid black, flowing hair,
superb teeth, and great conversational power.   She died at the
residence of Honorable John Y. Mason in Richmond, a short
time prior to the civil war.

The Van Ness Mansion made its last public appearance in
the Assassination Conspiracy when its affable and inoffensive
proprietor, Mr. Green, was put into a military prison upon a
newspaper rumor that the mansion was to have been used as a
place of incarceration for President Lincoln preparatory to his
removal to Virginia by stealth.   It is a noble old property, and
when the Board of Public Works or whatever is responsible
hereabout arranges Seventeenth street and fills up the canal, the
ride around this mansion up the shaded river side to Braddock's
Rock and Camp Hill will be one of the best in Washington.

A word on the subject of the original proprietors of the site
of Washington.   To their titles all deeds for property in the
Federal city date, and I spent an hour looking them over one day
recently in the Room of the Commissioners.

The Carroll estate was divided into " New Troy," 500 acres,
Duddington pastures 431 acres, and Duddington Manor 497½
acres.   St. Thomas bay entered the Manor from the Eastern
branch and St. James's creek, behind it, separated Duddington
pasture from Notley Young's farm of 400 acres.   East of Duddington, and nearer the Navy Yard was " Houp's addition," laid
out for Madame Ann Young by Jeremiah Riley and his father,
Eliphas Riley in 1757.   Part of the same was resurveyed for
Charles Carroll, Jr., in 1759 and called ' Cerve Abbey Manor.'

The dwelling (70x22 feet), great smoke house, spring house and brick stable (95) at Duddington were erected after the city was laid out. A log house and a frame hen house in the corner nearest the Capitol were on the square previously.

Robert Peter's log mansion house (36x22), quarters and outbuildings stood on the square between 13th and 14th streets west of W and boundary.

Mr. Young's mill (36x24), stood between 1st and 2d streets East and M and N streets in what is now "Swampoole." The widow Digges had log houses in Delaware avenue near by.

John Davidson's heirs occupied his frame mansion and log wings (32x20) (12x12) between 12th and 13th streets west and K and L north; his family graveyard was at the corner of K and 13th.

Mr. Fenwick's house, 60 by 31, stood right on the space where Georgia Avenue intersects S. Capitol Street, at the water side; the graveyard was just by.

Messrs. Lynch and Sands lived in a "mansion house," 20 by 17 at the corner of L North, and 6th West, near the old Seventh Street Market.

The widow Young had a mansion house 36 by 23, with half a dozen tenements, right on the Eastern branch, between 17th and 18th streets East, at the burnt bridge.

James M. Lingan's frame mansion and office attached, 66 by 22 feet, was right in Ninteenth street, nearest N, at M and N North.

Samuel Davidson's log dwelling and kitchen (original) stood on square 183, at 17th and M streets, four squares north of Lafayette Square.

David Burns's house and graveyard, occupied then by James Burns, 20 by 16—graveyard 30 by 30—stood on H street North, between 9 and 10 West, identical with the subsequent Mausoleum.

The residence of Notley Young was a staunch and roomy brick, which stood near the Potomac side, upon the bluffs near the Washington wharves, and was taken away within a comparatively recent period, to accommodate a new street.

Notley Young's mansion (original proprietor) was in the middle of South G street (between Squares 389 and 390) and between 9th and 10th streets West, half way between the steamboat landing and Long Bridge. One of his barns was at 10th and D, and another at 7th and I. His graveyard was at the riverside where South II strikes the water.

Abramam Young's mansion house (22 by 22) and graveyard stood on North D, by 15th East, at the city boundary.

Samuel Blodget's mansion, 29 by 12, stood in 16th Street West, between P North and Massachusetts Avenue, half way between the White House and the boundary.

George Walker's mansion—53 by 82, graveyard, and log tenements stood between Maryland Avenue, North E, 6th Street East and 7th, Square 862, on the Bladensburg route.

Mrs. Prout's house—53 by 24, and graveyard stood on Square 90, M and 8th streets.

Mr. N. Young's dwelling, above referred to (42 by 52), stood in G street, between 9th and 10th, Square 389–90, and it had 27 cabins, sheds, houses, barns, etc., attached, between 7th and 11th, and F Street and the river.

At Alexandria, in 1798, Mr. Fairfax's house was on the opposite heights of Hunting Creek, opposite "Parry Hill." Cameron's Mills were just above the neck of the creek; Lee's house was on the first knoll back of the town, just opposite Cameron Street, if extended; the Episcopal Church was at Columbus and Cameron Streets; the Quaker meeting-house at St. Asaphe and Wolf; the Presbyterian and Methodist, on the same square, between Royal and Fairfax and Wolf and Duke. Catholic and Dutch Lutheran Churches were suggested at Church and Washington Streets.

Widow Wheeler's log buildings, and three distinct corps of graves, in rows, stood three squares above the Navy Yard bridge, between Virginia Avenue and 14th East, and South M Streets and the Eastern Branch, right behind the Commissioners' wharf, where also was the upper ferry.

One of the most notable estates around Washington is that

of the Calvert family, which existed in somewhat better than its present condition, before the District was laid out.

The estate of Mount Airy lies one mile north of Bladensburg, upon the Old Stage road to Baltimore, and the Washington Branch Steam Railway passes through the noble level park where once, I have heard "Porte Crayon" say, herds of deer roamed at will. Lodges of plastered brick, quaint to the eye, flank the main gate, and as the visitor canters down the drive to the mansion, he sees upon a low eminence to the left, within

MT. AIRY.

view of both lodge and villa, the burial ground of the family. Two flat tombs, vault-fashion, enclose the remains of John and of Rosalie Eugenia Calvert, and the memorial stone of Charles B. Calvert is an upright piece of marble,—the three substantial and plain, and thus inscribed:

In memory of Charles B. Calvert; Born August 23d, 1808, Died May 12, 1864.

Blessed are the merciful; for they shall obtain mercy.—Matt. v. 7.

Here lies the body of John Calvert, Esq., of Riversdale; youngest son of Benedict Calvert, Esq., of Mt. Airy, Prince George County, Maryland, and grandson of Charles Calvert, sixth Lord. Baltimore, who died January 28, 1838, aged 70.

Here rests the body of Rosalie Eugenia Calvert, wife of Geo. Calvert, and daughter of Henry J. Stric, Esq., of Antwerp.

May she be remembered among the children of God, and her lot be cast among the Saints.

> " We see the hand we worship and adore,
>   And justify the all-disposing power."

From this mound of sepulture a pleasant view is afforded of the picturesque negro cabins scattered over the estate, of the large barns and improvements which were in their prime about 1830, and of the blue and gray wooded hills of Prince George's, which almost enclose the estate, as well as that vista of declining terraces toward the Anacosta, at Bladensburg. The mansion is built of brick and stone, rough plastered, and in color, bright yellow. It is flanked with offices which are connected with the centre by short colonnades, and the grounds are tastefully ornamented with glass houses and fountains. This estate has been the home of one of the natural branches of the Calvert family for many generations—that of Benedict Calvert, son of Charles, Fifth Lord Baltimore, whose daughter Nelly became the youthful bride of the child of Mrs. George Washington, and Mother of George Washington Parke Custis, with whose estate of Arlington in Virginia, the fine old aristocratic coaches of the Calverts exchanged ceremonial visits, up to the periods of Jackson and Van Buren.

Following the fashions and opportunities of their time and station, the Lords Baltimore strewed natural offspring, even from the beginning. The pious George, first of the title, left Philip Calvert, born out of wedlock; Benedict Leonard, Fourth Baltimore, married the grandchild of a mistress of Charles II, and this lady bore illegitimate children whom the husband petitioned the House of Lords " to bastardize." Charles, the Fifth Baltimore, left Benjamin (called Benedict) Calvert, who is, in the above inscription, for some reason attributed to the Sixth Baltimore. Finally, Frederick, the last Baltimore, died without other issue than Henry Harford and his sister, both natural offspring. The family of Benedict Calvert of Mt. Airy, has always been honorably associated and held in high esteem in Maryland.

The great families of that early day in the vicinity of Washington were the Calverts of Mount Airy, the Curtises of Virginia and Georgetown, and the Carrolls of Duddington. Mrs. George Washington's son married Eleanor Calvert, and the eldest daughter of this marriage married Thomas Law, the second married Thomas Peter of Georgetown, and the son married Mary Lee Fitzhugh and moved to Arlington House after the death of his grandmother Washington. Here we have a family association both mutable and memorable.

Thomas Law, brother of Lord Ellenborough, a Lord Chief-Justice of the King's Bench, and son of a Bishop of Carlisle, made a great fortune by the aid of Warren Hastings in India, and his brother was one of Hastings' counsel. It was thought better for the interests of Hastings that Law should slip off to America, and as at that time an immense speculation was current in Washington City lots, Law embarked and lost the greater part of his fortune in building houses around the new Capitol. He erected several of the fine old edifices on New Jersey Avenue heights, and there he dwelt in widower solitude after his divorce from his wife, who had taken advantage of a visit he made to Europe in 1804 to assume male apparel and consort with officers at the marine barracks. The house where Law dwelt after obtaining the divorce was then a boarding house for Congressmen kept by Mitchel, a Frenchman. It was Law who obtained the consent of Congress to open the Tiber Creek by lottery. These points are derived from C. W. Janson's American book, published in London, 1807.

Miss Josephine Seaton tells us that Thomas Law was a younger brother of Lord Ellenborough, Lord Chief-Justice of the King's Bench and brother of the Bishop of Bath and Wells. He served in the civil list under Lord Cornwallis in India and came to America enraptured with Washington's character and Republican prospects. He married Anne Custis, sister of George Washington Parke Custis, of Arlington, and built blocks in the city with his India accumulations, and had a country house. Like Joel Barlow he was a deist. He had two sons, John and Edmund, and possessed considerable random genius. Jefferson wrote to him respectfully in 1822 from Monticello.

Colonel John Tayloe, one of the wealthiest land-holders in

Virginia, moved to Washington and built a town house in 1798. He had an income of $30,000 a year, was married to the daughter of Governor Ogle of Maryland, and was thirty years of age when his house was finished. It was called the Octagon.* The following year he established the Washington race, course nearly on the site of the present Columbia College. His income in 1804 was said to have been $75,000 a year, and he expended $33,000 annually in the purchase of land, having great tracts on both sides of the Potomac. He died in the Octagon, March 3, 1828, in the 58th year of his age; his widow lived until 1855. Tayloe was undoubtedly the wealthiest citizen of Washington in the first quarter of a century of its history. Probably no other person has had as much income since within the District limits, if we except Mr. Corcoran the banker. Tayloe was educated in England after the revolution. A considerable portion of his large property remains in the hands of his connections.

On the Maryland side of the Potomac within a few hours' ride of Washington are two great old mansions called respectively Notley Hall and Marshall Hall.

Notley Hall is referred to in the novel of Rob of the Bowl in these terms :

" Think of my ride all the way to Notley Hall—and round about by the head of the river too—for I doubt if I have any chance to get a cart over the ferry to-night. The boat-keeper is not often sober at this hour. Would you rather ride twenty miles (from old St. Mary's) to Notley, or twelve to Mattapany ?"

George Notley was mentioned in the remodeled school laws of 1723 as one of the seven trustees of the principal and better sort of inhabitants of Prince's Georges county named by the Assembly.

The Marshalls were a leading church of England family in St. George's Hundred as early as 1642. Marshall Hall is now (1872) a pic-nic resort owned by a Washington City inn-keeper. The Addison family of Oxon-Hill came to America between 1650 and 1660.

---

* Engraving of Tayloe's Octagon on page 118.

More than two hundred feet above the Potomac stands Arlington House, one of those huge adaptations of classical architecture to domestic uses which abounded in the Middle States and the South about the period of the Revolution. It shows to admirable advantage from Washington, with its front of a hundred and forty feet breadth, much of which is taken up with a heavy Doric portico, designed, as old Custis, its proprietor, used to say, in his affectation of art, after the Temple of Pæstum. But when the grandson of George Washington's wife got the great columns up, his patience, his money, or his art gave out, and he hastily covered the Temple of Pæstum with a barn roof. The house is not split up into so many small rooms as Mount Vernon, and some of its larger apartments are cool and spacious. It used to be the depositary of many Washingtonian trophies and portraits, and we owe to Custis an account of nearly all the pictures and casts of Washington that were taken. In the light of the late war Arlington House might have become a sort of rebel Mount Vernon had Lee been victorious, and its position is strikingly like that of Washington's homestead. It has the same yellow color of rough casting, a lawn and natural fresh timber, and Custis and his wife are buried together privately upon their estate, like George and Martha Washington. But by the reverse of fortune, and by the many thousand Federal soldiers buried around the mansion, Arlington is the Mount Vernon of that collective Washington of the second Union—the volunteer soldier of the people. Here are fifty or sixty acres of graves, a white head-board to every one; and the natural level of the grass rolls over all, so that the dismal coffin-like mound common to church yards is not manifest. The grounds are laid out in an unaffected way, and on the great carriage-drives the officers are buried. Amongst the soldiers' graves there are some rebels, laid away in honorable equity, but accredited to their cause upon their head-boards. The effect of the ceme_tery is to make one think of rest, neatness, and coolness. Overhead, the hickory, walnut, elm, oak, and chestnut trees, some of them a century old, make shadow without mourning. There are no funereal willows or cypresses.

The graves project their files of head-boards to the limit of the timber, and they ramble into the realm of sunshine, making the semblance of a silent encampment of tents in miniature. The disconnected remains of two thousand soldiers of Bull Run are laid away together under a single granite scroll, which bears a dignified descriptive title. The cemetery proper does not occupy more than a third of Arlington wood and park, which is probably composed of 200 acres, and is a fine instance of Virginia landscape, covered with great trees, containing springs and rills, and from many parts of it the city of Washington and the suburb of Georgetown are seen directly below, in all the clear chiseling of a Potomac atmosphere. The mansion of Arlington is merely an office for the Warden of the cemetery now. The old estate, of which it was the homestead, embraced eleven hundred acres, and was the property of Daniel Parke Custis, the first husband of Mrs. George Washington, and one of the richest men in the colonies. Washington left it to his wife's grandson and his own adopted son, George Washington Parke Custis, who died in 1857, leaving this estate to his daughter, Mrs. Colonel Robert E. Lee, during her life, and then to Custis and Fitzhugh Lee, his grandsons. Arlington could not be confiscated, therefore, as it was not the property of the traitor Lee, but by the accumulation of taxes upon it, the State of Virginia ordered it to be sold. Edwin M. Stanton, to whom we owe the purchase and preservation of a good many relics, such as Ford's theatre, resolved at any price to buy Arlington. He bid it in without opposition for twenty-six thousand dollars. Previous to this time all the Washington relics that had not been carried off by Mrs. Lee, were taken to the Patent-Office, that temple of sewing machines and martyrs' relics. The old house is naked of everything but flower-pots now.

"BRENTWOOD."

"Brentwood," the estate (1873) of Captain Carlisle Patterson, U. S. N., stands in the hilly woods north of the Capital. It was the farm of Robert Brent, Esq., a Maryland farmer, whose daughter married Joseph Pearson, Congressman from North Carolina. Soon after the Capital was pitched in the neighborhood.

The house was built in 1816 from designs by Latrobe, who threw his habitual dome over it, but devised a really elegant residence. The main building is three rooms broad, including a very elegant crosswise hall and the dome behind it as rooms, which they are, and of exquisite proportions at that. The wings are five rooms deep.

The Pearson Mill stood until the Civil War, on the Tiber near Boundary street, when it was pulled down, but not until a painting of it had been made by Mr. Cranch, the artist. Many years before the water had been diverted, to supply the Capital and its fountains.

Mr. Pierson was thrice married, and to Miss Worthington of Georgetown at last. One of the daughters of this marriage was wedded to Augustus Jay, grandson of Chief-Justice John Jay.

There remained of this estate in 1873 about 150 acres; ninety-six acres had been detached and turned into the Kendall Green, and Columbian Institute properties. The present owner, Captain Patterson, is the brother-in-law of Admiral David Porter.

Daniel Carroll, the first Commissioner of Washington, was born at Upper Marlbro,—an old Maryland court-house town, recently opened to the outer world by railway,—and he was sixty years of age when he became a Commissioner to locate the Capital City upon a part of his estate. He was a Catholic, and therefore for a small part of his life not eligible to political promotion. But his wealth, prudence, and patriotism, and the leading position of his brother, Bishop Carroll, and of the Carroll family at large, made him, to the end of his days, a prominent man in public counsels. He had been a member of Congress, and a member of the Constitutional Convention, and was near the close of his days when he became the Federal Commissioner. Reduced by infirmities he was unable to work with much energy upon the Capital site and he resigned his office in three or four years, and died May, 1796.

The Carrolls of the western shore of Maryland were a very numerous family, and much confusion has grown out of the similarity of their names. At Bishop Carroll's chapel, eight miles north of Washington, are tombs of Eleanor Carroll, relict of Daniel Carroll, Esq., who died in 1796 at the remarkable age of 92, so that she must have been born in 1704. What a remarkable old lady this would be to tell us about pre-Washingtonian incidents! In the same grave-yard lies Ann Brent, daughter of Daniel Carroll, and widow of Robert Brent, who was born in 1733, and died in 1804. In the same grave-yard lie the Digges, a notable family in their day, and patrons of Major L'Enfant.

At Georgetown College Cemetery, a cross of marble stands at the head of a slab which is said to cover the general remains of those elder Carrolls who were removed from Duddington at a comparatively recent period.. At the base of the cross is the inscription, set up over the son of the Simon Carroll :

TUDOR PLACE.

" Daniel Carroll, of Duddington, Obt. May 9, 1849, aged 84."

Tudor Place, of which we give an engraving, is the finest villa in Georgetown, and was built by Thomas Peter. Here Robert E. Lee paid his last visit to the District of Columbia, about 1869. It is now occupied by Thos. Beverley Kennon, of the Peter family.

Threckall's addition to Georgetown celebrates the name of a notable family, whose estate was near the convent, and is now destroyed.

" Kalorama," used to be a celebrated Washington villa, the seat of Joel Barlow, Esq., poet, diplomatist, soldier, and successful speculator.

Colonel William Washington lived at Kalorama prior to Barlow.

Another notable place in Georgetown is the Linthicum house, built by Colonel Dorsey, next owned by Robert Beverley and occupied for many years by John C. Calhoun, while in the height of his national reputation.

Thomas Lin Lee, who was at the time fifty years old, was addressed by Washington, in July, 1794, and asked to serve with Richard Potts, as Commissioner, in place of Governor Johnson and Dr. Stewart. " The year 1800," said the President, " is approaching with rapid strides, equally so ought the public buildings to advance. The prospect is flattering ; . . the crisis is, nevertheless, delicate." Washington then intimated that he wished to avoid past negligence by naming Commissioners who would reside on the Federal site and consider their salaries as paid to them with that understanding to defray their expenses.

Mr. Lee had been Governor of Maryland between 1779 and 1783, and an efficient co-operator with General Washington in supporting the armies of the country. He was a delegate both to the Continental Congress and the Constitutional Convention, and had just retired from the Governorship of the State when he received the nomination of Federal Commissioner. He died in 1810.

Richard Potts, another Commissioner, lived at Fredericktown, and had been a patriot and Governor of Maryland between the early terms of Governor Lee, and was a United States Senator. He was an educated gentleman.

Frederick, in Maryland, was a flourishing place, with an arsenal, five churches, and about seven hundred houses, in the last year of Washington's administration. Travelers in those days describe the portion of Maryland intermediate between Frederick and Washington, as nearly reduced to the condition in which it remains, to a great degree. Yellow clay and gravel, tilled with the hoe instead of the plough, worn out with tobacco culture, and often lying in naked prospects, with scarcely an herb to cover it. The people, however, were prying and inquisitive, compared to that phlegmatic German population on the Monocacy, whose fields were thrifty and green with wheat. An English traveler, who visited the Great Falls as early as 1796, turned off at Montgomery Court-house, and crossed about three miles above them, by a ferry, one mile and a quarter wide, to the Virginia shore.

Thomas Johnson, another Commissioner, had been a delegate from Maryland to the Constitutional Congress, and Governor during the early part of the Revolution. Between 1791 and 1793 he was Judge of the Supreme Court of the United States. He died at the age of eighty-seven, in 1819.

Alexander White, Commissioner as above, had been a delegate from North Carolina to the Continental Congress, and a representative up to 1793; he is said to have been an ardent and eloquent man, and he died at Woodville, Virginia, 1804.

Mr. Commissioner Scott died in the year 1800, and his place was filled by W. Church.

Analostan Island, in the Potomac, opposite Georgetown, containing 70 acres, was the celebrated residence of General John Mason, where was entertained Louis Philippe, by the descendant of George Mason, of Gunston Hall. The house was burned down during the civil war, and the island is now a pleasure resort. Jas. M. Mason, rebel Commissioner to Europe, passed his childhood here. Government built a causeway, connecting this island with the Virginia shore. The novelist and poet Paulding wrote as follows, in 1825, on "Anadostan:"

> " On either side, and all around,
>   The weltering wave is seen to flow,
> Noiseless, or, if you hear a sound,
>   'Tis but a murmur, soft and low.
>
> The great trees, nodding to and fro
>   In stately conclaves not a few,
> Whisper as secretly and slow
>   As bashful lovers ever do.
>
> The tinkling bell, the plashing oar,
>   The buzzing of the insect throng,
> The laugh that echoes from the shore,
>   The unseen thrush's vesper song—
>
> And when I count the earthly hours
>   That I shall cherish most of all,
> That walk in Anadostan's bowers
>   Will be the first that I recall."

A few sketches of the early Commissioners of the city are appended:

In Georgetown College Cemetery is this tombstone bearing reference to the family which owned a part of the river front where the city was pitched.

"To the memory of the Rev. Notley Young, who departed this life August 1st, 1820, aged 54 years."

Opposite Oak Hill Cemetery in Georgetown is what is called the Colonel Carter place, on which the houses burned down about the close of the war. Here lived the French minister Sartiges and M. Mercier, with whom Prince Napoleon stopped on his visit to this country. Governor Henry D. Cooke bought the grounds and ruin for $50,000 and laid the foundations of a large mansion on which work has been suspended for several years.

The following inscriptions are in Glenwood Cemetery.

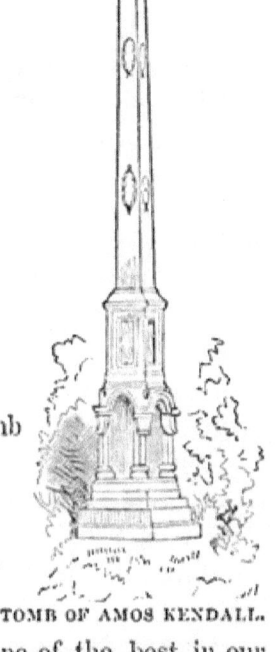

> Our father JOHN LESSFORD,
> The Chronicler of Washington,
> Died Feb. 23d, 1862.
> Aged 36.

> AMOS KENDALL.
> Born August 16th, 1789.
> Died Nov. 12th, 1869.

> JANE KYLE,
> wife of Amos Kendall,
> Born October 12th, 1807.
> Died June 25th, 1864.

On Postmaster General Kendall's tomb
are these mottoes :

> "Charity is love in action."
> "Blessed are the dead who die in the Lord."
> "The path of the just is as the shining light."

TOMB OF AMOS KENDALL.

As a public official, Mr. Kendall was one of the best in our
service, and he may truthfully be called the great Postmaster
General. He went into his office poor and left it very poor.
Every cent that he has made was acquired subsequent to his
resignation, and it was gained almost entirely by his business
association with Mr. Morse, the inventor. When Kendall took
the Post-Office in charge he turned out every clerk, and for a
week had the books of the department overhauled. Those
clerks whose accounts were straight were re-appointed, and the
derelict dismissed. He was so poor that a tempter appeared to
him in the person of a subordinate and clerk, who pertly said :

"Mr. Kendall, I am aware that you have no money. I have
an account in the bank, and will lend you some when you are
in need of it."

"Thank you," said Kendall coldly, "I don't know that I

have need to borrow any money, but when I have, I certainly shall not borrow it from a subordinate."

This clerk wanted some favors in the way of pickings. Next morning he was turned out of the Post-Office.

Morse, the inventor, lacking business qualifications entirely, had made up his mind to secure Amos Kendall to popularize his telegraph apparatus. Kendall set to work with rigid method, and, proceeding to organize companies, arranged that Morse should have so much stock in each company, according to its capital, and that he (Kendall) should have a certain portion of Morse's revenue. In this way both of them grew speedily to riches, but Kendall had business thrift and vigilance, and at this time he is probably richer than Morse—unless he be dead. Kendall has been in two things consistent all his latter days— he has been a Jacksonian Democrat, and a rigid member of the Baptist Church.

I met him at the close of the Impeachment trial, and interrogated him as to Johnson's criminality.

"I take little sympathy in politics these days," he said; "neither with Mr. Johnson nor his opponents. I never admired him."

Last New Year's day the old man stood among his married daughters, receiving visitors, the handsomest septuagenarian in Washington. His residence, until of late, has been in a grove, called Kendall Green, on the borders of the city, and he is rich in real estate all round about here. The Baptist Church, with the high iron spire, at the corner of Eighth and H streets, has cost him probably $150,000. Kendall was a Northern man who began life a school teacher in Kentucky, and he never lost sight of the New England economical virtues, while he was conservative in politics. I asked him last New Year's day what he thought, after this long interval. of the character of Andrew Johnson.

"He grows larger as he recedes," said Kendall; "he was the greatest American I ever looked upon, and second to only him to whom all greatness is subordinate, the first President."

15

The later life of Mr. Kendall has been troubled by but one considerable loss, that of his son, who was shot dead in a street collision with the son-in-law of his old friend, John C. Rives. He made no upbraidal nor mutiny, but laid away vindictiveness with the bones of the lad, who was at fault.

Kendall was not a man that the nation will weep over. He was too strict, too well-balanced, too much guided by pure, cold human judgment to wring from men affectionate regrets that he never desired. Sufficient unto himself, within his own resources, architect of the wealth he evolved, his life has been so complete and fortunate that there is no urn upon his tomb for tears. Heaven makes some men exceptionally perfect in life, that, dying, it may show how poor they were, lacking weaknesses.

A few hours ride by rail from Washington will take the visitor to Charlottesville, the home of Jefferson of which I shall give a short description.

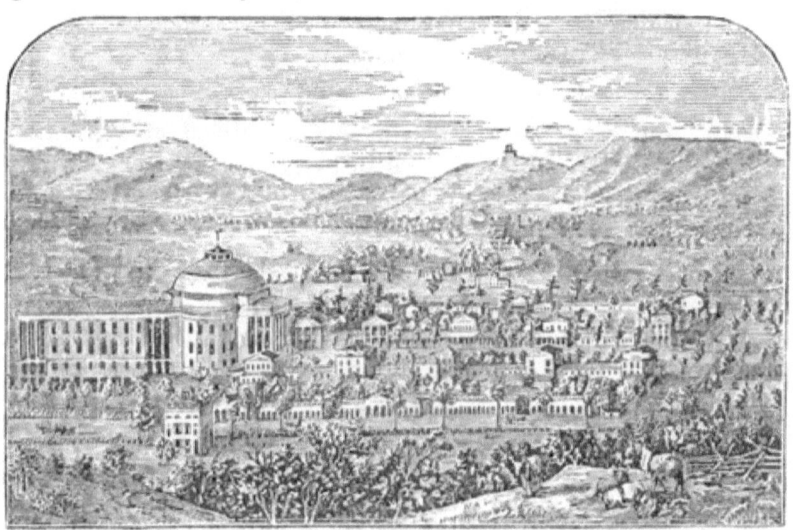

JEFFERSON'S UNIVERSITY AND HOME.

Leaving Washington at 7 o'clock A. M., I breakfasted at Alexandria, and crossed Bull Run before 9. There are two Northern settlements on the weird old stream,—its deep pools and frequent eddies lying gloomily among the rocks,—one set-

tlement completely new, and hewn out of the timber and underbrush lying beside the railroad, and its neat frame cottages
and warehouses standing upon smart boulevard streets, with per-
spectives of bold hills in the street vistas; the other village is
at Manassas Junction, amongst Beauregard's old forts, and it
contains five hundred traders, tavern-keepers, and mechanics.

The view at Manassas is the first of the great series of Blue
Ridge landscapes, which make what is called the Piedmont
terrace of Virginia so entrancing. Manassas is a bold, open
plateau, bounded by blue mountains, which make the landscapes look wide and stately. Bull Run is the gulf to the
northward where the plateau drops away. Nothing now
remains of the battle fought here but certain redoubts,
breastworks, and forts, overgrown with sedge or dribbling off
to weed. The Rappahannock and its outlying stations—every
one the site of a battle—soon passed by. I saw the pretty
soldiers' cemetery at Culpepper, and then Cedar Mountain arose,
where I had wandered bareheaded on the night of the fierce
battle there, feeling the first paralysis of the fear of death.
All the crops of oats, wheat, potatoes, and corn were thriving,
and the wheat harvest was nearly over. I dined at Gordons-
ville, a town of railway junction, which the rebels held during
nearly the whole of the war—a pretty, struggling, whitewashed
town at the foot of hills; and here leaving the Richmond road
to the left, I passed through the Southwest Mountains, under
the base of Monticello, and crossing the Red Ravenna River,
was at Charlottesville.

Being here to attend commencement, I took advantage of
the proximity of Monticello to ride there. It is only three miles
from the town, and on the side opposite to the site of the
University. It is a doomed mansion, standing on the crest of
a conical mountain, the promontory of a ridge of such, and
the Ravenna River washes the base of the hill.

Hiring a horse for one dollar and a half, or at the rate of half
a dollar an hour, I rode briskly out the south road, forded
Moore's Creek, and turned up the base of Sneed's Mountain.

Fine forest trees shaded the way; the fields were tinted blue
with the stalks of weeds; the wheat, all cut and shocked, stood
on the shoulders of the hills, and slipped into the dips and
curls of rich valleys; the streams were heard saying liquid
things to the dry air, and rabbits, tame as the mice that play
round a baby's crib, cocked up their plump bodies in the road
and looked sideways archly and squintingly. All the streams
caught a reddish tinge from the oxides of iron in the clay, and
yet they reflected the sky and their banks like crystal; locust
trees grew amongst the stone walls that enclosed the fields;
some large oaks stood in the barest vistas, and the loose horses
rested beneath them from the sun; I heard few birds or grass-
hoppers singing, and my whole attention and cestacy felt the
impression of the expanding sceneries, which widened as I
mounted, showing the humped backs of blue mountains, and
loftier ranges further off, which were swung across the sky like
a scarf of gauze. The forms of these nearer mountains were
like the postures of Michel Angelo's marbles, unique, sinewy,
startling, elbowed, and hipped, and bending and yawning, and
their strong outlines· were filled in with the bluest, grayest,
sweetest mists and herbages, while between the isolated cones
and spines the valleys rolled like the Illinois prairies, and,
wherever there was a depression, you could guess a stream.
Rising higher and higher, the narrow roadway became a terrace
on the brink of a ravine, and at times there were deep creases
and rocky shelves over which the way had to be carefully
picked, but the higher I climbed the purer and rarer grew the
air, the nobler the stature of the oaks and ash trees, and the
deeper the sense of majesty in nature round about. I pictured
the tall, strong, buoyant man who had ridden over this road so
often, looking away at the plains and eminences, and feeling in
his spirited nature the inspiration of their rolling freedom.
Like the backs of bisons thundering along in herd and suddenly
arrested by some alarm, they stood silent, picturesque, and
gigantic along the plain. Glimpses of other mountains were
seen through the foliage, as I rose into the purer air, and at

last, gaining the crest of the ridge, I turned along the mountain spine and began to climb Monticello. No fence nor wall lined the road, which wound round and round through the timber, till, suddenly, in the wildest part of the wood, I came to a tall, brick enclosure, partly broken down and pierced in the middle to make place for a panel of iron rods, through which I saw a rough granite obelisk and some granite slabs. This I knew to be the family cemetery of Jefferson.

It was a part of the natural woods, and tall locusts, linden, and hickory trees grew amongst the graves, while an abundance of small herbage, bushes, weeds, and climbing vines grew upon the walls and amongst the slabs and vaults. The enclosure was about one hundred feet square, the wall was ten or twelve feet high, and within it were, perhaps, thirty vaults and tombs. No words can convey to you an idea of the desolation of the scene as associated with such a man. The first glimpse through the bars filled me with a sense of pity and indignation. The bars contained no wicket, and a barred gate on another side was fastened with a large padlock, so I climbed over the *grille* and the tottering wall, and let myself down amongst the graves. A thunder storm which had been gradually moving and muttering overhead now began to bellow, and some lightning attended it, but not a drop of rain fell.

Jefferson's tomb is made of granite, and is about eight feet high; almost every letter is gone from it, chiseled and chipped off by vandal students, and it looks battered and nondescript, like a Druid stone. Under the monument is a plain slab, more perfect, covering the remains of his favorite daughter, Martha, and this, like almost every other stone in the grave-yard, contains a religious or poetic inscription. One or two of the slabs have fallen off the brick vaults, and some are cracked or overgrown with moss. The grave-yard seems to have no keeper, and to be falling to decay unregretted; weeds grow under the trees; the road to the gate is blocked with bushes; the great President's tomb itself is simply frightful. He has many living descendants, but, as the livery stable man said to me :

"You know how it is down yur, now. It's every man for himself, and 'Ole Tom' being dead, has no friends."

Mounting my horse anew, I passed through the remainder of the wood of Monticello, entered a cornfield, and finally drew near a garden fence and some vineyard poles; before me stretched a straight and narrow orchard lane, with some out-buildings at the further end; to my left, on the crest of the mountain arose the dome of Monticello. You must understand that Jefferson's house is set upon a lawn, made by shaving down the cap of the mountain, and that it stands probably five hundred feet above the little town of Charlottesville and the Ravenna River. This house was not finished when the Revolutionary War began, but Jefferson inhabited it while he was Governor, the Legislature at that time meeting at Char-lottesville, and here were entertained nearly all the officers captured with Burgoyne at Saratoga, as well as Lafayette, and all the great leaders of troops and opinions for fifty years.

Monticello, like almost every celebrated Virginia mansion of the old planter time, wears a look of dilapidation, and, as you draw near it, you feel a sense of shiftlessness, of old black imported bricks, of gates unhinged and hats stuffed in windows, of threadbare stateliness and imposing imposition, bankruptcy, reduction, failure, woe, these are the impressions.

The style of the house is that of a Corinthian villa, with a dome over the middle, and with two irregular wings, one portico opening into a green lawn, littered over with carts, harness, rotten benches, and beautiful shade trees,—of the latter, par-ticularly lindens, poplars, and locusts. The portico on the reverse side of the house looks out upon a sort of *parterre*, which is enclosed on three sides by the state stables and by a continuous underground passage which, after an old notion, had connected the whole series of stables, dry wells, and so forth, with the mansion. The stable wings are concluded at the two ends by two-story pavillions, one of which was Jeffer-son's library in the Summer time, and the other was his office in the Winter. The house is large, roomy, and manorial, but it is in a sad state of dilapidation. The shingles on the roof are so rotten that the rain drives in at every frequent shower, and all the wood work of the place is decayed; the paint of a former time has left no vestiges; therefore all the woodwork has a whitish dun-color, but the well-blackened English bricks are said to be as durable and as good as ever.

A shambling boy, who had lost one arm at the battle of Little Rock, fighting with Sterling Price, told me to tie up my horse, and he charged me fifty cents to enter the old mansion. Over the door, under the portico, was a great clock, balanced with cannon balls, which had not been going for forty years. The great hall of the house is partly surrounded above by a gallery or balcony, where it is the tradition that the President used to show himself to crowds of students and admiring visitors.

From this room I passed into the dining-room, with deep butteries, pantries, and so forth, where there was no particle of furniture and a bad smell of funky wood. On the other hand, I walked into a great, naked drawing-room, where there were two large mirrors, made of different pieces of glass set in the wall, and as my face skimmed over them, I had a melancholy presentiment of the many historic visitors whose countenances had also rested there, and—perished. The room under the dome was an octagonal ball-room, with a place at one side where the ladies could descend into the pediment of one of the porticoes, and use it for a dressing-room.

I said to my guide at this spot: "I believe Jefferson never danced?"

"Oh, I expect that he did," said the guide, "for he was a rale infidel, fotched up by old Voltaw."

The indescribably humorous pronunciation of "Voltaw" compelled me to laugh.

Said I: "Was Jefferson really brought up by Voltaire?"

"Oh, yes, he raised him."

Now, this sort of anecdote is just as true as the mass of things related of Jefferson by orthodox people.

Voltaire died in 1778, while Jefferson did not visit France until 1784; so that he never saw Voltaire at all. But Franklin was a friend of Voltaire, and Jefferson succeeded Franklin as Minister to France, and he probably had a higher admiration for Franklin than for any man of his time.

I observed, all through the low, uncomfortable bed-rooms of Monticello, that Franklin stoves were ubiquitous,—real, genuine, original Franklins,—and the guide said that these same stoves could be found in broken pieces all over the farm.

There was never a bedstead in all Monticello, alcoves having been substituted in the walls, and slats were fixed to staples in these alcoves. On one of these uncomfortable beds Jefferson's wife died, and they were obliged to lower her body out of one of the semi-circular windows which abounded there, because there was no stairway commodious enough to permit them to take out the coffin.

I wandered through these old bed-rooms, walking out upon the dangerous roof, haunted the rotten old stables, peeped through the dry walls and the covered walks; saw the front of the house, all chopped and chiseled over with names of boys and boors. In some of the rooms the farmer's wife was drying apples and making raspberry jam; in others farm-gear, harness, and old barrels were strewn about. In one room a dog had littered; the man of the house had the rheumatism; not far off they pointed out the house of Mr. Randolph, Jefferson's chief grandson, and looking southward, we could see Willis' Mountain, said to be 150 miles away. I think in all America there is no such landscape for size and beauty equal to this from Monticello. It far surpasses the view from the terrace of St. Germain. At one time Jefferson owned nearly the whole country round about, but toward the end of his life he became in debt, and sold parcel after parcel, until now the estate is reduced to about 250 acres, which rents for $250 a year. A field hand is capable of possessing the home of the richest President.

Monticello belonged to Captain Levey, a Hebrew, and a

Commander in the United States Navy, who was a rich man, and who had a romantic attachment to the great leader; for he not only took Jefferson's house and dwelt in it, but he had a statue of that chieftain made and presented to the United States, and it now stands in front of the White House. Levey, I am told, married his own niece, which was contrary to the laws of Virginia, and he left the State before the war, whereupon the rebel Commonwealth confiscated his property. It is now in litigation. Levey is said to have expressed in his will the desire that it should be repaired, and made an institute for the children of United States Navy officers. The neighbors consider the estate valued at about twelve thousand dollars. It is now occupied by a farmer named Wheeler. Jefferson's nail factories, grist-mills, and various other expensive enterprises, are now extinct or in ruins. The neighbors say that Monticello will make the finest vineyard hill in America, but at present tumbles more and more to ruin every year, and seems to possess neither master nor patron.

As a change from old times to new, I would relate a passage of a ride recently taken to the Great Falls of the Potomac, passing on the way the celebrated Cabin John bridge.

The name of Jefferson Davis has been obliterated from this bridge, as from almost every piece of architecture and engineering in the country.

The hollow ruin of a hotel at the Great Falls is kept by one Jackson, the brother of that inn-keeper who, at Alexandria, shot Colonel Ellsworth dead; and the survivor is a good specimen of a tavern-keeper in an old settled, pro-slavery region; a slouchy, shiftless, greasy-haired man, whose humor is chiefly an appalling exhibit of his manifold offences, seasoned up with a wild amiability and familiarity. His black hair falls in snaky long locks, behind his ears, and his gray eye has the light of desperation in it. Behind his bar stand a pair of double-barreled rifles and game-bags, and one of the guns he shows as the identical weapon which slew Ellsworth. Jackson says that the gun was not the property of his brother, but borrowed. I

took up the rifle, giving it the benefit of the doubt, and found it
to have been purchased in the year 1836, at a hardware store in
Alexandria, and used for many years as a favorite par-
tridge-piece.

It was on deposit at the time at the Marshall House, and
had been loaded with slugs by its fraternal borrower, with the
intent of killing two men with it—a man with each barrel.
The first barrel was aimed fairly at the heart of Ellsworth, and
in an instant the second would have slain Brownell, but the
Zouave threw up his musket, so that Jackson's shot passed
over his head, and at the same time the desperate assassin was
both shot and bayoneted.

" Where is your brother buried ? " I asked of the inn-keeper
at Great Falls.

" In the family burying-ground, sir, over in Fairfax County,
Virginia.   The widow lives on a nice little property she owns
at Fairfax Court House."

" I believe there was afterward a military company formed
called the " Jackson Avengers ? " "

" Yes, sir.   And they had it reported that I was sworn to
kill Brownell.   That ain't so, sir.   I left him to a just
Gord.   I never bore him no hate.   He was afterwards
in Washington City, and at last he was killed at the
second Bull Run.   I had one other brother in the rebel
army, but I kept out to make money.   Ha! ha! ha!
There is a picture of the shooting of Ellsworth; somebody
came along and gave it to me, and I stuck it up behind the
bar.   Some people says it will make people dislike me, but I
think not.   Everybody knows I'm his brother, and it's a sort
of eppropriarte."

The Aqueduct authorities ordered Jackson away in 1872.

The Loudon Valley, above Great Falls, which runs parallel
with the Shenandoah, was the haunt of Moseby's men, and
the great conduit of treasonable information and contraband
goods, from Washington and Baltimore to Lynchburg and
Richmond.   Leesburg was the nearest den of runners to the

Capital of the country—thirty-four miles—and it was, perhaps, the most lawless village in Virginia. The rebels several times passed to and fro between Virginia and Maryland this way, as they had no railway lines to advance upon, while we generally moved by the lines of rail, and paid little attention to the ferry passengers, between Point of Rocks and Chain Bridge, except to patrol and picket them. Leesburg was illuminated the night of the defeat of Ball's Bluff, and it was the scene of many of the debauches of Moseby's men. The wild torrent region between the mouth of Goose Creek and Great Falls was signally adapted to blockade running, and the dangers of fording and navigating in the roaring river of dark nights, lent a terrible interest to the enterprise of the smugglers and spies. These crossed most generally in small, flat-bottomed scows, hastily nailed together during the day, to evade the order forfeiting every private boat on the Upper Potomac, and the cargo was generally whisky and drugs.

Jackson told me that he had been fifteen times confined in the Old Capitol Prison for running the blockade, and, on one occasion, he walked straight from the jail to the hand-ferry, below the Great Falls, and paddled across with five barrels of whisky. He had been threatened with execution, if he were caught again, but he sent a boy half a mile down stream to fire off pistols, and, being himself shot at several times, finally re-crossed the river with his cargo twice before he could manage to run it into Leesburg. There it was sold to officers and guerrillas for $1, in gold, a gill.

Such opposite social passages as have been given, bring to view the changes wrought amongst the old Potomac people by pitching the national Capitol amongst them. There is a cemetery in Georgetown—the most beautiful suburb of Washington—which is worthy of a visit from anybody. It stands on the green heights, where they decline in steep terraces to Rock Creek, and ravines making up from the base, describe inexpressibly cool amphitheatres, on whose successive shelves the obelisks of the dead stand motionless and white among the

foliages.   Here are buried old citizens, whose village existence
the nation invaded, and planted the Capital City upon their
fields, so that they grew often rich and married their daughters
to shrewd Congressmen, whose intelligence made the best of
every foot of ground.

Marriage is the destiny of an accident.   Shipwrecked so-
cially upon this marshy island, many a politician made the
best of the site and married Sukey Brown or Betsy Wilson,
who became the mother of Indian contractors and foreign ministers, instead of bearing a herd of young sovereigns who could
fight a game chicken, burn an abolitionist, or wallop a nigger,
without the aid of the art of reading, or the distress of knowing
how to write.

It has occurred to me that in all this running narrative I
have not given the distant reader a description of the Capital
town, as you might have approached it, any time within the
past fifteen years.

Here is the city, as you come to it by the oldest railway from
the North.   First, a series of grassy hills, with sandy creeks
at their passes; then Bladensburg, an angular stretch of old,
gable-chimneyed, bent-roofed houses half a mile from the rail;
then a line of red clay breastworks, worming up to the hill tops,
where stand dismantled forts; then an octagonal building with
a cupola on it; standing out in the country next to a farm-
house and beside a great green imitation bronze horse on a
pedestal in the lawn; the home and foundry of Clark Mills,
sculptor; then the uneasy outlying landscapes of a city, cul-
verts planted nowhere, streets graded to no place, brick-kilns
and pits, a cemetery, frame shanties on goose pastures disputed
by cows made sullen by overmilking; boys, babies, friendless
dogs, and negro women " toting " great bundles on their heads,
no more fence, the smell of apparent garbage and ash heaps,
signs of ground-rents and dirt throwing invitations; and all
this time you are descending into basin land and down the valley of a bare creek; at last a dome, such majesty and whiteness
as you never saw elsewhere, appears sailing past the clouds:
the Capitol!

Out of the long, cramped, green-painted saloon-cars you descend, into a depot that is first a shed, then a dark, dull, dirty vestibule; for the republican government is not yet independent enough to make corporations, erect buildings here worthy of the Capital City. The exterior of this depot is also mean and squatty. Backed up against the depot are omnibusses and cabs, whose drivers, white and negro, bully you with whip-handles. Over this pirate body you see close by like a marble majesty, the Capitol, dome and wing, stand silent, sentient, scintillant, regardless of the bare lots, shanties, barracks, machineries, marble slabs, and unfinished dirt terraces that surround it.

To comprehend this city further, climb to the dome of the Capitol. It is enveloped by a range of fort-capped hills, half in Maryland, half in Virginia. Through these hills the Potomac makes two broad clefts, coming down from the West and departing to the South. Down where it departs, a point stands out in the water, the City of Alexandria, Virginia, near where it comes in, on a hill-top, connecting with Washington, is Georgetown, Maryland. Between Alexandria and Washington, a river makes up acutely from the Potomac, the East Branch, whose real name—the Anacostia—is now nearly obsolete. In the angle between the Potomac and the Anacostia lies the Capital City, about fifteen miles from the tomb of the patriarch who selected the site and gave it the name. The dome where you stand is nearly in the geographical centre of the city, yet by the force of circumstances, the actual, settled city lies away from the junction of the two rivers, between the Capitol and Georgetown, and in a lower, baser site. Out on the extreme cape, between the rivers, lies the Arsenal, connected with the city by a straggling line of houses; it was the place of the trial and execution of the assassins of President Lincoln. Further up the East Branch, where the only bridge crosses it, lies the Navy Yard, a walled in and busy area of twenty-eight acres; over this bridge Booth and Harrold escaped to Surratsville and lower Maryland; still further up the East Branch lies the Congressional Burying Ground, and to both the Navy Yard and the cemetery, lines of disconnected houses radiate from the Capitol. Around the Navy Yard there is a large and elderly settlement, to which a street railway runs, and amidst it the town tower of the oldest church in Washington, where worshiped Jefferson and Madison. The front of the Capitol inclines this way, and over the high, thickly settled plateau looks out the Statue of Liberty over your head.

CONGRESSIONAL BURYING GROUND.

Its back is toward the real city; behind it eighty-nine thousand people live; in front of it not more than fifteen thousand.

Now turn yourself around, with your back against the back of the statue, and look away from the Navy Yard:

Beneath you are the terraces of the Capitol and the lawn. From the bottom of the lawn great avenues radiate; that to the left leads to the Long Bridge and indices Arlington Mansion, far up the Virginia Hills, a steam railroad passes along it and crosses the bridge to Alexandria. The second avenue is a canal, straight as a sunbeam, and it points to the white, chalky stump of the abandoned Washington Monument. The third is the famed Pennsylvania Avenue, dense with the costly shops and hotels, revealing at the bottom the granite Treasury building; the fourth to the right is a short avenue, and it leads to the City Hall, the seat of municipal government. Half lost in houses beyond this are the great marble piles of the Post-Office and Treasury, which lie in the densest centre of the city. Other avenues to the right go out to the open Northern country and the far forts which Early invested in 1864. Away off, on the crest of one of these hills, you see dimly the white tower of the Soldiers' Home, Mr. Lincoln's summer residence.

Objects between this latter and your eye are the brick block where General Grant resided, the dingy brick factory of Government Printing, and the Church of St. Aloythus, with the highest tower and the merriest bells of Washington.

Now, return your eye to the Patent-Office, which stands on its own separate though inferior hill. A great market-house lies on each side of it, nearly equi-distant. The market-house to the left is on the Avenue. Between this market-house and the Potomac are the fine towers of the Smithsonian Institute. Continuing South to the Potomac, you come to the Ferry to Virginia, and the shipping piers

Follow out the Avenue to the Treasury, and beyond it are the President's House, the War and Navy Departments, General Grant's head-quarters, and the elegant residences of Lafayette Square, where live most of the ambassadors and rich officials. Beyond these a stream called Rock Creek falls through a deep valley to the Potomac, and on the other side of it is Georgetown. Another creek, immediately beneath the Capitol where you stand, is called the Tiber ; it bends around the base of Capitol Hill, and, by a long detour nearly parallel with the Potomac, gets an outlet not very far from the mouth of Rock Creek. This Tiber makes, with a canal leading from it to the East Branch, an island of one-fourth the city.   .

All the forts around or overlooking the city are dismantled, the guns taken out of them, the land resigned to its owners. Needy negro squatters, living around the forts, have built themselves shanties of the officers' quarters, pulled out the abattis for firewood, made cord-wood or joists out of the log platforms for the guns, and sawed up the great flag-staffs into quilting poles or bedstead posts. Still the huge parapets of the forts stand upright, and the paths left by the soldiers creep under the invisible gun muzzles. Old boots, blankets, and canteens rot and rust around the glacis ; the woods, cut down to give the guns sweep, are overgrown with shrubs and bushes. Nature is unrestingly making war upon War. The strolls out to these old forts are seedily picturesque. Freedmen, who exist by selling old horse-shoes and iron spikes, live with their squatter families where, of old, the army sutler kept the canteen ; but the grass is drawing its parallels nearer and nearer the magazines. Some old clothes, a good deal of dirt, and forgotten graves, make now the local features of the war.

Meantime the too ambitious monument to the *pater patriæ* stands like a stunted giant, the superfluous blocks at its base grown over with grass, and few approach it, even in curiosity. Its foundations are said to be defective, and no money has been voted toward building it this long time. A few boxes, in various parts of the country, receive dimes and quarters towards its completion, but, standing as it now does, a hundred and thirty feet in the air, it has probably reached its highest. I heard a humorous explanation of the failure of this monument, from an Irishman.

" They broke the Pope's block of stone," he said, " it was an onlucky act. The holy Father cursed the whole thing, and immediately the foundation settled."

I have spent part of a day in the shaft and workshops of the Washington Monument, a mournful instance of the short life of public impulse, and of the defects in the machinery of miscellaneous private enterprise.
This monument is already raised to the height of 175 feet. It has already cost nearly $250,000, and is raised to more than one-third its total height. The foundations are perfectly secure, and capable of supporting all the height yet to be added. There are stones from all parts of the world ready to

WASHINGTON MONUMENT.

be inserted in the shaft or subsidiary temple ; but work has been suspended upon it for about twelve years.

The monument was discouraged, because the people believed

that the contributions, being dropped into Post-office boxes all over the country, were stolen, and never applied to the edifice, and also because the artists and art critics kept up a steady fire of deprecation upon the plan of the monument. This plan was an obelisk, surrounded with a Greek Temple. There is no notion, at present, of adding the temple, but the Monument Association hope to raise enough money to finish the obelisk. It is easy to do this, and it ought to be done ; for the unfinished shaft in the Capital City is a record of popular impotence, worse than if a monument to Washington had never been begun. This age and people are no exception to the human passion for monumentalization. If ten thousand churches and schools would give twenty-five dollars a-piece, this monument could be finished. The interior of the shaft is of twenty-five feet diameter, between the inner sides of the walls, and so thick are the walls, that the exterior diameter is fifty-five feet. The material is marble from Maryland. Within there is a yawning chasm of shaft, very impressive to look up into, and see, at the farthest height, a scaffold hung, from which a rope droops dizzily, and on the floor the dampness splashes and the darkness lies all around the year, save when some melancholy visitor puts his head within, and feels dejected over the suspended gratitude of the land of Washington. I hope no more great monuments will be commenced, but I hope a feeling will be revived to see this one finished. The memorial stones, to decorate some portions of the shaft, represent all companies, lands, and ages—lava, from Vesuvius ; aerolites, shaken out of crazy satellites or planets ; rocks of copper and of porphyry; stones from Jerusalem and Mecca ; everything but the Pope's stone, which, not the builders, but the mob rejected.

If the Washington monument ever be reared 600 feet high, according to the original plan, it will be of the weight of 125,800,000 pounds ; the portion already completed exceeds 80,000,000 pounds.

CHAPTER XX.

JOBBING COEVAL WITH GOVERNMENT.

We can get little comfort by consulting the early records of the country, to show that there were some bad things done in those days. There is less apology for evil in a great and prospered nation, than in a series of jarring colonies, where few local leaders sought after the revolution to remedy their desperate fortunes. Early in the history of the country we were without organization, authority, or means. Able men in those days had few resources, unless endowed with estates, or surrounded with family influence. But it never was true of the United States, that corruption got to be organized, flagrant and backed by a large part of public opinion, until a few years prior to the civil war. The Confederate Government was as corrupt at Richmond, considering its opportunities, as the Federal Government at Washington. Both were swindled by currency printers, contractors, quarter-masters, and beset by rapacious Congressmen, who endeavored to retard the general cause where they could not take the advantage. What is called the scalawag element in the South, has to some degree been the development of the stealing element at Richmond. In the North the big army contractors have gone to railroad building, and the naval harpies are trying to restore American commerce with the old hulks which were four or five times paid for when chartered by the nation.

It was also true at the close of the Revolutionary War, that contractors, clothes-furnishers, and others, endeavored to spoil the new government, but we can nearly count up on our fingers the early scandals in the history of our country. Let us look at some of them:

1789. The State of Georgia was the first to inaugurate a land swindle. It sold out to three private companies preemption rights to tracts of land; these companies were called the South Carolina Yazoo, the Virginia Yazoo, and the Tennessee Yazoo; the whole amount of land disposed of was fifteen and a half million acres, and the sum agreed to be paid was upwards of $200,000. Subsequently the same lands were sold to other companies, because the first purchasers insisted upon making their payments in depreciated Georgia paper. Hence arose the controversy on the celebrated Yazoo claims, so called.

1790. Mr. Jefferson, who is not good authority on a question of the Treasury, in the first administration, thus speaks of what he believes to be corruption, under General Hamilton, after the Federal assumption of State debts:

" The base scramble again. Couriers and relay horses by land, and swift-sailing pilot-boats by sea, were plying in all directions. Active partners and agents were associated and employed in every State, town, and country neighborhood, and this paper was bought up at five shillings, and even as low as two shillings on the pound, before the holder knew that Congress had already provided for its redemption at par. Immense sums were thus filched from the poor and ignorant, and fortunes accumulated by those who had themselves been poor enough before."

1790. Mr. Jefferson is authority for the statement that Robert Morris, and other advocates of the national assumption of the State debts, made a lobby amongst the Federal Congressmen, to concede for this point the latitude for the Capitol in 1790. Two Virginia members changed their votes on the financial subject; therefore the seat of government was given to the South. If this was the case, both Morris and Hamilton were well punished for the intrigue. Mr. Hamilton closed his public career before the middle of his life, and Mr. Morris is commemorated in the local history of the seat of government as the victim of the most tremendous speculative failure ever recorded in that city. His houses, put up on the spot since called for his partner, Greenleaf's Point, tumbled to ruins before the public buildings were complete, and he himself spent a venerable portion of his romantic history in the debtor's jail at Philadelphia. The funding bill was then adopted as an act of barter, and twelve millions of dollars were authorized to be borrowed to pay the foreign debt, and twenty-one millions, five hundred thousand dollars, to pay off the State debts. The tariff was immediately pushed up to meet these obligations, and here began the manipulation of duties in the interest of domestic manufacturers.

1791. The same year that the Capital was conceded to the banks of the Potomac, Mr. Hamilton's proposition for a National Bank was brought forward. It passed the Senate in Philadelphia, without division. In the house it was attacked by James Madison and others, but it finally passed by a vote of 39 to 20. President Washington required the written opinions of the members of his Cabinet, as to its constitutionality, and Hamilton and Knox endorsed it with vigor, while Jefferson and Randolph took the opposite side. Its charter was limited to twenty years, and its capital was to consist of $10,000,000, of which the United States subscribed $2,000,000. The bank was to be established in Philadelphia, and was to be managed by twenty-five directors. The bank stock was the favorite speculation of the day, and within a few hours after opening the books the whole amount was subscribed, with a surplus. Branches were established in the chief commercial towns of the republic. This bank and its successors, as we shall see further on, was assailed as one of the corrupt influences of the early period of the republic.

1793. The first charge of general corruption was made in Congress by John F. Mercer, of Maryland ; he intimated that the first assumption of State debts had been dishonestly engin-

cered, and that members of the House had not been wholly
guiltless. To this Theodore Sedgwick replied, saying that the
ears of the House had already been more than once assailed by
insinuations of the base conduct of individual members in
speculating in their own measures. " If," said Sedgwick, " there
be so base and infamous a character within these walls, if
there is one member of this House who has been guilty of
plundering his constituents in the manner represented, let his
name be mentioned, let the man be pointed out."

Another member admitted that speculation had been carried
to a very great extent during the pendency of the funding
system, but that could not be avoided. The matter
was then dropped, but Secretary Hamilton was attacked
by Mr. Giles, of Virginia, and charged with failing to account
for upwards of a million and a half of the public money. He
was called upon to explain this as well as his mismanagement
and intrigue in the negotiation of loans. Hamilton replied
that the alleged defalcations were made up by reckoning bonds
as money, and omitting deposits, etc. Hamilton had, however, borrowed too much money through the forwardness of
the American bankers in Holland. Mr. Giles and his associates introduced nine resolutions of censure, charging Hamilton
with exceeding his powers, with dereliction of duty, with misappropriating loans, deviating from his instructions, and violating the law. A debate followed in committee of the whole,
and although Madison voted to censure Hamilton on all
counts, the resolution of censure failed.

1795. The first charge of personal bribery was made in
1795, and was brought up on the question of a breach of privilege. The charge was very similar to that made against
Mr. Oakes Ames, nearly eighty years later. Two persons
named Randall and Whitney, from Maryland and Vermont,
respectively, had formed a scheme for obtaining from Congress,
for the sum of $500,000, the right to purchase of the Indians
twenty millions of acres, in the peninsula of Michigan. The
proposed purchase was divided into forty shares, some of which
were offered to members of Congress, who were guaranteed

that the shares would be taken off their hands if they should
lose confidence in the speculation. Randall boasted that he
had secured thirty members. Mr. Murray, of Maryland, explained the attempt at bribery to the House, and Randall was
ordered to be arrested and put on trial at the bar. His defence
was that he had been misunderstood, and that his conduct was
merely foolish and imprudent, and not corrupt. He was
declared guilty of a high contempt, in attempting to influence
members as to their legislative functions, and only 17 votes
were cast against the resolution, amongst them Mr. Madison's;
he maintained that the members had no privilege against such
attempts except in their own integrity. Randall was sentenced
to be reprimanded by the Speaker, and was put in custody.

1796.   In 1796 a transaction in Congress of a disgraceful
nature occurred, growing out of the Georgia or Yazoo land
speculation, which would look, in our times, quite like a piece
of corruption. Mr. Baldwin, of Connecticut, of the lower
House, had received a memorial, to be presented to Congress,
asking it to do nothing recognizing the validity of the Yazoo
sale until an investigation could be had. Amongst the Senators who had personal interest in this Georgia speculation
were Frederick Frelinghuysen, the grand-uncle of the present
Senator from New Jersey, and James Gunn, Senator from
Georgia.   Gunn, who was represented to have been a fire-
eater, demanded that Baldwin show him the memorial, before
its presentation, and give the names of the signers up to his
vengeance.   When Baldwin refused, Gunn sent him a challenge, through the precious Frelinghuysen aforesaid. Baldwin
laid the challenge before the House, and the matter was referred to a committee, which reported that both Gunn and
Frelinghuysen had been guilty of a breach of privilege. The
land-speculating Senators made apologies to the House, and
the matter was allowed to languish.

1797.   The first case of the expulsion of a Senator was that
of William Blount, of Tennessee, a very popular man in that
new State. He was exposed by President Adams in 1797,

who sent to Congress some papers showing the condition of the country concerning Spanish intrigues in the south-west, and amongst these papers was the copy of a letter from Blount to a Cherokee Indian agent, written while the former was governor of the American territory south of the Ohio. The agent sent the letter to the President, who asked the British Minister what it meant. It then appeared that Blount had played the traitor to the British, in order to right himself in a desperate land speculation. He had designed selling his lands to an English Company, and was afraid that the non-commercial French nation would come into possession of them, by a re-transfer, before he could complete the sale. To anticipate this, Blount had proposed to raise a force of barbaric back-woodsmen and Indians, to co-operate with a British naval force, and put the English into possession on the Gulf. This scheme had avarice for its motive and cool treason for its instrument. The House of Representatives voted to impeach Blount, and the Senate put him under bonds amounting to $50,000. The House also asked that he be " sequestered " from his seat in the interim, which the Senate interpreted to mean expulsion, and forthwith set Governor Blount outside the door, with much less delicacy than the Senate lately showed Messrs. Caldwell, Pomeroy, and Harlan. Blount's sureties, one of whom was his brother, surrendered him into custody, but the case was postponed until the next session, and after the fashion of Mr. Colfax at South Bend, a great reception was prepared for Blount at Knoxville; he was elected to the State Senate, and chosen president thereof. Blount's brother, in the House, meantime sent a blackguard letter and challenge to Mr. Thatcher, of Massachusetts. Strife ran so high at this period that gentlemen of different politics would not speak to each other on the street. Senator Blount died unexpectedly, before his constituents had an opportunity to disgrace themselves by giving him enlarged honors.

The first great scandal against a public official was made public while the Capital was pitched in Philadelphia, in 1797.

Its object was no less a personage than Alexander Hamilton.
One Callender had published a book containing a quantity of
correspondence and documents which seemed to show that
Hamilton and one Reynolds had been buying up old claims
against the United States, and that the latter had received
advances of money from the former to make these purchases.
Reynolds, and a man named Clingman, had some time before
been prosecuted for perjury, and for seeking to obtain fraudulent payment from the Treasury of an alleged debt due them
from the Government.   By Hamilton's influence the Controller
of the Treasury stopped the prosecution.   This Reynolds was
the son of a Revolutionary officer, and some letters which he
and his fascinating wife possessed seemed to indicate that a
dark affair was going on.   Three members of Congress who had
explored the matter, went frankly to General Hamilton and
laid the proofs before him, and required an explanation.   This
was given but it was hardly less astounding than if Hamilton
had been detected in corruption.   He confessed to having paid
one thousand dollars hush money to Reynolds not on account
of any peculation, but to avoid exposure in a very shameless
intrigue between Hamilton and the wife of Reynolds.   Hamilton resolved to take a desperate step and save his official honor,
at the expense of his private reputation and happiness.   He
published certified copies of the correspondence.   We take a
few paragraphs of his tolerably bulky pamphlet from an autograph copy owned by William Duane, and inscribed with his
name, March 28, 1799.   The title is "*Observations on Certain
Documents Contained in Nos. V. and VI. of ' The History of
the United States for the year 1797,' in which the charge of
speculation against Alexander Hamilton, late Secretary of the
Treasury, is fully refuted.   Written by Himself.   Philadelphia, printed for John Fenno, by John Bioren.   1797.*"
    Hamilton shows in this pamphlet all his graces of literary
composition, and strikes from the shoulder at the outset :
    "The charge against me," he says, "is a connection with
one James Reynolds for purposes of improper pecuniary spec-

ulation. My real crime is an amorous connection with his wife, for a considerable time with his privity and connivance, if not originally brought on by a combination between the husband and wife, with the design to extort money from me."

The next salient point is this, well-worded:

. "This confession is not made without a blush, I cannot be the apologist of any vice because the ardor of passion may have made it mine. I can never cease to condemn myself for the pang which it may inflict in a bosom eminently entitled to all my gratitude, fidelity, and love. But that bosom will approve that, even at so great an expense, I should effectually wipe away a more serious stain from a name which it cherishes with no less elevation than tenderness."

These must, indeed, have been hard passages to commit to print, and it argues nobly for woman that, having been assured from the lips of her husband of his offences against her, she could forgive him for his honor's sake, and, when he came home wounded to die, receive him in her arms as if he were stainless. Men never do these acts of forgiveness.

The gist of Hamilton's confession is in these paragraphs:

" Some time in the summer of the year 1791 a woman called at my house, in the city of Philadelphia, and asked to speak with me in private. I attended her into a room apart from the family. With a seeming air of affliction, she informed me that she was the daughter of a Mr. Lewis, sister to a Mr. G. Livingston, of the State of New York, and wife of a Mr. Reynolds, whose father was in the Commissary Department during the war with Great Britain; that her husband, who, for a long time, had treated her very cruelly, had lately left her to live with another woman, and in so destitute a condition that, though desirous of returning to her friends, she had not the means; that knowing I was a citizen of New York, she had taken the liberty to apply to my humanity for assistance.

" I replied that her situation was a very interesting one; that I was disposed to afford her assistance to convey her to her home, but this at the moment not being convenient to me

16

(which was the fact), I must request the place of her residence, to which I should bring or send a small supply of money. She told me the street and the number of the house where she lodged. In the evening I put a bank bill in my pocket and went to the house. I inquired for Mrs. Reynolds and was shown up stairs, at the head of which she met me and conducted me into a bedroom. I took the bill out of my pocket and gave it to her. Some conversation ensued, from which it was quickly apparent that other than pecuniary consolation would be acceptable.

"After this I had frequent meetings with her, most of them at my own house, Mrs. Hamilton, with her children, being absent on a visit to her father.

"In the course of a short time she mentioned to me that her husband had solicited a reconciliation, and affected to consult me about it. I advised to it, and was soon after informed that it had taken place."

The next thing was that the husband wrote to Hamilton that he had discovered the intrigue, and that his heart was crushed; but he wrote shockingly bad English. He reproached Hamilton with having taken advantage of his wife's necessities, and Mrs. Reynolds wrote that he had meant to assassinate the Secretary of the Treasury. Hamilton found himself considerably demoralized. He says:

"In the workings of human inconsistency, it was very possible that the same man might be corrupt enough to compound for his wife's chastity, and yet have sensibility enough to be restless in the situation, and to hate the cause of it."

Of course, after Hamilton let the real facts out right candidly, his enemies discredited him.

"It is showed," he says, "that the dread of the disclosure of an amorous connection was not a sufficient cause for my humility, and that I had nothing to lose as to my reputation for chastity, concerning which the world had fixed a previous opinion."

He goes on to show that, having first black-mailed him for

nearly ten thousand dollars, the panel-thieves then accused him of taking money from the Treasury, and entering into speculation with Reynolds and others. This pamphlet is signed Alexander Hamilton, Philadelphia, July, 1797, and in the appendix to it are all the amorous epistles to and fro, which must have made "live" reading when they first saw the light.

1798. The House of Representatives, during this session refused to pass a resolution previously adopted in the Senate to authorize Thomas Pinckney to receive certain presents which in accordance with custom had been tendered him by the Courts of Madrid and London at the close of his missions thither, and which he had refused to accept because of the Constitutional provision relating to presents from foreign powers. The resolution was rejected on grounds of public policy as was afterwards declared by unanimous vote of the House.*

We will now make a step out of the past, and come to a memorable claim of the present day—that of Mrs. Gaines:

Mrs. Gaines is the great female character in New Orleans. She is a small, plump, bright-eyed woman, and she has been the heroine of the very heroic law suit which she has personally conducted, raising money for the purpose to the amount of half a million, recovering nearly a million, and with all the probabilities in her favor of getting a million more. But, if she were to get what she would receive under other conditions than those of democratic public opinion, she would possess half the city of New Orleans in its most valuable part, and be a wealthier woman than Miss Burdett-Coutts, whom Wellington endeavored to marry out of covetousness to her fortune.

The home of this lady is in New York City, but she spends much of her time in New Orleans, where she has strong friends and strong enemies, almost equal in number. Her suit has involved many of her intimate friends, from whom she has borrowed money to pay lawyers' fees and court fees. Her second husband, General Gaines, believed implicitly in the merits of her case, and gave her $200,000 to fight

* Additional matter illustrating this Chapter may be found in Chap. VII.

it out. She has been twice married, and to excellent
men both times ; and I was told that the brother of her first
husband had helped her with nearly the whole of his funds.
There is a dash, piquance, and nimbleness about this woman
which distinguishes her as one of the queens of her sex. She
is said to be about 60 years of age, but would pass for 40 ; and,
while her education is defective, she is a natural authoress and
lawyer, and can write a stinging brief where sauce and justice
are mixed together.

She is just the sort of woman to be identified with New
Orleans—Provincialism and Cosmopolitanism mingling in her
as amongst many of these old *habitans*. Her mother had married
a French bigamist, and, discovering the fact after she reached
New Orleans, presumed to marry again the great Daniel Clarke,
one of the wealthiest men of the South. He was one of the
earliest property-holders in New Orleans, and represented that
territory in Jefferson's administration. Clarke was smitten
with the beauty of the French lady, and contracted a secret
marriage with her—made secret in order to anticipate a divorce from his French predecessor. But, while he was absent
in Washington City, his relatives and connections, who had
expected to get his money, told him that his wife was unfaithful, and hired her lawyer to tell her that her marriage with
Clarke was not legal. Having a natural affection for man, the
French lady proposed to take a third husband. This offended
Clarke, and it seemed to confirm the lies which had been said
against his lady ; and meantime his daughter was born—the
present Mrs. Gaines—for whom he maintained affection, so
that, while he let the wife slide, he gave a very considerable
sum of money to a man in Wilmington, Del., to be used,
and applied to educate his daughter, and at her maturity to
present her with the principal. Thus the banks of the Brandywine, where Thomas LaFayette, Harry McComb, and your humble
correspondent passed their youth, became the playground of the
future Mrs. Gaines. As they had no penitentiary in the State,
and never whipped white people at the post, the custodian of

the baby saw no business reason why he should not squander her money. He did squander it, and history has made no mention of the innumerable fried chickens, roast capons, and deviled crabs which this unfaithful guardian devoured out of the inheritance of the babe in the woods. A Mr. Croasdale, who is the best journalist in Delaware, some time ago collected the story of Mrs. Gaines's childhood in Wilmington, and it was published, over another name, in the *Galaxy Magazine*.

When the guardian had squandered all the money, and both his liver and conscience were disordered, some faint recollection of her childhood inspired a dream in the little ward.

She dreamed that her father was another person than the man she called father; that he was rich and lived in a distant State, amongst negroes, molasses, and such other things as children like. She came down to breakfast the next morning, where the unfaithful guardian was thinking, in a morose way, how fortunate it was for him that the State had no penitentiary, and how unfortunate that there were no other little girls to be let out with endowments. Unhappy Delawarean. For him no longer the fried oyster gamboled, or the chicken fricaseed! While he was thinking over this thing the little girl told her dream. He immediately fainted, and they had to borrow some old Delaware rye, next door, to bring him to consciousness.

As he came to, he said, "Myra [he pronounced it Myrie, as did the future gallant husband of the little girl], who has been putting that nonsense into your head?" He answered his own question by confessing, like an honest criminal in one of the fairy books.

The little girl was at once put in possession of a law suit. She became a heroine, married two husbands, and has living grandchildren. Both her husbands were devoted men, who believed in her claim; she does the same, fighting it out.

I have a theory that Nature's chief use for us in this life is employment; and that, like the flies which convert into healthy motion the mortification and decay in the atmosphere, we are all right enough when something is given us to do. But Nature makes a very unhappy fly of us when she leaves us a vast law suit, and at the same time impresses us with the fact that we are after our rights. Who would know much about Daniel Clarke, or the man in Delaware, if it were not for Mrs. Gaines?

To show how the public service and the lobby come into collision, it may be well after reciting such matters as the above, to relate a conversation which I had in 1873 with one of the most gallant and distinguished men in the army, whose name I shall not give, because he might be injured by the political harpies of that service.

" What is our relative position amongst the navies of the earth?" said I.

" We stand not above the *sixth* in rank.

" Great Britain could whip all the navies of the earth to-day, one after the other. Her salvation lies in keeping up her commercial supremacy. I have seen a single vessel in her navy, in the China Seas, which could take in detail, the whole American fleet, and beat every ship successively. The iron-clad to which I allude cost about $1,500,000, whereas we have just voted $3,000,000 to build ten ships. Next to England comes France in the perfectness of her navy. Russia and Spain have enormously improved their efficiency upon the seas. North Germany, since she has acquired seaports, has become very ambitious, and not only are her vessels-of-war remarkable, but her naval officers are of a remarkably shrewd and vigilant description. Even Turkey has a better navy yard than the United States, strange as it may appear."

" Do you think that we are defenseless in our great cities by reason of the prostration of our navy?"

" Well, New York City might be defended, because of its remarkable natural defenses. A ship or two sunk in the channel, at the Narrows, or in the Lower Bay, would prevent an entire fleet from getting up to the city; but an iron-clad navy could go right into Boston harbor or into Portsmouth or San

Francisco. A few months ago, we barely missed getting into a war with Spain, and the State Department had really got us right in, when suddenly it was suggested that we examine our naval resources for the moment. Word was sent that three or four ships might be ready in twelve months, and two or three more in eighteen months. It is needless to say that we backed right out of the war matter; and the Government, to-day if it knows anything, knows that even Spain could drive right into us, because now-a-days men do not count, but mechanism in ships does all the business. Anticipating trouble with us on the Cuban account, Admiral Paolo, now Spanish Minister, visited the United States, and took an inventory of the armored navy. He had all the points; and, by George! we would have been humiliated in the estimation of the earth. You see, about 1864 or '5, we were the first naval power in the world, having gotten up the earliest iron-clads. But that navy was created for an emergency, constructed of green timber, and a late investigation shows that every shot fired into those old rotten iron-clads would have crumbled the whole framework.

The English and other foreigners built upon our suggestions, and they have made a series of ships which can steam 13 knots an hour. Prior to the war, our old wooden vessels were also the best afloat. The Minnesota, and such other great ships in the American navy, made good speed, and gave our sailors confidence; but, as we stand, to-day, we must keep mum, or be terribly humiliated."

" What is the best opinion in the navy—I mean amongst the large and high-minded officers—on the proper method of building a ship-of-war, whether in a navy-yard or in private yards ?"

" There is but one way," responded my informant, " of constructing a legitimate vessel-of-war, and that is in the National navy-yards. Private shipbuilders work only to complete a job, get their money, and show the ship, which will be good enough for a short period. But the greatest thing to be looked to in a ship-of-war is the timber; which must be thoroughly seasoned;

for green timber warps, rots, and is unable to hold its outer armor in a very little time. The English build of that magnificent teak; and I have seen, in the Japanese Seas, one of Nelson's old ships, which had come out in eighty days from Great Britain, as sound and buoyant as he found it at Trafalgar. We built for an emergency, in private navy-yards, of green oak, which has no longevity. The corrupt shipbuilding interests of the country press forward whenever we want new ships, and, under the tariff system, rob the Government, and, under the modern job system, carry off the prize from the navy-yards, where we should have work of the best class slowly and surely made. The tariff interests, in the estimation of the honest officers of the navy, will some day be our scorn as a people, and get us such a flogging that we will cut the throats of these jobbers in the public necessities. The great iron-clad ships of Russia, Prussia, and Spain have been built by the English, under free-trade, and the work superintended by Commissioners from the respective nations which wanted the vessels. We cannot build a ship-of-war for our lawful needs in any foreign ship-yards, without an act of Congress, and that act never will be granted under the horrible system of the modern tariff. I have heard naval men say that, if the United States got into a war, and was flogged out of its life, so that the whole bluster would be taken out of her, and we should have to begin, like France, from the bottom, and work out an honest salvation, we would be better off. Something calamitous is necessary to stop the unpatriotic excesses of our business people."

I asked the gentleman who spoke thus intelligently what the leading men of the navy thought of Secretary Robeson and Admiral Porter.

"For Robeson," said he, "there is such contempt that I do not care to relate the character of it. Instead of demanding, like a man, that Congress give the country a navy sufficient to protect us, he begs for everything, as if he were apologizing for making the demand.

"Admiral Porter reduced himself in the estimation of all men of courage when he wrote those sycophantic letters to the President. But he is equal to his position. He always was a shrewd, prying, suggestive fellow, and no portion of the navy has come under his supervision but he has improved it. There is no fear of him. Robeson is a mere shyster, and the civil head of the navy is the disgrace and contempt of every genuine officer in it. We have no navy whatever. Every one of those monitors and iron-clads built during the war is rotted, and an appropriation of $3,000,000 will do nothing more than build some fair iron-clad coasters for defense."

Some of the scandals so-called of modern Washington partake of the marvelous and get little consideration from people who demand testimony as well as theory. Let me give an instance:

You have probably met, amongst your acquaintances, this kind of a man: An agreeable, decorous, thrifty well-to-do gentleman, who will talk with you intelligently about the growing evils of the country and of the general corruption of politics, but will, at the same time, inflexibly pursue his private purposes against the Government, under the belief that, in the destruction imminent over everybody, the best way to anticipate it is to make one's stake and share so big that it can bear one up above the common calamity. The country is full of people who deprecate corruption, but do not arrest their personal scheme, which is a part of it.

The gentleman in this case referred to was taken with a communicative mood. He knew perfectly well that he could tell me nothing of consequence which I would not print, but it is queer that very many careful men have somewhere concealed about them a hidden desire to give points against their class to newspaper men. Said this gentleman:

"I am one of the oldest engravers in this country. There is an investigation one day to be made into the currency of the country, which will startle you, and your newspapers and

all their readers. There is a $10 bill. Take it,—look at it!
Do you see anything notable about it ?''

I looked the bill all over, and then the man all over, and
saw nothing to excite a remark in either. '' There is nothing
particular about that bill,'' he said, '' except that it is counterfeit. There are eighteen distinct counterfeits on the $10 bill,
and, as an engraver, I know that they represent eighteen different counterfeiting gangs. I got this bill from a street-car
conductor in New York. ' I got into his car, and, as he came
along, I said, ' My friend, I am sorry to ask you for so much
change, but really I have nothing less than $20.' ' O !' said
he, ' I'll oblige you,' and, in a smiling way, he gave me this
bill and a quantity of 50-cent fractional currency. I put the
whole away in my pocket, and, being an engraver, I got to
looking at the number 37 on the lantern window of the car.
Thought I to myself, ' That's a remarkably handsome 7 for a
common painter to make.' You know that an engraver notices
such things. Well, that evening I went into the Astor House,
and, going up to the fine, old, white-haired man who sells
cigars there, and is known to everybody in New York, I tendered him one of the 50-cent papers. Old Jimmy looked at it
and said to me, ' I am sorry, Mr. Robinson, but that stamp is
counterfeit. It's a very well-executed one, but I have nothing
better to do in my leisure time than to look over such things.'
At this Jimmy handed me the stamp, and I looked at it, and
then at the others, and, sure enough, they were all counterfeit.
I quietly stepped outside the Astor House, and looked for No.
37, amongst the cars. I found that the conductors ran eight
hours off and on, and that my man would not come on till next
morning. There I found, at the appointed time, my conductor, and stepped up to him, and said in a low tone, ' Young
man, you changed a bill for me yesterday, and gave me a
quantity of counterfeit money. Now I want you to take it
back without any noise.' He affected to grow indignant, but I
said, ' Stop ! stop ! Do you see that policeman ? If you don't
return me in good money the amount which you changed for

me, I will have you under arrest in two minutes !' Well, it was interesting to see the promptness with which that ' shover of the queer' gave me all of my money, and forgot to ask for his own.

" Mr. Gath, you newspaper men know nothing whatever about the duplication of United States Bonds, and about the quantity of counterfeit scrip afloat. If you, as a newspaper-man, were to go to Gen. Spinner and to the heads of the Treasury, and ask how much counterfeit currency was in cir-culation, they would probably tell you 10 per cent. ; but I tell you, as an engraver, that they have admitted to me that there is 25 per cent., or one quarter of the whole amount of the stamps current in this country, which are fraudulent. Do you know, sir, that the postal currency is renewed six times every year ? That is the case, and see the possibilities for its in-creased duplication and counterfeiting. We could better afford to pay 50 per cent. premium, and use gold, than have to deal as we do with a lot of paper which is beyond the control, to a great extent, of the Government officials. The extravagantly high prices, and the corruption in our politics and life, hinge upon the currency. The duplication of the United States bonds will some day be found such an alarming matter that it will bring the whole country to its feet. That crime began in the Treasury so far back as Chase's time. John Covode and others in Congress made strenuous efforts to expose it, but they were gagged by the gavel and a party majority. An official, who at that time was connected with the printing, had, in some way, got a grip upon the Secretary, and could not be budged from his place by any power in the country. His ac-counts were short one year $63,000, and he could not tell where the money had gone. They kept after him, however, and, on one occasion, he appeared before the examiners with his arms full of bonds, and throwing them down, said, ' There are your $63,000 !' Now, there was a press used for printing at that time, and it ran repeatedly in the night. The official himself was seen to emerge after dark, on two occasions, with a great tin box in his hand, which he put into his buggy and carried away. Now, how much duplication of bonds do you suppose it required to make $63,000 worth of coupons so as to equalize that account?"

"Several hundred thousand, I suppose."

"No, sir; it took between $18,000,000 and $19,000,000 of bonds; and about that time happened the first duplication.'"

I looked suddenly into the old gentleman's eyes, and was in great doubt whether I was speaking to an intelligent lunatic or a great reformer.

If one-tenth of the propositions annually considered in the committees of Congress was to be passed, the burden of taxation would be felt immediately at every fireside of the country, and it is much to be feared that the people will never be sufficiently earnest until the iron enters into the flesh, and jobbery makes them howl.

In order to give an idea of the magnitude of the plunder involved in the schemes of the lobby, which have been defeated in the Congress of 1873, Senator Chandler has employed some of his leisure moments to make out the following list of attempted steals:

Soldiers' Bounty Bill, . . .	$400,000,000
Agricultural Lands bill, . .	90,000,000
Cotton Tax refunding, . . .	72,000,000
Compound interest to States, .	32,000,000
Australian subsidy, ...	5,000,000
Oriental subsidy, ...	13,000,000
Ship-yard subsidy, ...	6,000,000
Other subsidies, ...	5,000,000
The two per cent. job, . . .	1,500,000
Total, ...	$624,500,000

The Soldiers' Bounty Bill and the Agricultural Lands bill were passed by the House, but squelched by the Senate. The

Treasury has had a narrow escape of several of these plundering schemes. Taking into account the stupendous jobs that have been carried through, with the aid of an unscrupulous lobby, plain folk may well stand aghast at the costliness of Congressional legislation.

Those members of Congress who are always looking out for a " spec." have come to despise the constituency. They see that the people soon forget a dishonored public man, and hence the audacious villainy known as back pay passed the Congress of 1873, its champions not scrupling to register themselves in black and white. In order to involve the whole government, judicially and administratively, in this villainy, the general pay of all was increased and made retroactive.

The following table shows the new salaries provided by the bill. The increased salaries of the Speakers of the House and of all other officials took effect on the 4th of March:

The President,	$50,000
Vice-President,	10,000
Chief Justice of the United States Supreme Court,	10,500
Justices of the United States Supreme Court,	10,000
Cabinet officers,	10,000
Assistant Secretaries of the Treasury, State and Interior Departments,	6,000
Supervising Architect of the Treasury,	5,000
Examiner of Claims in State Department,	4,000
Solicitor of the Treasury,	4,000
Commissioner of Agriculture,	4,000
Commissioner of Customs,	4,000
Auditor of the Treasury,	4,000
Commissioner of the Land-Office,	4,000
Assistant Postmaster-General,	4,000
Superintendent Money Order System,	4,000
Superintendent Foreign Mails,	4,000
Speaker of the House of Representatives,	10,000
Senators, Representatives, and Delegates,	7,500

The salaries of all the clerks, doorkeepers, messengers, and other employees of the House were increased from 15 to 25 per cent.

All sorts of ingenious excuses had been manufactured, and were ready at hand, to defend back pay ; amongst other pleas was that against the old mileage system.

Under the system of mileage the grossest inequality in the compensation of members of Congress has always prevailed. Just before the war the father of the present Senator Bayard, of Delaware, who received about $200 mileage, sat by " Duke " Gwinn, of California, who got $19,000. To make the matter more uneqal and unjust the fact was that, although receiving this immense amount on account of travel, Mr. Gwinn actually did not go to Callifornia for years. After the war when Reverdy Johnson was Senator from Maryland, he received $128 mileage for a Congress, while Messrs. Nye and Stewart, of Nevada, received about $10,000 apiece. A few years ago so much complaint was made about this unjust discrimination between members, that a modification of the mileage rates was established, but it has still worked very unequally.

It appears that for the Congress just expired the mileage paid to Senators from the States named was as follows : California, $4,029.60 ; Oregon, $6,492.80 ; Nevada, $3,513.60 ; Texas, $3,000 ; Louisiana, $2,531 ; Arkansas, $2,400 ; Minnesota, $2,475.25 ; Kansas, $2,352.10 ; Nebraska, $2,147.20 ; Mississippi, $2,160.

The idea of making an Omnibus bill to include with the long talked-of increase for the President, the Supreme Court Judges, and the Heads of Departments, the never before talked-of increase for members of Congress, apparently originated with Butler, of Massachusetts, the Guy Fawkes of Congress. He brought the bill back from the Judiciary Committee, on the 7th of February, 1873, with a long report,—historical, argumentative, and didactic,—in which he labored hard to prove that there were strong reasons of justice, morals, and public economy for raising the salary to $8,000 per annum. In the

same report he advocated the increase of the President's salary
to $50,000, and proposed to raise the pay of the Judges and
the heads of Departments to $8,000. His bill to accomplish
all this was recommitted without action. Some time before,
Sargent had tried to put an amendment on the Executive and
Legislative Appropriation bill, raising the President's salary to
$50,000. Dawes, who was in the chair, ruled it to be in
order, but an appeal was taken, and the House, by a vote of
60 yeas to 67 nays, refused to sustain the ruling.

Butler's next move was to get his bill hitched on to an ap-
priation bill. He made the first effort to accomplish this on
Feb. 11, when he moved to suspend the rules so as to instruct
the Appropriations Committee to bring in the bill as a part of
the Miscellaneous Appropriation bill, then about to be reported
to the House. He was beaten by a vote of 81 yeas to 119
nays, but he gained a point—he got a showing of hands ; he
knew the strength of his forces, and could see how many
recruits he must get to win. He had foreseen that it was essential to secure the help of the outgoing members, who numbered nearly 100, and there was only one way to do this : by
allowing them to share in the profits of the proposed raid on
the Treasury. He therefore inserted the words, " including
members of the XLIId Congress," the effect of which was to
make the increase retroactive—going back two years.

Up to this time comparatively few members had faith in the
process of the movement, and very little had been said about
it in the informal canvasses in the lobbies and cloak rooms,
which influence the disposition of bills far more than the
debates upon the floor. Now it was seen that the bill had a
strong backing of pledged supporters, and an active canvass for
recruits began. Late in the night of Monday the 25th, Butler
sprung his bill upon the House, as an amendment to the Executive, Legislative, and Judicial Appropriation bills, which
had come back from the Senate with amendments. No one
but the friends of the measure had notice of his intention. A
large number of members had gone home on the assurance of

Garfield that the bill would be called up only to get it in place, and that he expected no action upon it. Garfield protested, but Butler insisted on a vote on his amendment, and carried it by a vote of 71 to 67, on a vote by tellers in Committee of the Whole. The Crédit Mobilier debate intervened next day, and it was Friday before the question came up again. Butler's amendment, adopted in Committee of the Whole, was rejected by the House, on a call of the yeas and nays, by a vote of 69 to 121. Butler changed his vote to No, in order to move a re-consideration.

Next morning he made the motion, and promised if it was carried to admit an amendment, prepared by Sargent, fixing the salary at $6,500, with no allowance for traveling expenses. This seemed a fair proposition, and the recommendation was carried without much opposition. Sargent offered his amend-ment, but by the time it began to dawn upon the minds of the members who opposed an increase, that, if any change were made in the salary, the whole question would, in the end, go to a Conference Committee of six men, who could put in any amount they pleased, and then force the House to agree to their report, or run some risk of losing the entire Appropriation bill, which would make an extra session necessary. Sar-gent's amendment narrowly escaped defeat, the vote being 100 to 97. Amendments offered by Garfield were adopted, raising the salaries of all the clerks in the House, and adding 15 per cent. to the pay of all other employees, and adding $2,000 a year to the salaries of the Assistant Secretaries of the General Departments.

The bill went to the Senate, and when the question arose on concurring in the salary admendment, some Senators opposed it because it did not increase their pay enough, and others because they thought it wrong to make any increase. Both these elements of opposition united to defeat a motion to con-cur. The vote stood 23 to 36.

The bill then went, of necessity, to a conference committee. Speaker Blaine now took a hand in the game, and appointed as the House conferees Garfield, Butler, and Randall, knowing that the two latter were in favor of a larger increase of salary than the House had, at any time, endorsed. They were both advocates of a beaten proposition, and it was in violation of a well-recognized principle of parliamentary practice to appoint either of them on the Committee. The Senate conferees, named by the Vice-President, were all high-salary men, who insisted that $6,500 was not enough, and would be less than the Pacific Coast Senators got already, with their mileage. The Conference agreed to put another $1,000 on, making the salary $7,500, and they restored Butler's provision for the payment of actual traveling expenses, and retained the retroactive clause, dating the increase back to March 4, 1871. The President's salary, and those of the other officials, they left as passed by the House. The report was made to the House on Monday morning, March 3. It was vehemently denounced by Farnsworth and others, and freely defended, on the ground that the Senators were so stubborn that the House conferees had to yield for fear of losing the bill. The shameful retroactive clause did not find a single apologist, either in this or in any previous debate. It was vigorously assailed and denounced, but no one had the hardihood to say a word in its favor. Everybody knew that it was a barefaced robbery of the Treasury of nearly $1,500,000—a bribe of $5,000 a piece to induce outgoing members to vote to increase the pay of their successors. The provision doubling the President's salary escaped with very little criticism. Members were so much occupied with the question of their own pay that they gave small attention to the portions of the bill relating to other officials.

The conference report was finally adopted by the House by yeas, 103 ; nays, 94. This was a fair test vote, although the high salary men, tricky to the last, tried to make it appear otherwise by falsely saying that the bill would be lost if the report was rejected. The effect of rejecting the report would have been to send the bill to a new conference committee, which could have reported back in an hour with the salary

amendment stricken out.   Every member who voted yea must,
therefore, be held to have favored the salary grab, retroactive
clause and all.   It was late Sunday night before a vote was
had in the Senate on adopting the report.   The result was
yeas, 36 ; nays, 27.   The bill was signed by the President the
same night.   Under the retroactive provision dating the increased pay to Congressmen back two years, every member received $5,000 as extra compensation for services in the Forty-
second Congress, less sum already drawn by him as mileage.
The amount of money taken from the Treasury for this purpose we cannot give with accuracy, because we do not know
the exact amount of the mileage to be deducted.   At a moderate estimate it was $1,400,000.

No justification was attempted in either the Senate or the
House for dating back the increased salary.   It was so disgraceful a proceeding that it admitted of no defense.   The
members of Congress, in accepting their offices, agreed to
serve for the salary provided by law.   On the last day but one
of their term of office, they voted themselves nearly $5,000
apiece as additional pay.   They had the power to do it, and
are amenable to no punishment except such as their constituents may provide for them at the next election ; but their conduct in a moral point of view is very little better than that of
a merchant's clerk who should increase his salary by helping
himself from his employer's cash drawer.

Observe the effect of the back-pay and other swindling
schemes of its class :

The total amount of the various appropriation bills passed at
that scandalous session of Congress exceeds the amount of the
previous session about fifty-four millions of dollars : The
details of the various appropriations of 1873 are as follows :
Preliminary deficiency, $1,699,833 ; Texan border commission,
$18,490 ; pension, $30,480,000 ; American and British claims
commission, $613,500 ; Indian, $5,512,218 ; fortification, $1,-
899,000 ; consular and diplomatic, $1,311,359 ; Military Aca-
demy, $344,317 ; legislative, executive and judicial, estimated,

\$19,500,000 ; naval, \$22,275,757 ; army, \$31,796,008 ; Post-Office, \$3,529,107 ; river and harbor, \$6,112,900 ; sundry civil, \$32,175,415 ; deficiency, \$9,242,871—total, \$195,310,-839.

Truly the 43d Congress was a shameless body. The corrupt members from the extreme Puritan states exceeded in effrontery those from Pennsylvania or Kansas. In the last hours of the session after the Crédit Mobilier case had been disposed of in the House, we had the most extraordinary spectacle of the session presented by a colleague of Oakes Ames, of John B. Alley, of Samuel E. Hooper, of Mr. Dawes, and of Senator Wilson, another Representative from Massachusetts, the Hon. Ginery Twichell, openly and actively lobbying on the floor of the House for the passage of a bill, introduced by himself, in favor of a railroad corporation of which he is president. When the point of order had twice been made upon him, that he could not vote in favor of a bill in which he was personally interested, the Hon. Ginery Twichell left his own desk to take a seat beside the tellers, upon the final division of the House on the question of the passage of the bill, and personally expostulated with members who were voting "nay." Evidently the example of Oakes Ames and the lessons of investigation were utterly thrown away upon the Hon. Ginery Twichell."

Midst all of this scandal the moral and Christian world was doing nothing to show its disgust at what was going on at Washington. The great business house of Phelps, Dodge & Co., of New York, whose leading partner was the patron of orthodox philanthropy, was at the same time paying \$271,000 to the government to be let out of prosecution for smuggling, and the moral newspapers were pompously parading the following solemn declaration of Mr. John Alexander, of Philadelphia:

"By the Grace and Providence of God enabling me, I will contribute to the treasury of the National Association for securing the amendment of the Constitution of the United States, the sum of *five hundred dollars* annually, *until an amendment (in substance such as at present proposed by the Association) shall be made to the Constitution of the United States.*

"If this amendment is not made during my lifetime, I shall hope to continue the aforesaid annual payments through the agency of the legal representatives of my estate.

"I can do all things through Christ which strengtheneth me."

After such an exhibition of pious stupidity we may answer the question which every reader is probably putting in his mind : What can we do about it ?

And this we answer in the words of that admirable review, the New York *Nation*, with whose advice we shall close our chapter :

"We maintain, and with increased confidence," says the *Nation*, "that the shameful corruption in the Government which is showing itself side by side with overwhelming Republican majorities all over the country, is a fresh proof that the Republican party is a common human organization, for the ordinary political purposes—namely, the embodiment in legislation of a small cluster of ideas ; that that purpose was carried out at the close of the rebellion ; that the party is now *functus officio*, and has for several years been kept in office by the popular dread of " reaction " and the force of the great patronage and enormous handling of money resulting from the war ; and that in the absence of any great controlling ideas, of real work, and of a powerful and respectable opposition, its leading men, who, for all practical purposes, are the party and represent it, have grown careless, and insolent, and indifferent to public opinion, and finally corrupt. There is nothing ecclesiastical about them or it. It has no divine mission, and they have no personal consecration. *It* is simply the consensus of a large body of the American people on a few points of home policy, and *they* are a number of not very remarkable gentlemen, whom the American people has put in charge of its affairs.

" The remedy is to be found in the formation of another organization for other purposes. What these purposes are we have frequently intimated. We may venture to repeat them— the reform of the civil service ; the restoration of the judiciary to its old position of independence and respectability ; the simplification of political machinery, so that honest and industrious citizens can attend to their political affairs without the help of professional tricksters; the release of the States from the constant interference and supervision of the central authority; the purification of Congress by the reform of the tariff, and the prohibition of grants, subsidies, bounties, "protective" duties, and the total exclusion of Congressmen from a share in the appointing power. These objects can only be obtained by a party formed for that purpose, and for nothing else. Whether we are near the formation of any such party we do not know. We acknowledge with sorrow and disappointment that the events of last year undoubtedly postponed it, but we would fain believe that those who last year honestly strove to bring about a better state of things, have not abated one jot of heart or hope. We are sure that they must find in what is now passing both abundant justification for their course and abundant reason for trying again, whenever the opportunity offers. It is needless to say, of course, that any such organization would contain, if successful, whatever good elements the Republican party now contains, and many good elements which that party does not contain, and nothing short of this combination of the good of all parties will save us. The good Republicans are not likely to be removed in chariots of fire when the party organization disappears."

CHAPTER XXI.

THE WHISKEY FRAUDS.

In February, 1875, there was received at the Treasury Department, information which led to an exposure scarcely less startling than the famous *Crédit Mobilier* transactions, and which in its final results has been far more decisive, and in that sense, far more satisfactory. Like the *Crédit Mobilier*, it reached close to the doors of the White House; but in this case, too, no sufficient evidence was discovered for believing the President dishonest. He was evidently only the tool of his friends. The country congratulates itself that though its chief magistracy has been so thoroughly belittled by the President, it has not been stained by his corruption.

In the early stages of the preparation of this book, the author gave a detailed account (page 152) of the manner of operation of the "Whiskey Ring." In the light of the recent trials, and those yet to come, it will be seen that the operations of these distillers were very correctly given. This circumstance shows that all parties the least familiar with affairs at Washington, were fully apprised of this thoroughly organized effort to defraud the government. Why, then, have not these frauds been punished before? Simply because, until the advent of Bristow, we have lacked a public official, who either had the moral courage to fight the "Ring," or whose record was sufficiently unstained to render such a fight effective. It was well known that the "Ring" possessed unlimited means; that they could hire the most skillful counsel, and could also " hire" almost any kind of witnesses that they desired. There was too, another great obstacle. It was one thing to *know* that these frauds were being perpetrated, and another, and very different matter to *prove* them so conclusively that a jury could not do otherwise than convict. The " Ring" cared little that it was known that they were defrauding the revenues, so long as they could successfully stop any effort to bring them to justice. So long had they succeeded in doing this, that they became so confident of their power, that they did not believe that they could be disturbed. They had either ignored or quieted Boutwell and Richardson, and supposed they could do the same with Bristow. So surprised were they at their mistake, that Bristow had matters well in his own hands, before they recovered themselves and were ready to act.

Our previous account did not exhibit either the magnitude or the impudence of the Ring in anything like the true proportions. The great difficulty with which it seems to labor was not that some of the government officers were corrupt, but that there were some honest ones, who occasionally, though very rarely, gave them trouble. Even the efforts which were at first made in behalf of honest administration of the laws were rendered useless by the thorough system with which the operations were carried on. Every movement about the distilleries was so guarded, that the parties who were collecting evidence, were maltreated, and even threatened with death ; while at Washington, some of the officers highest in the government service, were in the pay of the " Ring." Consequently, whenever there was any plan devised, these parties in the pay of the Ring immediately telegraphed the news to where the investigation was to take place, and the distillers and collectors would be ready to have everything going perfectly right. When the government detectives retired, they would resume their regular operations.

With these parties who thus kept them informed, the Ring, of course, divided equally. The regular tax levied by Congress is fifty cents per gallon. The distillers paid the collectors thirty cents. These collectors, by fixing the returns, paid a small portion to the government, (it need hardly be said that the portion was as small as it was safe to make it,) and divided the balance among themselves. How much this amounted to, to these corrupt officials, may be estimated from a paragraph published in the *Chronicle* (Washington) of May 8th, 1876. It says: "One of the effects of breaking up the whiskey rings of the country has been a large increase in the internal revenue receipts for the month of April. The increase has been over three and a half millions as compared with the same month last year, which can be attributed to no other cause than the faithfulness and vigilance which now mark the collection of the revenue."

To the distillers, this difference in the tax amounted to a practical monopoly. Of course distillers who paid the regular tax of fifty cents could not begin to compete with those who paid only thirty cents. They must either join the Ring or quit the business.

Secretary Bristow labored for a long time to correct these evils, but the paid servants of the Ring, within his own force, thwarted him. At one time, it was determined to make a general transfer of the collectors, sending, for instance, those at St. Louis to Philadelphia. This, of course, would probably have brought exposure, as faithful officials would, in some cases, have gone where corrupt ones had been. But immediately the representatives flew to Washington, and soon the President was influenced to revoke the order, and the "Ring" was happy.

This proved conclusively to Mr. Bristow, that whatever was done, must be done secretly, and without even the knowledge of his subordinates. A happy discord occurred in St. Louis, which aided him greatly. The two leading papers of St. Louis had a disagreement which resulted in February, 1875, in the receipt, by Secretary Bristow, of a message from Mr. Fishback, owner of the St. Louis *Democrat*, confidentially informing him that if he (Bristow) would appoint a reliable agent, he himself would give him such aid as would expose the St. Louis Whiskey Ring. Mr. Colony, commercial editor of the *Democrat*, was thereupon appointed, and at once began operations. All communications were made with Bristow personally, or with solicitor Bluford Wilson. Such secrecy was necessary in conducting the investigations, that only a very few persons were taken into confidence, and much of the correspondence was conducted in a new cipher, through a citizen of Washington totally unconnected with the government. In this way legal proof and matters of record were fully obtained before an arrest was made.

Mr. Colony, and his assistants, went to work by appointing twenty men to watch the distilleries and rectifying houses, and determine the amount and character of the work done after dark, all of which is illegal. These watchmen were many of them assaulted and beaten; but enough was discovered to piece out the other revelations, which were mainly as to the amount of whiskey shipped from the city. Mr. Colony, to ascertain this, made an exhaustive examination of all the freight shipments by all the lines for quite a period, professedly in his capacity as commercial editor. These returns show the excess of fraudulent whiskey. The fraud itself was consummated in various ways, all of which require connivance on the part of the revenue agent.

We cannot better show the opposition which these parties met with, than by quoting the testimony of the detective who went to the Pacific coast to unearth the frauds there.

Special Agent D. L. Phillips of Illinois, detailed to investigate the Whiskey Rings supposed to exist on the Pacific coast, made a report to the House of Representatives. The main facts are as follows: Mr. Phillips reached San Francisco on the 14th of September, 1875, and one of the first discoveries which he made was that men earnestly intent upon enforcement of law, if they hailed from States east of the Rocky Mountains, were not regarded with favor, either by those in office or by distillers or liquor dealers on the Pacific coast. He also found

17

great demoralization in the civil service, which was caused by
the partisan and despotic authority of those in California who
control Federal patronage at Washington. Honest and upright men who have self-respect and moral worth do not want
office in California, nor could they find employment in public
service if they desired. The remote situation of the Pacific
coast from the seat of government, and the general understanding that appointments to office are really made by Senators
and Representatives in Congress, inspired, he said, in all office-
holders a very lively and grateful sense of loyalty, not to the
Government or any of its departments, but to the Senator or
Representative through whom such appointments are held, and
the results are that so long as offices can be held under such
circumstances and surroundings the civil service must be utterly
debased, venal, and purely personal, and such, he says, in his
judgment, is the condition of affairs in California.

It was assumed almost everywhere he went that there was a
Whiskey Ring in San Francisco, and that to build up its interests, protect its members, and secure its immunity, the interests of brandy and whiskey distillation in all other portions of
the State were oppressed and well-nigh destroyed. The distillation of whiskey from wheat has for many years been a
favored interest. It has been more or less mixed up in all political struggles, and spending its money freely, it had its share
of political recognition.

Mr. Phillips says he investigated carefully the accusations
made by Senator Sargent against Revenue Agent Clark, now
on duty at San Francisco. He found that the affidavits upon
which the charges were based were made by distillers, whiskey
dealers, and one Johnson, a Revenue Agent, who was admitted
to have been a spy upon Clark. The attacks upon him were
intended, he thinks, to impair the confidence of the Department in his honesty, and thereby secure the removal of a public servant who was proving troublesome in California to revenue officials and distillers engaged in plundering the Government. Mr. Phillips thinks that Clark had abundant reason

for urging the Collector to seize the Antioch distillery, notwithstanding the fact that it was owned by Charles Joel, who had been a member of the California Legislature, and had voted for Mr. Sargent to be United States Senator.

Mr. Phillips says that the Executive has made many removals and appointments, without consultation with members of either House of Congress, and asks why not make the rule uniform and apply it to California. Until this is done, there will be no improvement in the public service in that State.

The following extract from Mr. Phillips' report is very interesting :

"About the time that Senator Sargent filed his charges against Clark, it was learned that one Chas. Warner, formerly engaged in distilling at Atlanta and Canton, Ill., and now residing in the town of Watsonville, Cal., was in possession of important information concerning frauds on the revenue in the distillation of whiskey, at San Francisco. After protracted efforts and earnest protestations on his part of personal danger, Warner was prevailed upon to surrender certain books kept by him, which disclosed most startling frauds on the revenue in 1865-6 and 1868-9, and these frauds were perpetrated by the very men who have since, and do now, control the distilling and liquor business of California, especially in San Francisco.

" The details of these frauds, explained at length and sworn to by Warner, are on file in the office of the Commissioner of Internal Revenue, and need not be set out in this report. The amount of these frauds approaches to nearly $1,500,000, and covers a little over two years' time. The men who perpetuated them are men who met Mr. Clark with insolence, abuse, and threats, and some of their affidavits form the basis in part of the charges of Mr. Sargent against him.

" Mr. Warner, from whom I was mainly instrumental in procuring information, and whose testimony was taken in my room in the night, at his earnest request, with no one present but Supervisor Hawley and myself, has been threatened with death for his disclosures, and informed of men who will murder him. He has written to Hawley to furnish him protection, and says to escape assassination he expects to be forced to leave California. It is well known that hired spies in the liquor interests the past Winter, watched by day and night every step of Hawley, Clark, and myself, and every word incautiously uttered was known and reported to Government officials and Whiskey men continually."

Mr. Phillips details at considerable length the attempts made by himself and Supervisor Hawley to prosecute persons engaged in defrauding the Government, but failed, as he says, because of the failure of the District-Attorney's office to do its duty. He became convinced, not only of a total disinclination to prosecute distillers and liquor dealers for the violation of law, lest officials should be found involved, but of a fixed determination in the District-Attorney's office not to do so, if escape therefrom was possible. He closes this branch of his report as follows:

"After a long and careful observation, I am convinced that, under the present Federal officials on the Pacific coast, the prosecution and conviction of guilty distillers and whiskey dealers in San Francisco are out of the question. I wish, however, to say that in the Federal Judges, the Government has great reason to take an earnest, honest pride. They are able, learned, patriotic, and just; and no man can more keenly feel than they, the impossibility of faithfully executing law and vindicating the just claims of the Government as matters now stand."

After all the evidence had been carefully collected, "the lightning" struck with a vengeance. Distilleries were seized in St. Louis, Chicago, Milwaukee, Indiana, New Orleans, and a few in other smaller places. In St. Louis over thirty parties were at once indicted, and many of them were of the most respectable men in the city, moving in the best society. In Chicago over sixty were indicted at one time, and over one hundred indictments in all, including some of the most prominent men in the city. The trials were speedy, impartial, and decisive, resulting in almost every case in the conviction of the accused. Avery, Chief Clerk of the Revenue Bureau at Washington, a man high in the Government service, together with Joyce and McKee, were sent to the penitentiary and heavily fined. A host of minor lights in [the "Ring" have gone to keep them company. It is hardly necessary to say they will not be so jolly a band as when they were filling their pockets with Government greenbacks.

The interest of the country has centered in the trials at St. Louis, as that city seemed to be the head-center of the work, and as the whole fraud has been there laid before the public in the trials of the most important conspirators; we cannot give a clear idea of the ways in which these things were carried out in any other way so well as by giving the testimony of the man who confessed.

In the trial of McDonald and Avery, Deputy Collector McGrue testified as follows; I came to St. Louis in June, 1871, and remained until November, 1872. I had repeated conversations with McDonald and Joyce about making money out of illicit distilling, the substance of which was, that the distillers should be protected in making crooked whiskey on condition that they should give a certain part of the taxes saved to certain parties. From September, 1871, to November, 1872, I collected money from the distillers, Bevis & Frazer, Thompson, Curran & Ulrich, to pay to other parties. I had a talk with all the distillers mentioned, and assured them that they could run in violation of law, and they would be protected by Government Officers on the conditions mentioned. I did this on the authority of Joyce and McDonald. The amounts were collected every Saturday night and averaged $8,500 per week.

The distillers brought it to me at my room, generally about noon, and I disbursed it. A certain sum was taken out to pay the gaugers and the storekeepers, and the balance was divided into five parts. The money for the subordinates was given to

John Leavenworth for disbursement. Of the other five pack-
ages, I kept one, McDonald got one, Joyce got one, and the
other two were given to Leavenworth with the understanding
that McKee got one, and Ford the other. This work began in
the first part of September, 1871. McDonald complained once
that Joyce ought not to receive as much as the rest, and so on
one occasion I gave him $200 more than the rest, without giv-
ing Joyce his full one-fifth. By the arrangement the distillers
were to retain one-half of the profits on crooked whiskey.
Leavenworth was a gauger, and part of the time, storekeeper.
The tax on whiskey at that time was fifty cents per gallon,
and I collected about thirty cents per gallon. It was understood at the supervisor's office, that the gaugers, store-keepers,
and other subordinates were to receive from $1.00 to $1.50 per
barrel, but generally Leavenworth paid them more. I took
the money for the main members of the ring to the supervisors,
and there was no particular disguise about my delivering it to
them. I always set aside a portion of the money; part of the
time, $100 per week, and part of the time $300 per week for
Wm. O. Avery, Chief Clerk of the Internal Revenue Bureau at
Washington. The increase was made at the instance of Joyce,
who came from Washington once and said that Avery was
complaining of not receiving enough money; hence we increased it to $300 per week.

Randolph W. Ulrich, one of the most prominent distillers in
St. Louis, testified that he had talked several times with Joyce
in 1871, about making crooked whiskey, but that he declined
entering into any arrangement. Subsequently, however, when
he found that several other distillers were in the illicit business,
he went in and remained till October, 1872. He had several
talks with Fitzroy, and paid him money several times. He
reported the amount of crooked whiskey to McGrue and
afterwards to Fitzroy. He paid thirty and thirty-five cents per
gallon. He did not know where the money went and did not
care.

Alfred Bevis, of the firm of Bevis and Frazer, one of the

witnesses, testified to the crooked whiskey operations of his firm, carried on with the knowledge and collusion of McDonald and Joyce, and said that the firm paid the Ring from $3,000 to $5,000 per week, and previous to the last presidential election he paid the Ring from $10,000 to $20,000.

His firm, he said, went into the crooked whiskey business with the understanding that they were subserving political purposes and would be protected by the officers there and at Washington. The witness said he was in the Collectors' office *when the records were destroyed*, the destruction of which was arranged by Joyce and Con. Cannon, the latter Chief Clerk of the Collectors' Office. The witness had been shown letters by Joyce, purporting to come from Avery and from Babcock, the President's private secretary, giving assurance of protection from seizure; witness had one of these in his possession about twelve hours, having taken it to show to Frazer. The witness said that he did not remember reading the Babcock letter, but thought it was signed " Bab!" The Avery letter was given him by Joyce in his office. There were reports that the Ring was in danger and Joyce showed these letters to convince them that they were protected and that he kept posted. They were frequently shown letters of that kind.

What a sad commentary on humanity! What a discouraging thought for the enthusiastic believer in Republicanism, that her citizens combine together to forward a scheme of wholesale fraud, and that the most trusted officers of the Government are leagued with them. But still more stunning to our national pride to know that the officers of our Government actually inaugurated this plan of wholesale fraud and compelled those to go into it whom they could not persuade. It is an ugly fact that officers sworn to support the Government and faithfully execute its laws, are in the main responsible for these frauds. They rendered it impossible for a man to pay the honest tax and live. Those who were paying but thirty cents per gallon tax could drive out of the market and into bankruptcy those who honestly paid the full fifty cents.

Against all the parties the evidence was so conclusive as to produce a conviction except in the case of Babcock. The country has this consolation at least, that however much it may have been degraded by the treachery of its chosen officers, it *did* convict and punish them. Most of them are now serving out *contracts with the Government* in the Penitentiary.

The case of General Babcock who was private secretary to the President has been an exception to the otherwise uniform success of the Government in convicting the accused. Very strong accusations were made, that he being private secretary to the President, and thus knowing almost the first, any movement about to take place, informed the Ring. The charges failed of proof sufficiently conclusive to cause the jury to convict, but the general way that Babcock's defense was managed showed the public quite conclusively that he was guilty. His counsel seemed to rely on the inability of the prosecution to prove his guilt rather than their ability to prove his innocence. The very fact that he, on a very moderate salary, was living in the style and extravagance of a large income did not help the case in his favor, at least in the popular mind.

Since his acquittal it has come to light that this method of proceeding followed by his counsel, was with good reason. It transpires that just before his trial a letter was written by the Attorney General to the various prosecuting officers, that no terms must be made with any guilty man. This sounds very well, but when it is remembered that it is only by the confessions and testimony of guilty parties that any prosecution could have been sustained, it is equally clear that no guilty man would confess and testify for the benefit of the Government unless he could be secured from punishment himself. He would have no object in doing so. This letter was in some way left, so that Babcock's counsel got it, and straightway it was telegraphed to the various papers throughout the land. Of course those who would otherwise have testified for the Government sealed their lips, and the prosecution was too weak to convict. Why the Attorney General wrote such a letter at that particular time, and why it was left so that Babcock could get hold of it, can only be accounted for, that Grant and Pierrepont are very stupid men, or that there was a belief among our very highest Government Officials that Babcock was guilty, and a determination that he must be acquitted.

CHAPTER XXII.

OUR NATIONAL DISGRACE.

As if the arrest and conviction of some of the most trusted officers of the Government was not enough to almost shake one's faith in the stability of republican institutions, the whiskey frauds were followed by the discovery of wholesale corruption in the Secretary of War's office, the accused person being no less than the Secretary himself, General William W. Belknap.

Gen. Belknap was comparatively an unknown man until President Grant nominated him for Secretary of War. He came of good stock, his father, Gen. William G. Belknap, having been an officer in the regular army from 1813 to 1851, served with marked gallantry through the Florida and Mexican wars, and enjoyed the intimate friendship of Gen. Scott. William Worth Belknap was born at Newburg, N. Y., on the 22d of September, 1829, and graduated from Princeton College in the class of 1848, among his college acquaintances, singularly enough, being Messrs. Clymer and Blackburn of the committee that has just exposed his guilt, as well as Secretary Robeson. He studied law at Georgetown, D. C., and in 1851 began the practice of his profession at Keokuk, Ia. He served one term, in 1857–8, in the Iowa Legislature as a democrat, but being unwilling to give countenance to the Lecompton swindle, he separated from the radical wing of his party, and was known as a Douglas democrat up to the outbreak of the Rebellion. He entered the army as Major of the 15th Infantry, and served with his regiment in the army of the Tennessee, rising through the various grades and participating in the battle of Shiloh, siege of Corinth, campaign and siege of Atlanta. After the capture of that place, he marched with Sherman to the sea, and finally to Washington, taking a prominent part in all the actions of these brilliant campaigns. He was promoted to the rank of Brigadier-General for special gallantry in the memorable battle near Atlanta, in which his regiment fought from either side of the line of breast-works, was afterwards breveted Major-General, and, at the date of his muster-out, on the 24th of August, 1865, was regarded by Gen. Sherman and his companions as one of the most accomplished and promising officers of the army. Shortly afterward, he was appointed Collector of Internal Revenue for the First District of Iowa, and, upon Gen. Rawlins' death, soon after Gen. Grant entered upon the Presidency in 1869, he became Secretary of War. His second wife was then living, but she died of consumption in the latter part of 1870, and about three years ago he was married to his present wife, her sister, Mrs. Bowers, at Harrisburg, Ky., her birth-place, at the residence of her brother, Dr. William Tomlinson, her kinsman John H. Pendleton of Ohio, giving away the bride. She was understood to have property, and he soon rented a large house, and they launched out into a very extravagant style of living. Mrs. Belknap has been one of the handsomest and most elegantly dressed ladies in Washington, and received many of her dresses from Worth, the Paris milliner.

It is probable that the extravagant living and the "Paris milliner" are in a great degree responsible for the awful fall which is best given in the testimony of Mr. Caleb P. Marsh before the Congressional Committee, appointed to examine into this corruption.

"In the summer of 1870 myself and wife spent some weeks at Long Branch, and on our return to New York, Mrs. Belknap [the Secretary's second wife, who died in the following December] and Mrs. Bowers [the present Mrs. Belknap, who is a sister of the second Mrs. Belknap], by our invitation, came for a visit to our house. Mrs. Belknap was ill during this visit, some three or four weeks, and, I suppose in consequence of our kindness to her, she felt under some obligation, for she asked me, one day, in the course of a conversation, why I did not apply for a post-tradership on the frontier. I asked what they were, and was told that they were many of them very lucrative offices, in the gift of the Secretary of War, and that, if I wanted one, she would ask the Secretary for me. Upon my replying that I thought such offices belonged to disabled soldiers, and besides that I was without political influence, she answered that politicians got such places, etc., etc. I do not remember saying that, if I had a valuable post of that kind, I would remember her. But I do remember her saying something like this: 'If I can prevail upon the Secretary of War to award you a post, you must be careful to say nothing to him about presents, for a man once offered him $10,000 for a tradership of this kind, and he told him that, if he did not leave the office, he would kick him down stairs.' Remembering, as I do, this story, I presume the antecedent statement to be correct.

"Mrs. Belknap and Mrs. Bowers returned to Washington, and, a few weeks thereafter, Mrs. Belknap sent me word to come over. I did so. She then told me that the post-tradership at Fort Sill was vacant, that it was a valuable post, as she understood, and that she had either asked for it for me, or had prevailed upon the Secretary of War to agree to give it to me; at all events, I called upon the Secretary of War, and, as near as I can remember, made application for this post on a regular printed form. The Secretary said he would appoint me, if I could bring proper recommendatory letters, and this I said I could do. Either Mrs. Belknap or the Secretary told me that the present trader at the post, John S. Evans, was an applicant for re-appointment, and that I had better see him, he being in the city, as it would not be fair to turn him out of office without some notice, as he would lose largely on his buildings, mer-

chandise, etc., if the office was taken from him, and that it
would be proper and just for me to make some arrangement
with him for their purchase, if I wished to run the post myself.
I saw Evans, and found him alarmed at the prospect of losing
the place. I remember that he said that a firm of Western
post-traders, who claimed a good deal of influence with the
Secretary of War, had promised to have him appointed, but he
found on coming to Washington this firm to be entirely without influence."

"Mr. Evans first proposed a partnership, which I declined,
and then a bonus of a certain portion of the profits, if I would
allow him to hold the position and continue the business. We
finally agreed upon $15,000 per year. Mr. Evans and myself
went to New York together, where the contract was made and
executed which is herewith submitted. During our trip over,
however, Mr. Evans saw something in the Army and Navy
Journal, which led him to think that some of the troops were
to be removed from the post, and that he had offered too large
a sum, and before the contract was drawn, it was reduced by
agreement to $12,000, the same being payable quarterly in ad-
vance. When the first remittance came to me, say probably
in November, 1870, I sent one-half thereof to Mrs. Belknap,
either, I presume, by certificate of deposit or bank notes by
express. Being in Washington at a funeral (the funeral of
Mrs. Belknap) some weeks after this, I had a conversation
with Mrs. Bowers to the following purport, as far as I can
now remember, but must say that just here my memory is exceedingly indistinct, and I judge in part perhaps from what followed, as to the details of the conversation: I went up-stairs
in the nursery with Mrs. Bowers to see the baby; I said to her,
' This child will have money coming to it before a great while.'
She said, ' Yes. The mother gave the child to me, and told
me that the money coming from you I must take and keep for
it.' I said, "All right,' and it seems to me I said that perhaps the father ought to be consulted. I say it seems so, and
yet I can give no reason for it, for, as far as I knew, the father

knew nothing of any money transactions between the mother and myself. I have a faint recollection of a remark of Mrs. Bowers that, if I sent the money to the father, then it belonged to her, and that she would get it any way. I certainly had some understanding then or subsequently, with her or him, for, when the next payment came due and was paid, I sent the one-half thereof to the Secretary of War, and have continued substantially from that day forward to the present time to do the same.

"About, I should say, a year and a half or two years after the commencement of these payments, I reduced the amount to $6,000 per annum. The reason of this reduction was, partly because of the combined complaints on the part of Mr. Evans and his partner, and partly, as far as I now remember, in consequence of an article in the newspapers, about the time, reflecting on the injustice done to soldiers at this fort, caused by the exorbitant charges made necessary on the part of the trader by reason of the payment of this bonus.

" The money was sent according to the instructions of the Secretary of War, sometimes in bank notes by Adams' express; I think on one or two occasions by certificates of deposits on the National Bank of America in New York. Sometimes I have paid in New York in person. Except the first payment in the fall of 1870, and the last in December, 1872, all were made to the Secretary in the modes I have stated, unless perhaps on one or two occasions, at his instance, I bought a government bond with the moneys in my hand arising from the contract with Evans, which I either sent or handed to him.

"The first payment to me by Mr. Evans was made in the fall of 1870, at the rate of $12,000 a year. He paid at that rate about a year and a half or two years, and since then at the rate of $6,000 a year. It would aggregate about $40,000, one-half of which I have disposed of as above stated."

" Usually when I sent money by express I would send Mr. Belknap the receipt of the company, which he would either return marked "O. K.," or otherwise acknowledge the receipt of the same. Sometimes I paid to him in person in New York, when no receipt was necessary. I have not preserved any receipts or letters. When sent by express, I always deposited the money personally, and took a receipt for it."

There are some facts in the Belknap business not developed even in this testimony. Prior to the present peculiarly " centralized" national administration, the wants of the officers and soldiers of the army on the frontier were supplied by " sutlers," who were chosen by the officers at each station, and the prices of their commodities controlled by well-defined regulations. The buyers had the power of preventing imposition and extortion on the part of the seller. But very soon after the President's discovery of his late war minister, an act was passed by Congress, under administration influence, abolishing the old and quite satisfactory sutler system, and substituting these " post-traders," to be appointed and removed at the pleasure of the Secretary of War solely. The management of these trading posts has been but one of the many arbitrary acts which have characterized the last administration of the war office, and caused general comment and open criticism in army circles on the frontier, where it is a serious offense to speak disrespectfully of the powers that be at Washington. For several years these positions as post-trader have been known to have a fixed market value, and the amount of the bonus paid annually by the actual traders at each of the more important stations to the nominal incumbents, friends of the Secretary of War, has been an open secret on the frontier. It should be borne in mind that this Fort Sill tradership, for which $40,000 has been paid during the last five or six years, is but one of a number. How about the others? The newspapers have already had a good deal to say about one in the Northwest held by a Mr. Orville Grant.

The case of the Fort Sill trader, Mr. J. S. Evans, thus made prominent, is an excellent one to illustrate the whole system and its bearings. Fort Sill was first established in the southwest part of the Indian Territory in the winter of 1868-9. It

soon became one of the largest and most important of the
army stations. Mr. Evans of Kentucky, an experienced and
fair-dealing merchant and a gentleman,—far above the typical
army sutler,—opened the first store there upon the authority
of the troops. When the change was made, he became trader
on the recommendation of the officers of the post, and proceeded to erect buildings and lay in a stock of general merchandise. This required a large capital, as the nearest railroad
was then the Kansas Pacific, and much of his building material, as well as all his merchandise, had to be hauled in wagons
for hundreds of miles through a country without roads. In
most classes of goods the transportation costs more than the
merchandise itself. Had the Secretary appointed his friend
Marsh to the original vacancy in the Fort Sill tradership, it
would not have effected the desired object; the appointee
would have been obliged to command large capital, and then,
conducting the business in person or by deputy, be contented
with fair profits. So Mr. Evans was permitted to establish
himself with a large and valuable stock, investing his whole
fortune, get the business well established, and then, although
giving full satisfaction to those for whose accommodation, the-
oretically, the place is provided, he was unexpectedly notified
of the appointment of a successor. To have quietly stepped
aside would have ruined Mr. Evans; he could not have removed his goods to the nearest settlement at less than their
cost. He was at the mercy of Belknap's appointee, and the
latter well knew it.

Mr. Evans could do nothing but comply with the terms dictated by Mr. Marsh. And so he returned to his frontier store
under obligations to add to the selling price of his goods *one
thousand dollars a month*, to be paid in advance to the figure-
head at New York. Now it is a sad fact that these post-traders
make their profits on the sales to the enlisted men of the army
rather than on sales to the officers. The latter have various
other means of procuring supplies, and the traders favor them
also. Practically, therefore, this bonus had to be taken from

the pockets of the soldiers of the seven companies at Fort Sill.
Those troops then consisted of colored men of the 10th regiment of cavalry, about 600 in number.   Each of these poor
fellows, many of them freedmen earning their first wages, had
to contribute from his monthly pay of thirteen dollars, about
two dollars toward this bonus fund.   In other words, during
the last five years, the enlisted men in the army of the United
States serving at this post of Fort Sill have had extorted from
them, with the knowledge and consent of the Secretary of War,
the sum of *forty thousand dollars*, half of which has helped
toward the brilliant social display of that Secretary at Washington, while the other half has remained with the friend in
New York as hush-money.   At how many other places the
same thing has been done, remains to be seen.

The facts of the case cited, now first made public, have been
well enough understood all along out at Fort Sill.   Mr. Evans
was obliged to tell his friends of the state of affairs to justify
his exorbitant prices.   The former commander of a company
of the colored troops at that station, who were thus mercilessly
bled to pay those bills of the Paris dress-maker, visited Fort
Sill in the summer of 1872, and, finding that appeals through
the military channels had been fruitless, he reported the facts
fully to Senator Sumner, in behalf of the freedmen-soldiers.
A similar letter was written at the same time to Hon. F. W.
Bird.   But, as the *Republican* aptly remarks, to-day, although
the military ring in 1871–2 was too strong to be broken by
Senators Sumner and Schurz, its time had to come.   Four
years have brought changes, indeed.   Two departmental heads,
that withstood assaults far more formidable then, now fall before " a Mr. Marsh."

After Gen. Belknap saw that his friend Marsh was bound to
tell the full truth, he called on the President, and in great
excitement offered his resignation, which the President un-
wisely accepted.   This unwise step may save Belknap from
punishment for his crime, as Congress has not yet been able
to convince itself that it has a right to impeach a man after he

ceases to hold office.   Whatever flimsy excuse may save Belknap from the full punishment for his crimes, the fact that he has so publicly branded himself as thoroughly wanting in honesty and honor, and that he stands disgraced in the eyes of the world, is the worst of punishments.

CHAPTER XXIII.

THE REPUBLICAN CONVENTION OF 1876.

The Convention which was to nominate candidates for the Republican party for the office of President and Vice-President, met in Cincinnati on the 14th day of June, 1876.

The Convention was called to order at noon by Ex-Governor Morgan of New York, and made a brief statement of the duties of the Convention. After this speech the temporary organization was at once completed by the choice of Theodore M. Pomeroy, Chairman.

The various committees were then appointed. The Committee on Organization presented Honorable Edward McPherson of Pennsylvania.

The Chairman of "The Committee on Resolutions" was Honorable Joseph R. Hawley of Connecticut. The platform which was adopted as a sign-board in the coming political campaign was mostly his work. After due deliberation General Hawley on the second day presented the following platform:

THE PLATFORM.

When, in the economy of Providence, this land was to be purged of human slavery, and when the strength of the Govenrment of the people, by the people, for the people, was to be demonstrated, the Republican party came into power. Its deeds have passed into history, and we look back to them with pride, incited by their memories and high aims for the good of our country and mankind; and, looking to the future with anfaltering courage, hope, and purpose, we, the representatives of the party, in National Convention assembled, make the following declaration of principles.

I. The United States of America is a nation, not a league. By the combined workings of the National and State Governments, under their respective constitutions, the rights of every citizen are secured at home and protected abroad, and the common welfare promoted.

II. The Republican party has preserved those Governments to the hundreth aniversary of the Nation's birth, and they are now embodiments of the great truths spoken at its cradle—that all men are created equal; that they are endowed by their Creator with certain inalienable rights, among which are life, liberty, and the pursuit of happiness; that for the attainment of these ends governments have been instituted among men, deriving their just powers from the consent of the governed. Until those truths are cheerfully obeyed, and, if needed, vigorously enforced, the work of the Republican party is unfinished.

III. The permanent pacification of the Southern section of the Union, and the complete protection of all its citizens in the free enjoyment of all their rights, are duties to which the Republican party are sacredly pledged. [Applause.] The power to provide for the enforcement of the principles embodied in the recent constitutional amendments is vested by those amendments in the Congress of the United States, and we declare it to be the solemn obligation of the legislative and executive departments of the Government to put into immediate and vigorous exercise all their constitutional powers for removing any just causes of discontent on the part of any class, and securing to every American citizen complete liberty and exact equality in the exercise of all civil, political, and public rights. [Applause.] To this end we imperatively demand a Congress and Chief Executive whose courage and fidelity to these duties shall not falter until these results are placed beyond dispute or recall. [Applause.]

IV. In the first act of Congress signed by President Grant, the National Government assumed to remove any doubts of its purpose to discharge all just obligations to public creditors, and solemnly pledged its faith to make provision at the earliest practicable period for the redemption of the United States notes in coin. [Applause.] Commercial prosperity, public merits, and National credit demand that this promise be fulfilled by a continuous and steady progress to specie payment. [Loud and long-continued applause.]

V. Under the Constitution the President and heads of Departments are to make nominations for office; the Senate is to advise and consent to appointments, and the House of Representatives is to accuse and prosecute faithless officers. The best interests of the public service demand that these distinctions be respected; that Senators and Representatives who may be judges and accusers should not dictate appointments to office. The invariable rule for appointments should have reference to the honesty, fidelity, and capacity of appointees, giving to the party in power those places where harmony and vigor of administration require its policy to be represented, but permitting all others to be filled by persons selected with sole reference to efficiency of the public service, and the right of citizens to share in the honor of rendering faithful service to their country.

VI. We rejoice in the quickened conscience of the people concerning political affairs. We will hold all public officers to a rigid responsibility, and engage that the prosecution and punishment of all who betray official trusts shall be speedy, thorough, and unsparing. [Cheers.]

VII. The public school system of the several States is the bulwark of the American Republic, and with a view to its security and permanence we recommend an amendment to the Constitution of the United States forbidding the application of any public funds or property for the benefit of any school or institution under sectarian control. [Great cheering, continuing several minutes.]

VIII. The revenue necessary for current expenditures and the obligations of the public debt must be largely derived from duties upon importations, which so far as possible should be so adjusted as to promote the interests of American labor and advance the prosperity of the whole country. [Cheers.]

IX. We re-affirm our opposition to further grants of the public lands to corporations and monopolies, and demand that the national domain be devoted to free homes for the people.

X. It is the imperative duty of the Government to so modify existing treaties with European governments that the same protection shall be afforded to adopted American citizens that is given to native-born, and all necessary laws be passed to protect immigrants in the absence of power in the State for that purpose.

XI. It is the immediate duty of Congress to fully investigate the effect of the immigration and importation of Mongolians on the moral and material interests of the country. [Applause.]

XII. The Republican party recognize with approval the substantial advance recently made toward the establishment of equal rights for women by the many important amendments effected by Republican Legislatures in the laws which concern the personal and property relations of wives, mothers, and widows, and by the appointment and election of women to the superintendence of education, charities, and other public trusts. The honest demands of this class of citizens for additional rights and privileges and immunities should be treated with respectful consideration. [Applause.]

XIII. The Constitution confers upon Congress sovereign power over the Territories of the United States for their government, and in the exercise of this power it is the right and duty of Congress to prohibit and extirpate in the Territories that relic of barbarism, polygamy; and we demand such legislation as will secure this end and the supremacy of American institutions in all the Territories. [Applause.]

XIV. The pledges which our nation has given to our soldiers and sailors must be fulfilled. The grateful people will always regard those who perilled their lives for the country's preservation in the kindest remembrance.

XV. We sincerely deprecate all sectional feeling and tendencies. We therefore note with deep solicitude that the Democratic party counts as its chief hope of success upon the electoral vote of a united South, secured through the efforts of those who were recently arrayed against the nation, and we invoke the earnest attention of the country to the grave truth that a success thus achieved would re-open sectional strife and imperil the national honor and human rights.

XVI. We charge the Democratic party as being the same in character and spirit as when it sympathized with treason, and with making its control of the House of Representatives the triumph and opportunity of the nation's recent foes; with re-asserting and applauding in the National Capitol the sentiments of unrepentant rebellion; with sending Union soldiers to the rear; with deliberately proposing to repudiate the plighted faith of the Government; with being equally false and imbecile upon the overshadowing financial question; with thwarting the ends of justice by its partisan mismanagement and obstruction of investigation; with proving itself, through the period of its ascendency in the Lower House of Congress, utterly incompetent to administer the Government. We warn the country against trusting a party thus alike unworthy, recreant, and incapable. [Cheers.]

XVII. The National Administration merits commendation for its honorable work in the management of domestic and foreign affairs, and President Grant deserves the continued and hearty gratitude of the American people for his patriotism and his immense services in war and in peace. [Cheers.]

After the reading and accepting of the PLATFORM, balloting commenced.

The candidates proposed were: Hon. Marshall Jewell, of Connecticut; Hon. Oliver P. Morton, of Indiana; Hon. Benjamin H. Bristow, of Kentucky; Ex-Speaker James G. Blaine, of Maine; Hon. Roscoe Conkling, of New York; Gov. R. B. Hayes, of Ohio; Gov. Hartranft, of Pennsylvania.

These proceedings occupied the second day of the Convention, and early on the third the balloting commenced. Seven ballots were cast. We give these in full, as they are valuable for reference.

FIRST BALLOT.

Whole number of votes cast,	759
Necessary to a choice,	380
Blaine,	291
Morton,	125
Bristow,	113
Conkling,	96
Hayes,	65
Hartranft,	58
Jewell,	11

SECOND BALLOT.

Applying the rule adopted by the Convention to the second ballot it stands as follows:

Whole vote,	747
Necessary for a choice,	374
Blaine,	298
Bristow,	114
Morton,	111
Conkling,	93
Hayes,	64
Hartranft,	63
Wheeler,	3
Washburne,	1

THIRD BALLOT.

There being no choice a third ballot was ordered. The clerk called the roll of States. The third ballot resulted as follows:

Whole vote,	755
Necessary to a choice,	378
Blaine,	293
Bristow,	121
Morton,	113
Conkling,	90
Hartranft,	68
Hayes,	67
Wheeler,	2
Washburne,	1

FOURTH BALLOT.

There being no choice the fourth ballot was then taken as follows :

Whole vote,	759
Necessary for a choice,	378
Blaine,	292
Bristow,	126
Morton,	108
Conkling,	84
Hartranft,	71
Hayes,	68
Washburne,	3
Wheeler,	2

FIFTH BALLOT.

The Chair (Lieut.-Gov. Woodford) announced the result of the ballot as follows :

Whole vote,	753
Necessary for a choice,	377
Blaine,	287
Bristow,	114
Hayes,	102
Morton,	95
Conkling,	82
Hartranft,	69
Washburne,	3
Wheeler,	2

SIXTH BALLOT.

Whole vote,	754
Necessary for a choice,	378
Blaine,	308
Hayes,	113
Bristow,	111
Morton,	85
Conkling,	81
Hartranft,	50
Washburne,	4
Wheeler,	2

SEVENTH BALLOT.

The Chair announced the vote as follows:

Whole vote,	756
Necessary for a choice,	378
Hayes,	384
Blaine,	351
Bristow,	21

After Gov. Hayes had been nominated, the convention quickly proceeded to nominate a candidate for vice-president. Mr. Stewart L. Woodford and Mr. William A. Wheeler of New York; Gen. Joseph R. Hawley of Connecticut, were nominated, but before the first ballot was finished the balloting was suspended, and William A. Wheeler nominated by acclamation.

The Republican Convention of 1876 having put forth as its centennial ticket,

FOR PRESIDENT,

RUTHERFORD B. HAYES, of Ohio;

FOR VICE-PRESIDENT,

WILLIAM A. WHEELER, of New York,

Adjourned.

18

CHAPTER XXIV.

Rutherford B. Hayes was born at Delaware, Ohio, October 4, 1822. His birth, as far as one can see, was in no way responsible for his rapid rise to the summit of American fame. His parents were respectable, thrifty people, born in New England, who migrated to the West carrying with them that industry which has characterized New England people and which has helped so much to develop the West.

Like all New England people, the parents of young Hayes were anxious to give their children a thorough education. This he received at the schools of his native place and at Kenyon College, finishing his professional studies at the celebrated law school at Cambridge, Mass. From his early youth he showed marks of good abilities, and in his college course, was the first scholar in his class—a result more of industry than genius. During his youth, as in his manhood, he has always been characterized by genial manners and a hearty good fellowship, which have always won for him the love of all of those with whom he has come in contact. These characteristics were the result of a hearty good will towards his fellows, and an earnest interest in all matters, rather than any zeal for the interests of others and the success of public or private matters, in order that reputation might accrue to himself. While a youth he never *sought* any preëminence, but often it was accorded to him as the natural results of his industry, intelligence, and practical common sense.

From the Cambridge Law School, he entered the law office of Thomas Sparrow, of Cincinnati, and completed his legal studies. After scarcely a year at this, he opened an office for himself, and began to build up his own business, and a career for himself, little thinking at that time that he would ever be a candidate for the highest office within the gift of the American people. His genial manners and fine voice at once commended him in his profession, and he soon built up a fine legal practice. In 1858, his reputation had become so good that he was elected city solicitor.

At the outbreak of the war, Hayes entered the service at once. With his practical nature he saw at once the nature of the contest, and the need of every able-bodied man in the field. He was appointed Major of the 23d Ohio Infantry. This was one of the first regiments in the field, and was commanded by the distinguished leader, Col. William S. Rosecrans. Early in June, 1861, the regiment was mustered into service for three years, but before it started for the seat of war, its colonel received the commission as brigadier-general in the regular army.

Late in July, the regiment was ordered to Clarksburg, W. Va., and had its first active service in hunting down the guerrillas that infested the spurs of the Rich Mountain range. Major Hayes served temporarily as Judge-Advocate on Gen. Rosecrans' staff, and in November, 1861, received his commission as lieutenant-colonel. In April, 1862, the regiment, under command of Lieut.-Col. Hayes, left its winter quarters and moved in the direction of Princeton. After two weeks of skirmishing and foraging, the force was attacked by four regiments of infantry under command of Gen. Heath, and after making a determined stand, was compelled to retire. In the heart of August, orders were received to march with all possible dispatch to the Great Kanawha. The regiment made 104 miles in about three days, embarked on transports for Parkersburg, and took the cars for Washington, where it joined Gen. McClellan's army.

The first shots at South Mountain were fired by Col. Hayes' command. The regiment was ordered to ascend the mountain at an early hour by an unfrequented road. The enemy were posted behind stone walls, and greatly out-numbered their assailants, and the regiment was exposed to a murderous fire of musketry and grape at short range. Out of the 350 men who went into action, 100 soon lay dead or wounded on the field. Lieut.-Col. Hayes was badly wounded, his arm being broken, and the command devolved upon Major Comly. The commander, however, was not ready for ambulance or hospital; there was still a good deal of fight in him, for he re-appeared on the field undaunted, with his wound half dressed, and fought until he was so weak that his men had to carry him away. After the battle of Antietam the regiment was ordered to the Kanawha Valley. Lieut.-Colonel Hayes was appointed to the colonelcy of the regiment, and in December, 1862, was placed in command of the First Brigade of the Kanawha division. During the campaign of 1863, his division was exposed to arduous rather than dangerous service, but in 1864 he won his promotion by his gallantry at Winchester, Fisher's Hill, and Cedar Creek. In the battle of Opequan, Col. Hayes' brigade, after advancing across several open fields, gained the crest of a hill and caught a glimpse of the enemy's line. Moving forward under a heavy fire, the brigade dashed through a fringe of underbrush and halted on the edge of a slough 40 or 50 yards wide and nearly waist deep. When he saw the whole line wavering, Col. Hayes plunged in under a shower of bullets and grape, and dragged his way through. He was the first man over. The infantry floundered through the morass, and the enemy were driven back. Col. Hayes exposed himself recklessly, and was half the time in advance of the line. At Winchester his horse was shot under him, and he narrowly escaped with his life. As he lay on the field stunned by his fall, and wondering why the troops were not ordered to charge the enemy's line, there was a cloud of dust on the Winchester turnpike, and Sheridan rode into camp on his magnificent horse in time to save the day. During this terrible campaign, Col. Hayes had three horses shot under him and was wounded four times. In the Spring of 1865, he was given the command of an expedition against Lynchburg, and was preparing to cross the mountains of West Virginia when the war was brought to a close. For his bravery at Fisher's Hill and Cedar Creek he was breveted major-general.

Throughout the war, General Hayes not only showed himself to be an able general and a brave soldier, but what has still more of a bearing on his present condition, he proved himself a thorough patriot and a commander who had at heart the welfare of the members of his command. His courage was shown only in the battle. In camp he was quiet and unobtrusive, attending to the duties of his position with the same assiduous zeal which had characterized his previous life. Every soldier of his command loved him, and it has been remarked, by those who have had an opportunity of knowing, that in his canvass for the governorship of Ohio, he met his most enthusiastic support from his old soldiers, who knew him best.

We have, during the present administration, had too much of the spirit which animated too many of the commanders of the army, which may be best termed *selfish zeal*. Their own interests were first considered, the interests of the country afterwards, if at all. It is one of the gratifying hopes in this campaign that our candidates are men who will have some regard for the wishes of the people and the interests of the country.

Before Gen. Hayes left the army, he was nominated by the Republicans for Congress. He was urged to obtain a furlough and take the stump in his own behalf. To the letter he sent this characteristic reply : " Thank you. I have other business, now. Any man who would leave the army to electioneer for Congress, ought to be scalped." He was elected easily to Congress. His career there is briefly described by a correspondent of the New York Tribune, in the following words:

" In the fall of 1864, Gen. Hayes was elected to Congress
from Cincinnati by a large majority. He seldom appeared on
the floor of the House, not making any elaborate speeches,
nor taking a prominent part in the reconstruction measures
which engrossed the attention of Congress. He was a member of the Committee on Private Land Claims, and was Chairman of the Committee on Library. The delegation from Ohio
at that time, was a very strong one, including Gen. Schenck,
John A. Bingham, James M. Ashley, Samuel Shellabarger,
and Columbus Delano, and it is not surprising that the inex-
perienced member took a lower seat than his brilliant colleagues, and was content to be a listener. In 1866, he was
reëlected, but resigned the position in 1867, in order to accept
the Republican nomination for Governor."

This brief resumé would be very incomplete and inadequate
if we did not add that Gen. Hayes accomplished a great deal
of silent, effective work. He at first was considered a good
party man, but of no very positive characteristics ; but it was
soon discovered that whenever a conference or consultation
was held, Hayes was called in ; that his opinions were always
given quietly and briefly, but that the final conclusion always
coincided with them. This has always been a characteristic of
his life, and all his work has been quiet but effective.

The Democratic nominee for the governorship was Judge
Thurman, and the contest was a very close one, as Judge
Thurman is one of the ablest and most popular leaders of
his party. He was the only man whom many western democrats thought able to beat Hayes in the coming campaign,
and whom they consequently desired the St. Louis Convention to nominate. The Republican platform that year had
several unpopular planks, and the Democratic candidate was
an exceedingly strong one, but Gen. Hayes entered upon
the canvass with unwonted vigor, won hosts of friends by
his bearing on the stump, and was elected by a majority of
nearly 3,000 votes. In 1869 he was re-nominated, his opponent
being Mr. Pendleton, and he increased his lead by several

thousand votes. After his retirement from office he resumed the practice of his profession. In 1872 he was a candidate for Congress, but was defeated by Henry B. Banning, a Liberal Republican, by 2,500 votes. In April, 1873, he was nominated for Assistant Treasurer at Cincinnati, but the Senate adjourned without confirming the appointment. In 1875 he was nominated for Governor in the face of his letter of withdrawal in favor of Judge Taft. The canvass which followed was almost without parallel in the political annals of Ohio. After manifesting a strong disposition to screen themselves behind the school question the Republicans assumed the offensive on the currency question, came out boldly for hard money, and with the aid of Carl Schurz won the day. During this heated canvass Gov. Hayes was constantly on the stump, and the great victory for hard money which was won last October was due in large measure to the zeal and fire of the Republican leader.

Thus it will be seen that Gov. Hayes has been kept constantly in public life ever since he first entered it, except while he was in the army. As soon as the presidential strife began to fill the air, his name was mentioned as a candidate by the Republicans of Cincinnati, and endorsed by many prominent men, all of whom have re-echoed the testimony of Senator Sherman, who says: "I believe the nomination of Gov. Hayes would give us more strength, taking the whole country at large, than any other man. He is better known in Ohio than elsewhere; but the qualities that have made him strong in Ohio will, as the canvass progresses, make him stronger in every State. He was a good soldier, and though not greatly distinguished as such, he performed his full duty, and I noticed, when traveling with him in Ohio, the soldiers who served under him loved and respected him. As a member of Congress he was not a leading debater or manager in party tactics, but he was always sensible, industrious, and true to his convictions and the principles and tendencies of his party, and commanded the sincere respect of his colleagues. As a Governor thrice elected he has shown good executive abilities and gained great popularity, not only with Republicans, but with our adversaries. On the currency question, which is likely to enter largely into the canvass, he is thoroughly sound, but is not committed to any particular measure, so as to be disabled from coöperating with any plan that may promise success. On the main questions, protection for all, equal rights, and the observance of the public faith, he is as trustworthy as any one named. He is fortunately free from the personal enmities and antagonisms that would weaken some of his competitors; he is unblemished in name, character, and conduct, and he is a native-born citizen of our State. I have thus, as you requested, given you my view of the presidential question, taken as dispassionately as if I was examining a proposition in geometry, and the result drawn from the facts not too strongly stated is that the Republican party in Ohio ought, in their State Convention, to give Gov. Hayes a united delegation instructed to support him in the National Convention. Not that we have any special claim to have a candidate taken from Ohio, but that in Gov. Hayes we honestly believe the Republican party in the United States will have a candidate who can combine greater popular strength and greater assurance of success than other candidates, and with equal ability to discharge the duties of President of the United States in case of election."

To Senator Sherman is due the honor of first bringing Gov. Hayes' name prominently before the country as a candidate.

From this sketch it will be seen that the candidate of the Republicans has a record to which he can appeal with much confidence and pride.

In personal appearance Gov. Hayes is strong, and a very large man, weighing about 190 pounds. He has a family of which he is very fond. His wife is a truly amiable woman, and of great intellectual and social power. If her husband should be so fortunate as to receive the honor for which he is nominated, she would preside at the White House with eminent grace and good sense.

Gov. Hayes' letter of acceptance will complete the record

of an eventful and so far successful life, for the present. What will be the next chapter of it, the *fall elections* alone can tell :

COLUMBUS, O., July 8, 1876.

Honorable Edward McPherson, Honorable William A. Howard, Honorable Joseph H. Rainey, and others, Committee of the Republican National Convention :—

Gentlemen : In reply to your official communication of June 17th, by which I am informed of my nomination for the office of President of the United States by the Republican National Convention at Cincinnati, I accept the nomination with gratitude, hoping that, under Providence, I shall be able, if elected, to execute the duties of the high office as a trust for the benefit of all the people.

I do not deem it necessary to enter upon any extended examination of the declaration of principles made by the Convention. The resolutions are in accord with my views, and I heartily concur in the principles they announce. In several of the resolutions, however, questions are considered which are of such importance that I deem it proper to briefly express my convictions in regard to them.

The fifth resolution adopted by the Convention is of paramount interest. More than forty years ago, a system of making appointments to office grew up, based upon the maxim, "To the victors belong the spoils." The old rule, the true rule, that honesty, capacity, and fidelity constitute the only real qualifications for office, and that there is no other claim, gave place to the idea that party services were to be chiefly considered. All parties in practice have adopted this system. It has been essentially modified since its first introduction. It has not, however, been improved. At first the President, either directly or through the heads of departments, made all the appointments, but gradually the appointing power in many cases passed into the control of members of Congress. The offices in these cases have become, not merely rewards for party services, but rewards for services to party leaders. This system destroys the independence of the separate departments of the government. It tends directly to extravagance and official incapacity. It is a temptation to dishonesty. It hinders and impairs that careful supervision and strict accountability by which alone faithful and efficient public service can be secured. It obstructs the prompt removal and sure punishment of the unworthy. In every way it degrades the civil service and the character of the government. It is felt, I am confident, by a large majority of the members of Congress to be an intolerable burden and an unwarrantable hindrance to the proper discharge of their legitimate duties. It ought to be abolished. The reform should be thorough, radical, and complete. We should return to the principles and practice of the founders of the government, supplying by legislation, when needed, that which was formerly established by custom. They neither expected nor desired from the public officer any partisan service. They meant that public officers should owe their whole service to the government and to the people. They meant that the officer should be secure in his tenure as long as his personal character remained untarnished and the performance of his duties satisfactory.

If elected, I shall conduct the administration of the government upon these principles, and all constitutional powers vested in the Exective will be employed to establish this reform.

The declaration of principles by the Cincinnati Convention makes no announcement in favor of a single Presidential term. I do not assume to add to that declaration, but, believing that the restoration of the civil service to the system established by Washington and followed by the early Presidents can be best accomplished by an Executive who is under no temptation to use the patronage of his office to promote his own re-election, I desire to perform what I regard as a duty in stating now my inflexible purpose, if elected, not to be a candidate for election to a second term.

On the currency question I have frequently expressed my views in public, and I stand by my record on this subject. I regard all the laws of the United States relating to the payment of the public indebtedness, the legal-tender notes included, as constituting a pledge and moral obligation of the government, which must in good faith be kept. It is my conviction that the feeling of uncertainty inseparable from an irredeemable paper currency, with its fluctuations of values, is one of the great obstacles to a revival of confidence in business and to a return of prosperity. That uncertainty can be ended in but one way—the resumption of specie payment. But the longer the instability connected with our present money system is permitted to continue, the greater will be the injury inflicted upon our economical interests and all classes of society. If elected, I shall approve every appropriate measure to accomplish the desired end, and shall oppose any step backward.

The resolution with respect to the public school system is one which should receive the hearty support of the American people. Agitation upon this subject is to be apprehended, until by constitutional amendment the schools are placed beyond all danger of sectarian control or interference. The Republican party is pledged to secure such an amendment.

The resolution of the convention on the subject of the permanent pacification of the country, and the complete protection of all its citizens in the free enjoyment of all their constitutional rights, is timely and of great importance. The condition of the Southern States attracts the attention and commands the sympathy of the people of the whole Union. In their progressive recovery from the effects of the war, their first necessity is an intelligent and honest administration of the government, which will protect all classes of citizens in all their political and private rights. What the South most needs is peace, and peace depends upon the supremacy of law. There can be no enduring peace if the constitutional rights of any portion of the people are habitually disregarded. A division of political parties resting merely upon distinctions of race, or upon sectional lines, is always unfortunate, and may be disastrous. The welfare of the South, alike with that of every other part of the country, depends upon the attractions it can offer to labor, to immigration, and to capital. But laborers will not go, and capital will not be ventured, where the constitution and the laws are set at defiance, and distraction, apprehension, and alarm take the place of peace-loving and law-abiding social life. All parts of the constitution are sacred, and must be sacredly observed—the parts that are new no less than the parts that are old. The moral and material prosperity of the southern states can be most effectually advanced by a hearty and generous recognition of the rights of all, by all—a recognition without reserve or exception. With such a recognition fully accorded, it will be practicable to promote, by the influence of all legitimate agencies of the general government, the efforts of the people of those states to obtain for themselves the blessings of honest and capable local government. If elected, I shall consider it not only my duty, but it will be my ardent desire, to labor for the attainment of this end.

Let me assure my countrymen of the Southern states that, if I shall be charged with the duty of organizing an administration, it will be one which will regard and cherish their truest interests, the interests of the white and of the colored people, both and equally, and which will put forth its best efforts in behalf of a civil policy which will wipe out for ever the distinction between North and South in our common country. With a civil service organized upon a system which will secure purity, experience, efficiency, and economy, a strict regard for the public welfare solely in appointments, and the speedy, thorough, and unsparing prosecution and punishment of all public officers who betray official trusts, with a sound currency, with education unsectarian and free to all, with simplicity and frugality in public and private affairs, and with a fraternal spirit of harmony pervading the people of all sections and classes, we may reasonably hope that the second century of our existence as a nation will, by the blessing of God, be prominent as an era of good feeling and a period of progress, prosperity, and happiness.

Very respectfully, your fellow-citizen,

R. B. HAYES.

CHAPTER XXV.

William A. Wheeler, the Republican candidate for Vice-President, was born in Malone, Franklin County, New York, June 30, 1819, and is consequently fifty-seven years of age and but a few days the senior of Samuel J. Tilden, the Democratic candidate for the Presidency. His early life was the same as that common to the large majority of the early settlers of that part of New York State which was at that time almost the frontier section.

His early education was gained under great difficulties, which are fitly set forth in his address to the people who welcomed him home on his return to Malone after his nomination. Speaking to the young men, he said:

"I know every phase of the struggle of young men seeking to make their way; years ago I trampled through the storms and snows of winter to my first district school in an adjoining town. In the log houses of the neighborhood, through the shrunken roofs of the humble farmers' houses, I have at night literally been a star gazer; but in my wildest dreams and highest building of castles in the air, so great an honor as that now conferred upon me never occurred to me. This result shows that in this country every man of character is the equal of every other man."

Despite all difficulties he succeeded in getting, what in those days was then considered a good common school education, and before he attained his majority he was elected Town Clerk, and he says the emoluments—$60 per year—were more to him than the thousands he has since earned. He was early chosen District Attorney in his own county, and was then chosen member of the Assembly for two terms.

At the age of seventeen years he entered the University of Vermont. He remained there two years, and then concluded to leave college and enter upon the study of law. When he had completed his course he was admitted to practice, and at once opened an office. His first pleadings were very successful, and he became very popular with his clients and neighbors, so that after a few years he was nominated by the Democrats to be District Attorney of Franklin County—a position which he continued to fill during several years.

His first election occurred immediately after the adoption of the new Constitution, being the first that was held under its provisions. He became a candidate for the Assembly at the close of his last term as District Attorney, and was elected on the Whig ticket, the county having cast a tie vote at the last election between the Locofoco and Whig candidates. Mr. Wheeler was again chosen to represent his county in the Legislature, and at the close of his term gave several years to his profession, and became cashier of the local bank, a position which he held for fourteen years. He became President of the Ogdensburg and Rouse's Point Railroad, and continued to be the active and supervisory officer for eleven years. When the Republican party was formed from the Whig organization, he followed its fortunes, and in 1858 was elected State Senator. He was chosen President pro tem. for two terms, the Senate in 1858 being the first in this State in which the Republican party had control.

In the Fall of 1859 he was a candidate from the XVIth Congressional District, composed of the Counties of Clinton, Essex, and Franklin. This was the XXXVIIth Congress, memorable for its grave responsibilities at the war crisis. The three counties were all slightly Republican, and gave Mr. Wheeler a majority of about 1,000. During the long and active sessions of this Congress Mr. Wheeler acted with his party in the Anti-Slavery measures and in the prosecution of the war.

Mr. Wheeler retired to private life, where he remained for four years. In 1867 he was elected a member of the State Constitutional Convention, which assembled in June, 1868. In the Republican caucus, preliminary to the election of the officers of the Convention, Mr. Wheeler's name was mentioned for presiding officer with those of Thomas G. Alvord of Syracuse, and Charles G. Folger of Geneva, now one of the Judges of the Court of Appeals. Mr. Wheeler was elected. His position as the presiding officer removed him from participation in the debates which gave opportunities for a display of legal abilities. His opening speech on taking the chair was about the only effort calculated to attract public attention. It had an important bearing upon the subject of negro suffrage, and the Committee before whom this question came reported an article embodying the proposed change in the Constitution. In the Autumn following the adjournment of the Convention, Mr. Wheeler was again a candidate for Congress in the XVIIth District, composed of the counties of Franklin and St. Lawrence, and was elected. This was the XLIst Congress, of which Mr. Blaine was chosen Speaker for the first time. Mr. Wheeler was appointed by him Chairman of the Committee on the Pacific Railroad, and upon his re-election in November, 1870, with very little opposition was appointed to the same position. To the XLIId Congress he was elected by a very large majority, and was returned in the succeeding contest. He was at that time appointed a member of the Committee on Appropriations, but the most important achievement of his Congressional service, and that which gave him prominence before the country, was the "Wheeler Compromise." Previous to this a sub-committee of the Select Committee on Louisiana Affairs, consisting of Charles Foster, William Walter Phelps, and Clarkson N. Potter, had visited Louisiana, and presented a unanimous re-

port to the effect that the government of which William Pitt
Kellogg was the head, was largely responsible for the misfortunes
of the people in that State. This report was accepted by all
but the blindest of partisans in the North as a truthful presentation of the situation. The other members of the Select Committee took the extraordinary step of going to Louisiana and
repeating the work already done. The result was that one of
the other members of the Committee, Samuel S. Marshal,
agreed with Messrs. Foster, Phelps, and Potter that the Kellogg
Government was a usurpation, and should not be recognized,
and that the action of the Returning Board was illegal, but
stated that a compromise was desirable.

This was the majority report. Messrs. Hoar, Wheeler, and
Frye, as a minority, also presented a report which contained
little that was new, reciting the events in Louisiana before
1874, and concluding that a main source of trouble lay in sufficient education not being provided for the negro. Out of
these reports grew the "Wheeler Compromise," from which
the complexion of the Louisiana Legislature became Republican
in the Senate and Democratic in the House, while Mr. Kellogg
retained the office of Governor.

CHAPTER XXVI.

THE DEMOCRATIC CONVENTION OF 1876.

The Democratic Convention was unlike the Republican in almost every particular. Gov. Tilden, like Ex-Speaker Blaine, was largely the favorite, but unlike him, was speedily nominated.

The Convention assembled on the 27th of June, 1876, and its work was speedily accomplished. The only matters of its history worth recording are THE PLATFORM, and the ballots for the candidates.

After spending the first day in preliminary work, the Convention met on the second day, and adopted the following platform:

THE PLATFORM.

We, the delegates of the democratic party of the United States in national convention assembled, do hereby declare the administration of the federal government to be in urgent need of immediate reform. We do hereby enjoin upon the nominees of this convention and of the democratic party in each state, a zealous effort and co-operation to this end, and do hereby appeal to our fellow-citizens of every former political connection, to undertake with us this first and most pressing patriotic duty of the democracy of the country. We do here reaffirm our faith in the permanency of the federal Union, our devotion to the constitution of the United States with its amendments, universally accepted as a final settlement of the controversies that engendered civil war, and do here record our steadfast confidence in the perpetuity of republican self-government in absolute acquiescence to the will of the majority, the vital principle of republics; in the supremacy of the civil over the military authority; in the total separation of church and state, for the sake alike of civil and religious freedom; in the equality of all citizens before the just laws of their own enactment; in the liberty of individual conduct unvexed by sumptuary laws; in the faithful education of the rising generation that they may persevere, enjoy, and transmit these best conditions of human happiness and hope. We behold the noblest product of a hundred years of changeful history, but while upholding the bond of our union and the great charter of these our rights, it behooves a free people to practice that eternal vigilance which is the price of liberty.

Reform is necessary to rebuild and establish in the hearts of the whole people the union, eleven years ago happily rescued from the danger of a corrupt centralism, which, after inflicting upon ten states the rapacity of carpet-bag tyrannies, has honeycombed the offices of the federal government itself with incapacity, waste, and fraud, infected states and municipalities with the contagion of misrule, and locked fast the prosperity of an industrious people in the paralysis of hard times. Reform is necessary to establish a sound currency, restore the public credit, and maintain the national honor. We denounce the failure for all these eleven years to make good the promise of the legal tender notes which are a changing standard of value in the hands of the people, and the non-payment of which is a disregard of the plighted faith of the nation. We denounce the improvidence which, in eleven years of peace, has taken from the people in federal taxes thirteen times the whole amount of the legal tender notes, and squandered four times this sum in useless expense, without accumulating any reserve for their redemption. We denounce the financial imbecility and immorality of the party which, during eleven years of peace, has made no advance toward resumption; that, instead, has obstructed resumption by wasting our resources and exhausting all our surplus income, and while annually professing to intend a speedy return to specie payments, has annually enacted fresh hindrances thereto. As such a hindrance we denounce the resumption clause of the act of 1875, and we here demand its repeal. We demand a judicious system of preparation by public economies, by official retrenchments, and by wise finance which shall enable the nation soon to assure the whole world of its perfect ability and its perfect readiness to meet any of its promises at the call of the creditor entitled to payment. We believe such a system well devised and above all, intrusted to competent hands for execution, creating at no time an artificial scarcity of currency, and at no time alarming the public mind into a withdrawal of that vaster machinery of credit by which ninety-five per cent. of all business transactions are performed; a system open, public, and inspiring general confidence, would from the day of its adoption bring healing on its wings to all our harassed industries, and set in motion the wheels of commerce, manufactures, and the mechanical arts, restore employment to labor, and renew in all its natural force the prosperity of the people. Reform is necessary in the sum and mode of federal taxation, to the end that capital may be set free from distrust and labor lightly burdened. We denounce the present tariff, levied upon nearly 4,000 articles, as a masterpiece of injustice, inequality, and false pretence. It yields a dwindling, not a yearly rising, revenue; it has impoverished many industries to subsidize a few; it prohibits imports that might purchase products of American labor; it has degraded American commerce from the first to an inferior rank on the high seas; it has cut down the sale of American manufactures at home and abroad and depleted the returns of American agriculture—an industry followed by half our people; it costs the people five times more than it produces to the treasury, obstructs the processes of production, and wastes the fruits of labor; it promotes fraud and fosters smuggling, enriches dishonest officials and bankrupts honest merchants. We demand that all custom house taxation shall be only for revenue.

Reform is necessary in the scale of public expenses, federal, state, and municipal. Our federal taxation has swollen from sixty millions gold in 1860 to four hundred and fifty millions currency in 1870, or in a decade from less than five dollars per head to more than eighteen dollars per head. Since the peace the people have paid to their tax gatherers more than thrice the sum of the national debt and more than twice that sum for the Federal government alone.

We demand a vigorous frugality in every department and from every officer of the government; reform is necessary to put a stop to the profligate waste of the public lands and their diversion from actual settlers by the party in power, which has squandered 20,000,000 of acres upon railroads alone, and out of more than thrice that aggregate has disposed of less than a sixth directly to tillers of the soil.

Reform is necessary to correct the omissions of the Republican Congress and the errors of our treaties and our diplomacy which have stripped our fellow citizens of foreign birth and kindred race recrossing the Atlantic of the shield of American citizenship, and have exposed our brethren of the Pacific coast to the incursions of a race not sprung from the same great parent stock, and in fact now by law denied citizenship through naturalization as being neither accustomed to the traditions of a progressive civilization nor exercised in liberty under equal laws. We denounce the policy which thus discards the liberty-loving German and tolerates the revival of the Coolie trade in Mongolian women imported for immoral purposes and Mongolian men hired to perform servile labor contracts, and demand such modification of the treaty with the Chinese empire, or such legislation by Congress within a constitutional limitation as shall prevent the further importation or immigration of the Mongolian race.

Reform is necessary and can never be effected but by making it the controlling issue of the elections and lifting it above the two false issues with which the office-holding class and the party in power seek to smother it. The false issues with which they would enkindle sectional strife in respect to the public schools of which the establishment and support belongs exclusively to the several states, and which the Democratic party has cherished from their foundation and resolved to maintain without partiality or preference for any class, sect, or creed, and without contribution from the treasury to any of them, and the false issue by which they seek to light anew the dying embers of sectional hate between kindred peoples once estranged, but now reunited in one indivisible Republic, and a common destiny.

Reform is necessary in the civil service. Experience proves that the efficient economical conduct of the governmental business is not possible if its civil service be subject to change at every election, to be a prize fought for at the ballot box, to be the brief reward of party zeal instead of posts of honor assigned for proved competency and held for fidelity in the public employ, that the dispensing of patronage should neither be a tax upon the time of all our public men nor the instrument of their ambition. Here again professions falsified in the performance, attest that the party in power can work out no practical or salutary reform.

Reform is necessary even more in the higher grades of the public service. President, Vice-President, judges, senators, representatives, cabinet officers—these and all others in authority are the people's senators. Their offices are not a private perquisite; they are a public trust. When the annals of this Republic show the disgrace and censure of a Vice-President, a late Speaker of the House of Representatives, marking his rulings as a presiding officer, three senators profiting secretly by their votes as law makers; five chairmen of the leading committees of the House of Representatives exposed in jobbery, a late secretary of the treasury forcing balances in the public accounts, a late attorney general misappropriating public funds, a secretary of the navy enriched or enriching friends by percentages levied off the profits of contractors within his department; an embassador to England censured in a dishonorable speculation, and the President's private secretary barely escaping conviction upon trial for guilty complicity in frauds upon the revenue, a secretary of war impeached for crimes and confessed misdemeanors, the demonstration is complete that the first step in reform must be the people's choice of honest men from another party, lest the disease of one political organization infest the body politic, and lest, by making no change of men or party, we can get no change of measures and no reform. All these abuses, wrongs, and crimes, the product of sixteen years' ascendancy of the republican party, create a necessity for reform confessed by the republicans themselves, but their reformers are voted down in convention and displaced from the cabinet. The party's mass of honest voters are powerless to resist the eighty thousand office-holders, its leaders and guides.

Reform can only be had by a peaceful civic revolution. We demand a change of system, a change of administration, a change of parties, that we may have a change of measures and of men.

After but little discussion, the platform was adopted, and the Convention proceeded to ballot for a candidate for President. The candidates were Samuel J. Tilden, of New York; Thomas A. Hendricks, of Indiana; Gen. Hancock, of Pennsylvania; Ex-Governor Parker, of New Jersey; Ex-Governor William Allen, of Ohio; and Senator Bayard, of Delaware.

FIRST BALLOT.

Whole number of votes cast,	713
Necessary for a choice,	476
Samuel J. Tilden had	403
Thomas A. Hendricks,	134
General Hancock,	75
William Allen,	56
Senator Bayard,	27
Joel Parker,	18

SECOND BALLOT.

Whole number of votes cast,	726
Necessary for a choice,	484
Samuel J. Tilden,	508
Thomas A. Hendricks,	75
General Hancock,	60
William Allen,	54
Senator Bayard,	11
Joel Parker,	18

and Governor Tilden was declared elected.

On the third and last day of the Convention Governor Hendricks was nominated on the first ballot with so much unanimity that the Indiana delegation which refused to have him considered for any but the first place on the ticket acquiesced, and the Democratic Centennial Ticket stands

FOR PRESIDENT,

SAMUEL J. TILDEN OF NEW YORK.

FOR VICE-PRESIDENT,

THOMAS A. HENDRICKS OF INDIANA.

CHAPTER XXVII.

SAMUEL J. TILDEN.

Governor Tilden was born at New Lebanon, in the county of Columbia and State of New York, in the year 1814—the year which ruined the fortunes of the great Napoleon. One of his ancestors, Nathaniel Tilden, was Mayor of the city of Tenterden, Kent, England, in 1623. He was succeeded in that office by his cousin John, as he had been preceded by his uncle John in 1585 and 1600. He removed with his family to Scituate, in the colony of Massachusetts, in 1634. His brother Joseph was one of the merchant adventurers of London who fitted out the Mayflower. This Nathaniel Tilden married Hannah Bourne, one of whose sisters married a brother of Governor Winslow, and another a son of Governor Bradford.

Governor Tilden's grandfather, John Tilden, settled in Columbia County. The Governor's mother was descended from William Jones, Lieutenant-Governor of the colony of New Haven, who in all the histories of Connecticut is represented to have been the son of Colonel John Jones, one of the regicide judges of Charles I, who is said to have married a sister of Oliver Cromwell and a cousin of John Hampden. The Governor's father, a farmer and merchant of New Lebanon, was a man of notable judgment and practical sense and the accepted oracle of the county upon all matters of public concern, while his opinion was also eagerly sought and justly valued by all his neighbors, but by none more than by the late President Van

Buren, who till his death was one of his most cherished intimate and personal friends.

From his father Governor Tilden inherited a taste for political inquiries, and in his companionship enjoyed peculiar opportunities for acquiring an early familiarity with the bearings
of the various questions which agitated our country in his
youth.

In early youth Governor Tilden showed a strong love for
study, and a determination to be the master of every subject
which came to his notice, which has marked his life at every
step of his upward course. From a very early age there has
been every evidence that no position was beyond his powers,
and that with favorable circumstances he would become one of
the great men of his day.

Young Tilden entered college in his eighteenth year. The
fall of 1832, when he was to enter college, was rendered memorable by the second election of General Jackson to the Presidency and Martin Van Buren to the Vice-Presidency of the
United States, and of William L. Marcy to the Governorship
of the State of New York. In that contest an effort was made
to effect a coalition between the National Republicans and the
Anti-Masons. The success of the Democracy depended upon
the defeat of that coalition. Samuel heard the subject discussed in the family, and was especially impressed by what fell
from the lips of an uncle who deplored his inability to "wreak
his thoughts upon expression." Samuel disappeared for two or
three days, and in the seclusion of his chamber proceeded to
set down the views he had gathered upon the subject, and in
due time brought the result to his father, at once the most ap-
preciative and the least indulgent critic of his acquaintance.
The father was so highly pleased with the paper that he took
his son to see Mr. Van Buren, then at Lebanon Springs, to
read it to him. They found so much merit in the performance
that they decided it should be published with the signatures
of a dozen or more leading Democrats, and it shortly after
appeared in the Albany *Argus* as an address, occupying about half

a page of that print, and from which it was copied into most of the Democratic papers of the state. The *Evening Journal* paid it the compliment of attributing it to the pen of Mr. Van Buren, and the Albany *Argus* paid it the greater compliment of stating "by authority" that Mr. Van Buren was not the author.

Mr. Tilden had not been long at Yale College before his health gave way, and obliged him to leave. After some rest he was enabled to resume his studies, and in 1834 entered the University of New York, where he completed his academic education. He then entered the law office of the late John W. Edmunds, in the city of New York, where he enjoyed peculiar facilities for the prosecution of his favorite studies of law and politics.

The accession of Mr. Van Buren to the Presidency in 1837 was followed by the most trying financial revulsion that had yet occurred in our history. During that summer appeared the Presidential message calling for a special session of Congress, and recommending the separation of the Government from the banks and the establishment of the independent Treasury. This measure provoked voluminous and acrimonious debate throughout the country, even before it engaged the attention of Congress.

Mr. Tilden, though still a student, sprang to the defense of the President's policy, and wrote a series of papers, marked by all the characteristics of his maturity, and advocating the proposed separation and the redeemability of the Government currency in specie. These articles were signed "Crino."

In the fall of 1838, Nathaniel P. Talmadge, a Senator of the United States from New York, who had separated from the Democratic party and joined the Whigs in opposition to the financial policy of President Van Buren, was announced to speak on the issues of the day in Columbia County. A meeting had been arranged very quietly, at which it was hoped he might exert an influence upon the doubtful men and change the political complexion of the party. The Tildens heard of the proposed meeting about noon of the day upon which it was to be held. They promptly sent word to all the Democrats of the vicinity, and the result was one of the largest meetings ever known in that region. Talmadge, in the course of his speech, took great pains to convince his audience that it was the Democrats that had changed their position, but that he and his friends were unchanged. At the close of his remarks one of the Whig leaders of the movement offered a resolution, which passed without opposition, inviting any Democrats in the assembly that might be so disposed to reply to the Senator. The young Democrats, who had mostly gathered in the rear of the hall, regarding this as a challenge to them, shouted for Tilden. Samuel, yielding to the obvious sentiment of the meeting, came forward, and took the place just vacated by the Senator.

After discussing the main question of the controversy, he adverted to the personal aspects of the Senator's speech, and especially to his statement that the Democrats had changed position, while he himself had remained consistent. By way of testing the truth of this declaration, he turned to the Whigs on the platform and, pointing to each of them in turn, asked if it was they or if it was the Senator who had opposed them in the late contest for the Presidency, that had changed. Finally, fixing his eye upon the chairman, Mr. Gilbert, a venerable farmer and almost an octogenarian, he said, in a tone of mingled compliment and expostulation: "And you, sir, have you changed?" By this direct inquiry the honest old man was thrown off his guard, and stoutly cried out: "No!" Mr. Tilden skillfully availed himself of this declaration of his old neighbor and friend, and applied it to the Senator in a strain of masterly sarcasm and irony. The effect was electric; it thrilled the assembly and completely destroyed the objects of the meeting.

The spectacle of a *young* college student so easily vanquishing in an intellectual contest, a United States Senator had not then been witnessed. How often it might now be done is not so certain.

In these times, when the whole business of the country is utterly prostrated we can realize what an excitement attended the financial debate of 1837, and after; all who read this speech must be convinced that even if Webster and Nicholas Biddle were the champions of a system under which the revenues of the nation were made the basis of commercial discounts there was another very strong side to the case and that young Tilden ably presented it.

Mr. Tilden, who had watched this financial revolution of 1837 from the beginning, and knew its merits as thoroughly, perhaps, as any man of his time, undertook a defense of the President's scheme and to overthrow the sophistries of his enemies in a speech which he delivered in New Lebanon on the third day of October, 1840. It is marvelous, that in so short a time our people should have forgotten, as to a very considerable extent they appear to have done, the lessons taught in this speech, and those still better taught by the war then waged by the Democratic party with the policy of inflation, irredeemable currency and irresponsible credits. At the time this speech was delivered the Whigs were meditating the re-establishment of the United States Bank if they could succeed in dividing the Democrats on the Sub-Treasury scheme. This effort provoked Mr. Tilden to review the history of the bank and expose its ill-founded claims to be regarded in any sense as what it claimed to be, " a regulator of the currency." What he says upon that subject possesses to the reader of to-day not only considerable historical interest, but is pregnant with lessons which will never be out of season.

Upon his admission to the bar Mr. Tilden opened an office in Pine street, in the city of New York.

In 1844, in anticipation and preparation for the election which resulted in making James K. Polk President, and Silas Wright Governor of the State of New York, Mr. Tilden, in

19

connection with John L. O'Sullivan, founded the newspaper called the *Daily News*.

In the fall of 1845 he was sent to the Assembly from the city of New York, and while a member of that body was elected to the convention for the remodelling of the constitution of the State, which was to commence its sessions a few weeks after the Legislature adjourned. In both of these bodies Mr. Tilden was a conspicuous authority, and left a permanent impression upon the legislation of the year, and especially upon all the new constitutional provisions affecting the finances of the State and the management of its system of canals.

The defeat of Mr. Wright in the fall of 1846, and the coolness which had grown up between the friends of President Polk and the friends of the late President Van Buren, resulted fortunately for Mr. Tilden, if not for the country, in withdrawing his attention from politics and concentrating it upon his profession. He inherited no fortune, but depended upon his own exertions for a livelihood. Thus far his labor for the State, or in his profession, had not been lucrative, and, despite his strong tastes and pre-eminent qualifications for political life, he was able to discern at that early period the importance in this country, at least, of a pecuniary independence for the successful prosecution of a political career. With an assiduity and a concentration of energy which have characterized all the transactions of his life, Mr. Tilden now gave himself up to his profession. It was not many years before he became as well known at the bar as he had before been known as a politician. His business developed rapidly, and though he continued to take more or less interest in political matters, they were not allowed after 1857 to interfere with his professional duties.

At the New York municipal election held in November, 1855, a desperate attempt was made to defeat Azariah C. Flagg, one of the candidates for City Comptroller. Mr. Flagg was of the same school of politics as Mr. Tilden, and was renowned throughout the State, as well as in the city, for his fidelity to public trusts. The seekers after profitable jobs from the publie had nominated as his opponent a popular mechanic of gentle manners by the name of Giles, whom they hoped to control by the usual persuasives in case of his election. He ran upon what was then known as the "Know-Nothing" or "Native American" ticket. The returns gave Mr. Flagg the office by a small plurality of 117—20,313 against 20,134 for Giles. His opponent was to prosecute a *quo warranto*, and Mr. Flagg's title to the office was tested at a Supreme Court held before Judge Emott and a special jury.

The claimants seemed to have monopolized all the proof attainable, and to have left little or nothing for the defense. Add to this the original canvass had been made, as usual, upon distinct papers commonly called tallies. The split tally comprised three foolscap sheets, which contained the original canvass of the split votes, and tranfers from the tally of the regular vote and the aggregate result, showing the number of votes that each candidate had received. The tally of the regular votes had disappeared, at least could not be produced, and its loss was accounted for. The papers of split tallies, transfers, and summaries that were produced corresponded with the oral testimony, and confirmed the relator's theory of the alleged error in the return.

Such was apparently the desperate attitude of the Comptroller's case, when Mr. Tilden was called upon to open for the defense. The defense, if any could be made, had to be constructed upon the basis of the testimony offered by the relator, for other testimony there was none. The return showed, as the law required, the entire number of votes given in the district, and the regular varieties of what are called regular votes appeared from the prosecutor's own oral evidence. On this slight basis of actual testimony Mr. Tilden constructed an impregnable defense. In his opening, and after reviewing the weak points in the testimony of the relator which he was enabled to discover by the light of his midnight researches, he, for the first time, gives an intimation to his adversaries of the weapon he has improvised in a night for their destruction!

Before Mr. Tilden took his seat the case was won and Mr.
Flagg's seat was assured. Within fifteen minutes after the
case was submitted to the jury they returned with a verdict in
his favor.

Two years later Mr. Tilden achieved another, and in some
respects, even a more signal professional triumph, in the Bur-
dell-Cunningham contested will case. Soon after Mrs. Cunningham's acquittal on the trial for the murder of Dr. Burdell
she applied to the Surrogate for letters of administration and a
widow's third, on the ground of a private marriage shortly
before Burdell's death. Mr. Tilden was retained by the heirs
of Dr. Burdell to contest the fact of the alleged marriage. In
this, as in the case of Mr. Flagg, his adversaries had all the
affirmative testimony, the marriage certificate, the positive oath
of the clergyman who solemnized the marriage, of the daughter
Augusta, the only witness of the alleged ceremony, and the
subscribing witness to the marriage certificate, and of the two
serving girls employed in the house. For the defense there
was no affirmative testimony whatever. Its only resource was
the evolution of sufficient internal and external evidence on the
cross-examination, to overthrow the compact and careful array
of the testimony of the petitioners. Though satisfied in his
own mind that Burdell had been murdered, and by Mrs. Cunningham, and never married, Mr. Tilden found himself unable
to produce a single witness who, from personal knowledge,
could testify as to any important fact about either the murder
or the marriage. He had besides to contend with the indefatigable energy of the petitioners in producing "willing" witnesses ready to supply any defect in her case as fast as it was
exposed. Mr. Tilden adopted a course which, though not entirely original in the profession, was probably never more skil-
fully and effectively put in practice. Proceeding upon the
principle which guided him in his defense of Mr. Flagg, that
the truth in regard to any particular fact was in harmony with
every other fact in the world, and that a falsehood could only
be even apparently harmonized with a limited number of facts,

he determined to conduct his defense by a species of moral triangulation.

There is probably no case in which Mr. Tilden has been employed that required the exercise of so high a range of metaphysical powers, or in which his penetration of character appeared to greater advantage. His defense seemed almost a creation, and the result produced the more profound impression as it removed whatever doubt existed in the minds of the people as to Mrs. Cunningham's participation in the murder of Burdell.

The conviction took immediate possession of the public mind that had Tilden conducted the case for the prosecution when she was under indictment she would undoubtedly have been convicted. It is scarcely necessary to say that the Surrogate did not confer letters of administration upon Mrs. Cunningham, or leave her any further pretext for wearing the widow's crape.

His defense of the Pennsylvania Coal Company in its suit with the Delaware and Hudson Canal Company is another illustration of his legal abilities. The Delaware and Hudson Canal Company had a contract with the Pennsylvania Coal Company by which, among other things, it was agreed in case of the enlargement of their canal the coal company should pay for the use of their canal extra toll equal to such portion of one-half the reduction in the expense of transportation as might result from such enlargement. In due time the canal company put in their claim for extra toll. The coal company denied that the cost of transportation had been reduced, or that they had derived any advantage whatever from the enlargement. After tedious and futile negotiations suit was instituted by the canal company and Mr. Tilden was retained for the defense. The case was tried before Judge Hogeboom, of the Supreme Court, sitting as referee. Seventy odd days were consumed in the hearing, and testimony offered by the plaintiff fills several large printed volumes. As in the Flagg case, the plan of the defense, as advised by Mr. Tilden, was a surprise both to Court and counsel.

The amount claimed was 20 cents a ton on an annual transportation of five or six hundred thousand tons a year for some ten years, besides a royalty of the same amount for an indefinite future. It was a crisis in the fortunes of the Pennsylvania Coal Company, through which it was successfully conducted.

Among the more important cases in which Mr. Tilden has been concerned, one in which his strictly professional abilities appeared to special advantage, was the case of the Cumberland Coal Company against its directors, heard in the State of Maryland in the year 1858. Mr. Tilden's success in rescuing corporations from unprofitable and embarrassing litigation, in reorganizing their administration, in re-establishing their credit and in rendering their resources available, soon gave him an amount of business which was limited only by his physical ability to conduct it.

Since the year 1855 it is safe to say that more than half of the great railway corporations north of the Ohio and between the Hudson and Missouri rivers have been at some time his clients. The general misfortunes which overtook many of these roads between 1855 and 1860 called for some comprehensive plan for relief. It was here that his legal attainments, his unsurpassed skill as a financier, his unlimited capacity for concentrated labor, his constantly increasing weight of character and personal influence found full activity, and resulted in the re-organization of the larger portion of the great net-work of railways, by which the rights of all parties were equitably protected, wasting litigation avoided, and a condition of great depression and despondency in railway property replaced by an unexampled prosperity. His relation with these companies, his thorough comprehension of their history and requirements, and his practical energy and decision, have given him such a mastery over all the questions that arise in the organization, administration, and financial management of canals, as well as railroads, that his influence more than that of any other man in the country seems inseparably associated with their prosperity and success, not only in his own country but abroad. It is, we believe, an open secret that his transatlantic celebrity brought to him quite recently an invitation from the European creditors of the New York and Erie Railway to undertake a reconciliation of the various interests in that great corporation, which the proprieties and duties of his official position constrained him to decline.

Till the war came Governor Tilden made every effort to avert the rebellion. When his efforts, combined with those of other prominent patriots, had proved abortive, his convictions of duty were perfectly decided and clear. They were to maintain the integrity of our territory and the supremacy of the constitutional authorities. He had been educated in the school of Jackson, and had been a diligent student of the lessons taught by the nullification controversy of 1833. He had studied carefully and profoundly the relation of the Federal and State governments, and of the citizens of those governments. He had thus early formed perfectly clear and settled opinions, about which his mind never vacillated. They were the opinions of Jackson, of Van Buren, of Wright, and of Marcy, with whom, during most of their public lives, he had been on terms of personal intimacy.

During the winter of 1860–61 he attended a meeting of the leading men of both parties in the city of New York, to consider what measures were necessary and practicable to avert an armed collision between what were then termed the free and the slave States. To the north he urged reconciliation and forbearance, appreciating as he did more clearly than most of those around him the fearful and disastrous consequences of a civil war, whatever might prove its ultimate result. To the South he urged a deference to the will of the majority and a respect for the provisions of the Federal Constitution, within which they would be sure of adequate protection for themselves and for their property; but he warned them that outside of the Constitution they could expect protection for neither.

When the war did come Mr. Tilden associated himself with and was the private adviser of Mr. Dean Richmond, then at the head of the Democratic party of this State, and who was accustomed on all important questions to visit Mr. Tilden in his retirement and seek his counsel.

At a meeting held at the house of General Dix, just after the first call of President Lincoln for 75,000 troops, Mr. Tilden was present and participated in the discussions which took place. He then and there expressed the opinion that they were on the eve of a great war, and maintained that instead of 75,000 troops Mr. Lincoln should have called out at least 500,000, half for immediate service and the other half to be put in camps of instruction and trained for impending exigencies. Unhappily that generation had seen so little of war and had such limited means of comprehending the rapidity with which the war spirit, once lighted, will spread among a people, that it was not competent to appreciate the wisdom of this advice, which, if adopted, would probably have prevented the necessity of any further increase of military force.

To Secretary Chase and his friends, Mr. Tilden insisted that the war ought to be carried on under a system of sound finance, which he did not doubt the people would cheerfully sustain if the Government would have the courage to propose it. At a later period of the war he was invited by the Government at Washington to give his advice as to the best methods for its further conduct. He said to the Secretary of War:

"You have no right to expect a great military genius to come to your assistance. They only appear once in two or three centuries. You will probably have to depend upon the average military talent of the country. Under such circumstances your only course is to avail yourself of your numerical strength and your superior military resources resulting from your greater progress in industrial arts and your greater producing capacities. You must have reserves and concentrate your forces on decisive points, and overwhelm your adversaries by disproportionate numbers and reserves."

His advice was not taken, but he had the satisfaction, within a year after it was given, of hearing the Secretary of War acknowledge its wisdom and lament his inability to secure its adoption.

With the peace, came to Mr. Tilden the most important political labor of his life. With the assistance of Charles O'Conor, who followed the members of that band of conspirators with all his usual vigor and adroitness until it was not only broken up, but its leading members scattered to the four quarters of the globe, he assailed and overthrew the combined Republican and Democratic Ring which ruled and ruined New York. This "ring" had its origin in an act passed by the Legislature of the State of New York in 1857, in connection with the charter of that year, which provided that but six persons should be voted for by each elector and twelve chosen. In other words, the nominees of the Republican and Democratic party caucuses should be elected. At the succeeding session of the Legislature their term of office was extended to six years. This gave a Board of Supervisors, consisting of six Republicans and six Democrats, to change a majority of which it was necessary to have control of the primary meetings of both of the great national and State parties for years in succession—a series of coincidences which rarely happens in a generation.

This was doubly a "ring." It was a "ring" between the six Republican and the six Democratic Supervisors. It soon grew to be a "ring" between the Republican majority in the Legislature and the half-and-half Supervisors and a few Democratic officials of the city. It embraced just enough influential men in the organization of each party to control the action of both party organizations—men who in public life pushed to extremes the abstract ideas of their respective parties, while secretly they joined hands in common schemes for personal power and property. It gradually transferred its seat of operations to Albany. The lucrative city offices—subordinate appointments, which each head of department could create at pleasure, with salaries in his discretion, distributed among the friends of the legislators; contracts, money contributed by city officials, assessed on their subordinates, raised by jobs under the departments, and sometimes taken from the city treasury, were the corrupting agencies which shaped and controlled all legislation.   Year by year the system grew worse as a governmental institution—more powerful and more audacious.   The Executive Department swallowed up all the local powers, which gradually became mere deputies of legislators at Albany, on whom alone they were dependent.   It became completely organized on the 1st of January, 1869.   But its power was enormously extended by an act passed on the 5th of April in the following year, giving the power of local government to a few individuals of the "ring" for long periods, and freed from all accountability.

Within a month after the passage of this Tweed charter the Board of Special Audit—one of the fruits of this Legislature —were making an order for the payment of over six millions of money, of which it is now known that scarcely 10 per cent. in value was realized by the city.   Tweed got 24 per cent., and his agent, Woodward, 7 ; the brother of Sweeny, 10 ; Watson, Deputy Collector, 7 ; 33 per cent. went to mechanics who furnished the bills, though their share had to suffer many abatements; and 20 went to other parties.   Over $250,000 were sent to Albany to be distributed among the members of the Legislature.

The percentages of theft, comparatively moderate in 1869, reached 66 per cent. in 1870, and later, 85 per cent.

The Senators who voted on the 6th of April, 1870, with but two dissenting voices, to deprive our great commercial metropolis, with its million of people, of all power of self-government, as if it were a conquered province, to confer upon Tweed, Connolly, Sweeny, and Hall for a series of years the exclusive power of appropriating all moneys raised by taxes or by loans and an indefinite power to borrow—who swayed all the institutions of local government, the local judiciary and the whole machinery of elections—did not come again within reach of the people until the election of the 7th of November, 1871, when their successors were to be chosen.   All hopes of rescuing the city from the hands of the freebooters depended upon recovering the legislative power of the State, in securing a majority of the Senate and Assembly. To this end Mr. Tilden directed all his efforts. In a speech at the Cooper Union in New York, he stated Mr. Tweed's plan, which was to carry the Senatorial representation from that city, and then re-elect eight, and, if possible, twelve of the Republican Senators from the rural districts whom he had bought and paid for the previous year, and thus control all the legislation that might be presented there which involved his freebooting dynasty.

A party in power is naturally disposed to risk the continuance of abuses rather than hazard the extreme remedy of "cutting them out by the roots." The executive power of the State and all its recently enlarged official patronage were exerted against the latter policy. And since the contest of 1869 the "Ring" had studied to extend its influence in the rural districts, and had showered legislative favors as if they were ordinary patronage: But fortune favors the brave. Without an office or a dollar's worth of patronage in city or State to confer, Mr. Tilden planted himself on the traditions of the elders, on the moral sense and forces of Democracy, and upon the invincibility of truth and right. That undaunted faith in the harmony of truth and its irreconcilability with error, which we have found sustaining him at the bar and carrying him from victory to victory against more desperate odds, sustained him here. As always happens to those who battle for the right, Providence came to his aid. The thieves fell out, and one of their number betrayed them. A clerk in the Comptroller's office copied a series of entries—afterwards known as "secret accounts"—and handed them to the press for publication. They showed the dates and amounts of certain payments made by the Comptroller, the enormous amounts of which, compared with the times and purposes of the payments and the recurrence of the same names, awakened suspicions that they were the memorials of the grossest frauds. Mr. Tilden soon became satisfied of this, from the futility of the answers received from the city officers when questioned about them and from other sources, and reached the conclusion that the city had been the victim of frauds far transcending anything ever suspected. He immediately formed his plan, for the execution of which—as it involved the control of the approaching State Convention— the co-operation of several leading Democrats was first secured. He accepted an arrangement by which he was to be sent to the convention from his native district, Columbia County, which had always during the "Ring" ascendency afforded him that opportunity of being heard.

Early in September he issued a letter to some seventy-six thousand Democrats, reviewing the situation and calling upon them "to take a knife and cut the cancer out by the roots." But before the meeting of the convention an event happened which could not have been foreseen, but which was pregnant with the most important consequences.

To the eternal honor of the Democratic party of the city and State, on the issue thus made up by Mr. Tilden they gave gave him their cordial and irresistible support. The result was overwhelming, and not only changed the city representation in the legislative bodies of the State, but, in its moral effect, crushed the "Ring."

Mr. Tilden was one of the delegates chosen to represent the city in the next Legislature. In deference to the views of his principal coadjutors, Mr. Tilden devoted the six weeks' interval between his election and the meeting of the Legislature to the prosecution of its investigation in the city departments and in preparing the vast mass of accurate information which was the basis of nearly all the judicial proofs that have since been employed successfully in bringing the members of the "Ring" to justice or driving them into exile.

Mr. Tilden gave his chief attention during the session of the Legislature to the promotion of those objects for which he consented to go there, the reform of the judiciary and the impeachment of the creatures who had acquired the control of it under the Tweed dynasty.

Mr. Tilden had thus by his bold acts made himself prominent in the work of reform, and recognized as the man to lead it in the State. Prominent friends of reform urged him to accept the nomination for Governor. They said he could be nominated without difficulty and elected triumphantly, and in his triumph the great cause of administrative reform would receive an impulse which would propagate it not only over the whole State, but over the Union.

Mr. Tilden ultimately consented to take the nomination for Governor, his objections to which were overcome by a single consideration. It was the only way in which he could satisfactorily demonstrate that a course of fearless and persistent resistance to wrong will be vindicated and sustained by the masses of the people; that honesty and courage are as serviceable qualities and as well rewarded in politics as in any other profession or pursuit in life. He was unwilling to leave it in the power of the enemies of reform to say that he dared not submit his conduct as a reformer to the judgment of the people; to say that his course had ruined his influence; that his name should be a warning to the rising politicians of the country against following his example. He felt that, whatever might be the result of his administration, the moral effect of his election would be advantageous, not only in his own State, but throughout the country. But for these considerations, Mr. Tilden would have allowed himself to be made the candidate of the Democratic party for the Senate of the United States, a position more congenial to his tastes, and for which his personal preferences were well-known.

He was nominated and elected, and whatever lessons or eloquence could be expressed in big majorities were not wanting to lend their eclat to his triumph. Mr. Tilden's plurality over John A. Dix, the Republican candidate, was 53,315. Mr. Dix had been elected two years previously by a plurality of 53,451.

The first message of Governor Tilden foreshadowed with distinctness the controlling features of his administration.

First—Reform in the Administration.

Second—The restoration of the financial principles and

policy which triumphed in the election of Jackson and Van Buren, and which left the country without a dollar of indebtedness in the world and a credit abroad with which no other nation could then compete.

In furtherance of his policy of administrative reform, he recommended a revision of the laws intended to provide criminal punishment and civil remedies for frauds by public officers and by persons acting in complicity with them. These recommendations, during the same session carefully wrought into the legislation of the State, bore especially upon those forms of administrative abuse which the exposure and arrest of William M. Tweed had recently revealed, and also upon another and kindred class of abuses in the management of our canals, with which the Governor was already acquainted, but of which the public as yet had only an imperfect realization.

But the feature of the message which produced, perhaps, the most profound impression, not only upon his own immediate constituents, but upon the whole nation, was that which related to the financial policy of the Federal Government. A generation had grown up who had never seen or used any other money than a printed promise of the Government, and it had become a widespread conviction among the aspiring politicians of both the great parties that the current public opinion in favor of an inflated and irredeemable currency would overwhelm and destroy any public man who would attempt to stem it. No convention of either party in any State of the Union had ventured the experiment; the active leaders of both had either avoided or yielded to the current. Mr. Tilden deemed it his duty to lose no time in advocating the only financial policy which ever had insured or can insure a substantial and enduring national prosperity.

On the 19th of March, and as soon as he had secured from the Legislature such additional remedies for official delinquencies as were requisite for his purpose, the Governor in a special message invited the attention of the Legislature to the mismanagement of the canals.

He pointed out, in this communication, with considerable

detail, the fraudulent processes by which, for an indefinite number of years, the State had been plundered, its agents debauched, its politics demoralized, and its credit imperilled. The fullness, boldness, and directness of his statements produced a profound impression, not only throughout the State, but throughout the country.

The Legislature, though containing in both branches many of the most notorious canal jobbers, and constituted largely in that interest, was obliged to yield to the irresistible public sentiment which the Governor's policy and message had awakened, and granted him the authority to name such a commission. The results of the investigations, communicated to him from time to time during the summer of 1875 and to the succeeding Legislature of 1876, arrested completely the system of fraudulent expenditure on the canals which he had denounced at the bar of public opinion.

Through the adoption of various other financial measures upon his recommendation, and by the discreet but vigorous exercise of the veto power, the Governor was fortunate enough to secure a reduction of the State tax—the first year of his administration, about 17 per cent.—and to inaugurate a financial policy by which the State tax, which was $7\frac{1}{2}$ mills on the dollar of the assessed valuation, when he came into office, will be reduced to 4 mills at least at the expiration of his term of two years, and at the expiration of the next succeeding year to not exceeding 3 mills.

Mr. Tilden is now in the sixty-third year of his age. He is five feet ten inches in height, and he has what physiologists call the purely nervous temperament, with its usual accompaniment of spare figure, blue eyes, and fair complexion. His hair, originally chestnut, is now partially silvered with age.

For some reason best known to himself (and the gossips), Mr. Tilden is a bachelor, and should the suffrages of the people send him to the White House, we may perhaps compromise with the female suffragists who presented their case so persistently to the convention, by allowing them to elect a matron of the White House.

CHAPTER XXVIII.

THOMAS A. HENDRICKS,

Nominated as the candidate for Vice-President of the United States, was born in Muskingum county, Ohio, September 7th, 1819, and reaped the advantages of the common schools of his boyhood days, completing his education in South Hanover College. He studied law at Chambersburgh, Pa., in 1843, and shortly afterwards settled in Indiana and practiced his profession in the courts of that state. His reputation for ability and fairness in dealing with his clients made him very popular, and attracted the attention of the people of his state, and in 1848 he was elected a member of the legislature by the Democratic party. Of that body he at once became a leader. He declined a re-election. In 1850 he was elected a member of the constitutional convention, and distinguished himself by imparting in committees and debate in convention a thorough knowledge of the theory of government. In 1851, Mr. Hendricks was elected by the Democratic party a member of the United States House of Representatives, and served in that capacity until 1855, when President Pierce appointed him Commissioner of the General Land Office. He continued in that position, by re-appointment by President Buchanan, through most of the term of that President.

In 1863, the legislature of Indiana, having a Democratic majority, elected Mr. Hendricks to the United States Senate, and he took his seat at the special session which was convened on the 7th of December of that year. He entered upon his duties when a majority of the Senate was supporting the Administration, which Mr. Hendricks had opposed. He, nevertheless, viewed the war waged against the government by the Confederate forces as against the life of the nation, and disregarding it as a party matter, voted with the Administration party for army supplies. From these facts Senator Hendricks took his place among the progressive statesmen of those times, who were familiarly known as "War Democrats." Mr. Lincoln always counted upon Senator Hendricks as one of the men in the Democratic party upon whom he could confidently rely in the darkest hour of the nation's peril.

In the Senate Mr. Hendricks was never demonstrative. He was always a hard worker and valuable man in committees. He brought to its business a considerate judgment, large experience, and great patience. In debate his speeches were ever marked by candor, coolness, and dignity, carrying conviction. His whole public record in the senate, the legislature, and as a land commissioner, stands unchallenged in point of capacity and honesty.

In 1868 he was one of the prominent candidates named for the presidency, but gave way for the sake of harmony.

A Democratic State Convention held at Indianapolis, on the 12th of July, 1872, nominated Mr. Hendricks as a candidate for Governor. He accepted in a speech in which he took occasion to give his hearty endorsement to the Cincinnati platform and nominees, saying " Henceforth offices shall be filled and laws administered, not for individual profit or personal aggrandizement but for the common weal." His term of office as Governor expires January 1, 1877.

Such is the public record of Gov. Hendricks as it is impartially recorded. Like his associate Gov. Tilden, he will suffer in the coming campaign many aspersions, especially as to his views during the war and the currency question. During the war, his desire that the difficulties might be settled without recourse to arms, caused him to delay too long to suit the fiery ardor of the aroused North, but the cool, unimpassioned historian will accord to Gov. Hendricks probably a juster name, as one who had at heart the welfare of his country, though differing from the views then controlling the Administration.

His views on the currency question represent those of the western wing of his party, and while many may not coincide with them, these many must remember that he is by no means alone in cherishing them.

Gov. Hendricks is well known and held in high esteem by his fellow citizens of Indiana, and if the wheel of fortune should throw him into power, Indiana would vouch for him to the country.

CHAPTER XXIX.

VARIOUS POLITICAL STATISTICS.

ELECTORAL VOTE FROM 1824 TO 1872.

1824	Andrew Jackson. 99	John Q. Adams....84	W. H. Crawford.41	Henry Clay......57
1828	Andrew Jackson 178	John Q. Adams....83		
1832	Andrew Jackson.219	Henry Clay.........49	John Floyd......11	William Wirt.....7
1836	Mart. Van Buren.170	Wm. H. Harrison..73	Hugh L. White.26	Daniel Webster..14
1840	Wm. H. Harrison.234	Martin Van Buren..60		
1844	James K. Polk...170	Henry Clay........105		Will. P. Mangum.11
1848	Zachary Taylor. .163	Lewis Cass........127		
1852	Franklin Pierce.254	Winfield Scott....42		
1856	James Buchanan.174	John C. Fremont..114	Millard Fillmore.8	
1860	Abra'm Lincoln..180	J. C. Breckinridge..72	John Bell......39	Step.A. Douglass.12
1864	Abra'm Lincoln..212	Geo. B. McClellan..21		
1868	Ulysses S. Grant.214	Horatio Seymour. 80		
1872	Ulysses S. Grant.300	Thos. A. Hendricks 42	B. Gratz Brown.18	Scattering........6

POPULAR VOTE FOR PRESIDENT FROM 1851 TO 1872.

STATES.	1852.			1856.		
	Scott, Whig.	Pierce, Dem.	Hale, F. Soil.	Frem., Rep.	Buch'n, Dem.	Film., Amer.
Alabama......................	15038	26881	.....	.....	46739	28552
Arkansas.....................	7404	12173	.....	.....	21910	10787
California....................	35407	40626	100	20691	53365	36165
Connecticut..................	30257	33249	3160	42715	34095	2615
Delaware.....................	6293	6318	62	308	8004	6175
Florida	2875	4318	.....	.. ...	6358	4833
Georgia......................	16660	34705	9996	.....	56578	42228
Illinois......................	64934	80597	9996	96189	105348	37144
Indiana......................	80001	95340	6929	94375	118670	22386
Iowa.........................	15856	17763	1604	43954	36170	9180
Kentucky....................	57068	53806	.....	314	71642	67416
Louisiana....................	17255	18647	.....	.....	22164	20709
Maine	32543	41609	8030	67379	39080	3325
Maryland....................	35066	40020	54	281	39115	47460
Massachusetts................	52683	44569	28023	108100	39240	19626
Michigan....................	33859	41842	7237	71762	52136	1660
Minnesota...................	.....	.....	....	.....	.....	.....
Mississippi..................	17548	26876	....	.....	35446	24195
Missouri.....................	29984	38353	.....	.....	58164	48524
New Hampshire..............	16147	29997	6695	38345	32789	422
New Jersey..................	38556	44305	350	28338	46943	24115
New York...................	234882	262083	25329	276007	195878	124604
North Carolina..............	39058	39744	.....	.....	48246	36816
Ohio	152526	169220	31682	187497	170874	28126
Oregon......................	.....	.....	.....	.....	.....	.....
Pennsylvania................	179174	198568	8525	147510	230710	82175
Rhode Island................	7626	8735	644	11467	6680	1675
Tennessee...................	58898	57018	.....	.....	73638	66178
Texas.......................	4995	13552	.....	.....	31169	15639
Vermont.....................	22173	13044	8621	39561	10569	545
Virginia.....................	58572	73858	.....	291	89706	60310
Wisconsin...................	22240	32658	8844	66090	52843	579
Total................	1386578	1601474	155825	1341264	1838169	874534

POPULAR VOTE FOR PRESIDENT FROM 1854 TO 1872—CONTINUED.

STATES.	1860.				1864.			
	Linc'ln, Rep.	Doug., Dem.	Breck., Dem.	Bell, Union.	McClel. Dem.	Linc'ln, Rep.	Dem. maj.	Rep. maj.
Alabama.............	......	13651	48831	27825	......	......	......	......
Arkansas............		5227	28732	20094				
California...........	29173	38516	34334	6817	43841	62134	......	18293
Connecticut.........	43692	15522	14641	3291	42285	44691	......	2406
Delaware............	3815	1023	7347	3864	8767	8155	612	......
Florida..............		367	8543	5437				
Georgia..............		11590	51889	42886				
Illinois..............	172161	160215	2404	3913	158730	189496	......	30766
Indiana..............	139033	115509	12295	5306	130833	150422	......	20189
Iowa	70409	55111	1048	1763	49506	89075	......	39479
Kansas...............	......	......	......	......	3821	16441	......	12750
Kentucky............	1364	25651	53143	66058	6301	27786	36515	......
Louisiana	......	7625	22681	20204	......	......		
Maine	62811	26693	6368	2046	44211	61808	......	17592
Maryland............	2294	5905	42482	41760	32739	40153	......	7414
Massachusetts	106533	34372	5939	22331	48745	126742	......	77997
Michigan............	88480	65057	805	405	74604	91521	......	16917
Minnesota	22069	11920	748	62	17375	25060	......	7685
Mississippi.........		3183	40797	27040				
Missouri............	17028	58801	31317	58372	31678	72750	......	41072
Nebraska...........	......	......	......	......				
Nevada..............					6594	9826	......	3232
New Hampshire.....	37519	25881	2112	441	32871	36400	......	3529
New Jersey.........	58324	62801	......	......	68024	60723	7301	......
New York...........	362646	312510	......	......	361986	368735	......	6749
North Carolina.....	......	2701	48539	44990	......	......		
Ohio................	231610	187232	11405	12194	205568	265154	......	59586
Oregon..............	5270	3951	3046	183	8457	9888	......	1431
Pennsylvania........	268030	16765	178871	12776	276316	296391	......	20075
Rhode Island........	12244	7707	......	......	8470	13092	......	5222
South Carolina......	......	......	......	......	......	......		
Tennessee	......	11350	64709	69274	......	......		
Texas...............			47548	15438				
Vermont............	3883	6849	218	1969	13321	42419	......	29098
Virginia............	1929	16290	74323	74681				
West Virginia.......	......	......	......	......	10438	23152	......	12714
Wisconsin	86110	65021	888	161	63884	83458	......	17574
Total........	1866352	1375157	845763	589581	1808725	2216067	44428	451770

STATES.	1868.				1872.			
	Seym. Dem.	Grant, Rep.	Dem. maj.	Rep. maj.	Greel'y, Liber'l.	Grant, Adm.	Lib. maj.	Adm. maj.
Alabama.............	72088	76366	......	4278	79441	90272	......	108218
Arkansas............	19078	22112	......	3034	37927	41373	......	3446
California...........	51077	54588	......	506	40718	54020	......	13302
Connecticut.........	47782	50695	......	3043	45880	50638	......	4758
Delaware............	10980	7053	3357	......	10306	11115	......	909
Florida.............	......	......	......	......	15487	17763	......	2276
Georgia..............	102722	57134	45588	......	76356	62550	13806	......
Illinois.............	199143	250293	......	51160	184938	241944	......	57006
Indiana.............	166980	176548	......	9568	163632	186147	......	22515
Iowa...............	74040	120399	......	46359	71196	131566	......	60370
Kansas.............	13600	31048	......	17058	32970	67048	......	34078
Kentucky...........	115890	39566	78324	......	99995	88766	11229	......
Louisiana...........	80225	33263	46962	......	57029	71663	......	14634
Maine..............	42460	70426	......	28833	29087	61422	......	32335
Maryland...........	62357	30438	31919	......	67687	66760	927	......
Massachusetts.......	59408	136477	......	77069	59260	132272	......	74212
Michigan...........	97069	128550	......	31481	78355	138455	......	60109
Minnesota..........	28075	43545	......	15470	24423	55117	......	30694

POPULAR VOTE FOR PRESIDENT FROM 1854 TO 1872—CONTINUED.

STATES.	1868.				1872.			
	Seym. Dem.	Grant, Rep.	Dem. maj.	Rep. maj.	Greel'y, Liber'l.	Grant, Adm.	Liber'l maj.	Adm. maj.
Mississippi.........	......	......	......	......	47288	82175	......	34887
Missouri...........	65628	86860	......	21232	151434	119196	32238	......
Nebraska..........	5439	9729	......	4290	7812	18329	......	10517
Nevada............	5218	6480	......	1262	6236	8413	......	2177
New Hampshire.....	31224	38191	......	6967	31424	37168	......	5744
New Jersey..	83001	80131	2870	......	76156	91656	......	15300
New York....	421883	410883	10800	......	387281	440736	......	53155
North Carolina..	84601	96769	......	12168	70094	94769	......	24675
Ohio.....	238606	283223	......	41617	244321	281852	......	37531
Oregon...........	11125	10961	164	......	7739	11819	......	4089
Pennsylvania......	313382	342280	......	28898	212041	349589	......	137548
Rhode Island.......	6548	12993	......	6445	5329	13665	......	8336
South Carolina.....	45237	62301	......	17064	22703	72290	......	49587
Tennessee.........	26129	56628	......	30499	94391	85655	8726	......
Texas............	......	......	......	......	66500	47406	19094	......
Vermont...........	12045	44167	......	32122	10927	41481	......	30554
Virginia..........	......	......	......	......	91654	93468	......	1814
West Virginia......	20306	29175	......	8869	29151	32315	......	2864
Wisconsin	84707	108857	......	24150	86477	104997	......	18520
Total......	**270913**	**3045071**	**217184**	**522512**	**2834079**	**3597070**	**86030**	**849021**

Lincoln's maj. over McClellan, 407342; Grant's over Seymour, 305458; Grant's over Greeley, 762991.

VOTE OF OHIO FOR GOVERNOR IN 1875 (By Counties).

COUNTIES.	MAJORITIES.		Dem. Allen.	Rep. H'yes	COUNTIES.	MAJORITIES.		Dem. Allen.	Rep. H'yes
	Allen.	H'yes				Allen.	H'yes		
Adams............	386	....	2239	1853	Hancock.........	274	....	2833	2559
Allen............	769	....	2920	2151	Hardin..........	81	....	2608	2527
Ashland..........	550	....	2800	2250	Harrison.........	....	285	2069	2324
Ashtabula........	....	4120	1962	6092	Henry	682	....	2905	1323
Athens..........	....	782	2410	3192	Highland.........	55	....	3215	3160
Auglaize.........	1750	....	2851	1161	Hocking.........	688	....	2082	1394
Belmont	74	....	4588	4514	Holmes.........	1779	....	2838	1059
Brown...........	1319	....	3677	2358	Huron..........	....	1186	2637	3873
Butler...........	2295	....	5290	2935	Jackson.........	....	287	2297	2494
Carroll..........	....	457	1453	1896	Jefferson........	....	895	2826	3721
Champaign.......	....	482	2620	3102	Knox...........	297	....	3182	2885
Clarke	....	997	3292	4389	Lake...........	....	1558	1120	2678
Clermont........	556	....	4036	3480	Lawrence	....	647	3089	3736
Clinton.....	....	1216	1938	3154	Licking........	1525	....	5142	3617
Columbiana......	....	966	3971	4940	Logan..........	....	794	2102	2896
Coshocton.......	592	....	2913	2321	Lorain.........	....	2770	2097	4767
Crawford....	1779	....	3834	2064	Lucas..........	....	1384	4481	5865
Cuyahoga	....	6046	10966	17012	Madison........	....	85	2028	2113
Darke...........	1394	....	4233	2929	Mahoning.......	159	....	3947	3788
Defiance.........	1295	....	2483	1218	Marion.........	772	....	2306	1534
Delaware........	....	127	2708	2835	Medina.........	....	899	1960	2859
Erie............	....	234	1312	2891	Meigs..........	....	590	2843	3483
Fairfield.........	1553	....	2657	2639	Mercer.........	1569	....	2500	1000
Fayette..........	....	575	1871	2246	Miami..........	....	767	3229	4006
Franklin........	1109	....	7951	6842	Monroe.........	2113	....	3129	1016
Fulton..........	....	991	1314	2303	Montgomery.....	812	....	8014	7202
Gallia..........	....	520	2388	2908	Morgan.........	....	200	2004	2201
Geauga..........	....	1939	726	2665	Morrow.........	....	130	2606	2156
Greene..........	....	1933	2308	4141	Muskingum......	330	....	5218	4888
Guernsey........	....	893	2131	2824	Noble..........	....	67	2037	2104
Hamilton........	....	1295	22921	21916	Ottawa	719	....	1781	1062

VOTE OF OHIO FOR GOVERNOR IN 1875—Continued.

COUNTIES.	MAJORITIES.		Dem. Allen.	Rep. H'yes	COUNTIES.	MAJORITIES.		Dem. Allen.	Rep. H'yes
	Allen.	H'yes				Allen.	H'yes		
Paulding........	....	14	1130	1144	Trumbull........	....	2352	3301	5653
Perry...........	945	....	2708	1853	Tuscarawas.....	789	....	4048	3259
Pickaway.......	747	....	3144	2397	Union...........	....	644	1952	2596
Pike...........	610	....	1940	1330	Vanwert........	125	....	2233	2108
Portage.........	....	513	2859	3402	Vinton.........	409	....	1906	1497
Preble..........	....	222	2389	2611	Warren.........	....	1175	2513	3688
Putnam	1112	....	2756	1304	Washington.....	86	....	4230	4144
Richland........	765	....	4050	3285	Wayne..........	454	....	4301	3847
Ross...........	226	....	4216	3990	Williams........	....	137	2362	2399
Sandusky	744	....	3573	2609	Wood...........	....	723	2808	3531
Scioto..........	....	259	3620	3879	Wyandot........	670	....	2305	1735
Seneca..........	604	....	4315	3721					
Shelby	954	....	2701	1757					
Stark..........	235	....	6630	6395					
Summit.........	....	1100	3528	4628	Total.......	37016	12557	292273	297817

Per cent....................................	....	....	49.53	50.47
Majority....................................	5541	....	....	5541
Total vote..................................	590,000		590,000	

VOTE OF NEW YORK STATE FOR GOVERNOR IN 1874 BY COUNTIES.

COUNTIES	Dem. Tilden.	Rep. Dix.	COUNTIES.	Dem. Tilden.	Rep. Dix.
Albany, ...	15466	12234	Onondaga,............	9380	11610
Allegany,...............	3268	5187	Ontario, ...	4449	4536
Broome,................	4296	4881	Orange,..............	7878	7519
Cattaraugus,...........	4517	5255	Orleans,.............	2567	3147
Cayuga,...............	5318	5077	Oswego,.............	6440	7580
Chautauqua,...........	5555	7827	Otsego,..............	6083	5320
Chemung,..............	4226	3453	Putnam,.............	1706	1478
Chenango,.............	4242	4296	Queens,.............	6257	4961
Clinton,...............	3094	5065	Rensselaer,..........	10702	9881
Columbia,..............	5780	4134	Richmond,...........	3021	2150
Cortland,..............	2268	2927	Rockland,..........	2632	1817
Delaware,.............	4592	4508	St. Lawrence, ...	3866	9406
Dutchess,.............	8767	5254	Saratoga, ...	4953	6364
Erie,.................	15536	15146	Schenectady, ...	2648	2203
Essex, ...	3191	3395	Schoharie, ...	4545	2712
Franklin,..............	2339	2786	Schuyler,...........	2260	2110
Fulton,...............	2913	3523	Seneca,.............	3282	2569
Genesee,..............	2672	3088	Steuben,............	7088	7072
Greene,...............	3368	3043	Suffolk,.............	3729	3901
Hamilton,...	463	246	Sullivan,............	3681	2294
Herkimer,.............	4377	4728	Tioga,..............	2357	3502
Jefferson,.............	5026	6828	Tompkins,...........	3310	3370
Kings, ...	28849	26841	Ulster,..............	8303	5884
Lewis,................	3219	2761	Warren,.............	2430	2231
Livingston,............	3753	4347	Washington,.........	4346	5419
Madison,..............	2978	5450	Wayne,.............	4017	5103
Monroe,...............	10534	9701	Westchester,.........	9466	7145
Montgomery,..........	4159	3773	Wyoming,...........	2416	3434
New York,.............	87436	44958	Yates,..............	1721	2234
Niagara,...............	4579	4925			
Oneida,...............	11137	11488	Total, ...	416391	366074
			Per cent,...........	53.22	46.78

VOTE FOR GOVERNOR OF CONNECTICUT.

COUNTIES.	GOVERNOR, '75.			Gov. '74.		Gov. '73.		Gov. '72.		Gov. '71.	
	Dem. Ingersoll.	Rep. Greene.	Temp Smith.	Dem. Ingersoll.	Rep. Harrison.	Dem. Ingersoll.	Rep. Haven.	Dem. Hubbard.	Rep. Jewell.	Dem. English.	Rep. Jewell.
Fairfield,..	9448	7003	522	8274	6937	7867	6792	7767	7645	8428	7800
Hartford,....	11988	9654	506	10714	8367	9407	9038	9290	9830	9728	9712
Litchfield,...	5678	3968	168	5078	2886	4852	3893	4804	4428	5134	4820
Middlesex,.	3297	2950	325	2892	2452	2627	2736	2857	3075	2924	3139
New Haven,	13210	9649	546	10672	9054	12338	7084	10991	10544	11701	10322
New London,	5427	5739	491	4687	4739	4081	4800	4783	5568	5174	5682
Tolland,	2165	2078	185	2009	1898	1947	1945	1893	2188	2001	2293
Windham,	2539	3231	189	2429	2710	1940	2957	2068	3295	2209	3615
Total, ...	53752	44272	2932	46755	39073	45059	39245	44562	46563	47970	47473
Per cent.,...	53.24	43.85	2.91	53.91	46.09	53.45	46.55	48.90	51.10	49.95	50.05
Majority,....	6548	.....	.....	6782	.....	5814	.....	.....	2001	.....	103

VOTE FOR GOVERNOR OF NEW JERSEY.

COUNTIES.	GOVERNOR, 1874.		GOVERNOR, 1871.		GOVERNOR, 1868.	
	Dem. Bedle.	Rep. Halsey.	Dem. Parker.	Rep. Walsh.	Dem. Randolph.	Rep. Blair.
Atlantic, ...	1158	1412	1003	1343	1096	1632
Bergen, ...	3680	2549	2878	2648	2780	2149
Burlington, ...	5527	5542	4887	5648	5206	5891
Camden, ...	4359	5279	3737	4330	3656	4126
Cape May, ...	684	829	538	728	688	946
Cumberland, ...	2965	3513	2434	3411	2394	3712
Essex, ...	13067	13694	11360	10847	11720	12902
Gloucester, ...	2343	2127	1960	2591	1796	2160
Hudson, ...	13346	8128	10237	7281	11301	7103
Hunterdon, ...	4829	3386	4663	3023	4795	3384
Mercer, ...	5432	5198	4594	4621	4180	4338
Middlesex,...	5455	4164	4367	4175	4325	3912
Monmouth, ...	6051	4179	5224	4021	5303	3706
Morris, ...	4305	4571	3733	3771	4074	4210
Ocean, ...	1382	1610	1112	1556	1080	1856
Passaic, ...	4047	4051	3222	4141	3431	4632
Salem, ...	2518	2445	2348	2961	2230	2553
Somerset, ...	2784	2552	2457	2264	2539	2179
Sussex, ...	2906	1729	3148	1849	3211	2219
Union, ...	5062	4275	4304	3767	3789	3573
Warren, ...	4263	2217	4056	2117	4122	2640
Total, ...	97283	84050	82362	76383	83955	79323
Per cent., ...	53.65	46.35	51.88	48.12	51.42	48.58

Joseph D. Bedle's majority, 13,233; Joel Parker's majority in 1871, 5,979; Theodore F. Randolph's majority in 1868, 4,632. Total vote in 1874, 181,333; in 1871, 158,745; in 1868, 163,288.

PRESIDENTS AND VICE-PRESIDENTS FROM THE FIRST CONTINENTAL CONGRESS TO THE PRESENT TIME.

PRESIDENTS.

I.—*Prior to the Adoption of the Constitution.*

NAME.	State.	Date of Appointment.	Died	NAME.	State.	Date of Appointment.	Died
Peyton Randolph.	Va.	Sept. 5, 1774	1775	John Hanson....	Md.	Nov. 5, 1781	1783
Henry Middleton..	S. C.	Oct. 22, 1774	...	Elias Boudinot..	N. J.	Nov. 4, 1782	1821
John Hancock....	Mass.	May 24, 1775	1793	Thomas Mifflin..	Penn.	Nov. 3, 1783	1800
Henry Laurens,...	S. C.	Nov. 1, 1777	1792	Rich'd Henry Lee	Va.	Nov. 30, 1784	1794
John Jay..........	N. Y.	Dec. 10, 1778	1829	Nathan'l Gorham.	Mass.	June 6, 1786	1796
Sam'l Huntington.	Conn.	Sept. 28, 1779	1796	Arthur St. Clair..	Penn.	Feb. 2, 1787	1818
Thomas McKean..	Del.	July 10, 1781	1817	Cyrus Griffin.....	Va.	Jan. 22, 1788	1810

II.—*Under the Constitution.*

NAME.	State.	Term of Service.	Died.	NAME.	State.	Term of Service.	Died.
George Washington.	Va.	1789—1797	1799	John Tyler........	Va.	1841—1845	1862
John Adams.......	Mass.	1797—1801	1826	James K. Polk,....	Tenn.	1845—1849	1849
Thomas Jefferson...	Va.	1801—1809	1826	Zachary Taylor....	La.	1849—1850	1850
James Madison......	Va.	1809—1817	1837	Millard Fillmore...	N. Y.	1850—1853	1874
James Monroe......	Va.	1817—1825	1831	Franklin Pierce....	N. H.	1853—1857	1869
John Quincy Adams.	Mass.	1825—1829	1848	James Buchanan...	Penn.	1857—1861	1868
Andrew Jackson....	Tenn.	1829—1837	1845	Abraham Lincoln..	Ill.	1861—1865	1865
Martin Van Buren...	N. Y.	1837—1841	1862	Andrew Johnson...	Tenn.	1865—1869	1875
William H. Harrison.	Ohio.	1841—1841	1841	Ulysses S. Grant...	Ill.	1869—1876	....

VICE-PRESIDENTS.

NAME.	State.	Term of Service.	Died.	NAME.	State.	Term of Service.	Died.
John Adams.........	Mass.	1789—1797	1836	John Tyler.........	Va.	1841—1841	1862
Thomas Jefferson...	Va.	1797—1801	1826	George M. Dallas...	Penn.	1845—1849	1864
Aaron Burr..	N. Y.	1801—1805	1836	Millard Fillmore...	N. Y.	1849—1850	1874
George Clinton.	N. Y.	1805—1812	1812	William R. King...	Ala.	1853—1853	1853
Elbridge Gerry.....	Mass.	1813—1814	1814	J. C. Breckinridge,..	Ky.	1857—1861	1875
Daniel D. Tompkins.	N. Y.	1817—1825	1825	Hannibal Hamlin...	Me.	1861—1865	...
John C. Calhoun....	S. C.	1825—1832	1850	Andrew Johnson...	Tenn.	1865—1865	1875
Martin Van Buren..	N. Y.	1833—1837	1862	Henry Wilson.....	Mass.	1869—1875	1875
Richard M Johnson.	Ky.	1837—1841	1850	....	.....	....	....

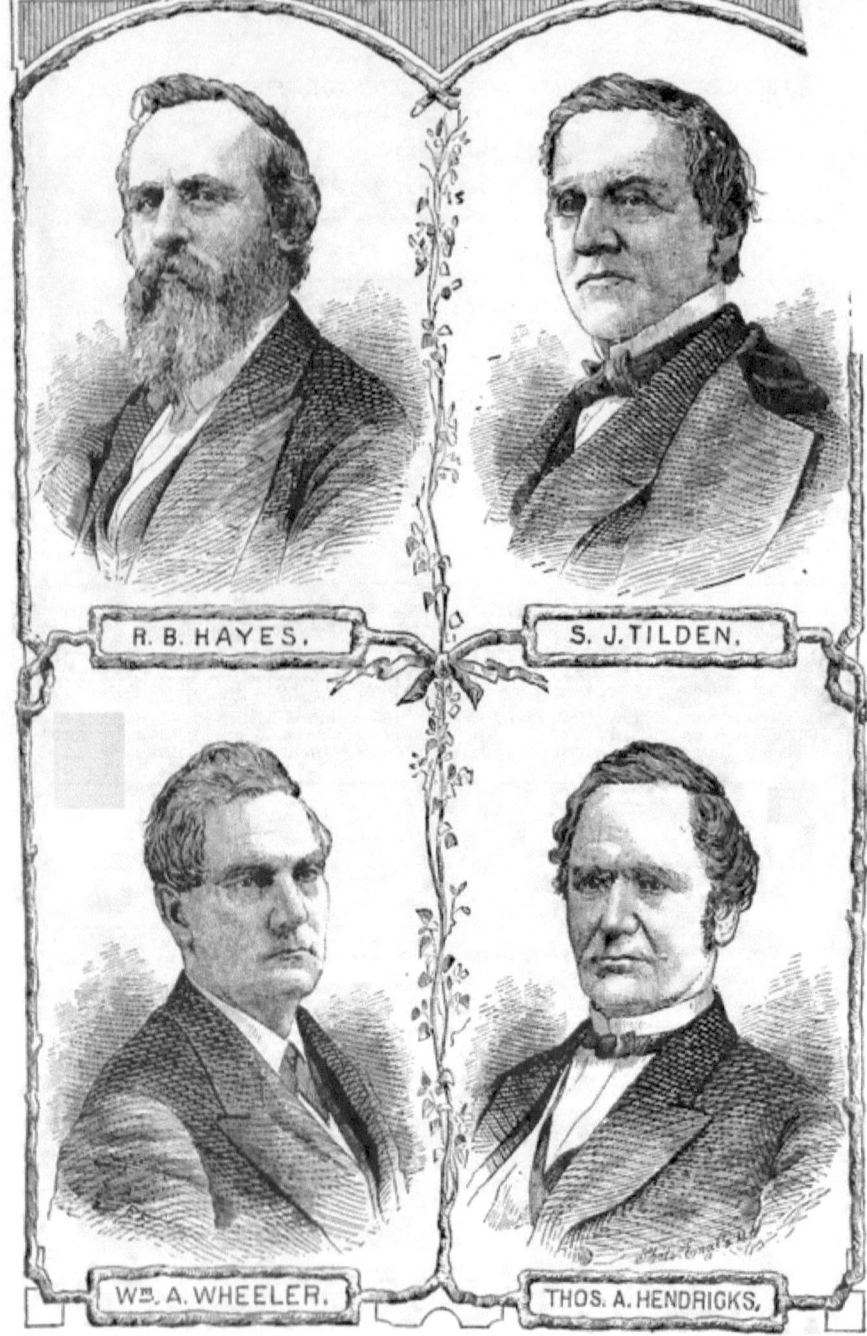

R. B. HAYES.

S. J. TILDEN.

Wᵐ. A. WHEELER.

THOS. A. HENDRICKS.

www.ingramcontent.com/pod-product-compliance
Lightning Source LLC
Chambersburg PA
CBHW032010110726
47901CB00004B/1029